TAKE ME HOME TO KELSEA SANDS

SHARON BOOTH

Boldwood

First published in Great Britain in 2026 by Boldwood Books Ltd.

Copyright © Sharon Booth, 2026

Cover Design by Debbie Clement

Cover Images: Shutterstock

Chapter icons: Shutterstock

A CIP catalogue record for this book is available from the British Library.

Paperback ISBN 978-1-83656-778-3

Large Print ISBN 978-1-83656-777-6

Hardback ISBN 978-1-83656-776-9

Trade Paperback ISBN 978-1-80656-135-3

Ebook ISBN 978-1-83656-779-0

Kindle ISBN 978-1-83656-780-6

Audio CD ISBN 978-1-83656-771-4

MP3 CD ISBN 978-1-83656-772-1

Digital audio download ISBN 978-1-83656-775-2

This book is printed on certified sustainable paper. Boldwood Books is dedicated to putting sustainability at the heart of our business. For more information please visit https://www.boldwoodbooks.com/about-us/sustainability/

Boldwood Books Ltd, 23 Bowerdean Street, London, SW6 3TN

www.boldwoodbooks.com

For my mother, Janet.
September 1941–October 2025
You were there when I took my first breath,
and I was there when you took your last.
Loved and remembered always.

xxxx

1

'Well, Alison,' the nurse said cheerfully, 'your blood pressure's definitely up since your last health check. We're going to have to do something about that, aren't we?'

She released the pressure from the arm cuff and Alison slumped in the chair, relieved that it was over even if the results weren't what she'd hoped. She hated having her blood pressure monitored.

'It makes me feel a bit queasy,' she told the nurse. 'That horrible tightening on my arm is so uncomfortable. You know, I'm pretty sure it's that which sends my blood pressure soaring. Bet it's much lower really.'

'Yes, a lot of people say that,' the nurse replied. 'White coat syndrome. Isn't it funny?'

Hilarious.

'Well, that's you done for today, my love. If you give us a ring in a few days, we'll have the results of your blood tests for you and let you know if you need an appointment. Have you still got your own BP machine at home?' As Alison nodded, she said, 'Smashing. Well, in the meantime, can you monitor your blood pressure for us over the next four days and let us know the readings? Then we'll discuss whether you need your medication increasing. Okay?'

It wasn't really a question. Alison was dismissed. She nodded her thanks and stumbled out of the consulting room feeling as deflated as the cuff that now lay, harmless-looking, on the nurse's desk. You'd never believe it could grip with such ferocity. Bloody thing.

She gave a half-hearted smile to the receptionist then hurried out of the building, eager to get as far away from the place as possible. She dreaded visiting the surgery. Doctors and nurses and monitors and tests...

Unfortunately, it was January, which meant it was her birthday month and time for her annual health check. She'd skipped it last year and had hoped she could get away with it this year, too, but there'd been a few text messages from the surgery, and even the chemist had pointed out to her that there was a note on her prescription saying she needed to book an appointment before she could get any more blood pressure tablets.

There had been no escape.

At least it was over with now, she thought, as she unlocked the car door and slid into the driver's seat, glad to get out of the drizzle that had persisted all afternoon. Slamming the door shut, she took a deep breath and leaned back against the headrest for a moment, closing her eyes as she tried to still the panic.

'It's done,' she murmured. 'The worst bit's over with now.'

Except she knew that wasn't true because she still had to take her own blood pressure for four days and it was an ordeal she really wasn't looking forward to. And then there was the waiting for the blood test results.

'Don't think about it now,' she said firmly. 'Come on, let's go home. I'll treat you to a posh coffee and a slice of that Victoria sponge.'

She wondered vaguely if anyone else had conversations out loud with themselves. Maybe it was just her. One thing to talk to yourself in your mind, but to say it out loud?

'I think you might be a bit daft,' she told her reflection in the rear-view mirror as she wrestled with the seat belt.

'Hey, me too!' it replied.

She shook her head, laughing, and started the car.

At least she had the whole evening to herself tonight. No late shift at the petrol station. No babysitting duties. Just the latest episode of her favourite soap and a few chapters of the book she'd been trying to read for the last three weeks.

'And a bath,' she decided, as she navigated her way out of the car park and on to the main road. 'Not a shower. A nice long soak in the tub, with my posh bubble bath, and maybe even candles.'

She knew it would never happen. She'd seen it in the films but had never actually had a soak with candles around the bath in her life and probably wouldn't start now. Besides, her hair really needed washing, and a shower was so much quicker...

The drive home took forever. Rush hour, with the world and its wife making their way home after a hard day's graft. She'd managed to leave work a couple of hours early so she could go to the doctor's but had forgotten about the busy main roads through Hull at teatime.

She finally pulled up outside her house thirty-five minutes after leaving the surgery on what should have been a ten-minute drive. She was feeling frazzled and anxious and had no doubt that her blood pressure had just climbed to even greater heights.

'Why are some drivers such morons?' she wondered aloud as

she unclipped her seat belt, reached for her bag and finally stepped out on to the pavement.

'There you are, stranger! Thought you were never coming home.'

For a split-second Alison thought the voice was her daughter's and her heart sank, but it was only Rosie, sitting on the doorstep, the light from the wall lamp revealing her beaming face as Alison moved closer.

God, she thought, *what an awful way to feel about my own daughter! I'm a horrible person, I really am.*

'What are you doing here?' She couldn't help smiling as her cousin jumped to her feet. It was hard not to smile when Rosie was around.

'I've been sat on your doorstep for bloody ages,' Rosie told her. She peered round at her behind and said, 'Is my arse wet? Just have a look for us, will you?'

She spun round so Alison could check the back of her jeans.

'No, you're fine,' Alison reassured her, resisting the urge to correct Rosie's grammar and tell her she'd actually been *sitting* on the doorstep. All those years of teaching, she supposed. Hard habit to break but not a very likeable one, especially as she hardly spoke with perfect grammar herself, despite her writing skills. She unlocked the front door and switched on the hallway light. 'Go on in. I'll put the kettle on. You still haven't said why you're here.'

'Well, why do you think?' Rosie held up a carrier bag and shook it. 'Your birthday cards! Belated happy birthday, Ali!'

Alison paused in the act of hanging up her coat and stared at her. 'You never came all this way just to bring me those!'

'What else was I supposed to do? We felt awful. We thought you'd be at your mam and dad's last weekend, so we all left your cards there, and then you didn't turn up, so... Hey, you've got pressies too. There's even one in there from Mam and Dad. Mind you, I wouldn't like to guess what it is. You know what Mam's like.'

She grinned and Alison grinned back. She adored her cousin and always felt cheerier in her presence. At forty-three, Rosie was nineteen years younger than Alison, and was a lively, bubbly woman with a glorious mop of thick, wavy strawberry-blonde hair that tumbled over her shoulders, and large, heavily made-up blue eyes that usually twinkled with humour. Despite the weather she was wearing tight jeans, trendy trainers and a denim jacket.

Alison, whose own fine light-brown hair wouldn't know what a wave was, usually kept her style simple by putting it in a pony-tail or a bun, and her eyes, although blue like most of her family's, were pale like her dad's and uncle's, rather than the vibrant blue Rosie and her brother boasted. At five foot three she was an inch taller than Rosie, but while the younger woman's curves were in proportion, Alison was most definitely pear-shaped. Her flat chest and broad hips had been the bane of her life.

In short, Alison had every reason to envy her cousin but didn't. She couldn't muster a single negative thought about her.

When Rosie was born Alison had been at university, though still living at home, and she'd been all too keen to babysit for extra money. She'd watched her cousin grow up, and for most of the time she'd been fond of her – apart from the tricky teenage years when Rosie had really got on Alison's nerves for a while.

When Alison became a mum herself, it was Rosie's turn to babysit as soon as she was old enough. Alison would get home from wherever she'd been – usually with her husband, Drew – and while he'd wander into the living room to give them space, she'd sit in the kitchen and listen to Rosie's latest news, her joys, her woes, her worries and secrets. And Alison began confiding in Rosie, too, and discovered her cousin had become a good listener.

Over the years, Alison had come to feel that Rosie was the sister she would have loved to have. Having her as a cousin was the second-best thing.

Impulsively she threw her arms around Rosie and hugged her.

Rosie blinked. 'Bloody hell, what's up with you?'

'I've missed you, and it's so good of you to come all this way to bring my birthday cards.'

'I'm a saint, me.' Rosie gave her a worried look. 'Are you okay, Ali?'

'Yeah, of course.' Alison hurried through to the kitchen where she immediately flicked the light and the kettle on and pulled two mugs from the cupboard. 'Isn't the weather miserable? Bloody drizzle all afternoon. Sick to death of grey skies, aren't you?'

'Well, you can't expect anything else in January,' Rosie pointed out, sitting at the table. 'Never sunbathed in the New Year in my life. Ooh, your kitchen's lovely and warm.' She gazed around, an appreciative look on her face. 'I do love your house.'

'Are you still at your mam and dad's or have you gone back to the caravan?' Alison queried.

'Still at Mam and Dad's.' Rosie wrinkled her nose. 'Park doesn't open again until 1 February. Bit of a pain but there you go.'

'Oh, of course. I don't know how you cope in a caravan through the winter,' Alison said, shivering at the thought of it. 'You know, I've offered before but I'll say it again. I've got a spare room. You can always come and live here with me, you know. I'm sure you could get a job locally. You'd be very welcome.'

'Aw, I know, and it's really good of you, but I've spent enough time away from Kelsea Sands. I don't want to leave again. Besides, I've had enough of living in a city, thanks all the same. Twenty years in Sheffield with Craig was enough. Too far from the sea for my liking. And the Humber.'

Alison nodded. Twenty years had been more than enough for her, too. She'd missed Rosie so much during those years, even though they'd spoken on the phone regularly and visited each other at least once a month. Of course, they both had other friends, but it wasn't the same. She'd been relieved when Rosie came home, although sad for her that her long-term relationship had ended.

'I'm hardly far from the Humber myself,' she pointed out. 'And it's only a fifteen-minute drive to the sea.' It was the one thing she'd insisted upon when they'd bought this house. She'd wanted a view of the river, and this new estate on the site of an old dock had been the perfect compromise if she couldn't live in Kelsea Sands.

'Yeah, but you know what I mean.'

Alison nodded, understanding. The air was different in a city. Any city. You could breathe properly in Kelsea Sands. Given the choice, she knew where she'd rather be, and if it hadn't been for Drew's job in the west of the city, and the heavy traffic going across the River Hull at rush hour every morning and evening, she'd have insisted that they buy in the village, or at least as close to it as possible.

Her heart lay in the countryside of Holderness and always would. This remote area of East Yorkshire, edged on one side by the North Sea and by the Yorkshire Wolds on the other, with the

Humber Estuary marking its southern boundary, was the only place she ever felt truly at home.

Even so, she didn't like to think of Rosie staying in a caravan, as nice as it was. Not in winter. Tide's Reach Caravan Park was open eleven months of the year, so its residents were sent packing on 31 December and not allowed back until January was over. Something to do with its licensing conditions, according to Gavin Hewson, who owned it.

Since Rosie had broken up with Craig four years ago, she'd spent every January at her parents' house, just across the road from the park. They'd offered to let her live there permanently, but she'd refused. She'd rather have her own space, even if it was a caravan. Still, it was handy to have a permanent address, and they clearly didn't mind her using theirs.

'Them next door but one from you have still got their Christmas decs up! Have you noticed? Bad luck, that,' Rosie said, nodding knowingly. 'Should have taken them down on Monday at the latest, and here we are on Friday. Wouldn't like to be in their shoes. Hey, you're a bit late home from work, aren't you?' she added, glancing at the clock on the wall as Alison handed her a mug of tea, strong with two sugars, just as she liked it.

The clock was shaped like a chicken and Alison had bought it about thirty years ago when she'd had a sudden and inexplicable desire to decorate her kitchen like a rural farmhouse. All the other things from that era had long since been replaced with something more suited to a home on a reasonably modern city estate, but the chicken clock had stayed. Alison couldn't really say why.

'I've been to the doctor's,' Alison admitted, wondering why she'd shared that information. It would have been much easier to say that the traffic had been bad. She put her own mug of tea on a coaster with shaking hands.

Rosie's expression changed to one of concern. 'Are you all right? Nothing's wrong, is it?'

'No, honestly. Everything's fine. Well...' Alison blinked away sudden tears. 'I mean, I think it is. Mostly.'

She turned away and rummaged in the cupboard. 'Cake?'

'Always,' Rosie confirmed. 'But what aren't you telling me, Ali?'

Alison carried two small plates, each holding a slice of cake and a fork, and placed them carefully on the table before taking a seat next to Rosie.

'I swear, it's nothing. Just a routine health check with it being my birthday month.' Her eyes drifted to the carrier bag that Rosie had propped against her chair leg, and, without warning, she burst into tears.

'Oh, God!' Rosie put her arm around Alison's shoulders and pulled her closer. 'What is it? What's happened? You can tell me, you know. Mind my cake,' she added, hastily nudging the plate away as Alison's elbow moved scarily close to her precious Victoria sponge. 'What did the doctor say?'

'It was the nurse,' Alison said with a sniff. 'It's not about that anyway. Well, not really. My blood pressure was up a bit, and I've gained another seven pounds since I last got weighed and I got told off like I was a naughty kid.'

Rosie nodded wisely. 'They're trained to talk to you like that, you know. Did she call you poppet? I'd have had words if she did.'

Through her tears, Alison couldn't help but laugh. 'No. She was really nice, to be fair. It's me. I feel so washed up. I'm sixty-two!'

'I know,' Rosie said. 'It was your birthday the other day, remember? Are you going to open your cards or are you going to cry all over your cake? Cos that's a crime, if you ask me. It looks ever so nice.' She gazed longingly at her plate. 'Can I stop hugging you now? I'm starving.'

She gave Alison a wink.

Alison shook her head. 'What are we like? Yeah, let's have the cake. Although I shouldn't by rights. The nurse would have a fit.'

'Oh bugger it,' Rosie said. She ignored the fork and picked the cake up in her hands, taking a big bite and chewing blissfully. 'Mm, mm, this is gorgeous,' she managed eventually. 'M&S?'

'Maister's,' Alison told her. She scooped some cake up on her fork and began to tuck in. Sod her blood pressure.

'So,' Rosie said, a few minutes later when the cake had been safely devoured, 'what's with the tears?' She licked her fingers and sighed. 'I must pop into Maister's on the way home.'

'I was just being stupid,' Alison told her. She reached over and opened the kitchen drawer. 'Here, have a baby wipe.'

'Trust you to have baby wipes handy. You're so organised.' Rosie wiped her hands gratefully. 'Thanks, love.'

'I don't feel very organised,' Alison admitted. 'I feel as if everything's falling apart, to be honest. Me most of all.'

'Just because you've turned sixty-two? It's only a number. I don't remember you getting all upset about turning sixty, and surely that was a bigger deal?'

'I'm on the fast lane to seventy now,' Alison said bleakly. 'It's all downhill from now on.'

'It's all downhill from twenty-nine, if you ask me,' Rosie said with a shrug. 'You can't let it bother you. What does it matter? At least we're alive.'

Alison sighed. 'I've got a whisker on my chin,' she admitted at last. 'One wiry dark whisker. I keep having to pluck it out.'

Rosie giggled.

'It's not funny. What if it's just the first? I'll end up looking like Father Christmas!'

'Not if your whiskers are dark. You might end up looking like Hagrid, though.'

'Thanks for that.'

'What's really bothering you?' Rosie queried.

'Life,' Alison said with another, heavier sigh. 'I often wonder what Drew would think of me wasting it away like this.'

'Bless him,' Rosie said. 'He was a lovely fella.'

'He was, and he didn't deserve...'

'Nobody does,' Rosie said gently, squeezing Alison's hand. 'But that's life, isn't it?'

'Do you know, it was nine years in November. Can you believe that? I've been a widow for nine whole years.'

'I'm sorry I wasn't here for you,' Rosie told her for what felt like the millionth time. 'I tried to get back as often as I could, but I wish I'd lived closer.'

'You were brilliant,' Alison assured her. 'You all were. I'd have been lost without you.'

Her mam and dad had been towers of strength. Rosie had popped back from Sheffield as often as she could and had kept in touch by phone and text. Her aunt and uncle, Elaine and Christopher, had been quietly supportive, and her cousin Niall – Rosie's brother – had tried very hard not to be so vicar-ish and be more cousin-ish as he'd consoled and comforted her. Although he'd switched back to vicar mode when he'd performed the funeral service in his church – and a beautiful job he'd done, too.

All in all, she couldn't complain about any of them. She knew she was lucky to have them all.

'Maybe I shouldn't have given up teaching,' she mused, not really meaning it.

'You'd got completely fed up of teaching,' Rosie reminded her. 'You did the right thing.'

'But that was before I knew Drew was going to die! And before I knew I was going to be left all alone.'

'If you really wanted to go back to teaching, you'd have done so... afterwards, but you didn't, did you? You took that job at the petrol station. Don't you like it?'

Alison shrugged. 'I don't mind it, I suppose. It's easy and the people are friendly.' *And it's on the same retail park where Drew used to work so I feel closer to him there.* 'It's just that I can imagine Drew telling me I should be doing something more with my life than this.'

'Like what?'

'I don't know. I can't help thinking how he died so young, Rosie, while I got all this extra life. Shouldn't I be doing something with it? For his sake, if nothing else.'

'Not being funny,' Rosie said, 'but it won't make any difference to Drew what you're doing with your life. If you took up mountain climbing, became a nun, or spent your remaining years sitting in a corner, eating doughnuts and quietly growing your Hagrid beard it really wouldn't matter, would it? Drew wouldn't know one way or the other. Mind you, don't tell our Niall I said that, for God's sake.'

Alison spluttered with laughter. She could always rely on Rosie to tell it like it is. She had to admit that, deep down, she shared her cousin's belief that Drew wouldn't have a clue what she was doing now. There *was* no Drew. Not any more. Niall, bless him, had tried to comfort her with the assurance that his spirit had 'moved on' somewhere, but she'd only nodded and smiled to please him. Drew was gone. That was half the trouble.

They'd been together since their early twenties, and she couldn't say theirs had been a passionate love affair – the sort she'd read about in books and seen in films. It had been a quiet, steady companionship, really, but it had made them both happy enough and she missed him. She missed his lively chatter and his smile, and the way he caught spiders for her and put them outside, and how he cheerfully emptied the bins, so she didn't have to.

He'd been a lovely husband and a wonderful dad to Jenna, who'd adored him. Even so, she knew he'd have kindly but firmly dealt with their daughter's demands.

'Jenna doesn't help,' she said flatly.

Rosie nodded. 'Still babysitting every spare minute?'

'Yep. Don't get me wrong. I love Jenna so much, and I love Hallie and Ada. Of course I do. But sometimes I just wish I could have peace and quiet, you know? I seem to spend most of my time dashing from here to work, to school, or Jenna's house to mind the kids, or to Kelsea Sands to see Mam and Dad.'

'Speaking of your mam and dad,' Rosie said, 'are you going to open your birthday cards?'

'I guess so.'

'Wow, don't sound too thrilled. Have you got so many cards you don't need any more?'

The tears welled up again and Rosie groaned. 'Now what have I said?'

'Do you know what I got in the post for my birthday?' Alison demanded.

'Surprise me.'

'A bloody NHS bowel testing kit! That was my birthday post! Can you imagine?'

Rosie grinned. 'How very thoughtful of them.'

'Wasn't it?' Alison said. 'They also texted me to remind me to book a cervical smear.'

Rosie burst out laughing and handed her the carrier bag.

Alison decided she'd whinged enough and opened her cards. There was a lovely one from her parents, of course, and one from Uncle Christopher and Auntie Elaine, and one from Niall and his wife Kendra, plus a separate one from their children Ryan and Poppy, and one from Rosie.

'Open your presents,' Rosie urged. 'Mind you, don't get your hopes up.'

There was a necklace from her mam and dad, a beautiful, scented candle from Niall and Kendra, chocolates from Ryan and Poppy, and a gift box of soaps from Elaine and Christopher.

'Old lady soaps,' she said with a sigh.

'I know! Told you not to get your hopes up. Mind you, you *are* sixty-two,' Rosie said mischievously. 'I didn't get you a present as such, but I've written you a gift card. Look.'

She reached into the pocket of her jacket and handed Alison a note which read:

I owe you one trip to the cinema with nachos and dips thrown in, or a night out in the pub. Whichever's cheapest.

Alison put her arms around her. 'You're a star,' she told her.

'I know.' Rosie shrugged. 'So, what are you going to do about your Jenna?'

'What *can* I do? She works hard. Joel works hard. They need help with the girls, and they *are* my granddaughters.'

'Well, can't they put some childcare in place? After-school clubs or something? It's not fair dumping it all on you.' Rosie's eyes twinkled with mirth. 'Not at your age.'

Alison nudged her. 'Watch it! Oh, it doesn't matter really, except that I wanted to go home at the weekend and I had to miss it to take the girls to a birthday party at some fun palace. I'd hoped

I could just drop them off and make a getaway, but Jenna hadn't warned me we were expected to stay to supervise.' She pulled the band from her hair, freeing her ponytail and reflected how odd it was that, after all these years, she still thought of Kelsea Sands as home. 'Mam and Dad were very understanding but I know they wanted me there, especially with it being my birthday week.'

Rosie looked suddenly awkward, and Alison's eyes narrowed in suspicion.

'What is it?'

Rosie squirmed in her chair. 'Sorry, Ali. Truth is, I didn't just come to bring you the birthday cards. We were going to ring you, but your mam wanted me to tell you in person because she knew you'd worry, and she said you'd never believe anyone unless you could see their face.'

'Worry about what?' Alison asked, her nerves already kicking in.

Rosie gave her a pleading look. 'Now, don't get yourself all het up, but your mam's had an accident. A fall. She's all right,' she added quickly as Alison gasped. 'Well, mostly.'

'What does, "mostly" mean?'

'She's broken her arm,' Rosie admitted. 'Quite a nasty fracture. But you know your mam. She's staying cheerful.'

'But – but she must have come to Hull to the hospital! Why didn't someone tell me?'

'Dad tried,' Rosie said. 'Mam stayed at the A&E department with your parents, and Dad drove here to put you in the picture and maybe take you to the hospital if you wanted to go, but you weren't in. He didn't know where to find you so...'

'When was this?' Alison asked.

'Wednesday afternoon. Your mam said it was your afternoon off, but you must have been out.'

'I was,' Alison said grimly. 'I had to take Hallie to the dentist. Emergency filling. Joel and Jenna couldn't get away from work.'

'Aw, well, there you go.' Rosie looked sheepish suddenly. 'I'm sorry you're only just hearing about this. Truth is, I promised I'd come here to tell you yesterday, but I got an extra shift at the chippy last night and had to put off coming here. Your mam and dad are going to kill me when they find out. But look, don't worry about your mam, okay?'

'But how will she manage? You know how useless Dad is!'

'I'll pop in every day to make sure they have everything they need,' Rosie promised. 'And so will Mam and Dad. And Seb's lad Sam has offered to pick up any shopping for them and take them to the hospital if needs be, or anything else they need doing. You know how kind he is.'

Alison stared at her then promptly burst into tears.

'Not again! What's going on?' Rosie patted her arm. 'Since you turned sixty-two I think you've developed a faulty valve and sprung a leak.' She smirked. 'Good job it's only your eyes that are leaking, eh? Unless there's something else you haven't told me.'

'Let's not even go there,' Alison said, mopping her tears away with the sleeve of her jumper in a most unladylike manner. 'Poor Mam. It shouldn't be down to you, and Elaine and Christopher, to look after her and Dad. And it definitely shouldn't be down to Sam. It should be me. I should be there for them. Oh!' She gave an impatient shake of her head. 'Why are they so stubborn? Why do they have to stay in Kelsea Sands anyway at their age? I told them it's too remote. They should move somewhere closer to the shops and the doctor's surgery. There's not even a bus service there!'

'I just told you, Sam's offered,' Rosie told her. 'And there's me if I'm not working. And Mam and Dad. Stop worrying, Ali. Like I said, they'll be fine. We'll make sure of it.'

'If I could stay with them I would,' Alison murmured. 'You know that, don't you?'

'Of course. But you've got work, and the grandkids. We get it.'

'I'll be down to see them on Sunday,' Alison promised. 'I don't care if Jenna and Joel have other plans. I'm not changing my mind about this.'

'Great,' Rosie said. 'I'll probably see you there then. I'd better be getting off,' she added, glancing once more at the clock. 'I hate driving in the dark as it is, and the road back isn't exactly straightforward, is it?'

'Are you sure you want to go back tonight?' Alison stared out of the window, her brow creasing with anxiety. 'It's raining faster now. You can stay here tonight if you like. Go back in the morning when it's light.'

Rosie tilted her head, thinking. 'Tempting, but...'

'You can call your parents. Let them know you're staying here. They won't worry then.'

'I haven't got anything with me, though.'

'I can lend you some pyjamas. They'll probably fit you better than they do me. At least you've got boobs to fill the top and your hips won't strain the bottoms. And I have a new toothbrush in its packaging. You can have that.'

'I suppose it's something different to write in my journal... If I stay, can we watch that new Harlan Coben thriller on Netflix? I'm proper hooked on his stuff.'

'Really?' Alison wrinkled her nose. She didn't like thrillers. They made her too tense and anxious. 'I suppose so. As long as you'll sit through *Emmerdale* first.'

Rosie groaned. 'Aw no! You and your soaps.'

'One soap, and it's not up for negotiation,' Alison said firmly. 'I like the pretty scenery. Tell you what, I'll make you a posh coffee to help you get through it.'

'Ooh, one of those caramel ones? And do we get a hot chocolate before bedtime?'

'Naturally.' She'd start the diet tomorrow.

Rosie hesitated, clearly still not sure.

'And I still have loads of that cake left,' Alison said slyly.

Rosie grinned. 'Looks like you've got yourself a house guest for the night.'

2

It was only twenty-four miles from her home to Kelsea Sands, but it still took Alison nearly an hour to get there, and that was going by the quickest route.

Sometimes, if the weather was good and she had lots of time to spare and the mood took her, she'd go a longer way round, via Sunk Island, to gaze at the little boats at Stone Creek and look out over the Humber to Lincolnshire. Across the water she could see the Port of Immingham. With its cranes and chimneys and bustling activity it seemed a million miles away from this little haven of tranquillity.

It was a good place to walk along the riverbank, breathe in the fresh air and relax.

Today, though, she had no time for relaxing. Her mam and dad were expecting her and, despite her objections, had informed her they were taking her to The North Star for Sunday dinner.

She couldn't even remember the last time she'd been in the pub, even though it was only a few minutes' walk from her parents' home.

When, she wondered, had life got so hectic? When Hallie and Ada had started school she'd assumed that she wouldn't be needed so much for babysitting, but Jenna had begged her to take the twins to school on the mornings she wasn't working an early shift at the petrol station, and then she'd asked if Alison could pick them up afterwards and maybe take them home with her for a couple of hours because Jenna had so much work to do and it was far easier to get on with it while the twins weren't around.

Alison worked alternate Saturdays and Sundays and her weekend days should have been sacrosanct as Jenna, who was also a teacher, didn't work then and Joel only worked every other weekend at the large IT company he'd been with since leaving college, but somehow they both seemed to find things that needed doing. Joel was working overtime. He had a conference to attend. He was on a training course. Jenna had a pile of marking to get through. She had lessons to plan. She was feeling absolutely exhausted, and would Mum really mind...?

Somehow it had become normal. It was what happened. Jenna and Joel worked hard. Alison did the lion's share of the childcare, whether the girls were at school or not.

It wasn't fair and Alison knew it was time she did something about it. She just didn't know what. She loved Hallie and Ada with all her heart, but she was tired. She wanted – no, needed – a break. Besides, the twins should spend more time with their mum and dad, just as Alison should with hers.

She put all thoughts of her daughter and granddaughters aside for a moment as she passed Kelsea Wetlands – acres of grasslands, freshwater lakes and saltwater lagoons which provided a haven for birds and other wildlife – and drove along Weltringham Road.

On impulse, she drove past Sanderlings, her parents'

detached red-brick bungalow, and rounded the corner, heading towards the beach.

At the end of the road, she pulled into the little car park and turned off the engine. She needed to breathe in the sea air and shake off the dust of the city.

Alison made her way, with some difficulty, over the mound of grass and sand that formed a feeble barrier between the car park and the beach, and stood, hands on hips, gazing out to sea. The wide-open sky was vast above her, stretching out to meet the horizon where she could see the wind turbines off the coast of nearby Weltringham.

It was one of those crisp, cold, cloudless though blustery January days that made her feel grateful to be alive.

She turned her head to the left, where the crumbling cliffs began. There, the road she'd just driven down ended abruptly – bits of it tumbled into the sea every year thanks to the terrible coastal erosion.

The Tide's Reach Caravan Park stood just on the other side of the road, and she could see how close to the edge of the cliff some of the caravans were. She thought you'd have to be pretty brave to live in one of those, and surely it was time they were moved to safety. She supposed Gavin would see to it before the park reopened. He'd been fighting the battle against the hungry sea for a long time now, after all, and knew what he was doing.

Bits of concrete rubble still littered this part of the beach, but even so... There was something about this broken beauty that tugged at her heart. She closed her eyes and breathed in the salty air, glad to be home. Smiling, she threw out her arms, as if embracing the vast sky and the pounding waves. She felt freer than she had in months.

This tiny village, with no more than thirty residences, filled her with hope and optimism somehow. As she opened her eyes, she felt tears pricking and wasn't sure if it was emotion that was overwhelming her, or the salty sting of the sea carried on the increasingly gusty wind.

She drove slowly back down Weltringham Road, noting the bare hedges that lined the route, and the trees silhouetted against the blue sky, whose empty branches would, in a few short months, be lush and green and bursting with blossom. Ahead of her lay the Humber – the tidal estuary that fed into the sea. It was fast flowing today – hurried along by the impatient wind. On the other side of the water she could see the green banks of Lincolnshire.

As she pulled up outside Sanderlings, she saw the net curtains twitch, and smiled to herself. She'd known her mam would be waiting at the window, eager for her arrival.

No doubt the kettle would be boiling before Alison had even reached the front door. A broken arm wouldn't stop her mam from making tea.

She tapped lightly on the window, just to let them know she was about to enter the bungalow – although she had no idea why. Her parents had told her repeatedly not to bother.

'Not like we'll be getting up to something, is it?' her mam had chortled.

Even so, she felt it was the polite thing to do, although she never waited for a response. She pushed open the door into the hallway and, sure enough, she could hear the kettle even from here. The door to the living room was open, welcoming her in.

She took off her shoes, mindful of her mam's carpets, and headed into the surprisingly spacious room where she found her dad sitting in an armchair staring at a mobile phone.

Alison gaped at him. 'What are *you* doing with a phone?' she asked, hardly able to believe what she was seeing.

Her mam had bought herself a phone a few years ago

although she hated using it and had never really got the hang of it, preferring to use the landline. Whenever she used it to text Alison, she would always sign it with 'Love from Mam' as if Alison wouldn't know who the text was from, and the messages were as brief as possible.

Dad, though, had refused point-blank to entertain a mobile phone, so to see him sitting there with his eyes fixed on the screen of what looked to be a pretty up-to-date model was a shock.

He briefly glanced up at her and said, 'Hello, love. You made it, then,' before his attention switched back to whatever was so exciting on the screen.

Mam bustled into the room. She rolled her eyes and said, 'Is he still on that thing?'

Alison gently hugged her, aware of the arm that was encased in plaster and nestled in a sling. 'Surely that's not Dad's?' she murmured incredulously.

'Oh, it is. After my little fall our Christopher persuaded him to step into the twenty-first century in case of emergencies. That's Elaine's old phone but it's still quite modern. Your father's hooked. It's got the internet and everything, although it's a bit sporadic round here. Ask him what he's doing. Go on, ask him!'

Alison glanced at her father. 'What are you doing, Dad?'

He didn't reply, his fingers jabbing at the screen, his brow furrowed in concentration.

She tried again. 'Dad?'

He looked up, bemused. 'What?'

'What are you doing?'

'Oh.' He shrugged. 'A quiz.' His gaze lowered again, and Alison turned back to her mother who tutted in annoyance.

'Would you believe, he's answering a load of questions to find out which rabbit he'd be if he was a character in *Watership Down*? I ask you!'

'Oh, Dad!' Alison couldn't help but smile. After all his criticisms of other people using their phones too much he'd gone and fallen for that!

'Cup of tea, love?' Mam asked. 'Or would you prefer coffee? Mind, I haven't got one of them fancy machines like you have,' she warned, as she did every time Alison visited.

'Tea's fine, but I'll make it,' Alison said, ignoring her mother's protestations that she was perfectly capable.

'It *would* be your right hand,' she said, eyeing her mother worriedly as she reached for the teabags. 'How are you managing, really?'

'No problem at all,' Mam said cheerfully. 'I mean, it's a bit tricky doing some things, but I'm getting the hang of it. When you think about it, it's a blessing really. I'm learning to use my left hand after all these years. Never too late to learn a new skill.'

Trust her mother to look on the bright side, Alison thought, as she headed to the fridge for milk. You couldn't keep her down for long. She wished she'd inherited a bit of her parents' resilience.

Although not allowed to make the tea, Alison's mam soon dug out the biscuits and insisted on carrying the tin into the living room. Alison put a mug on the nest of tables beside her dad's chair just as he put his phone away with a sigh.

'I'm Bigwig,' he said. 'Is that good?'

'No idea,' Mam replied. 'I've never watched it.'

'Don't you know, Dad?' Alison asked, amused.

'How would I know? I've never watched it either.'

'Not read the book?' she asked cheekily.

He frowned. 'Why would I read a book about bloody rabbits? I'm not six!'

'Ignore him and have a custard cream,' Mam said, reaching for a biscuit from the tin she'd brought in.

'Aren't we going for lunch in the pub in half an hour?' Alison queried, checking the clock on the mantelpiece which said twelve thirty.

'Yes, but I haven't had any breakfast.'

'*Why* haven't you had any breakfast?' Alarm bells were ringing already. Mam liked a breakfast. 'Are you sure you're managing? Rosie said—'

'Rosie's been good as gold, bless her,' Mam assured her. 'You don't have to worry about me, love. Everyone's falling over themselves to help out: your auntie and uncle, Seb's lad Sam. Anyway,' she added dryly, 'I've got your dad to look after me. What could possibly go wrong?'

'I hope they've got the chicken and mushroom pie on,' Dad said hopefully. 'I do love a chicken and mushroom pie.'

'See what I mean?' Mam beamed at Alison. 'Never mind him. How was your birthday?'

'Oh, you know. I was working, so... Thanks for the card and the lovely necklace.' She pulled gently at the chain around her neck, which had a gold coffee bean attached. 'Very retro.'

'Is it? I just saw the coffee bean and thought of you with your passion for that machine of yours.'

Alison stifled a smile. It was hardly a passion. She maybe used it four or five times a month. But she supposed the thought was there.

'Rosie was so good to pop it all across to yours when you couldn't make it last weekend. We were so disappointed.'

'Sorry, Mam. I was working on Sunday, and on Saturday I had to ferry the girls around because Jenna and Joel were both busy.'

'They work too hard,' Mam said firmly. 'And so do you, by the sound of it.' She smiled suddenly. 'How are Hallie and Ada? I haven't seen them for weeks.'

'Lively,' Alison said wryly. 'Too lively for you, especially with your broken arm.'

'Oh, don't be silly! We'd love to see more of them. You can bring them here every weekend, you know. We wouldn't mind at all. Would we, Stan?'

Dad frowned. 'Would we what?'

'Mind about having Hallie and Ada here.'

'Who? Oh! No, of course not. I could take them to the beach. Show them the old Battery. I'm sure they'd be fascinated.'

Alison and her mother exchanged doubtful looks, unable to imagine the twins having any interest at all in the Battery.

It wasn't only the broken road that littered the beach with bits of broken concrete and rubble, but also the remains of the old Goodfellow Battery, a First World War military fort which, during the Second World War, had been enlarged with a hospital, gun emplacements, searchlights, barracks and officers' mess, most of which had been washed away by the sea thanks to the appalling coastal erosion.

What remained of it now ironically helped a little in the battle against that erosion, but it attracted attention from curious visitors and history buffs, and Alison had seen quite a few videos online of people who'd ventured inside the broken structure to film for their YouTube channel or social media sites.

Somehow, she doubted that seven-year-old twin girls would be as captivated.

'You'll have to bring them next weekend if you're not working,' Mam said. 'Don't worry. I won't let your dad anywhere near them. Maybe,' she added shrewdly, 'you can leave them here. Have the weekend to yourself for once.'

'Mam, you've got a broken arm!'

'Oh, so what?' Her mother glanced down at her plaster-encased arm and sighed. 'It's a bit of a nuisance, I must say, but I'm all right really. Mind you, your dad's had to fasten the button on my jeans. I couldn't manage it with one hand. Speaking of which, Elaine and Christopher are coming to the pub to meet us, along with Rosie, so that'll be nice, won't it?'

Alison frowned. 'Why did you say, "speaking of which" and go on about Elaine and Christopher when you were talking about the button of your jeans?'

'Why do you think? You just watch our Elaine's face when she clocks me wearing jeans again. You know what she thinks about me dressing inappropriately for my age.' She tutted crossly. 'Honestly, she'd have me dress like an old woman if she had her way.'

Alison bit her lip. Her mam was eighty-four. What age did she think you became an old woman?

She smiled fondly at her mother, who was nibbling happily on a custard cream. She still insisted on having her hair coloured every six weeks at the salon in the village of Hilderstead, around eight miles north-west of Kelsea Sands, covering the grey with a lovely ash blonde. She couldn't see a thing without her glasses so had stopped wearing make-up as she feared she'd end up looking like Lily Savage if she attempted it, but her skin wasn't in bad condition since she'd always used moisturiser, and she dressed quite fashionably despite her sister-in-law's disapproval.

It was strange, but sometimes it seemed her mother was younger than Alison. How had that happened?

Dad groaned. 'I'm starving. Did you hear my belly rumble then?' he demanded. There was a beep from his phone, and he beamed in delight. 'I've got a text message!'

'Aw,' Mam said fondly. 'His very first one. I'm so proud.'

'It's our Christopher,' Dad announced. 'They're already at the pub and they want us to hurry up because they're hungry and Rosie's already gone through two packets of crisps waiting.'

Alison laughed. 'Sounds like our Rosie. Come on then. To the pub!'

Odd, but as she helped her mam into her coat, Alison suddenly felt a whole lot brighter.

3

As blue as the sky was, it was decidedly cold outside, and the three of them hurried up the road to the pub as fast as Mam and Dad could manage.

They went past the front door of The North Star and round to the side door which, during the day, was the one everyone used. As they stepped inside, the familiar smell of beer mixed with cooking smells from the kitchen made them all relax instantly. Alison had forgotten how much she loved this place.

'I'll get the drinks,' Dad announced. 'You make sure you get your mam settled, Alison, there's a good lass.'

Alison sent a cheery wave to Seb's lad Sam, who was behind the bar, and herded her mother through to the main room of the pub.

The North Star had two sections: a large, quiet bar room running the full length of the main building, where people could sit by one of the two fireplaces and maybe select a book from either of the bookcases, or head to a table by one of the bay windows and gaze out over the river; and the restaurant, which was mainly used during the evening, or for private functions, or on exceptionally busy days. It was the only room that was carpeted. The bar room had its original slate floor.

The North Star was a large square building with a more recent rear extension. It had been built in the mid nineteenth century after the old village of Kelsea tumbled into the sea and the residents moved closer to the Humber.

A few decades ago, its red-brick walls had been rendered and painted white, while the inside was cheerfully decorated in shades of cream and teal. It had polished oak tables and fittings, teal Dralon chairs and banquettes, a large bay window on one side of the front door, and two slightly smaller bay windows on the other, all giving glorious views across the estuary to Lincolnshire. On its walls were maps and images of the Holderness coast, photographs of past lifeboat crew members, and even an old lifebelt.

It was warm and welcoming, and Alison's spirits lifted even further when she spotted the other members of her family sitting at a table by the window.

Rosie waved frantically at them, as if they couldn't possibly see her otherwise, even though there was currently no one else in the bar.

Christopher – a handsome, quiet man, with receding, wiry grey hair and gentle eyes – got to his feet as they approached the table, ever the gentleman. Alison often thought that he, a retired old-school police inspector, was like someone from another age. Sometimes it was hard to believe that he was her dad's younger brother. Her uncle was calm, cool, thoughtful and sensible. Dad was – not. What they had in common, though, was their kindness. They were both lovely men in their own way.

Elaine, she noticed, gave Mam a searching look, no doubt storing the jeans, trainers and Paddington Bear sweatshirt in her mental filing cabinet as evidence to be relied upon at a later date.

She hadn't worked all those years in admin at the police station in Millensea for nothing.

Short and stocky, with hair that was now more grey than the rose gold it had once been, she was wearing a very sensible dress and cardigan, as befitting a woman of seventy-four. Christopher, at seventy-six, was equally well-dressed in smart trousers, a shirt and tie, and a woollen sleeveless jumper. No one could ever accuse them of looking like they'd just rolled out of bed and thrown on the first things they could lay their hands on.

As Alison's dad strolled up to the table with a tray of drinks in his hands, she noticed his baggy jogging bottoms, and remembered that, under his coat, he was wearing a sweatshirt with a popular fashion logo partly obscured by a tea stain that he'd failed to remove properly that morning.

She looked down at her ancient black leggings and old grey jumper, and then at Rosie in her skinny jeans and low-cut, bright pink T-shirt, fingers adorned with rings, gold hoop earrings dangling from her earlobes, her eyelashes heavy with mascara and her lips pink and glossy and wondered how two branches of the same family could be so different.

'I thought you'd never get here,' Rosie told her. Without even waiting for her uncle to take off his coat, she grabbed the menus and began handing them out.

Her father lifted an eyebrow. 'Rosie,' he said quietly.

Rosie gave him a pleading look. 'Yes, but I'm hungry.'

'But you're not starving,' he said. 'Let them get settled before you start haranguing them, for goodness' sake.'

'Sorry, Dad,' Rosie said meekly, giving Alison a sideways eyeroll.

'And I saw that,' he added, his mouth twitching in amusement.

Rosie laughed. 'All right, all right, I get it. Behave yourself, Rosie.'

'Chance would be a fine thing,' her mother said, shaking her head. 'I think your brother must have got your share of the manners.'

To Rosie's credit she didn't bite. Although her mother had a habit of pointing out how saintly and wonderful Niall was, it had never bothered Rosie. Alison knew how much she loved her brother, and that she wasn't about to let her mother's uneven handouts of praise affect their relationship. Besides, Rosie realised her mam and dad adored her just as much. Her mam just had a funny way of showing it sometimes.

'To be fair,' Alison's dad said, handing her the Diet Coke she'd asked for and placing his wife's mango and pineapple juice in front of her, 'I *am* starving, so I'll have one of them menus, Rosie, if you don't mind.'

'See?' Rosie said triumphantly, handing her uncle the menu as she gave her dad a smug look. 'Not just me.'

Her father shook his head, but he was smiling.

Elaine raised her glass. 'To you, Alison. A belated happy birthday.'

Alison smiled as they all toasted her, resisting the urge to point out that she was far too old for birthdays, since she was actually the second youngest there.

'Thank you,' she said. 'And thanks so much for the lovely presents and cards. I really appreciate them. I've messaged Niall and Kendra to thank them, too.'

'They would have joined us,' Elaine said, 'but you know Sunday's a busy day for Niall.'

Niall, who at forty-six was three years older than Rosie, was the vicar at St Saviour's Church in Millensea, a small seaside town about ten miles and a twenty-minute drive up the coast. He and his wife, Kendra, lived in a modern vicarage with their two children, and it amused Alison and her mother no end how awed Elaine was, both by Niall's 'calling' and by Kendra's 'support and commitment to his calling'.

Rosie had told them that, whenever her brother and sister-in-law visited, her mam would buy fresh flowers for the sitting room, dust and hoover the house as if she was preparing it for a royal visit and bake a cake especially for the occasion.

'She puts a scented candle in the bathroom an' all,' she'd added. 'One day I hope Kendra drops by unannounced. Mam'll die of shame.'

'Chicken and mushroom pie,' Dad said, passing his menu back along the table. 'Can't beat it.'

'I don't know why you needed the menu,' Mam said. 'It's all you ever want anyway.'

'Are you not having a starter?' Elaine asked.

'I'd rather have a pudding,' Rosie told her.

The rest of them nodded in agreement, causing Elaine's face to fall in clear disappointment, as if she couldn't possibly have a starter if the rest of them weren't.

Gently, her husband pointed out that they had her favourite crème brûlée available and maybe she'd prefer to skip a starter in favour of pudding after all, so the crisis was averted. He placed their orders at the bar and informed them that he'd ordered them all another round of drinks as well and had settled the bill. 'My treat,' he added, holding up his hands as they protested. 'I insist.'

Everyone thanked him and Alison's dad raised his glass in his brother's direction. 'Fair enough,' he said comfortably. 'I'll get it next time though.'

'How's Jenna doing?' Elaine asked, after taking a polite sip of her white wine. 'Well, I hope?'

'Busy,' Alison said. 'New term. Back in the thick of it.'

'And Joel?'

'Oh, he's busy too,' she admitted. 'It seems he's determined to end up running the world. He's always off doing some training course or other.'

'I expect they just want what's best for the girls,' Mam said comfortingly.

'Mm.' Alison wondered what, exactly, *was* best for the girls. Surely having their parents at home a bit more would be preferable to finding out that their dad had got another promotion and their mum was hitting all her targets? What about their responsibilities to their daughters? She knew it was hard for modern parents and had every sympathy, but sometimes she felt that Joel and Jenna deliberately looked for reasons not to be available for the twins, although she'd never say so to her extended family. Well, except Rosie, but she didn't count.

'Our Niall and Kendra manage their family life so well,' Elaine said proudly. 'Being a vicar is such a demanding role. Niall is on call practically all the time. And of course, Kendra has her counselling work, even though she's an exceptional vicar's wife and takes that duty very seriously. I honestly don't know how they balance everything, but they do it somehow.'

'Lucky Niall and Kendra,' Alison murmured. Christopher gave her a sympathetic look, and she blushed, mortified that he'd heard her, though at least he seemed to understand.

'How's your arm today, Cherry?' he asked Mam, who held up the limb in question so they could all examine it to their satisfaction.

'Not too bad,' she told him. 'I'm getting quite good at using my left hand – well, for some things anyway. Mind you, Stan's had to help me out a bit, haven't you, love? I've had to ask him to do things for me that no husband should have to do for a wife. By heck, the things you've seen lately, eh, Stan?'

Rosie spat her cider back into her glass as Elaine groaned, 'Oh, Cherry, must you? We're about to eat.'

As if on cue, Briar, a young woman from the village who was currently working for Sam, delivered the first of the meals to their table.

'Thanks, love,' Mam said cheerfully, as a plate of scampi and chips was put in front of her. 'How are you doing? And how's your mam?'

'All right, thanks, Mrs Wainwright,' Briar said. 'Her op went fine and she's coming out of hospital tomorrow, all being well. I told her about your fall, and she said to send you her love when I saw you.'

'Aw, tell her thank you. Glad her operation went okay. You tell her from me to take it easy when she gets home.'

'Oh, don't worry about that. Mam's never been one for doing anything else, has she?' Briar said with a grin. She put the last of the plates on the table and hurried off to get the rest of the meals.

'What happened to her mam?' Alison queried, reaching for the salt. She knew Mrs Chambers well and hadn't heard she'd been ill.

'Women's things. A bit of lifting up and tucking in, I expect. Certain things end up where they shouldn't when you get to her age.'

Elaine gave her a pained look. 'Cherry! We're eating!'

'Yours hasn't even arrived yet,' Mam pointed out indignantly. 'Ooh, did I tell you about Sheila MacMillan, Alison?'

'You mean that she died?' Alison asked. 'Yes, you told me before Christmas.' She gave her mother an anxious look. Was she getting forgetful or something?

'Not that she died, you daft ha'p'orth! About her will.'

Elaine forgot that she was annoyed with her sister-in-law and leaned forward eagerly. 'Ooh, yes. I heard all about that, too. Stella's furious, apparently.'

'What's this about?' Rosie asked, agog. 'What have I missed?'

'Well, you know everyone assumed that she'd have left Watersmeet to both her children? She didn't. She left it all to Ian.' Mam turned to Alison, her eyes bright. 'Do you remember Ian, love? He was in your class at primary school. Left here years ago.'

Alison knew who she meant. A brown-haired boy who always looked immaculate and had a penchant for trying to show her up.

'He was a proper goody-two-shoes,' she told Rosie, who was digging into her roast beef, despite her mother's pained expression which made it clear she felt her daughter should wait for everyone to be served.

'Aw, don't say that,' Mam rebuked her. 'He was a lovely little boy. Ever so bonny.'

Rosie pulled a face and mouthed, '*Bonny*?'

Alison grinned. 'He used to get picked on cos he had a posh satchel when the rest of us had them cheap cloth bags. It had his name written on it on a little card in the front pocket. He was a Cub. And a Boy Scout.'

'Ah,' Rosie said, nodding as if that told her everything she needed to know.

'Don't be mean,' Mam said.

'Don't be mean? He tried to show me up every Friday for weeks,' Alison said indignantly.

'I'm sure he didn't,' Mam said firmly, sprinkling vinegar liberally over her chips.

'Oh yes he did.' Alison turned to Rosie, who was clearly more ready to believe her. 'We used to have a spelling test every Friday morning. We had to go round the classroom, taking it in turns to ask one of our classmates to spell a word out of this book the teacher had given us. Most of us chose straightforward words, like *continue*, or *earthquake* or something. Do you know what words he gave me? *Archaeologist* and *miscellaneous*! I still remember the terror to this day.'

'Did you spell them right?' Rosie asked, enthralled.

'Well, yes. I wasn't even going to try, but I remember looking in horror at Miss Sayers—'

'Aw,' Mam interrupted. 'She was a lovely woman.'

'Yes, she was. And she just nodded and smiled at me and said, "Go on, Alison." So I did. And,' she finished smugly, 'I got them right and he was gutted.'

Miss Sayers had looked so proud of her. Alison remembered how happy it had made her feel for ages afterwards. Like she could achieve anything. She thought Miss Sayers had probably had a lot to do with her wanting to become a teacher herself.

'I'm sure Ian only asked you because he knew you could do it,' Mam mused.

'Because he fancied you, more like,' Rosie said gleefully.

They all broke off as Briar returned with the remaining plates of food. 'Sorry for the delay,' she said. 'Enjoy your meals. Is there anything else I can get you?'

They all assured her they had everything they needed, and she rushed back to the kitchen.

'Why is she in such a hurry?' Dad pondered. 'We're the only ones here.'

'Never mind that,' Mam said. 'What do you mean, Ian fancied her?'

'Isn't it obvious?' Rosie shrugged. 'He singled her out every week and he deliberately got her attention by giving her such hard words that she'd remember him forever.'

'We were ten!'

'What's that got to do with it? I had my first boyfriend at seven.' Rosie sighed. 'Aw, little Jon Day. He followed me round like a puppy for months, bless him. If his dad hadn't got that job near Blackpool, who knows what might have happened? Maybe I'd have been Mrs Day by now.'

'Well, if he'd actually married you, he'd have got my blessing,' Elaine said heavily. She'd never approved of Rosie and Craig 'living in sin' for twenty years, especially with Niall being a vicar, and him with a reputation to uphold.

Rosie ignored the jibe. 'Point is, it was clearly a strategy on Ian's part. Quite clever really.'

'Hardly!' Alison said with a snort of laughter.

'Worked, didn't it? How long is it since you left primary school? Fifty years or thereabouts. Yet here you are, still talking about it.'

'This is the first time I've mentioned it! Anyway, forget it. We were talking about Sheila's will.'

'Oh yes.' Elaine's eyes brightened. 'So, like your mother said, Sheila left Watersmeet to Ian, lock, stock and barrel.'

'It doesn't seem fair,' her mam added. 'He left Kelsea Sands to go to university and never came back, whereas Stella's been in the area the whole time, and did all sorts for her mother, didn't she?'

'Exactly,' Elaine said. She shook her head as she stuck a fork in her bacon-wrapped chicken breast. 'It's not right at all. But then, Ian always was her golden boy, wasn't he? She spoke about him in such glowing terms, whereas her daughter never really got a look-in. Poor Stella never had a chance.'

Rosie and Alison exchanged knowing looks. Alison

wondered how Elaine could be so lacking in self-awareness. Good job Rosie was so understanding.

'Didn't you ever go out with him then, Ali?' Rosie asked.

'Who, Ian? God, no. To be honest, I don't even remember seeing him after we left primary school and went up to Millensea High.'

'According to Sheila he did ever so well for himself,' Mam said. 'Went to university, got a degree, had his own business. She was so proud of him, wasn't she, Stan? Photos of him all over that house. I know cos I used to pop by when she was poorly, just to see if she needed anything. Still doesn't make it right, though. I mean, Stella did all right, too, and there were no photos of *her* – well, not recent ones any road. And what I want to know is, what will happen to Watersmeet now?'

'It will be sold, I expect,' Christopher said. 'It's a terrible shame. It's a lovely property, but I can't see Ian wanting to come back after all this time to live here, can you?'

'But what about her animals?' Rosie demanded.

'Oh crikey, yes,' Alison gasped. Sheila was well known for rescuing waifs and strays over the years. 'Please tell me someone's been feeding and watering them all.'

'Stella's been popping by when she can to check everything's okay, but as soon as her mother passed, she paid the Fosters at Carr Farm to see to the animals' physical needs. That's what I mean,' Elaine said primly, 'about it not being fair. I can imagine—'

But what she imagined was something she never revealed, as she let out a yelp and glared at her sister-in-law. 'Did you just bloody kick me?' she demanded, forgetting her rule about swearing in public.

Alison watched in surprise as her mother frantically nodded her head towards the bar. Everyone's gaze turned in that direction and Alison saw a man in jeans and a wax jacket standing at the counter, chatting to Seb's lad Sam.

'What?' she asked, seeing her mam's expression. She looked fit to burst.

'It's him!' she whispered dramatically. 'That bloke over there. It's Ian MacMillan!'

Alison frowned. 'Don't be daft. It looks nothing like him.' If it was, he'd certainly changed a lot since primary school. Mind you, she'd no doubt he'd say the same about her. It would be a bit worrying if they *hadn't* changed, wouldn't it?

'Of course it is. I'd know him anywhere. I told you, Sheila's walls were covered in framed photos of him. Aw, he's still bonny, isn't he?'

Rosie stifled a giggle. 'Has he got his satchel with him?'

'What's he doing?' Elaine whispered, not daring to look towards him.

'Well, since he's at the bar, I should imagine he's ordering a drink,' Dad said. 'This chicken and mushroom pie's bloody lovely, you know. Can't you ask Sam for the recipe, Cherry?'

'Hey, he's not getting a drink,' Rosie said, making no attempt to hide the fact that she was staring intently at the poor man. 'Ooh, look! Sam's passing him some foil tubs. Do you reckon he does takeaways now?'

Alison's dad brightened instantly. 'Takeaways? You mean I could order this pie any night of the week?'

'Will you shut up about that bloody pie?' Mam snapped. 'Honestly, you're a – oh! Hello, Ian!' She waved as the man at the bar turned to face them, as if she expected him to recognise her after all those years.

Alison watched, mesmerised, as he straightened and seemed to stare straight at her. He was dressed very casually in jeans and heavy boots, and his short brown hair was peppered with grey. If he really *was* Ian his face was thinner than she remembered, and of course the smooth baby skin was now lined. Had his eyes always been that startlingly blue? Surely she'd have remembered that.

For a moment she thought he was going to come over and speak to them, but then he seemed to have second thoughts. He nodded at them, then muttered something to Sam, who leaned over and said something back. The-man-who-might-be-Ian straightened, then headed out of the pub with his foil tubs.

'What a shame,' Elaine said. 'I'd love to have talked to him.'

'I'll bet you would,' Rosie mumbled.

'I expect he had to hurry home before his food went cold,' Christopher said.

'I must ask Sam if he does deliveries,' Dad mused.

Alison said nothing. Just when, she wondered, had Ian MacMillan got so – well – *hot*? It was impossible. It *couldn't* be him.

Rosie nudged her. 'You never know your luck. Maybe he still fancies you and he was so overcome at seeing you again that he had to flee before he gave himself away.'

'You missed your vocation,' her mother told her. 'You should have been writing films for the Hallmark Channel.'

Rosie cheerfully cut a roast potato in half. 'You can mock,' she said. 'I'm right about this. You just wait and see.'

4

Mac had fed Robert Carne that morning, but no one would have believed it if they'd observed the hungry way the Jack Russell watched him as he dished out his takeaway meal of roast beef with all the trimmings and carried his plate over to the table.

'You only get breakfast and dinner, not lunch,' he told the little dog, trying not to feel guilty. 'I have written proof,' he added, nodding at the handwritten list stuck to the fridge door with a magnet from Millensea. Instructions for the feeding of each one of the animals he was now responsible for. He wasn't about to deviate from them. He wouldn't dare.

Carne uttered a pathetic whine as if he'd been starved for weeks, which Mac knew wasn't true. Gilly Foster from Carr Farm had been at great pains to assure him that she and her husband, Keith, had taken great care of each animal, and had followed the directions that Sheila herself had left for whoever was to take temporary responsibility for their wellbeing. Carne was just very good at pulling on the heartstrings. No doubt Mac's mother had fallen for it every time, but he was made of sterner stuff.

'Thing is,' he explained to the little dog, as he lightly sprinkled salt on his roast potatoes and Yorkshire puddings, 'you might think I'm being cruel to you but I'm actually being kind. I have a duty of care to you, you see.' His hand paused in mid-air. 'God help you,' he muttered and put the salt back on the table.

He still couldn't believe what his mother had done. He'd been almost as shocked about it as his sister, the day they'd discovered the terms of the will. Almost, but not quite.

As if on cue his phone beeped and he took it out of his jeans pocket and glanced at the screen before laying it on the table, face down so he couldn't see it.

Talk of the devil.

> **STELLA**
> Have you followed the instructions today? Don't forget Mrs Beddows is due to be wormed tomorrow. We need to talk, Ian.

He sighed as he picked up his knife and fork. 'No, we don't.'

Not today. He really couldn't face it. Neither of them was likely to shift their position, so what would be the point? It would only end in yet another scene, with her screaming at him and him refusing to budge and one or the other of them walking away.

'And my name's Mac now,' he muttered. 'Don't call me Ian.'

He gazed around the big, comfortable farmhouse kitchen, aware of the flutter of nerves that had become a regular thing. In so many ways this was a dream come true. In others, it was a nightmare. What now?

'Now,' he said firmly, in answer to his own question, 'I eat my Sunday lunch.'

It had been good of Seb's lad Sam to let him have a takeaway. He'd popped into the pub a few nights ago to introduce himself, having heard that Seb – the former landlord – no longer worked at The North Star. Mac and Seb had been at school together, but they'd lost touch when Mac left for university. It was Seb's own father, Alby, who'd run the pub back in the day.

He and Sam had a friendly chat, and Mac had ordered a hot pasty to stave off the hunger pangs. He'd admitted he wasn't really one for cooking, which was when Sam had offered to let him order from the pub and take the meals home with him if he didn't fancy eating out.

He didn't intend to make a habit of it, but it had been a long time since he'd had a Sunday roast, and when Sam had suggested it, as a favour to his dad's old schoolfriend, he hadn't been able to resist.

Of course, if he'd known who'd be in the bar when he walked in, he would have cancelled the order. All those eyes staring at him then trying to pretend they weren't.

And Alison Wainwright among them.

He hadn't seen her for – how long had it been? There was no way he'd have known it was her if Sam hadn't told him who the strange woman was who'd waved and called to him as if they were best friends. Alison's mother. He hadn't seen any members of that family for decades, but as soon as he'd heard the word *Wainwright* he'd remembered.

He scooped up a forkful of mashed carrot and swede and ate without tasting it, his mind playing over his schooldays, so many, many years ago.

He'd adored Alison right through primary school, but she'd barely known he was there. He may have only sat across the table from her, but he might as well have been in another class-room for all the notice she'd taken of him. The only time she'd seemed to acknowledge his presence was when they'd done those spelling tests for Miss Sayers.

He smiled at the memory. Alison had been so clever, and

he'd known she'd be able to spell the difficult words. He wanted Miss Sayers and everyone else to know it, too. And he'd been right, hadn't he? He'd felt so proud of her when she haltingly spelled out whichever words he'd chosen for her. He couldn't remember what they were now, but he knew he'd picked the hardest ones in the book.

He'd thought he'd done a good thing, but for some reason Alison hadn't seemed to agree. She'd looked so furious that he'd thought she was going to thump him.

Then they'd gone up to high school and had been put into different streams, and he'd barely seen her after that. He'd caught glimpses of her across the playground, in the corridor, at school events, and in the hall for assembly, but she rarely glanced his way, and when she did it was as if she looked straight through him. Like he was completely invisible to her.

He jabbed idly at a sprout with his fork, remembering the pain of first love. If only he'd known what lay ahead of him. His angst over Alison had been nothing to what was to come.

His phone beeped again, and against his better judgement he picked it up and read the message.

STELLA

Don't ignore me, Ian! You can't avoid me forever. Mum made sure of that. That house should be at least half mine, and you know as well as I do that you won't stay there, so why don't you just do as I suggested and stop being a prat? Call me.

Robert Carne was sitting beside his chair now, staring hopefully up at him.

'Everybody wants something from me that I can't deliver,' Mac said.

Carne tilted his head, as if in sympathy.

'Don't look at me like that, as if you're any different. You only care about me because I know where the dog food is.'

He grinned as the dog gave a heavy sigh and lay down, his head on his paws.

'You're way too cute for your own good, you know that?' He rolled his eyes as the big, ginger cat, Alderman Mrs Beddows, strolled into the kitchen. 'Great. Reinforcements. If you're on the scrounge, too, you can forget it. You know the routine.'

Although, unlike Robert Carne, he had no doubt that Mrs Beddows could find her own food source if she wanted to. She was a hunter, after all. Besides, Sam had told him that she visited quite a few of the villagers and got way too many scraps for her own good. She didn't really need Mac at all, which was how he liked it.

And yet his mother had left not only this cat and dog in his care, but her other, more demanding, animals too. It had been quite specific. Watersmeet – this beautiful old farm on the edge of the Humber – was his, and his alone. And with it came her rescued Highland cow and bullock, her ageing New Forest ponies, her ex-battery hens and three ducks.

'I suppose I should be glad Ma Larkin passed away,' he said, then felt immediately guilty, knowing how much his mother had loved the old sow she'd looked after for years after saving her from the abattoir.

Since heading off to university he hadn't had any pets at all – not even a goldfish. Now look at him. Doctor Dolittle.

What if his mother had been wrong about him? What if Stella was right?

He closed his eyes and took a deep breath, then another, and another. *In through the nose, out through the mouth. You can do this. Remember what Doug told you. Don't think about the future. It's only now that matters. This moment.*

And at that moment all he had to think about was eating his lunch before it got cold.

"'Tomorrow is tomorrow. Future cares have future cures, and we must mind today.'"

It had been one of Doug's favourite quotes. Sophocles apparently.

He puffed out his cheeks, feeling a bit calmer. 'Right. Lunch.'

He would reply to Stella after he'd eaten and washed up, but it wouldn't be a long text. He'd simply explain that there was nothing to discuss, that he loved her, and didn't want to fall out with her, but that he intended to abide by his mother's wishes, and he was sorry if she was struggling with that.

'And,' he added firmly as he sliced through his roast beef, 'that my bloody name's Mac not Ian, and I shouldn't have to remind her of that fact every single time we speak.'

Ian was gone. A different person from a different time. He simply wasn't the same man any more, and his mother had obviously banked on that fact.

He couldn't let her down. Not this time.

5

Alison drove home the following Thursday afternoon feeling shattered. She'd done an early shift at the petrol station, having been roped in to cover bakery duty due to staff illness. With her usual early shift being on a Wednesday, two days in a row of early rises meant she now felt like she could sleep for a week.

One of the downsides of her job was that she was expected to cover at short notice. Even so, she liked the variety of her work. Sometimes she'd be manning the till. At other times she'd have to go in early to help with the food preparation, as the petrol station had its own bakery. She jet washed the forecourt, did stock rotation and whatever else she was asked to do and didn't really mind any of it.

What she'd refused, a year after starting work, was promotion. They'd wanted her to become a supervisor with a view to training for management. It was flattering but Alison wasn't tempted.

She didn't want any kind of responsibility. She'd done all that in her teaching job. All she wanted from this one was to go to work, do what needed to be done, go home and forget all about it. It suited her, but she had to concede it could be difficult when Jenna needed her.

She'd had to phone her daughter as soon as she got the call to explain she wouldn't be able to take the girls to school the next morning.

'But why didn't you just tell them you couldn't do it?' Jenna had demanded. 'You know I was relying on you to take the twins.'

'I couldn't,' Alison had explained apologetically. 'I would have if I could, but only a few of us are trained to cover the bakery, and one of them's doing a night shift tonight, so she can't work the early shift too, and apart from me and the one who rang in sick there's only Jean, and she's on holiday.'

'In January?' Jenna sounded as if she didn't believe a word of it.

'She's gone to Tenerife. She always flies out at this time of year to visit her sister.'

'Nice for some,' Jenna said.

Alison had bitten her lip, telling herself not to start an argument.

'Well, I'm sorry to let you down but I have to go to work tomorrow morning and that's that. I need an early night, so I'll say goodnight.'

'You'll still be able to pick the twins up, though?' Jenna had said quickly. 'After school, I mean.'

Alison sighed. 'Yes, of course.'

'Great. See you tomorrow then.'

The phone had gone dead, and Alison had held it away from her for a moment, staring at her contacts list and trying very hard not to feel angry with her daughter. Jenna knew the situation around shifts and covering for absent colleagues. Alison had made it very clear to her, and Jenna had promised she had backup in place. So why did she always make her feel guilty as hell whenever Alison put her job ahead of Jenna's demands? Would she prefer it if her mother got the sack?

Well, probably, because that way Alison would *always* be on hand to take the girls to school *and* pick them up, and probably have them at weekends, too. She wondered what would happen when she retired in five years' time. The twins would be twelve by then. Maybe she'd put off retirement for a couple more years. Working at the petrol station was a lot less hassle than rushing here, there and everywhere with Hallie and Ada.

In clear traffic, the petrol station was a twenty- or twenty-five-minute drive from her home. However, her granddaughters' school was ten minutes in the opposite direction.

The plan today was for her to collect the twins and take them back to their house, cook their tea – or dinner, as Jenna insisted on calling it these days – and get them settled before Jenna got home from work. Joel, apparently, was at a conference that weekend and would be heading south directly after finishing work.

At least it meant Alison would be home by seven. Quick shower, something to eat, and an evening in her PJs watching an old episode of *Lewis* or *Endeavour*, she decided, then an early night after her early start that morning. She was looking forward to it.

As her phone rang, she pressed the button on her steering wheel to accept the call. It was Jenna, sounding stressed.

'Sorry, Mum, change of plan. Would you be able to pick the kids up and take them back to yours for the night, please? Something's come up at work.'

Alison groaned inwardly. 'You want me to have them all night? Again?'

'It's my fault,' Jenna said hurriedly. 'I wouldn't ask but...'

'So what's come up?'

'I have a meeting I'd completely forgotten about. Like I said, my fault. And then a few of us are going to grab something to eat and do some brainstorming, so I won't be home until late. I wouldn't ask if it wasn't important. But look, I promise I'll pick them up from school tomorrow afternoon and have them on Saturday.'

She said it as if she was offering a favour, and not like it was something she should be doing anyway.

'You've got spare stuff at your house already, haven't you?' she continued. 'Pyjamas, toothbrushes, clean socks and underwear for tomorrow. That sort of thing.'

'Well, yes, but don't forget I've got work tomorrow and—'

'You're not on the early bakery shift again, are you?'

'No...' Alison sighed. She'd have time to drop them at school first, but it was bloody annoying. Even so, she could hear the desperation in Jenna's voice and knew she had no choice.

'Fine,' she said heavily. 'I'll take them home with me today and drop them at school tomorrow.'

'Oh, Mum, thank you! You're a lifesaver,' Jenna assured her. 'Give them my love. I owe you big time.'

'Yes, you do.'

The call ended and Alison tried to push aside her resentment. The last thing she wanted was for Ada and Hallie to feel they were a burden to her. None of this was their fault, and she did love them. It was just getting to be such a nuisance, and it was time Jenna and Joel got their acts together.

It was no good, she thought, as she headed down the road where the twins' school was located. She was going to have to be brave and have a talk to her daughter and son-in-law. They'd have to reach some sort of compromise. She didn't mind helping in emergencies, but she'd had enough of being at their beck and call every day.

Apart from anything else, she needed to get back to Kelsea Sands more often. Despite her mother's insistence that she was managing just fine, Alison knew how undomesticated her dad was and that he wouldn't have a clue about keeping the bungalow clean or cooking decent meals for the two of them while her mum's arm was mending.

Of course, she knew she could rely on her aunt and uncle and Rosie to make sure her parents were okay but she shouldn't have to. She wanted to be there for them herself and it should be fairly easy to work her visits around her job if only she didn't have to factor in babysitting duties every sodding day.

She couldn't remember the last time she'd done any baking or cooking. It had never been her strong point, and she was just as likely to have a Pot Noodle for tea as put anything in the oven. She'd meant to learn after she left teaching, but events had overtaken her. Her small garden was hardly inspiring, even making allowances for the fact that it was January. And other than slumping in front of the television when she got the chance, she had nothing else going on in her life. When had she last gone to the park? Or for a walk? No wonder she was gaining weight and her blood pressure was going up.

And that was another thing. Yesterday she'd had two missed calls from the surgery and today she'd received a text message asking her to make an appointment as soon as possible. Obviously, they'd seen the readings she'd submitted and had decided they needed to increase her medication after all. She simply hadn't had time to contact them and knew she couldn't put it off much longer.

Hallie and Ada came rushing out of the classroom, greeting

her with joy as always. She swept them both into a big hug and nodded at the teacher, who knew her quite well by now.

'Right then,' Alison said, ushering them across the playground towards the school gates, 'change of plan. You're staying the night at my house tonight. Is that all right with you?'

As expected, the girls were thrilled. It always seemed like an adventure to them when they stayed with Grandma, though Alison couldn't imagine why. It wasn't like they did anything exciting. She supposed it was just the novelty of sleeping in a bedroom that wasn't theirs – although, God knows, it might as well have been.

'We haven't got our tablets with us,' Ada realised, a look of horror on her face. 'Can we go home and get them?'

'No. You can do without them for one night.' It would do them good, she thought. They were far too attached to those devices for her liking and when they were with her she limited the time they spent on them. She wasn't confident that Jenna did the same.

'Can we have chicken dinosaurs for tea?' Hallie begged.

Alison shook her head. 'I don't have any chicken dinosaurs,' she admitted. Come to think of it, she wasn't entirely sure what she *did* have in her freezer. Not a lot, she suspected. She hadn't done a shop for well over a week. She was pretty sure she'd even run out of bread. 'We'll have to call at the supermarket on the way home,' she told them. 'I need to do some shopping, so maybe you'll get those chicken dinosaurs after all.'

The girls exchanged delighted looks, no doubt envisioning all the treats they predicted they'd be able to coax Grandma into buying for them.

Alison made sure they were securely fastened in their booster seats then climbed into the car. 'Right. Maister's here we come.'

Maister's was a supermarket not far from home, and Rosie often teased her that only posh people shopped there. It was true it was a fairly expensive option, and at some point she suspected she'd have to shop at a cheaper supermarket, but she and Drew used to do their weekly shop there and she had fond memories of them pushing a trolley down the aisles – Drew putting things in and her taking things out again. She knew where everything was; the layout was familiar despite the occasional revamp, and she was quite attached to the place, the staff and the brand.

Hallie and Ada loved it, too, as they demonstrated by running up and down the aisles, pointing excitedly to things they liked the look of, and finding something they couldn't live without every five minutes.

Leaving the shop some half an hour later, having spent at least ten pounds more than she'd planned to, Alison strapped the girls in the car, loaded the boot with her shopping, returned the trolley to the trolley park and got the hell out of there. She needed to get home fast before she ran out of energy to even cook those dratted chicken dinosaurs.

She couldn't be bothered to make something different for herself and sat down at the table around forty minutes later to enjoy a meal of glorified chicken nuggets, oven chips and baked beans.

The girls ate hungrily and with due appreciation for her efforts, and she felt justified in rewarding them with apple pie and tinned custard for afters. It was a dark, cold and miserable night, so pudding was definitely called for. After that she'd make sure they had a bath and got into their pyjamas, then they could have an hour of winding down before bed. Then... She closed her eyes for a moment imagining it. Peace!

'Oh no!' Hallie exclaimed suddenly. 'Ada! The topic!'

'The what?' Alison asked, alarmed at the look of horror on the twins' faces.

'Grandma! We're going to get into trouble,' Ada wailed.

'Of course you're not. Are you? Why?'

'Our topic's got to be handed in tomorrow.'

'Your topic?'

'Yes, Miss Mason said it had to be in by Friday or we won't get a mark for it and we've worked real hard on it all last term, too,' Hallie said.

'We have, Grandma,' Ada said, nodding furiously. 'We chose British birds and we've done loads of writing and pictures for it.'

'You mean a project,' Alison said, understanding. She vaguely remembered hearing them talk about it over the last few weeks. 'Well, okay, so it has to be handed in tomorrow? We'll pick it up from your house on the way to school then.'

The twins' expressions were almost comical. Although they looked very similar with their light-brown hair and grey eyes – so like their mother's – they weren't identical, but at that moment they looked like two peas in a pod. Guilt was written all over their faces.

'Go on,' Alison said suspiciously. 'What aren't you telling me?'

Ada squirmed and Hallie doodled an imaginary drawing on the table with her forefinger.

'We haven't *quite* finished it,' she admitted slowly.

'We nearly have,' Ada burst out. 'We just need to do a *really* little bit of work, don't we, Hallie?'

'Just a really *tiny* bit,' Hallie confirmed. 'Miss Mason gave us some questions to fill in about what we've learned doing the topic and stuff like that, but we forgot.'

'But you're not going to have time now, are you?' Alison said.

'We *would* if we had the topic here with us now,' Hallie pointed out.

'But you don't have it, sadly.' Alison had a sinking feeling in her stomach. She could see where this conversation was heading and didn't like it one bit. 'Maybe if I explain to Miss Mason in 'morning she'll understand and—'

'She won't,' Ada said. She glanced at Hallie, who blushed.

'All right,' Alison said heavily. 'What aren't you telling me?'

For a moment, the two of them looked at each other as if they were communicating telepathically. Alison really wouldn't have been surprised if they were.

'Our topic was supposed to have been handed in today,' Ada admitted at last. 'We told Miss Mason we'd forgotten it and she said she'd give us an extra day. We told her we'd finished it.'

'We nearly *have* finished it,' Hallie reminded her grandma, 'so it wasn't really a fib. But we're going to be in big trouble if we take it tomorrow and she finds out it isn't finished.'

'Especially since we've had an extra day,' Ada added.

Alison pursed her lips. 'Let me guess where this is going. You want me to take you back home to pick up your project. Tonight.'

The twins gave her a pleading look.

'We're really sorry, Grandma,' Hallie said.

'We wouldn't take very long to finish it,' Ada promised. 'And we'll go to bed straightaway afterwards.'

Alison sighed. 'I don't fancy going back out now. I'm tired. I just want a night of peace and quiet.'

'We'll never be able to sleep for worrying,' Ada told her. 'We'll probably keep you awake all night.'

Alison shook her head. For a seven-year-old the kid was an arch manipulator. She must take after her mother.

'All right, all right, I get it,' she muttered. 'Grab your coats.'

The girls gave a whoop of relief and climbed down from their chairs. Alison collected the plates and dumped them all on the draining board, then grabbed her keys. So much for a restful evening. *Endeavour* and *Lewis* would have to wait. Again.

6

'Oh, you like that, don't you? You really do.' Mac couldn't help but smile as Ellen MacKenzie leaned into him while he scratched her side, his fingers raking through her thick, ginger hair.

The beautiful Highland cow, along with her son, Jamie Fraser (named because, as his mother had pointed out, he was a handsome red-headed Highlander, so what else could she call him?) had been his mother's pride and joy.

According to the Fosters at Carr Farm, the tiny herd, or fold, of two usually grazed the field that edged the footpath along the banks of the Humber, devouring the grasses and fibrous plant matter and gazing out over the river, looking so magnificent and majestic that anyone walking beside Watersmeet would invariably stop to take photographs, exclaiming in surprise and wonder at such an unexpected sight.

In winter, though, the field sometimes became boggy, and the cows were transferred to the two-acre field that sat furthest away from the river. They were fed haylage in addition to their grazing, had a mineral lick and a supply of fresh water, and seemed quite happy together, taking cover when necessary in their purpose-built straw-bedded shelter.

The Fosters had assured him that Highland cows were hardy creatures and, compared with many breeds of cattle, easy to look after. If that was true, he dreaded to think how difficult it was to care for other breeds, given the extensive information sheets his mother had left for him about the various steps necessary to ensure their continuing good health. No wonder there were few farmers in Holderness who kept cows.

It seemed like an awful lot of responsibility to him. Although, as Ellen MacKenzie gave what sounded suspiciously like a loud sigh of pleasure and Jamie Fraser wandered over to find out what the fuss was about, he had to admit that the sight of these beautiful, placid creatures lifted his heart and made him feel that any hard work associated with their care would be worth it.

Maybe.

After leaving the barn to check on Jacob Armitage and Heatherstone, the two ageing New Forest ponies who were in a separate paddock with a shelter, he wandered to the large fenced-off area behind the garden where the five ex-battery hens lived, making sure they were securely fastened in for the night. The three ducks were also safely shut away. There were foxes around here and he didn't want to be the one responsible for letting his mother's beloved birds die an unnatural death.

With Alderman Mrs Beddows surprisingly at home and curled up by the fire, and Robert Carne trotting beside him, all the animals were accounted for and safe, but he had to admit there was a lot more to taking care of them all than he'd ever imagined. How had his mother coped on her own all this time?

He tried to ignore the familiar pang of shame that she'd had to. It wasn't, after all, true. Not really. She'd had the Fosters, who'd been good friends to her. And Stella, of course. His sister had visited her regularly and had, no doubt, done what she could to help their mother, even though she had never approved of her taking in so many animals.

Stella had a good heart. He had to remember that.

He glanced down at Robert Carne, who stared back at him, clearly wondering why they'd suddenly stopped halfway down the garden path when the warmth and comfort of home was so close.

'She deserves better,' he mumbled to the little dog.

Carne turned to look at the house then back to him. He clearly couldn't care less who deserved what. He was too focused on what *he* deserved, which was a nice warm fire and a snooze on the sofa.

Mac rubbed his forehead. What was he going to do about Stella? She was his sister, and he loved her, but right now she hated him, and who could blame her? Accepting his inheritance of Watersmeet was bad enough, but when you considered what had gone before...

He gazed up at the dark sky, wondering why his mother had put this on him. She'd known who he was. What he'd done. What if he let her down?

Finding no comfort in the night sky he turned to look out over the river, knowing that across the Humber lay the seaside town of Cleethorpes, and wondering how lively it was right now. Would the cafes, the shops, the amusements still be open? He doubted it, since it was January and out of season.

He felt a sudden stirring of something deep within him and, sickened, he turned away, calling to Carne as he strode rapidly back to the house.

Watersmeet *should* be Stella's, but his mother had left it to him. She'd trusted him to do the right thing. If he did as his sister wanted, he'd be letting his mother down yet again. If he sold the place to someone else, it would be just as bad.

He was trapped. The house he'd dreamed of and longed for so many times during the last few years had become his prison.

He had no idea how this was going to work because, unlike his mother, he had no faith in himself.

"'All shall be well, and all shall be well, and all manner of things shall be well.'" It was a quote by Mother Julian of Norwich, apparently, and another one that Doug had been fond of, designed to calm him down when his anxieties rose and his mind began racing.

He wasn't sure even Mother Julian herself would have had a solution to this dilemma.

After slipping off his wellies in the boot room, he entered the kitchen. The heat was comforting, like he'd just put a duvet around his shoulders.

'Maybe,' he said to Carne, 'I'll have a cup of tea first, and then I'll see if there's anything left in the freezer for dinner. I think there are some biscuits in the cupboard I can have while I think about it. I might even let you have one. What do you say?'

Carne yapped loudly and raced to the door that led to the hallway.

'All right, all right. You want to be by the fire. I get it.' Mac shook his head. There was no pleasing some people – even the ones that were dogs.

Before he could open the door to let Carne through, it opened and Stella stepped into the kitchen, her dark brown blunt bob cut to just the wrong length for her square face. She was dressed all in black for mourning – or to remind everyone that she'd just lost her mother and so much more besides. She gave the excited Jack Russell a perfunctory pat but her small, hazel eyes never left her brother's face.

'What the hell...' It was a shock to see her there. He hadn't set eyes on her since the reading of the will.

'You left the front door unlocked so I let myself in. You should be more careful.'

'Around here? Since when?'

She rolled her eyes impatiently. 'Times change.'

'Kelsea Sands doesn't. It's just as I left it. Like I never went away.'

She folded her arms. 'But you did, didn't you? For forty-four years.'

'Bloody hell, Stell. You been working that out in your head while you waited for me?'

'Didn't need to. It's embedded in my mind forever. Forty-four years of me being the only child in this family. To all intents and purposes.'

He turned back to the sink and filled up the kettle. 'Stop exaggerating. You were never the only child. Do you want a cup of tea?'

'I might as well have been!'

'Milk? Sugar?'

'Are you going to ignore me forever? Because I won't let you, you know. It's not fair, Ian! You know that deep down, so what are you going to do about it?'

He succeeded somehow in keeping his voice steady. 'It's Mac, Stella. I've told you so many times.'

'Mac!' She gave a scornful laugh. 'Since when?'

'Since I decided I'd had enough of being Ian,' he said quietly, flicking the switch on the kettle.

'Well, I can't blame you for that. I think we'd all had enough of Ian – Mum especially. Which is why this is so unfair.'

'So you keep saying, but it's what she wanted.'

'It's not what she wanted at all! She was just—'

'Just what?' He swung round to face her, feeling suddenly bitter that he'd been put in this situation. 'Deranged? Of unsound mind? You might well be right but try proving it in a court of law.'

'Sorry for you,' she hissed. 'She was just sorry for you.'

He gazed down at the floor. He thought it would have been better if his mother had been of unsound mind after all. Anything would have been better than her leaving him Watersmeet out of pity. Is that what she'd done?

Carne trotted over to him and sat by his side, gazing up at him with a solemn expression. Mac reached down and fondled the little chap's ears, feeling stupidly grateful for the warmth and affection in the dog's eyes. Right now, it felt as if Carne was the only person in the world who cared about him.

'It had nothing to do with pity,' he said, straightening as he remembered the other animals bedded down for the evening: the cows, the ponies, the ducks, the ex-battery hens, all safe and secure because he'd taken care of them and made sure they were. 'You know as well as I do why she left this place to me. You left her with no choice.'

'But you agree with me, don't you? Deep down you know I'm right, and before long you'll only do what I was going to do anyway. Why drag it out? Gavin will take it off your hands. You know he'll be fair and—'

'How many more times? I'm sure Gavin *would* take it off my hands, but the fact is that Mum didn't want him to. In fact, it's exactly what she tried so hard to prevent. Hence lumbering *me* with the place!'

'*Lumbering* you?' Stella's face was wet with tears, whether of anger, sadness or frustration Mac wasn't sure. Probably all three. 'That's how you see it? This beautiful house!'

'That's not what I meant,' he protested feebly. 'Look, I haven't got the energy to argue about this now, and I don't want to fight with you. Have a cup of tea with me. We can have a nice evening together catching up. I haven't seen you properly for so long and it would be good to chat. How are Ned and Crystal?'

Stella glared at him as she swiped the tears away with the back of her gloved hand. '*My* kids are fine. How are *yours*?'

He flinched as if she'd slapped him. 'Low blow, Stell.' She probably knew better than he did how Wyatt and Sarah were. Part of him longed to ask her if she'd heard from his children lately, but he didn't dare. Even if she had, would she tell him? And did he want to hear it anyway?

For a moment her face softened, as if she realised she'd gone too far. He seized upon the chance to start building bridges.

'Look, stay a while. I've got some biscuits somewhere,' he offered, trying to smile. 'We can have a proper catch-up. Forget all this business for one evening and just be... *us* again.'

Her mouth tightened and he knew he'd lost her. 'I'm not staying if you're not going to talk about Watersmeet,' she said coldly. 'When you've thought it over and decided I was right and you're willing to start negotiations then I'll come round and eat as many bloody biscuits as you've got. Until then, we have nothing to say to each other.'

'Stella,' he pleaded, but she turned and strode down the hallway towards the front door, ignoring him. He winced as she slammed it behind her, heading out into a night as bitter as she clearly still was.

'Oh, Mum,' he groaned. 'Look what you've done. As if I hadn't messed things up with her enough already.'

The kettle reached boiling point, and he went to the cupboard for a mug, noticing his mobile phone on the worktop. For a moment his hand hovered over it. His pulse raced. His heart thudded.

'"Tomorrow is tomorrow",' he reminded himself. '"All shall be well".'

Yes, he was mixing his quotations but so what? If it worked...

He turned his mobile phone over so he couldn't see the screen and busied himself making the mug of tea, half smiling as Mrs Beddows stalked in and wound between his legs, clearly on the scrounge for food.

'You two...' He shook his head as the dog and cat looked hopefully at him. 'You never stop, do you?'

But he was glad of their company. Glad of the interaction. Glad to be needed and wanted, even though a part of him screamed at the very idea of all that responsibility.

'I'm trying,' he told them. 'I'll do my very best not to let you down.'

It was as much as he could promise.

Yes, there was no doubt about it. The twins definitely took after their mother. Their attempts to manipulate Alison on the drive over to their house were shocking, as they remembered various other things they'd like to have with them overnight – 'But Grandma, we really *need* our tablets' – and decided that she should raid the fridge for a certain brand of yoghurt that Maister's didn't sell but which their mum had plenty of, and which they'd love to have for breakfast the following morning.

Fearing they'd be stuck in the house for hours while the twins did a massive search, Alison informed them they were to stay in the car and wait for her while she rushed in and picked up their project.

'But you won't know where it is. We should come in and get it,' Hallie said, while Ada nodded determinedly.

Alison pulled up outside their home and turned off the engine. 'Right,' she said, turning round to face them, 'let's get this straight. You two will stay here so that I can go in, get your project and leave again. I'm not spending the next two hours stuck in that house while you decide you want this, that and the other. You've still got the project to finish, remember? So tell me where I'll find it and I'll be out before you know it.'

Ada and Hallie gave her a mutinous look.

'It's that or we go straight back to my house, and you can face the wrath of your teacher tomorrow,' she told them, unmoved.

The twins sighed. 'All right. It's on the desk in our bedroom,' Ada said, sounding resigned. 'Oh, and our tablets are right next to it.'

'That,' Alison said firmly, 'is irrelevant.'

'It wouldn't take you long to get the yoghurts out of the fridge.' Hallie gave her a pleading look.

'You've just cost me a small fortune at Maister's. I think there's plenty for you to choose from for tomorrow's breakfast,' Alison said, unclipping her seatbelt. 'Now stay put or we go straight home, understand?'

The twins nodded and Alison removed her keys from the ignition, left the car and almost ran up the garden path to Jenna's front door. She hurriedly unlocked it thinking that if she found the project quickly enough, she might still have time to watch an episode of *Lewis* while the twins finished their work. She just hoped they wouldn't fall asleep in class tomorrow.

She flicked on the landing light and headed straight upstairs to the twins' room. It was at the back of the house, next to the family bathroom, and was a large, airy room, flooded with sunshine on bright days. She glanced around, noting with approval the bookcase loaded with classic children's books – she and Jenna were at least on the same page about encouraging the girls to read – and the large desk with two chairs, where the girls could do their homework.

The project! She spotted it almost immediately and grabbed

it from the desk, tucking it under her arm and heading, with relief, to the landing.

The bathroom door opened, and Alison let out a yelp of shock as she bumped into—

'Jenna!'

Her daughter looked horrified. 'Mum!'

'What are you doing here?' Alison, her nerves steadying, frowned. 'You're supposed to be at a meeting and...' Her voice trailed off as she stared at Jenna in astonishment. 'What the hell are you wearing?'

Jenna's face was scarlet and, as she clearly struggled to give her mother an adequate response, Alison suddenly realised what was going on.

'I don't believe this!'

She leaned against the banister, almost too stunned to support her own weight. Jenna was dressed like... like...

'Is Joel here, too?' Alison didn't want to imagine how *he* might be dressed. The mind boggled. 'Is this some sort of role play or something? Look, I don't mind you two wanting to spice up your sex life but at least do me the courtesy of being honest with me. All that meeting at the school rubbish. It's not fair, Jenna. And couldn't you have made it another night? What was the sudden urgency?'

Jenna pushed past her and shot into her own bedroom. Alison followed and plonked herself down on the bed while her daughter hastily reached for her dressing gown to throw over the black basque, lacy knickers, stockings and suspenders she was wearing.

'You've got a price label sticking out of that basque,' Alison said, reaching up to remove it. Her eyes widened. 'How bloody much?'

'Do you mind?' Jenna wrenched away and pulled the dressing gown on, wrapping it around her and fastening the belt tightly. 'What are you doing here anyway? You're supposed to be at yours and – oh God! Where are the twins?'

She looked fearfully at the door and Alison tutted impatiently. 'They needed to finish their school project for tomorrow. They're outside in the car, luckily for you. Imagine if they'd seen their mum looking like a—'

'Like a what?' Jenna challenged. 'A slut?'

'I never said that,' Alison said indignantly.

'You didn't have to. It's written all over your face.' She glanced at the clock on the bedside cabinet. 'You'd better take the project and get off, then. I don't want them up too late tonight.'

Alison gaped at her. 'You've got a nerve! I've got a better idea. Why don't I bring them in? Since you and Joel are clearly going to be at home all evening *you* can have them. They can finish their project in their own room then go straight to bed.'

'No!' Jenna gave her a terrified look. 'Not tonight, Mum. Please. Just take them back to yours.'

'Wow, you two really are desperate, aren't you? Do you pull this trick on me regularly? How many other times have I been conned into babysitting due to some big emergency when really you've been planning a bit of sexy time? I mean, don't get me wrong, I'm really glad that you two are clearly still having fun, but you could at least tell me the truth. It's not much to ask, is it?'

'Mum, can we discuss this tomorrow? You need to go!'

Jenna grabbed Alison's arm and began to pull her off the bed.

'All right, all right. Bloody hell! Word of advice, that's way too much make-up. Tone it down a bit. Hey, are you okay?' She realised her daughter was shaking and close to tears. 'Jenna? What's wrong?'

'Nothing! Nothing's wrong. I just – I need the loo.'

She darted out of the room and the bathroom door slammed shut. Alison waited, confused and worried. She didn't like to think it, but was it possible that Joel was making his wife do something she didn't want to do? Was this all his idea? She knew it wasn't really any of her business but something about Jenna's expression frightened her. If her son-in-law was making unreasonable demands, she'd have to get involved. She couldn't bear the thought of her daughter being part of something she wasn't happy about.

There was a beep and Alison realised Jenna's phone was on the bedside cabinet. Maybe it was Joel to say he was on his way. She leaned over and noticed his name, and without even meaning to, her eyes quickly scanned the brief message on the home screen.

JOEL

Arrived in Derby. Traffic horrendous as usual.
Give my love to the...

Jenna walked back into the bedroom, wiping her scarlet lipstick off with a tissue.

'Mum, I'm not being funny, but I don't like the girls being left alone in the car for long. Can we leave this for now?'

'Who are you expecting, Jenna?' Alison asked icily.

Jenna stared at her. 'What – what are you on about?'

Alison waved the phone at her. 'Joel's in Derby, as expected. He said to give the girls his love. So, for whose benefit is this get-up?' She waved a hand at Jenna's attire, even though it was hidden under the dressing gown. 'Wow, you really are a piece of work.'

Jenna sank on to the bed. 'It's not what you think.'

'So you're not having an affair?'

'No!'

'And you're not expecting a man round this evening?'

Jenna bit her lip.

'Is this the first time? Is that what you mean?'

Jenna's face was scarlet. 'I just – we haven't – I mean, yes. It's the first time.'

'You bloody idiot!' Alison leapt to her feet, glaring down at her daughter. 'What the hell are you thinking? You've got a husband who adores you and is working so hard to give you and the twins everything you could possibly want, and you've got two little girls outside who need their parents together.'

'You think I don't know that?' A tear rolled down Jenna's cheek, but Alison was having none of it.

'Save me the waterworks! I can't believe this. Of all the stupid, thoughtless, selfish things you've ever done, this takes the cake, it really does.'

Jenna wiped her cheek. 'What do you mean? What have I done?'

'Are you serious? How about dumping your kids on me every chance you get, and giving me a hard time when I have to work instead of babysit for you?'

'Dumping them on you? I thought you *liked* having them? I thought they were company for you.'

'Oh please, don't make that your excuse. I have a life of my own! Well, I would have if I could have five minutes alone. I put up with it because I thought you and Joel were busy working to pay the bills and build a better life for your family, but all the time you've been carrying on with God knows who! I mean, how many others have there been? Poor Joel.'

'Poor *Joel*!' Jenna spluttered, whether with anger or amusement Alison couldn't be certain. 'And where is Joel? Oh, of course. He's at a hotel for the weekend. Again.'

'Working! For you! For his family!'

Jenna lowered her head. 'I'd rather have him here.'

'So that's a good enough excuse to cheat on him? What time is this creep coming round, then? No wonder you were desperate to get me to leave.'

Jenna glanced at the clock. 'Any time now,' she said dully.

'Right.' Alison clutched the twins' project tightly to her. 'I'm going to take the girls home with me and make sure they get this finished. I suggest you take the opportunity to send lover boy packing and then spend the evening having a good long think about your future. You have responsibilities, Jenna. My God!' She shook her head. 'Your dad would be so ashamed of you.'

She didn't wait to hear any more of her daughter's feeble excuses but ran down the stairs and out of the front door, slamming it shut behind her.

Hallie and Ada waved cheerfully to her, and she swallowed down the lump in her throat. Jenna could blow these little girls' lives apart. What on earth was she thinking? Her heart broke as she contemplated the very real possibility that her granddaughters might soon be part of a broken family, with a mother and father at each other's throats. She couldn't bear it.

'Did you get it, Grandma?' Ada asked as Alison sat in the driver's seat and stuck the key in the ignition.

Alison forced herself to smile, for their sake, as she dropped the project in the passenger seat. 'Sure did. Now, let's get back home and get this finished, shall we? And I'll make you a lovely mug of hot chocolate as a reward when you're done.'

The girls cheered and she drove steadily out of the road, despite her racing heart and trembling hands, then turned towards home. It was the final straw. She couldn't carry on being taken advantage of by her daughter any longer, and she could see now that by allowing herself to be manipulated she'd enabled Jenna to start whatever this relationship was.

She needed to withdraw her help so that her daughter would be forced to spend more time with her family. Only then would Jenna realise what she was endangering. Maybe, with any luck, Alison would be in time to save the marriage from collapsing and ensure her granddaughters didn't have their hearts broken.

8

'I can't believe it! Our Jenna?'

'All right, keep it down!' Alison cast a furtive glance around The Driftwood Hub to make sure no one was listening. Not that there were many people who'd have heard her conversation with Rosie anyway. Apart from the two of them and Emmy, who had disappeared into the kitchen, the cafe/shop/information centre was empty.

'Are you sure? I mean, it just doesn't sound like her, does it?' Rosie frowned and shook her head before taking a sip of tea. 'She's not the type.'

'Clearly she is.' Alison was still smarting from the fact that her daughter had not only pulled the wool over her eyes, who knew how many times, but that she'd jeopardised her marriage and her children's happiness for what might well have been some cheap and meaningless fling. Judging by what Jenna had been wearing, Alison would put money on it being purely based on lust. 'I'm just grateful I made Hallie and Ada stay in the car. Imagine if they'd walked in on their mother looking like that?'

'Bloody hell, it doesn't bear thinking about.' Rosie sighed. 'I thought her and Joel were set for life. It's disappointing really, isn't it?'

'That's one word for it,' Alison said grimly.

'So what did you do? That was what? Ten days ago. Have you seen her since?'

Alison cradled her mug of tea, still seething. 'No. I dropped the twins at school the following morning and sent Jenna a text message telling her not to forget to collect them when they'd finished because I wouldn't be doing it again for the foreseeable. I also told her she'd better make some alternative childcare arrangements because I had a life to live and would no longer be available.'

Rosie gasped. 'You never did!'

'Do you blame me?' Alison demanded.

'No, of course not. I just never thought you'd actually do it. You've been threatening to tell her for long enough, but you always find a reason to back down.'

'Well, not this time. Like you said, it's been ten days now and she hasn't bothered to reply, so it looks as if I'm free at last.' Alison massaged the bridge of her nose, feeling far less happy about her new freedom than she'd expected to. 'This has really upset me, Rosie,' she admitted. 'I can't believe any daughter of mine would behave like that. I don't understand her, I really don't.'

Her sweet little girl. She'd always been so steady and responsible. Solemn even. Alison couldn't believe what had happened.

'Maybe she and Joel aren't as happy as we thought they were,' Rosie said thoughtfully. 'What a shame.'

'Perhaps if they spent more time together, they'd have a chance of making it work,' Alison said. 'Honestly, Jenna's always saying that she hasn't got time for Joel or for the girls, yet she's got time to seduce some creep from work.'

'You think he's a teacher?' Rosie asked, surprised.

'Well, she never goes anywhere to meet anyone else, does she?' Alison frowned suddenly. 'At least, I don't think she does, but what do I know? This proves that, actually, she could be going anywhere and doing anything while I'm looking after her children. And I've only got her word for it that this is the first time. She could have been having a torrid affair for months for all I know. Or a whole string of lovers!'

'Lucky bugger,' Rosie said, her eyes twinkling. 'Aw, don't look like that, Ali. You know I'm only messing. I wonder who's got the kids today then? Or is Jenna actually going to spend her Sunday with them for once?'

'Not my concern,' Alison said. *Yeah, keep telling yourself that, Ali.* God, she hoped they'd be okay without her. She blinked away tears at the thought. *I'm doing this for them, too*, she told herself fiercely. *They need their mum and dad to spend time with them. What else can I do?* She took a long swig of her tea and looked towards the counter. 'Might get Mam and Dad some of those blueberry muffins. They deserve a treat.' She smiled at her cousin. 'I'll get you one, too, as a thank you for listening to me ranting.'

'It's always a pleasure.' Rosie reached over and squeezed her hand. 'Aw, it's great to see you. You've missed that many weekends lately I'd nearly given up on you. Apart from that Sunday dinner in The North Star you've hardly been here.'

'I know. Don't make me feel more guilty than I already do.'

'I'm not trying to make you feel guilty. You mean about your mam? Honest to God, there's no need. It's like I told you, we've all kept an eye out and Seb's lad Sam has been smashing.'

'He's a nice lad,' Alison agreed. 'I never thought he'd stay here, did you? I mean, he seemed quite happy working for that builder in Weltringham and living in the flat in Millensea.

Fancy giving all that up to take over the pub cos his dad's retired.'

'I'm still surprised about that,' Rosie admitted. 'Seb retiring, I mean. I thought, after what happened, he'd find work a comfort.'

Seb, forever known as Seb from the pub, had run The North Star for decades, along with his wife, Donna. But when Donna passed away Seb had fallen into a serious depression, refusing to have anything to do with the pub. He'd even threatened to sell it. To everyone's surprise, Sam had given up his job and flat and moved back to Kelsea Sands, where he'd been acting as the landlord ever since, even though it was still Seb's name over the door.

'You were at school with Seb, weren't you?' Rosie asked. 'Funny, he always seems so much older than you when I see him now. Not that I see him much. He's practically a recluse.'

'Well, we all handle our grief in different ways, I suppose,' Alison said. She remembered the cheeky, lively little lad she'd been at primary school with and felt a sudden sadness for how life had treated Seb. She understood his grief. Thinking about it, she supposed she'd been lucky that Jenna and Joel had refused to let her wallow after Drew's death, even though they were grieving, too. And then when the twins came along, she'd been far too busy to let herself sink into the pit of depression that Seb had clearly found himself in.

Rosie's eyes lit up. 'Hey, guess who I saw yesterday?' Sometimes, her rapid change of subject was quite startling.

'Everyone you looked at?'

'Very funny.' Rosie stuck her tongue out. 'Your childhood nemesis. What's his name? Ian thingy.'

'Oh, Ian *thingy*. Yes, I remember him well.' Alison grinned. 'It's not surprising really, is it? Not if he's living at Watersmeet. Kelsea Sands is so tiny it's a wonder you don't see every single villager every single day.'

'I was walking down the road – on the way to your mam and dad's as a matter of fact – and he came out of St Helen's and nearly collided with me. Funny place to be, eh?'

'Not really. I often used to sit in the churchyard and think. It's a nice place to gather your thoughts.'

Rosie wrinkled her nose. 'Are you joking? It's creepy. Well, at this time of year especially.'

Alison couldn't see why. St Helen's was the village church – sadly redundant since the early 1990s, due to its dwindling congregation. Built in the mid nineteenth century, it had replaced the much grander fourteenth-century church of the same name that had fallen into the sea due to coastal erosion some thirty years before the new church's construction.

A compact red-brick building, it sat in a small graveyard that was gradually being reclaimed by nature. A bench was situated just to the side of the church porch, where visitors could sit and relax surrounded by bushes, shrubs and wild flowers. Most of the gravestones were so worn and weather-beaten they were illegible, but it was worth trying to read the inscriptions if you could manage it.

In the middle of the churchyard was a large stone cross which had belonged to the original church. It had been saved from the sea and stored safely away at a stately home near Hull, until the new village of Kelsea Sands took form and its brand-new church was built.

To the rear of the churchyard was a thick boundary of trees, and beyond it open fields that eventually adjoined the wetlands. Its location made St Helen's seem somehow even more wild and beautiful.

'Maybe he's going to buy it,' Rosie mused.

Alison looked at her, startled. 'The church? Why would he, when he's just been given Watersmeet?'

'Dad reckons it could be a lovely home, although I wouldn't fancy it myself. Not with all them graves around. And it's been up for sale for donkey's years, hasn't it? Cheap as chips. He says if things were different, he'd buy it himself.'

'By, "if things were different", I take it he means if this whole village wasn't about to fall into the sea?' Alison said glumly. Not that she was sure Kelsea Sands was even a village any longer. Was it, she wondered, a hamlet now, since there were no longer church services?

'Blimey, look on the bright side, why don't you? We're not done yet. Bet it will still be here when we're long gone.'

'It will probably outlast me,' Alison agreed. 'I'm falling to bits.'

'Oh, how did you get on at the doctor's?' Rosie said, with another of her sudden changes of subject. 'Did they alter your BP meds?'

Alison squirmed, wishing she'd been more careful with her choice of words.

'I'm, er, seeing the nurse tomorrow.'

'Tomorrow? But you said they'd messaged you to come in as soon as possible! That was ten days ago!'

'I know, but I've sort of had my mind on other things,' Alison pointed out. 'Don't look at me like that. I *have* made an appointment. I had to or they wouldn't give me my prescription.'

'Did you have those other tests?' Rosie asked suddenly.

'What other tests?'

'You said you got a cervical smear reminder and a bowel testing kit in the post. Did you sort them out?'

Alison sighed. 'No. I'm not going to bother.'

'Are you joking?' Rosie tapped her on the arm. 'Don't be so daft. You've got to do the tests, Ali! You can't ignore them, especially at your age.'

'Thanks very much for that,' Alison said. 'As if I needed reminding how old and decrepit I am.'

'You're not old and decrepit, but you know as well as I do that the older you get—'

'Yes, all right.' Alison shook her head. 'It's just all too much, you know? Since I turned sixty it seems to be one demand after another. You know how much I hate doctors and hospitals. Ever since...'

Rosie sighed. 'I know. But sometimes you've got to do things you don't want to do.'

'I just want them to leave me alone. I'm quite happy with my head buried in the sand.'

'Please, Ali. Do it for me. I'll be worried if you don't.'

Alison fought down the urge to snap at her cousin. It wasn't Rosie's fault that she was feeling swamped with all the requests for tests thrust upon her. It seemed the medical profession was determined to make her face up to the fear she'd had ever since Drew's illness.

'Okay,' she said reluctantly. 'I'll book a smear when I'm at the surgery tomorrow.'

'And you'll do the other test?'

'Yes, sure,' Alison said evasively. She drained her mug and picked up her bag. 'I'm going to get those muffins. I'll get one each for your mam and dad if you like.'

'Don't bother buying any for us,' Rosie said. 'Mam's been baking non-stop the last couple of days. Our Niall and Kendra and the kids are coming for tea, so you can imagine what it's been like. Do you fancy coming back with me? You haven't seen my sainted brother and his family for ages.'

'I'm going to grab a loaf and those muffins and go back to Mam and Dad's, but I can pop in for half an hour before I go home. It will be nice to see them all.'

'Great. They should be here in about an hour.'

They both got to their feet and wandered through a brick archway to the adjoining room where the village shop was located.

Once, Kelsea Sands had boasted a seafood restaurant, a cafe, a post office and a proper shop, as well as two pubs. Now there was just The North Star and The Driftwood Hub. The building used to be quite a distance from the beach, but now only a small car parking area stood between it and the sea.

The Hub stood on the crossroads with Kelsea Road, which led to the famous Kels Point – a three-mile long, constantly moving peninsula, curving out between the Humber and the North Sea, and affectionately nicknamed Yorkshire's Land's End. Directly opposite was the private lane that led to the Tide's Reach Caravan Park, which was strictly owners only.

The Hub was run by the Miller family. It consisted of a small cafe, a shop that sold general provisions, baked goods, and souvenirs of Kels Point, and an information section, with maps, leaflets and postcards, that was particularly popular with the nature lovers and birdwatchers who visited Kelsea Sands and adjoining Kels Point in droves.

Mr and Mrs Miller were Emmy's grandparents and had raised Emmy since she was a baby. Usually, one or the other of them was around, but today it seemed to be just Emmy, which was unusual for a Saturday. Then again, it was the end of January, and the weather was dismal, so they were hardly rushed off their feet.

'Emmy!' There was no standing on ceremony in this place. Rosie simply let out a holler and Emmy appeared from the kitchen, a wide smile on her face.

'You yelled?'

'Sorry about that,' Alison said, giving her cousin a sideways glance. 'She doesn't have much truck with manners. I'm just admiring those blueberry muffins and trying to decide whether to get one for myself. I want two for Mam and Dad, but I should really resist temptation.'

'You're going to get told off by the nurse anyway,' Rosie whispered. 'Might as well be hung for a sheep as a lamb.'

'You're so bad for me,' Alison said, though she didn't argue the point. 'Three then, please. And a loaf, too. I noticed Mam's nearly out.'

'Had someone asking about you yesterday,' Emmy said, as she bagged up three muffins.

'About me?' Alison frowned as she took a loaf from the nearby shelf. 'Who was that?'

'Ian!' Rosie squealed, delighted.

Emmy shrugged. 'No, I don't think that was his name. Was it Mark? No, Mac. That's it. Introduced himself as Mac. Said he'd just moved back here so I'm guessing he's Mrs MacMillan's son. Oh!' She beamed at them. 'Of course. MacMillan. Mac! What am I like? Anyway, he was asking if you still lived in the village. I told him not as long as I've been alive.'

'Great,' Alison said, feeling ancient. 'Thanks for the reminder.'

'You're totally missing the point,' Rosie pointed out. 'He asked about you! Didn't I tell you he still fancied you?'

'Will you give over? He never fancied me! We were just kids. Thanks, Emmy.' Alison took the bag of muffins and scanned her debit card. 'He must have recognised me in the pub and wondered if I'd moved back. Actually, come to think of it, I was still living here when he headed off to university, so he probably never knew I left at all. What else did he say?'

Emmy shrugged. 'Nothing much. He asked about the caravan park and if I saw much of the Hewsons. I told him hardly anything, but then the park's shut until next week and they just come and go without bothering with the rest of us, don't they?'

'I forgot the park was reopening next week,' Alison said to Rosie. 'You'll be able to move back to the caravan then.'

'I know!' Rosie beamed. 'I can't wait. Gavin's asked me to do a bit of cleaning at the clubhouse before they reopen, and I'll be getting my old job back, cleaning there after my shifts at the pub, so it's all extra cash.'

'So if he's Mrs MacMillan's son, he must be related to the Hewsons, right?' Emmy asked, clearly still thinking about Ian.

'Sort of.' Rosie nodded. 'His sister Stella was married to Gavin Hewson, and they've got two kids, so they're Ian's – Mac's – niece and nephew.'

'Did you, er, tell Ian anything about me?' Alison asked, suddenly nervous. She didn't want someone who, to all intents and purposes, was a total stranger, knowing about her life, such as it was. Especially someone as perfect as Ian bloody MacMillan.

'No, just that I hardly saw you and you lived in Hull as far as I knew.' Emmy winked. 'None of his business, is it? He seemed nice, to be fair, but I still think it's a shame for Stella. This whole will business, I mean. Gran does too. She's surprised Stella hasn't taken it to court.'

'Well, none of us really knows the reason, or the actual terms of the will,' Alison reminded her.

'Except the house is definitely his because Stella's been telling everyone who'll listen that she was robbed.' Emmy rolled her eyes. 'It's a bit embarrassing, to be honest.'

Rosie twirled a length of her hair around her fingers. 'I mean, I could always find out,' she said thoughtfully. 'I could get it out of Gavin, no problem. He's always fancied me rotten.'

Clearly seeing the expression on Alison's face, she let go of her hair and straightened. 'What? He does!'

'And what about Stella?' Alison demanded. 'They might be divorced but it's still too close for comfort.'

'Did I say anything about me fancying him back?' Rosie wrinkled her nose. 'Ugh! No way, ta very much.'

Alison shook her head then gave a weary smile to the girl behind the counter. 'Thanks, Emmy. Take care.'

She and Rosie stood outside The Hub and Rosie slotted her arm through Alison's. 'Never mind about me and Gavin anyway. I *knew* that Mac fella fancied you,' she insisted.

'*Mac*.' When and why, Alison wondered, had the name change come about? 'He also asked about Gavin. I suppose he fancies him as well?'

'Gavin's his ex-brother-in-law. He has to ask after him by law.' Rosie grinned. 'Well, I suppose I'd better love you and leave you.' She nodded down Kelsea Road to where her parents' four-bedroomed house stood, just a few doors away from The Hub. 'No doubt Mam will want me to give her a hand making the place immaculate for Saint Niall and the Heavenly Kendra. You *will* come by later?'

'Of course. I might even be able to persuade Mam and Dad to pop round with me.'

'Brilliant. I'll tell them to expect you all then.' She bobbed a kiss on Alison's cheek. 'And you'll let me know what happens at the doctor's, won't you?'

Alison sighed. 'I promise. Brownie's honour.'

'I got chucked out of the Brownies,' Rosie admitted sheepishly.

'I know. I know all your darkest secrets, remember?'

Rosie laughed. 'You'd be surprised. See you later, Ali.'

9

Alison managed to stifle a yawn and gave the woman sitting opposite her a sheepish look.

'They don't rush, do they?' the woman said, rolling her eyes. 'I've been sat here for over half an hour. Should have been seen twenty minutes ago.'

'Oh heck.' Alison hoped her appointment wouldn't be delayed for that long. She'd only been sitting in the doctor's waiting room for ten minutes and she was already tempted to get up and leave.

She glanced around, noting the depressing green shade of paint on the walls and the dark, functional carpet. A quick glance at the posters on the walls had already proved too much for her, warning of all sorts of nasty possibilities and making urgent demands that patients should take this test, ask for that referral, speak to a professional about this condition and that symptom. She felt like screaming and running out of the building.

Her heart was already thumping, and she knew her blood pressure would shoot up the minute she walked into the nurse's consulting room, if it hadn't already. Why couldn't they just increase her medication and be done with it? Why did she even need to see the nurse at all?

The consulting room door opened and a blonde woman of about thirty looked out, a bright smile on her face.

'Alison Parker?'

A different nurse this time then, Alison realised as she got to her feet, giving an apologetic look to the woman who was still waiting. The woman shrugged and popped a Polo into her mouth as Alison headed shakily to the consulting room.

'Take a seat, love,' the nurse said, settling herself in front of the computer. 'By, you're harder to track down than the Scarlet Pimpernel! It's been over three weeks since your blood tests.'

'I've, er, had a lot on,' Alison said, her throat dry with nerves. She eyed the blood pressure monitor with dread. Already she could imagine the cuff wrapped around her arm, and the panic building within her as it tightened its grip bit by bit. 'I didn't think it was that high,' she added, thinking aloud.

The nurse looked up from the computer screen. 'Sorry?'

'My blood pressure. I didn't think my readings were that bad.'

'Oh, no, they're not. I've shown them to the doctor, and he doesn't think you need to increase your medication – at least not this time. He'd like you to come back in three months and we'll see how you are then, and in the meantime keep an eye on it yourself at home. Don't get obsessed though, mind. Don't want you to get addicted to reading your blood pressure, do we?' She laughed and Alison thought there was fat chance of that happening.

'So, if it's not my blood pressure, why am I here?' she asked, puzzled.

The nurse swivelled round in her chair to face Alison fully, which she found deeply alarming.

'It's your blood tests, love. Well, your HbA1c to be exact.'

'My what?'

'Blood sugar levels. The test result shows you're at 49, which just tips you into the diabetic range.'

Alison stared at her. 'You're saying I'm diabetic?'

'Well, it's possible it's just a blip, which is why I'd like to do another blood test today, just to double-check. If the results come back the same, you'd need to make an appointment with the doctor to discuss medication, but we'll cross that bridge when we come to it. Now, can you take your coat off and roll up your sleeve for me, please?'

Feeling dazed, Alison did as requested, barely feeling it when the nurse took yet another sample of blood from her arm. Diabetic? This was a whole other ball game and not one she wanted to play. It must be a mistake, surely?

All right, she'd gained a bit of weight since Drew's death, and there had been a lot of comfort eating and microwave meals since she'd lived alone, and yes, she had developed quite a taste for sugary treats since looking after the twins... She remembered yesterday when she'd not only eaten the blueberry muffin at her parents' home but had helped herself to two enormous slices of Elaine's coffee and walnut cake at her aunt and uncle's house.

Thinking about it all now, as the nurse labelled the tube of blood and threw her gloves in the bin before washing her hands, she realised it maybe wasn't as surprising as she'd initially thought. Even so...

'I don't want more medication,' she said faintly. 'It's bad enough being on blood pressure tablets.'

'Well, like I said, we'll get these blood tests done and then we'll worry about what comes next once we know for sure,' the nurse said. 'Any other concerns you'd like to talk about today?'

She was already typing her notes up on the screen. Alison

said, 'And there's nothing else showing up in the blood tests? It's just the diabetes?'

Just the diabetes. Like that wasn't enough.

'Everything else has come back fine,' the nurse said cheerfully. 'Your cholesterol's a bit high, but not high enough to need medication. Basically, you need to take a bit better care of yourself. That's what it boils down to. We do run a weight loss clinic here, you know. Would you like me to refer you?'

Alison mentally shuddered, memories of her sporadic attempts to lose weight by attending Lightweights' meetings filling her with dread. 'No. No, thanks.' She considered for a moment. 'I read somewhere that diabetes can be reversed. Is that true?'

The nurse looked suddenly interested. 'That's right. Well, it's possible, with diet and weight loss.'

'I'd rather do that,' Alison told her. 'I don't want to take any more medication. If the results come back the same, can I ask the doctor if I can try to reverse it myself?'

The nurse considered. 'These tests show the amount of blood glucose over a period of three months,' she said slowly. 'I can give you three months, if you like. Three months to lose some weight and lower your glucose levels yourself. Then you'd have to come back in for a blood test, and we'll see what happens then. What do you think?'

Alison nodded. 'Thank you. I'll try that. So I should still ring for the results?'

'Yes. Call the surgery in a couple of days and I'll leave a message with the receptionist to tell her to give you the result, but that no appointment's necessary at this time. Even if this was a blip – and to be honest, I doubt it – it would do you good to try to get your blood sugar levels down. Best-case scenario is that you're pre-diabetic, and that's not a good position to be in either.'

'I'll do the diet whatever the result,' Alison promised.

The nurse smiled and scribbled something down, before handing her a piece of paper. 'A couple of reputable websites there with good advice and useful tips. Good luck.'

'Thank you.'

Alison stumbled out of the room and vaguely noticed that the woman who'd been sitting opposite her had gone, presumably into another consulting room unless she'd given up and gone home in disgust.

She headed downstairs and into the main reception area, nodding briefly at the receptionists before pushing open the door with relief and stepping out into normality. Her pulse was racing, and she felt sick with fear. Leaning against the wall, she took a few deep breaths to steady herself.

'I need to do something ordinary,' she said aloud. The supermarket wasn't far away. What was more ordinary than popping in there to buy something for tea? She needed to browse shelves, maybe treat herself to a magazine or a novel, see people pushing trolleys, struggling with baskets that they'd overfilled.

Her eyes filled with tears. She'd promised Rosie that she'd make an appointment for her cervical smear, and she'd intended to mention it at the reception, but her nerve had failed her. She'd just wanted to get out of this place, away from all the memories of Drew and the many, many appointments she'd attended with him, and all the things that had gone with that.

The other tests would have to wait. She had enough to deal with right now. She took another deep breath then strode purposefully towards her car.

A faint ping coming from her bag informed her that she had a text message. Initially tempted to ignore it, she realised it might be something to do with her parents, so against her better judgement she took out her phone, her heart sinking as she realised the text was from her daughter.

> **JENNA**
>
> Hiya Mum. Can we meet for a coffee in my lunch hour? 12.15 at The Park Cafe? Need to talk.

Alison groaned. What did that mean? Was Jenna going to try to convince her that she'd got it all wrong, and what she'd seen that evening at her daughter's house wasn't what she'd imagined? No doubt Jenna was getting desperate for her to take over the childcare duties again. Well, she wasn't going to fall for it. Not this time.

She climbed into the driver's seat of her car and tapped out a reply.

> **ALISON**
>
> I'll be there.

It wasn't much, but she felt it said enough for now. She'd have plenty to say in person if it came to it.

As if this day couldn't get any worse.

10

Jenna couldn't have looked more different as she sat at the table in The Park Cafe. Gone was the bright lipstick and the sexy lingerie. Today she was wearing a sensible pair of navy-blue trousers, a white shirt and a pale blue cardigan. No lipstick at all. Then again, she was hardly going to dress like some seductress to teach a class of twelve-year-olds, was she?

She'd obviously been looking out for her mum because she tentatively waved as soon as Alison entered the building and gestured to the two mugs that were already on the table. Evidently, she'd not waited for Alison to decide what she wanted to drink but had made the decision for her.

Alison took a seat opposite her daughter, warning herself not to give in even as she realised, to her surprise, how much she'd missed Jenna.

'Coffee, milky, one sugar,' Jenna said, as if expecting praise for remembering.

Alison was about to remark that she'd be knocking the sugar on the head from now on but didn't. They weren't here to talk about her possible diabetes diagnosis.

'Thanks,' she said grudgingly.

'Sorry I ordered for you, but I haven't got long. You know what it's like. Forty minutes for lunch and by the time I drive here and back...'

Despite her annoyance, Alison couldn't help but ask if Jenna would be having anything to eat.

'I'm not really hungry, to be honest, Mum,' Jenna admitted. She looked pale and tense and Alison's heart melted just a little.

'You can't go back to work without having something,' she said. 'Order a sandwich at least.'

'I won't have time.'

'Of course you will!' Alison motioned to a waitress who was hovering nearby. 'Excuse me, can we order some lunch, please?'

'Sure.' The waitress smiled at them expectantly and Alison turned to her daughter.

Jenna sighed. 'Just a sandwich, please. Ham and tomato will do.'

'Same for me,' Alison said, and the waitress nodded before heading off to give their order to the kitchen staff.

There was a chilly silence at the table. Alison wondered what it was that Jenna wanted to say to her and hoped she wouldn't allow herself to be fooled into picking the girls up from school that evening. This was supposed to be her day off from work, and she'd already wasted a chunk of it going to her appointment. She didn't need any more time carving out of her precious day.

On the other hand, she couldn't deny that she also missed Ada and Hallie. She was so used to seeing them every day that it was strange not having them around.

'How are the girls?' she asked reluctantly.

'Fine. Missing you, I think,' Jenna said.

'Don't try emotional blackmail on me,' Alison said immediately, her hackles rising at the thought that Jenna might be trying to manipulate her already.

Jenna's eyes widened. 'I wasn't! I was just saying, that's all.'

Alison sipped her coffee, not sure whether she believed her or not.

'Mum, what you saw that night...'

Jenna's voice trailed off as if she was waiting for her mother to interrupt, but Alison said nothing. She eyed Jenna steadily, wondering what sort of excuse her daughter was about to offer.

Jenna sighed. 'You're right. It was a stupid thing to do. I'm sorry.'

Alison leaned forward, forgetting all about keeping quiet. 'Sorry? It's not me you should be saying sorry to, is it? What about your husband? What about your daughters?'

'They don't know anything about it,' Jenna said. 'And I'd really appreciate it if it stayed that way.'

'I'll bet you would,' Alison said grimly. She gripped her coffee mug, still reeling from the fact that her daughter could do something so reckless. 'So who is he then? And how long's it been going on?'

'Does it matter?' Jenna asked wearily. 'And before you ask, nothing happened that night. In fact' – she gave a brittle laugh – 'he didn't turn up.'

'Sounds like a right charmer. Is he one of your fellow teachers? Is he married? Have you any idea how dangerous this could be for your career, never mind your marriage?'

'He's not married,' Jenna said angrily. 'I would never do that to another woman!'

'But you're okay doing it to your husband?'

Jenna bit her lip.

'So is it an affair?' Alison asked. 'Lust, love, what?'

'It was just a stupid mistake,' Jenna said. She ran a hand

through her hair, looking exhausted. 'We'd done a bit of flirting at work and just got carried away, I suppose. That night was the first time we were going to – you know. But he didn't show up. I guess he realised it was a mistake, too.'

'You guess?' Alison's eyes narrowed. 'Don't you know? Haven't you discussed it with him?'

Jenna shook her head. 'We've avoided each other ever since. I think we both feel a bit foolish.'

'So nothing happened? You didn't cheat on Joel?'

'No, Mum. I didn't cheat on Joel,' Jenna said heavily.

'Well!' Alison leaned back in her chair and puffed out her cheeks in relief. 'That's something, I suppose.' She couldn't bear the thought of her daughter losing her husband. She'd only regret it if she did. Alison knew what it was like to be alone and she wouldn't wish it on Jenna, not to mention what the twins would go through if the worst came to the worst.

The waitress returned with their sandwiches. They thanked her and spent the next few minutes eating in awkward silence.

'What you said about the girls,' Jenna said at last. 'About me dumping them on you. You didn't mean that, did you?'

Alison sighed. Here it was, then. The moment she'd been waiting for.

'I did actually, yes,' she said carefully. 'I'm sorry to say it, but that's how I feel.'

Jenna's eyes gleamed with tears. 'I thought you loved them.'

'Oh, Jenna, don't be daft, love! Of *course* I love them! This has got nothing to do with my feelings for my granddaughters, and everything to do with feeling like I'm being taken for a mug by my own daughter and son-in-law!'

'I thought you were happy to help,' Jenna insisted.

'I *was* happy to help! I *am* happy to help! But that doesn't mean I want to be at your beck and call every single day, and that's how it's felt to me for years now. I have a job, Jenna. I have parents who are getting on in years, not that you seem to care. When was the last time you visited them? You haven't even asked how your grandma's arm is.'

'There never seems to be any time!' Jenna shook her head and pushed her plate away, having only eaten one half of the sandwich. 'How *is* Grandma's arm anyway?'

'Healing slowly,' Alison said. 'I've been popping down to Kelsea Sands more regularly now I haven't had to babysit, and I've taken over the cleaning and cooking duties from your Aunt Elaine and Rosie. They've been brilliant, but they shouldn't have had to be, should they?'

'I doubt they minded,' Jenna said. 'You know how close they all are.'

'That's hardly the point, love.'

'No, I suppose not. I'm glad Grandma's getting better. I will try to pop down one weekend. Or maybe in half-term?'

'Why don't you all go down?' Alison asked impulsively. She squeezed Jenna's hand, feeling a sudden compassion for her overworked daughter. 'You, Joel and the kids. I'm sure they'd love to see you all, and it would do you good to be together as a family. A bit of sea air, or a walk along the river path. You can't beat it.'

'In February?' Jenna laughed mirthlessly. 'Even if I said yes, I can't see Joel wanting to visit Kelsea Sands at this time of year, or any time of year quite honestly. And the girls would get bored. It's not like there's anything for them to do there, is it? I don't know. Maybe I'll take them to see Niall and the family one day. At least there are amusements in Millensea.'

'Maybe you should go the whole hog and book a family holiday somewhere. Why not? Easter holidays, you, Joel and the twins. Go somewhere lovely where you can have fun and relax together. Actually talk. Take those bloody tablets away from the girls.'

'Mm. Maybe.'

Jenna shrugged and Alison bit down her frustration. You just couldn't help some people. 'Well, it's up to you. Just don't go getting distracted by any other men at work or anywhere else, for God's sake.'

'I won't. So...' Jenna gave her mother a pleading look. 'About the girls.'

'No.'

'But, Mum!'

'I said no, Jenna. I've done my childcare bit bringing you up, and then the last seven years with the twins. I've had enough. You and Joel earn enough money between you to pay for some sort of after-school club or something. It's not my responsibility.'

'Other grandparents do it,' Jenna said sulkily. 'Look, I've been giving this a lot of thought, and maybe you're right. Maybe we have been a bit unfair. But what if I pay you? The going rate – well, more or less. How would that sound? A proper job. Maybe you could even give up that job at the petrol station and look after the twins full time? What do you think?'

Alison stared at her. 'You're not serious?'

Jenna nodded eagerly. 'I'll bet you'd much rather be with Hallie and Ada than stuck behind that counter, wouldn't you? It's a win-win situation. You'll have a better job, and I won't have to worry about getting help with the twins because I know you'll be great with them, and far better than any paid child carer would be.'

'You're unbelievable,' Alison said. 'How can I make this any clearer? I do *not* want to look after the girls full time! I need my job at the petrol station. It's my independence.'

'But you don't even like it that much! You only took it because Dad died. You'd given up teaching, remember?'

How could she forget? They'd had such plans, she and Drew. But then he'd started to feel unwell, and just months after Alison had left her job, he'd been given a devastating diagnosis.

And when all hope had died, along with her husband, she'd been left alone and lonely in the house they'd planned to sell but had taken off the market while they focused on his treatment. The days had stretched on endlessly, and the nights – well, they were the worst.

After a year of tears and being trapped in a fog of indecision and fear, she'd finally applied for a job at a petrol station on the retail park where her husband had once worked as a manager of a large furniture store. The very petrol station where Drew had filled up the tank every week. She'd been surprised when she got the job, but it had brought her comfort – made her feel closer to him somehow.

And it had given her a reason to get up in the morning. There'd been no grandchildren to run around after then.

'That's not the point. Oh!' Alison gave an exasperated groan. 'You just don't get it, do you? Hallie and Ada are *your* children. Yours and Joel's. Your responsibility, not mine. I don't want to look after them every day. I want my freedom and they want – need – their parents. Why can't you understand that?'

Jenna watched her through narrowed eyes. 'So you don't want to see your own granddaughters?'

'Bloody hell! Of course I want to see them – but the same way any other grandparent would want to see their grandchildren, not because they're in my care twenty-four-seven. I'm tired, Jenna. They exhaust me. I love them to bits but, to be perfectly honest, I can only deal with them in short bursts. I'm fine to babysit for you once a week. That's not a problem. And if it's a genuine emergency then of course I'll help. But having them every day, having to juggle my job around the school run, having to fit my entire life around my commitments to your children – well, it just isn't on. Not any more. I'm done. I'm sorry.'

'Wow.' Jenna picked up her bag. 'Well, thanks a lot for making it so clear. I won't bother you again.'

Alison reached for her daughter's hand. 'I'm serious about babysitting them once a week. I'm happy to do that. I'll even take them to Kelsea Sands. Mam and Dad would love to see them and—'

'No, honestly, it's no trouble. I wouldn't want to interfere with your busy life,' Jenna said coldly.

Alison rolled her eyes. 'Jenna, stop being so stubborn and childish. Just because I don't want to make it my full-time job doesn't mean I don't want to see them at all. You know I love them.'

'Sounds like it,' Jenna said bitterly. 'When you can fit them in around your hectic schedule of course. I'll find my own childcare solutions, thanks, Mum. Nice seeing you.'

Alison stared, open-mouthed, as her daughter stalked out of the cafe without a backward glance.

She leaned back in her chair and shook her head. Well, that had gone well, hadn't it? She'd hoped, deep down, that they could come to some sort of understanding, that Jenna would see things from her point of view. It seemed that had been optimistic of her. Well, she'd tried. Time to go home and spend the afternoon catching up with all the little jobs she'd been putting off for far too long.

She picked up her bag and rooted inside for her purse, then let out a gasp of annoyance as it occurred to her that Jenna hadn't even paid for her own coffee and sandwich.

Bloody hell. Today really was the gift that kept on giving.

11

Evan Jones dried his hands on the towel and beamed at Mac.

'Well, the good news is that their teeth haven't deteriorated since the last check-up,' he said. 'I've had a good rummage around in their mouths and neither are in bad condition. Nor is the rest of them, come to that. I take it you've been following the feeding routine your mother and I agreed for them?'

Mac handed the vet the mug of tea he'd requested – 'three sugars, please, just enough milk to turn it from black to brown' – and nodded at the list stuck to the fridge-freezer. 'It's all on there,' he said. 'I've got to be honest. I hadn't expected the dental check-up to be so... thorough.'

He still felt queasy. It had all been a lot more clinical than he'd realised. The poor old ponies' heads had, in turn, been placed on a headstand, each one's mouth held open with a speculum while Evan, wearing a bright head light, peered inside with a dental mirror, poked and prodded with dental picks and probes, and even rasped a couple of sharp points on one of the elder pony's teeth. It had made Mac wince, though Jacob Armitage hadn't seemed to mind.

'They're getting on,' Evan reminded him. 'Just like with humans, teeth wear out as they get older. It's important ageing animals have regular check-ups. That's why your mother and I agreed on six-monthly calls. I'm pleased you've kept that up.'

Mac shrugged, not sure whether to confess that he'd had nothing to do with it. He'd simply received a text from Stella the previous day to tell him that the vet would be visiting for the ponies' regular dental check and that he'd better be in.

'I'm sorry about your mother,' Evan said, sitting at the table as if he was perfectly used to making himself at home in Watersmeet. Maybe he was. With all the animals and birds his mother had cared for over the years Mac had no doubt that she and the local vet had been on first-name terms. 'She was a good woman. Heart of gold. Couldn't bear the thought of any living creature suffering, could she?'

'No. She really couldn't.' Was that, Mac wondered, why she'd left him Watersmeet? To make sure that, like all her waifs and strays, he had a safe and secure roof over his head?

'It must all seem pretty overwhelming to you, though.' Evan surveyed him thoughtfully. 'Not used to animals, are you? Not since you got married any road, and how long ago was that? Thirty-five years or more.'

'You're very well informed,' Mac said cautiously.

'Your mother and I were good friends,' Evan said sadly. 'We shared a love for animals of course, and we talked. She said Lynne wasn't an animal lover.'

'She had allergies,' Mac said, sounding unconvincing even to himself. His wife had hated the thought of animal hair and all the other mess that came with having pets, and she'd made it very clear that, as much as her children begged and pleaded, a cat or a dog was out of the question.

'Ah. I see. Either way, your mother thought it a shame that you had no pets. Oh, don't look at me like that, lad! She just needed someone to confide in, you know. And Stella – Stella is a good woman, and your mother loved her to bits, but she wasn't always as...' He considered for a moment. 'As open-minded as she might have been,' he finished tactfully.

'No. Stella thinks what she thinks.' Mac sipped his black coffee, feeling ill at ease. How much did this big, burly man know about him? About who he was and what he'd done? Just how much had his mother confided?

'There's no judgement here, Ian,' Evan said, as if he'd read his mind. 'Things happen. The point is you did the right thing in the end, and you've come through it. That deserves some recognition and respect, if you ask me. What matters now is the future.'

Mac gave a half laugh. 'I don't think about the future. It's too much. I have enough on my plate getting through today, thanks very much.'

'Aye, well, they say that's 'best way,' Evan agreed. 'One day at a time.'

Mac said nothing. Sometimes, on the worst days, it was a question of one *hour* at a time. One *moment* at a time. He realised those darkest days were growing further and further apart, but they could still happen when he least expected them.

'It's Mac, by the way,' he said.

Evan frowned. 'What is?'

'My name. I don't answer to Ian any longer. I've left him behind with everything else.'

Evan nodded. 'Understood. Well, Mac it is then. Any other problems that I should know about? All the rest of your animal family okay?'

'I think so. The Fosters at Carr Farm have been brilliant, and I'm pretty sure that if there was anything wrong with any of them, they'd have told me.'

'I don't mind taking a look at them if you want to be really sure.'

Mac wasn't sure how to phrase his response, so he simply shook his head and said it was fine.

'I wouldn't charge,' Evan said quickly, obviously guessing what he'd been thinking. 'I meant as a favour to your mother really. I promised her, you see. I promised that I'd always keep an eye on things.'

Mac sighed. 'So, deep down she didn't really trust me with them?'

Evan frowned. 'That's not what I meant at all. Look, I won't lie to you. Your mother and I had a few long talks about the future: what would happen to the animals when she passed away. She knew Stella wouldn't keep them. Stella's got a good heart, but your mother was all too aware the lines your sister's thoughts would run along, and she couldn't take the risk. Stella would justify getting rid of the animals to herself. She'd tell herself it was for the best and she might even believe it. Your mother didn't want that. She wanted them to stay here at Watersmeet. The first place they'd ever had a secure, loving home. No more upheaval for them, that's what she said, and I agreed.'

'I get that,' Mac said heavily. 'But what do I know about animals? I mean, Highland cattle! Ponies. Ex-battery hens. Bloody ducks, for God's sake! I've enough on just with a cat and a dog.'

'Be grateful old Ma Larkin's gone to the great pigsty in the sky,' Evan said with a chuckle. 'Now, *she* was a handful! She'd have run rings round you.'

Mac grinned. 'So I heard. Mum used to write to me, telling me all about her.' His smile faded as he realised he wouldn't get any more letters from his mother. Even when he'd thought she'd never find him, somehow a letter would wing its way to him sooner or later, having bounced from one address to another. She never gave up. Good old-fashioned letters that had kept him anchored to home, somehow, more than any text or email ever could, all written on thick notepaper with a proper fountain pen.

He'd found the pen in her desk drawer last week. He'd sat and stared at it for ages.

'Bloody Ma Larkin,' he said, shaking his head. 'Where did she get these crazy names?'

'Literature! Your mother loved a good book, didn't she?' Evan said, laughing. 'Every single animal is named after a fictional character. Oh, she was one in a million, your mother, she really was.'

'I know,' Mac said quietly. 'She deserved a better son than me. Stella was so good to her. She's right to be angry. She should have Watersmeet really.'

'Like I said, your mother couldn't trust Stella with the animals. And the last thing she wanted was for her precious land to be sold off as an extension to that bloody caravan park. You know as well as I do that's what would have happened if she'd left it to Stella. Not because your sister's greedy or uncaring, but because of Gavin. Your mother said, divorce or no divorce, Stella would do what Gavin wanted, and he needs more land. He's losing bits of Tide's Reach to the sea every year. Sooner or later, he's going to run out of space for his caravans, and this place is as far away from the sea as it's possible to get in Kelsea Sands.'

He gave a contented sigh. 'By, you're a lucky man owning this place. Not the way you came to own it, obviously. That's a crying shame. But the fact that Watersmeet is yours. This lovely house. The land. The views across the Humber, and the curve of Kels Point straight ahead and beyond it the sea... I'd wake up every morning saying a prayer of thanks if I lived here.'

'Where do *you* live?' Mac asked, curious.

'Millensea,' Evan explained. 'Our practice is there so it makes sense. Nice house. Nice town. But very peopley, if you know what I mean. Holidaymakers. Day trippers. Not like here. Here you can hear yourself think.'

'Maybe we should swap houses,' Mac said, only half joking. 'I think it would be good to be in a place where you can't hear your own thoughts.'

Evan studied him for a moment, as if trying to decide how serious he was. 'Your mother loved you so much,' he said at last. 'She trusted you. She knew you'd do the right thing.'

'Of course she didn't trust me! How could she?' Mac asked brokenly. 'After everything I did! Everything that happened!'

'She never blamed you for that.'

'Well, she's the only one then,' Mac said bitterly. 'Everyone else did, me most of all. I don't blame our Stella for hating me.'

'Er, Stella didn't do too badly out of it,' Evan reminded him. 'She may not have got the house, but she got plenty of financial compensation.' As Mac raised an eyebrow, he nodded. 'Oh yes, I know. I was a witness to the will. Stella did all right, and it's not as if she was destitute in the first place, was it? Her divorce settlement was substantial, from what your mother told me. I mean, she's not a billionaire but she'll never have to work for a living, will she? Not that it's any of my business,' he added hastily, 'and I certainly wouldn't be saying any of this to anyone but you, but my point is, you mustn't feel too guilty about all this. Guilt can lead you on a downward spiral, and that's the last thing you need.'

'So you know about my monthly allowance, and the trust, too?' Mac asked wearily.

Evan nodded and took another sip of his tea. 'I'm aware that you got the house, but all the money you'll need to keep it running and to provide for the animals is locked away, with Stella holding the purse strings. She can't refuse you, though. If you need repairs doing to the house or outbuildings, if you need food for the animals or' – he nudged Mac with a grin – 'vet's bills paying, she's got to pay it. You needn't worry about that.'

'Like I said, Mum knew she couldn't trust me.'

'I don't think it was that,' Evan said kindly. 'But she knew you didn't trust yourself, and until you start to do that, you're still vulnerable. Plus, she had another reason for putting Stella in charge of the finances for this place. Don't you get it? She knew Stella would take it badly – losing Watersmeet. She was afraid the two of you would fall out for good, so she made damn sure that you'd *have* to stay in contact, whether you liked it or not.'

'Wily old bird, wasn't she?' Mac said, a wry smile playing on his lips.

'Canny,' Evan agreed fondly. He glanced around the kitchen. 'What about this place? The house, I mean. Anything need doing to it?'

'Well, I need a new bed, that's for sure,' Mac said with feeling. 'The bed in my old room must be the same one I used to sleep in when I was a kid, and to be honest, I don't fancy sleeping on Mum's old bed, even though it's fairly new. I thought I'd turn her room into a guest room just in case...'

His voice trailed off as he realised he didn't want to jinx things by putting into words the hope that, one day, his children would come to stay at Watersmeet. 'Anyway,' he finished, 'a new bed. I've been granted permission to buy one. Aren't I the lucky one?'

'I know your monthly allowance is probably enough to cover food and bills, but have you had any thoughts on what you're going to do with yourself now you've moved back here? Any job in mind?'

Mac shook his head. 'Like I said, I take one day at a time.'

Evan nodded. 'Well, I'm sure something will come to you in the end. You're still young enough to find your place in the world.'

'I'm sixty-two!'

'Exactly! Only sixty-two! I'm seventy, in case you're interested. Should have retired years ago but bugger that for a game of soldiers. I'm far too young and dynamic.' He drained his mug and wiped his mouth with the back of his hand. 'I enjoyed that. You make a right good cuppa. Nearly as good as your mother's.

'Now look, if you need anything – anything at all – you only have to ask. Here's my card, right? Even if you just want to call and ask for advice over the phone about the animals. But also if you ever want to talk about... Well, anything. You know. You mustn't be alone, Mac. Someone in your position – you need people to talk to. If you need a listening ear, I'm here. You understand?'

Mac smiled, seeing the genuine kindness and concern in the vet's eyes. 'Thank you. I'll remember that.'

'See that you do.'

Evan got to his feet and patted Mac on the shoulder. 'I can see myself out, no need to show me to the door. Just remember, I'm here, however lonely you might feel right now. I thought the world of your mother, and she thought the world of you, so that makes us pals in my eyes. I know you won't let her down.'

Mac couldn't reply, his throat was so tight with emotion. Evan nodded and smiled then picked up his bag and headed for the door.

'I'll send the bill to Stella,' he called over his shoulder. 'I'm sure she'll be delighted that the ponies are in the very best of health. We both know she'd hate for anything to happen to these precious animals.'

I'll send this bill to Phoebe,' he called over his shoulder. 'I'm sorry. We'll see to it that the poor creature is put out of its misery of death. We both know that those foxes are the real culprits in these predator unbalance.

12

Alison scooped up a spoonful of chicken fried rice and curry sauce, her eyes fixed on the television screen and an old episode of *Miss Marple*. She knew the plot off by heart, but it didn't detract from her enjoyment. She loved detective programmes – as long as they weren't too graphic or scary. She hated anything with too much tension. It was probably why she watched so many repeats of old series. That way she knew what to expect and there were no nasty surprises.

The Chinese takeaway had been a last-minute idea. A fond farewell to eating fast food. She'd rung the surgery that morning from work and had it confirmed that she was just within the diabetic range. It was time to do something about it. She had three months to turn things around, so what better way to mark the occasion than with her favourite Chinese dish?

'Tomorrow,' she murmured, as she wistfully eyed the vegetable spring rolls on her plate, 'it will be salad and vegetables and lean protein.' She couldn't say she was looking forward to it, but she was too scared not to give it a try. She wasn't going to roll over and accept that she was now a type 2 diabetic. No way. Not if she had a chance to do something about it.

The doorbell rang and Alison frowned. Rosie? But it was gone six o'clock and dark outside. Rosie didn't like driving in the dark, especially not on the lonely, winding roads between Hull and Kelsea Sands. Maybe it was someone wanting a donation or asking her to sign up for some raffle or other, or switch broadband providers or electricity companies. There'd been a lot of that just lately. Most of her neighbours had put signs in their windows, telling cold callers not to bother.

She put her plate on the coffee table and headed into the hallway, hoping whoever it was wouldn't keep her standing at the door too long, because there was nothing worse than cold chicken fried rice.

Making sure the chain was on the latch, she cautiously opened the front door, then heaved a sigh of relief and pulled back the chain, standing aside to let her son-in-law in.

'Joel! I wasn't expecting you.' She frowned, suddenly worried. 'Everything's okay, isn't it?'

'Apart from me and Jenna being well and truly dropped in it as far as childcare goes, you mean? Perfect.'

He sounded bitter and his eyes flashed with annoyance. Alison's worry evaporated, replaced with irritation.

'Has Jenna sent you?' she asked as she closed the door to keep out the cold January air.

'No. She doesn't know I'm here. She told me to leave it, and that I should stay away from you.'

I'll bet she did. Terrified I tell him what caused me to withdraw my labour, no doubt.

'Maybe,' she said, 'you should have listened to her.'

She'd been going to invite him through to the living room. Make him a coffee. Even offer him some of her fried rice. Seeing the disgust on his face, she changed her mind. She wished she'd left him standing on the doorstep in the cold now.

'Why are you being so selfish?' he snapped. 'You know how we're fixed. It's not easy, you know, both of us working with twins to look after.'

'Except,' she said coldly, 'you don't look after them, do you? You're always at bloody work or some conference or meeting or whatever. Jenna palms them off on me whenever she can, but you're even worse.'

'*Palms them off on you*?' He glared at her. 'So she wasn't lying then. You really do consider them a burden!'

'I never said that. Stop twisting my words,' she said crossly. 'Are you going to calm down and talk about this sensibly?'

'I'm perfectly calm. You know, we thought we were doing you a favour. After Drew died you were so miserable, and when the twins came along, we thought they'd be the perfect antidote for your depression—'

'My grief,' she said flatly. 'I think you'll find it was grief, and the only antidote to that is time, not looking after other people's kids.'

'Your grandchildren,' he reminded her, as if she needed reminding.

'I'm aware of that, and I love them both to bits,' she said. 'That doesn't mean I want my entire life to revolve around them. Surely you can see that? You clearly feel much the same way about them yourself.'

He puffed out his cheeks and shook his head. 'Wow! You're unbelievable. I'm working! I'm trying to build a better life for my family. Maybe that doesn't mean much to you, given that you threw away a perfectly decent career to sponge off Drew—'

'I beg your pardon?' Alison couldn't believe he'd just said that. She stared at him, hardly able to comprehend that the son-in-law she'd always got on well with could say something so cruel. '*Sponge* off him? What are you talking about?'

Joel's lip curled. 'You gave up your job to do what? Lounge about in the house while he drove himself into an early grave working to provide for you. How did you think he was going to make up the shortfall in your income, once you stopped teaching?'

'It wasn't like that at all!' Alison's eyes filled with tears, and she blinked them away angrily. She was *not* going to show any signs of weakness. 'Drew and I talked about it. We'd made plans.'

'*You* made plans, and he went along with them,' Joel said scornfully. 'He never liked letting you down, did he? You could have carried on working until you both retired. Instead, you quit your job, became a lady of leisure and let him work himself to death. Now you're trying to do the same to your daughter. How's she supposed to look after two kids and carry on working at the same time? Have you any idea how stressed she's been lately because of this? Or maybe you'd prefer it if she quit her job, too, and let me struggle to cover all the bills and mortgage?'

Alison had no words. She thought back to the discussions she and Drew had had about her leaving work. He'd been all for it. Hadn't he? He'd said they could easily manage on his salary, that she had no need to worry. He wanted her to be happy, he said.

Oh, God. Had she really driven him into an early grave?

'I think you should go,' she said shakily.

'Truth hurts, doesn't it?' he said unkindly. 'I'm glad you're upset. Jenna's been a mess for days, ringing round, organising after-school clubs and all sorts. Their gym club's probably out of the question now if you won't take them. Maybe the dance classes, too. We're probably going to have to look for a nanny now. Jenna's worn out trying to fix it all.'

'And I'm sure you did your best to help her,' she said sarcastically, knowing perfectly well that it would all have fallen on her daughter's shoulders. She felt a sudden guilt and shame. She should have considered that. She'd just made more hard work for Jenna.

'No wonder she doesn't want to see you again,' he snarled. 'You really take the biscuit, you know that? Not an ounce of compassion for her. When I think how forgiving she was, even though she really struggled after her dad died, knowing it was all your fault he got ill—'

'It was *not* my fault!' Alison pushed him away from her in fury, and he staggered backward, not prepared. 'How dare you say such a thing? He had cancer! I didn't cause that.'

'Cancer can be caused by stress. Everyone knows that. And his immune system was probably weakened by the extra work and the responsibility. But did Jenna ever have a go at you for it? No. She tried to get you through it all. She even trusted you with our babies, which is more than I would have done, considering the state you were in at the time.'

'Get out, Joel,' Alison said, unable to check the flow of tears now. She wanted him to leave because she hated the thought of him seeing how much he'd upset her. She didn't want him to have that power. She pulled open the door, her emotions making her oblivious to the icy blast that swept through the hallway. 'Leave, now.'

'Don't worry, I'm going. But I hope you're prepared for the fact that you won't be seeing the twins for a very long time.'

'You can't keep them away from me,' she gasped. 'They're my granddaughters.'

'Yes, when it suits you! If you're not prepared to look after them when we need you then you're not seeing them at all.

Simple as. And don't bother trying to harass Jenna about it because it was her decision. I'm just passing on the message.'

He pulled his coat tighter. 'I hope you're happy with yourself. You've really upset your daughter and now your granddaughters will be miserable, too. Nice work, Alison.'

The moment he stepped outside she slammed the door shut and dropped the latch, as well as sliding the chain across. For a moment she held her breath, half expecting him to try to get back inside, but she heard nothing until the front gate clicked shut, and a minute or so later his car started, and he drove away.

She leaned against the door, struggling for breath, her hands shaking. She couldn't believe that she'd just had a showdown with Joel, of all people. They'd always got along fine. Did he and Jenna really believe she'd been responsible for Drew's death? Is that what they'd thought all these years?

She staggered back into the living room and sank on to the sofa. She couldn't stop trembling and felt as if she was in shock. What just happened?

'It was Drew's idea for me to leave teaching,' she muttered to herself, shaking her head as if some invisible source was arguing the point. 'I admit I told him how unhappy I was, but it was Drew who said we could manage fine without my salary by that point. He was the one who dealt with the finances. He knew the situation. I didn't push him into anything. *I didn't!*'

But had she, without even meaning to? Drew had been such a kind man. He would have done anything to make her happy. And he knew how risk averse she was. The very fact that she was even mentioning how she'd like to leave her job – even though she had no intention of doing so then – would have signalled to him how unhappy she was feeling. Had he felt unable to ignore her misery? Had she emotionally blackmailed him, however unintentionally?

Biting back tears, she took her plate into the kitchen and scraped the takeaway into the bin. She couldn't face it now. Instead, she made herself a hot chocolate and carried it back into the living room, trying to calm herself down. She felt sick with anxiety. She hated confrontation of any kind, but to argue like that with her son-in-law! She couldn't believe she'd fallen out with her own family, and that she might never get to see Hallie and Ada again. Panic gripped her and she wondered for a moment if she should call Jenna, tell her she would give up her job and accept her offer to be the twins' nanny.

When the phone rang, she was almost afraid to look at it. What if it was Joel ready for Round Two? Or what if it was Jenna calling to add her tuppence worth? She really couldn't deal with any more accusations.

Daring to peer at the screen she almost sobbed with relief when she saw Rosie's name flash up on the screen. She accepted the call without even thinking about it, but it was some moments before she could manage to say hello, as she struggled to hold back the tears, her throat tight with emotion, her heart thudding.

'Ali? Ali, are you there?'

Alison desperately swallowed and managed to croak out a response.

'You sound awful. Have you got a cold? I was just ringing to tell you that I'm finally moving back into the caravan on Sunday, and I've just come here to give it a good clean. Wish I could stay here all night to be honest, but I daren't risk getting chucked out when I'm so close to escaping Mam and Dad's.' She laughed. 'Mind you, I'm in no hurry to go back to theirs yet. Just about to order meself a takeaway as a matter of fact and—'

She broke off as Alison let out a sob, even though she'd done her best not to.

'Ali? What's wrong?' Rosie asked anxiously.

'It's... it's Joel. He's just been round. Oh, Rosie, he said some awful things! It wasn't my fault, was it?'

'What wasn't your fault?' Rosie asked, sounding completely baffled.

'Drew! I didn't push him into an early grave, did I?'

'*What*?' Rosie's voice bellowed in her ear. 'Is that what Joel said? Is he there?'

'He left,' Alison managed. 'I asked him to leave.'

'Asked him to leave? I'd have kicked his sorry arse all the way down the Clive Sully,' Rosie raged. 'The bloody cheek of him! Why would he say something like that?'

'It's because of Jenna and the twins,' Alison said shakily. 'He's furious. He says... he says I can't see the girls any more because I've refused to babysit. He says Drew got cancer because he had to work so hard after I left teaching. That it was stress that made him ill.' She wiped her eyes with a trembling hand. 'It's not true, is it? I didn't cause his illness, did I?'

She really wasn't sure any more. Joel had certainly sounded convinced.

'Of course it's not true! Oh, Ali, don't let him get to you, please. Right, that's it, I'm on my way,' Rosie said.

'What? No, no you mustn't! You're about to have your tea,' Alison protested. 'Besides, it's dark outside and you hate those roads and—'

It was no use saying anything else. Rosie had hung up.

13

Alison was beginning to think she'd misunderstood the situation and that Rosie wasn't coming round after all, because almost two hours had passed since their phone call had ended.

She'd gone upstairs and taken a quick bath to try to soothe her frazzled nerves, then she'd got into her comfiest pair of pyjamas and settled in front of the television to watch the rest of *Miss Marple*, determined to put the whole sorry business out of her mind.

Unfortunately, it hadn't worked, because not only was she still fretting about the scene with Joel, the fact that her own daughter blamed her for her father's death and that she probably wasn't going to be allowed to see her own granddaughters for the foreseeable future, but now she had Rosie to worry about. If her cousin had really set off to visit her, she should have been there ages ago. What if something had happened to her?

It was almost eight o'clock. Alison nibbled her thumb nail and tried to decide whether she should try calling Rosie. But what if she was driving? The last thing she wanted to do was distract her.

She wandered over to the window and hesitantly pulled the curtain aside a little. It was dark and windy outside, but at least it wasn't raining. That was something. It had certainly got colder, though. She wouldn't be at all surprised if they had some snow. She patted the radiator and gave thanks for central heating.

The knock on the door a few minutes later made her jump. Whoever it was clearly hadn't noticed she had a doorbell – or didn't trust them. She grinned in relief. Rosie! Only her cousin would deliberately ignore what was right there in plain sight. She always said half the time they didn't work, and you were left standing outside pressing a useless button for ages like a numpty when you could have just banged on the door and saved yourself a great deal of time and bother.

Even so, as she opened the front door she kept the chain on to make absolutely certain that it wasn't Joel come back for Round Two.

'Bloody hell, Ali, let me in! I'm freezing me tits off here,' Rosie told her.

Alison laughed and slid back the chain. 'Aw bless you, you look nithered. Come in and get warm. I was getting worried about you. You've been ages.'

Rosie stepped inside the house and immediately kicked off her ankle boots before padding through to the living room in her thick socks. She was still wearing her jacket and had a woolly hat crammed down over her ears, her arms wrapped around a large paper bag, a tote bag slung over one shoulder.

'I come bearing gifts,' she said, slipping the tote bag on to the floor. 'Well, gifts and my night things. I'm all prepared this time. PJs, toothbrush, clean undies, make-up, the lot. I've even remembered to bring my own shower gel cos yours doesn't smell anywhere near as good.'

'Oh, I'm so relieved,' Alison admitted. 'Not about the shower gel. About you staying the night. But does Seb's lad Sam mind? You should be at work in 'morning, shouldn't you?'

Rosie had been cleaning at The North Star ever since she'd moved back to Kelsea Sands and sometimes had early starts.

'Swapped my shift with Bella. I'm doing the day after for her. It works out better for her cos she's got to go into Millensea to see the doctor about having her veins stripped.'

Alison thought she'd rather be cleaning than face discussing that, but she was glad Bella had agreed to swap her shift. 'That's great. I'd have hated you to drive back again tonight.'

'No chance of that,' Rosie told her with a dramatic shudder. 'Took my life in my hands coming here. I'm not risking it again.' She plonked the paper bag on the coffee table and Alison recognised the golden arches immediately.

'McDonald's?'

'Well, be fair, love. I didn't get to order that takeaway, did I? I'm starving. And there's no Maccie D's near us so I have to make the most of it while I'm here.'

Rosie took off her hat and jacket and tossed them casually on to an armchair. 'Right,' she said, 'I've got cheeseburgers and chicken sandwiches and fries and all sorts in here. Just help yourself to whatever you want.' She grinned. 'I'll send you the bill later.'

'Of course I'll go halves,' Alison said, even though she wasn't convinced she'd eat much. If a chicken fried rice had lost its appeal, she was doubtful burgers would tempt her.

In the event, she was staggered to discover that her appetite had come flooding back, and even though she wasn't much of a fan of burgers she managed to eat more than her fair share of Rosie's order – including apple pie washed down with a vanilla milkshake.

'God, I'm stuffed,' she said finally, leaning back on the sofa and patting her stomach. 'You do realise I'm diabetic and shouldn't be eating any of this?'

'You've had it confirmed then?' Rosie asked, wiping her hands on the serviettes provided. 'It's definite?'

Alison sighed. 'Yeah. Just tipped into diabetic range. They've given me three months to reverse it, and here I am eating junk food as if I hadn't a care in the world.'

'Sorry, Ali.' Rosie looked contrite. 'If I'd known...'

'It's not your fault!' Alison said quickly. 'To be honest, I'd ordered a Chinese takeaway earlier. I'd decided to start tomorrow, and I mean it this time.'

'You've already had a Chinese takeaway?' Rosie blew out her cheeks. 'Bloody hell! Even I couldn't manage both.'

Alison laughed. 'No, I threw the fried rice in the bin. I was too upset to eat it after what Joel said.'

'Yes, now you've eaten you can tell me exactly what he said. What happened from the moment you opened the front door and don't miss anything out.'

Trying to remember it as accurately as possible, Alison relayed her conversation with her son-in-law to Rosie, who said nothing but busied herself putting all the rubbish and wrappers back inside the paper bag.

'The cheeky get,' she said at last, when Alison had finally reached the point where she'd slammed the door on Joel and made sure the latch was down and the chain in place. 'Who the hell does he think he is? And what's got into our Jenna?'

'Is that what everyone thinks though, Rosie?' Alison asked, troubled. 'Tell me the truth. Don't give me any flannel. Do people blame me for Drew's illness?'

Rosie's eyes widened in shock. 'Don't be so daft! No one was to blame for that. It's just one of those things. And you were there for him through it all, by his side for every appointment, every test, every visiting hour. Imagine if you'd still been working! It would have been even harder for you and for him. As it was, you giving up your job turned out to be a blessing because you could spend every moment with him. Bloody Joel doesn't know what he's talking about.'

'Yes, but...'

Rosie sighed. 'Drew loved you, Ali, and he wanted you to give up your job if it made you happy, but he wasn't daft either. If it had put too much financial strain on you both he wouldn't have told you to go for it. You know that. You know Drew. And deep down, you know Joel's full of crap.'

'I can't believe they're not going to let me see the twins,' Alison said, feeling tearful all over again.

Rosie gave a snort of derision. 'Yeah, right. Let's see how long that lasts. Bet you anything you like that they'll come running to you before long begging you to babysit. You just watch!'

'You think so?'

'Why would they break the habit of a lifetime?' Rosie shook her head. 'Our Jenna wants a good talking-to. I've a good mind to go round there myself.'

'No, just leave it.' Alison sighed. 'I'm really sorry you had to come all this way to sort me out, Rosie. I shouldn't have got so upset.'

'You were bound to be upset, with Joel pushing his way in and yelling at you like that and saying all those awful things. And thinking Jenna blamed you for Drew's death – which I don't believe, by the way. I think that prat Joel's just found your weak spot and gone for it. All that on top of finding out about your diabetes. It's a lot, isn't it?'

'Too much,' Alison admitted. 'I just keep crying and that's not like me at all. I haven't really cried much at all since...'

'Well, not surprising. You cried so much then you must

have used up all your supply of tears.' Rosie eyed her sadly. 'I'm sorry you're having such a rough time of it, Ali. It's not fair.'

'I'm scared,' Alison admitted.

'Of Joel? Don't be scared of that long streak of piss. I'll drop-kick him into the River Hull. See how he likes that.'

Alison smiled, knowing that her cousin was the least violent person imaginable, and was clearly just trying to cheer her up. Alison loved her for it.

'Of the diabetes,' she said quietly. 'It's not a laughing matter, is it?'

'No,' Rosie said, the humour in her eyes fading. 'It's not. But it's reversible, that's what the nurse said, didn't she? So reverse it then.'

'What if I can't? You know how many times I've tried to diet before, and it never works. What if I can't stick to it?'

'You *will* stick to it because you know what's at stake,' Rosie said confidently.

'But when I'm here in the evenings I find myself picking at rubbish,' Alison admitted. 'Even when I'm not hungry.'

'So don't buy anything. If there's nothing in the cupboards you can't eat it,' Rosie said reasonably.

'It's not that simple. I can get a delivery of just about anything these days. One tap on my phone and I can order crisps, sausage rolls, sweets, ice cream, burgers...' She waved a hand at the paper bag stuffed full of their empty wrappers and bags. 'I'm so weak-willed.'

'You need someone to keep an eye on you,' Rosie said, nodding.

Alison hesitated. 'I don't suppose...'

'What?' Rosie shook her head. 'Aw, no love. I can't move in here for three months! I mean, I've got work. You know my shifts are all over the place like yours, and I'm here, there and everywhere. It would never work.'

That was true. Apart from cleaning at The North Star early most mornings, Rosie did a few evening shifts at a fish and chip shop in Millensea, and when Tide's Reach reopened, she'd be cleaning at Time and Tide, the clubhouse on site, straight after her shifts at the pub as well.

'Yeah, of course. Daft idea.'

Rosie pulled at a thread on the seam of her jeans. 'Mind you, there is an easier solution,' she said. 'You can come back with me to Kelsea Sands.'

Alison laughed, until it dawned on her that Rosie wasn't joking.

'There's no room for me,' Alison said, as her cousin gave her an intense look that told her she was deadly serious. 'Mam and Dad have turned my old room into a junk room. It would take months to clear that out, even if they let me get rid of anything. You know what they're like.'

'Not with your mam and dad,' Rosie said. 'With me!'

She sounded full of excitement and enthusiasm, while Alison stared at her, wondering if she'd lost the plot.

'But you live in a caravan.'

Rosie gave her an indignant look. 'A bloody luxury caravan, might I remind you. I ploughed every penny I had into that place. It's a little palace.'

After Rosie and Craig had decided to go their separate ways, they'd sold their house in Sheffield, and with Rosie's share of the proceeds she'd bought the caravan outright. Her parents had been horrified, warning her that it was a terrible investment, and reminding her that caravans began to lose their value the minute they were purchased.

'Save the money to use as a deposit on a house when you're

working,' Uncle Christopher had advised her, but Rosie wouldn't listen. She didn't want a mortgage, even if she could get one, which wasn't a certainty, and she didn't trust landlords either, so didn't want to rent. Not that there were any houses to rent in Kelsea Sands, and very few ever came up for sale. Rosie was adamant that she wanted to live in her old village and be close to her family again.

'I've missed it so much,' she'd told Alison. 'There were times when my heart literally ached for the place. I'm not going up to Weltringham or Millensea or further inland. I want to be in Kelsea Sands, and a caravan's my best option for that.'

No one could deny that was true, so Uncle Christopher and Aunt Elaine had gritted their teeth and let her get on with purchasing a brand-new two-bedroomed static caravan from Gavin Hewson. She'd have to vacate it every January, but other than that it was a home from home, and with her parents across the road and willing to let her live with them for the month she had to be offsite, Rosie hadn't seen any downside to the purchase, even though it now meant she had no savings and would probably never get on the property ladder.

'Who cares?' Rosie had said with a shrug as she proudly showed off her new home to her family. 'This is my home. I don't need another.'

'Until the land it's sitting on falls into the sea,' her mother said grimly.

'Gavin says if it gets too close to the cliff edge, we'll just move it to another plot,' Rosie said with a shrug. 'Easy.'

No one liked to point out that the caravan park didn't go back forever, and at some point, there was going to be nowhere to move the caravans that were teetering near the edge of the cliff to. Rosie wasn't daft and she must have known that. If she was choosing to look on the bright side, well, that was Rosie for you.

Alison had, to her shame, only been inside the caravan once, and that was when Rosie had first shown them all around, when the furniture was still covered in plastic protection. Caravans just weren't her thing, and she imagined it was quite poky and uncomfortable inside now that all Rosie's belongings were in situ.

She didn't want to hurt her cousin's feelings, though. 'Thanks, Rosie, but you wouldn't want me cluttering up the place for three months. It's okay, I'll manage somehow. Besides, it would take me about fifty minutes to get to work each day.'

Rosie, though, had got the bit between her teeth. 'But only four days a week! And it'll be smashing!' she cried excitedly. 'Think of it, Ali. You and me being housemates for three months while we get your life back on track.' She waved a hand in the air as if revealing a sign. 'Project Alison! Move in on Sunday with me. A new month. A new beginning. Twelve weeks to reverse your diabetes, make Jenna and Joel realise what twats they're being, and take back control. What do you say?'

Alison couldn't deny it sounded tempting. Twelve weeks wasn't really so long, was it? All right, the commute would be a long one, but it would be worth it in the end. And maybe, if she wasn't at home and at Jenna's beck and call, her daughter would realise that she had a point, and that she'd treated Alison unfairly. Maybe Joel would relent and let her see the twins. Maybe they'd organise proper childcare so that Alison's relationship with her granddaughters could be a more conventional one in the future.

Twelve weeks of having Rosie guarding her eating – because she knew her cousin would take this very seriously and help her stick to her diet. More importantly, twelve weeks of being by the sea, by the river, of country walks and fresh air, of seeing her parents and spending quality time with them, of mixing more with her aunt and uncle and maybe even seeing Niall and Kendra more frequently.

She'd missed Kelsea Sands. She understood the ache that Rosie had talked of because she'd felt it herself. She might only live twenty-four miles or so from the place, but sometimes it felt more like a million.

You either 'got' Kelsea Sands or you didn't, and if you didn't, you'd never understand the hold it had on so many people's hearts.

The mudflats of the Humber foreshore, the gleam of sunshine on the water that would dazzle you as you gazed at the horizon, the views across the wide expanse of the river to Lincolnshire, the vast open skies, the half-mile walk down the lane between the Humber and the North Sea, which took you past the church with its overgrown graveyard, along the narrow footpath edged with grassy verges that in spring were splashed with yellow daffodils and in summer bright with scarlet poppies.

The stark beauty of winter trees which, in May, modelled their pretty spring green dresses with lacy hawthorn trimmings. The tangled hedges. The wild grasses.

The North Sea with the wind turbines in the distance. The broken road that hung like a diving board over the crumbling cliffs. The sandy beach littered with rubble from another age.

The emptiness. The sheer simplicity and beauty of the place that could overwhelm you with emotion and reduce you to tears because it was just so bloody beautiful and you had no words to express how it made you feel.

This tiny little place, at the mercy of the tide, held Alison in its grasp forever, and as she thought about it, she experienced a tug of love and longing for home that couldn't be denied any longer.

Twelve weeks to change her life. Twelve weeks to take back

control. Twelve weeks to reconnect with her wider family, breathe in the fresh air and remember who she was.

Twelve weeks to find the old Alison.

'Okay,' she said, half laughing at the craziness of it all. 'You're on. I'll bring my stuff on Sunday night after work.'

Rosie gaped at her. 'Seriously?'

'Yes, seriously. I need to get my act together, Rosie. I can't carry on like this any longer, and where better to sort myself out than home?'

Because, she realised, Kelsea Sands had always been home. It was where she belonged. And she was ready to return.

Even if it did mean spending three months in a bloody caravan.

14

Alison eyed the Mars Bar with longing before forcing herself to turn away from the confectionery shelf. All day she'd been attacked by the sights and smells of delicious food at the petrol station. She'd been on a bakery shift that morning, and could still smell the sausage rolls and delicious sweet pastries from that section of the shop. Now she was working an extra shift to cover a colleague so there was no escape. It was enough to make her want to weep.

The last two weeks had been hard. Really hard. All the upheaval of packing her bags and moving down to Kelsea Sands on 1 February would normally have been enough to make her turn to food, but somehow, she'd mustered her strength and started her diet. So far, she'd managed to stick to it, though it had to be said that the bakery shifts were the hardest, especially after having to make such a long drive into work in the early hours of the morning.

If she'd had second thoughts about sharing the caravan with Rosie they'd quickly been dispelled – firstly by her parents' delight that she was going to be living so close to them for the next three months, and secondly by the pleasant surprise she'd received when she'd tentatively stepped into the caravan.

'Oh, wow!' She'd gazed around in surprise, noting how clean and tidy and spacious it was. There was a large open-plan kitchen, dining room and living room, complete with a proper sofa and armchairs, a large television on the wall, and a stylish fireplace with a pebble-effect electric fire.

'Dishwasher,' Rosie had said, proudly pointing it out. 'Bet you never expected that, did you?'

Alison hadn't, nor had she remembered the impressive cooker and hob, the beautiful ivory kitchen units with beech worktops, the double-glazed windows and the proper domestic radiators that indicated a fully functioning central heating system. No wonder the caravan felt so warm and welcoming.

'This is lovely, Rosie,' she'd said, gazing round in admiration. Bathed in lamplight and the glow from the fire, the caravan felt snug and cosy.

Rosie beamed at her. 'Come and see the rest of it.'

The shower room had a large, walk-in shower, and plenty of room to move around in, which wasn't something Alison had expected. There was even a heated towel rail. Rosie's bedroom had its own en suite which, although small, suited Rosie perfectly well.

'You can have the bigger shower room,' she said generously. 'I'm fine in this one.'

'Are you sure?' Alison asked doubtfully. 'It seems a bit unfair.'

Rosie had given her a worried look. 'Well, it's a sort of trade off. You haven't seen your bedroom yet.'

'Ah.'

To be fair, it wasn't a bad size, and at least the two single beds, separated by a bedside cabinet, were full-size ones, and not the usual caravan bunk-style beds that Alison had seen on the rare occasions she'd holidayed in a caravan. There was a single wardrobe at the end of the room, along with a tiny chest of drawers.

'I know it's not exactly huge,' Rosie had said worriedly.

'It's fine,' Alison assured her. 'It's only for three months, after all. Anyway, I'll only really use it for sleeping in so how big does it need to be?'

Rosie nodded, relieved. 'I mean, there's always the sofa if you'd prefer...'

'God, no! With us both coming and going with our shifts I'd never get a wink of sleep. No, I'm fine tucked away in here. Thanks, Rosie. It's perfect.'

Well, Alison reflected, as she restocked a shelf in the chiller cabinet with cans of cola, not perfect perhaps, but certainly much better than she'd anticipated. It really hadn't taken her long to feel at home in the caravan, thanks to Rosie's thoughtful gestures – not least the journal she'd presented Alison with that first night.

'Okay, so you know I like to keep a journal,' she'd said, as they'd settled themselves on the sofa in their pyjamas, mugs of tea in their hands as they'd valiantly resisted hot chocolate.

'Oh, do you?' Alison had grinned. 'You never mentioned.'

Rosie was obsessed with her journal. She wrote everything in it and decorated it beautifully with washi tape and stickers, torn pages from her favourite books (Alison almost cried in horror at the thought of it, though Rosie assured her she only ever used tatty old second-hand copies), bits of ribbon and lace, old greetings cards and anything else that took her fancy. What started as a fairly standard-sized – albeit stunningly beautiful – journal had ended up twice the thickness, so crammed full were its pages.

'Well,' Rosie said, ignoring the sarcasm, 'I got you a gift.'

She handed Alison a rather classy-looking cardboard box. Inside, under a layer of tissue paper, lay a pale blue hardback journal, embossed with silver waves. Its pages were thick and appealing, just waiting to be written upon.

'Got you these, too,' Rosie said, and handed Alison a bag which contained a whole assortment of stickers, washi tapes and other bits and bobs. 'Just spare ones,' she explained. 'I thought they'd do to start you off, and when you've got into it you can buy ones that really speak to you.'

'Oh, Rosie,' Alison breathed, 'they're lovely. This journal – it's absolutely gorgeous. But what am I supposed to do with it? You know me. I've never been one for arts and crafts.'

'I thought this could be your three-month diary of your time in Kelsea Sands. You could use it to chronicle Project Alison! Write about what happens every day. Maybe make your own weight loss chart, so you can colour in a square for every day you manage to stick to your diet. Write down your thoughts, and how you're feeling about everything. And you can stick things in it that reflect your mood. Whatever you like.'

She scrabbled in the bag and lifted out some of the washi tapes for her cousin to admire. 'Whenever you get peckish – especially on evenings cos we all know what a hard time that is when you're on a diet – you can take out your journal and start decorating a page or two. Honest, it's so absorbing that you forget all about food! Trust me.'

She paused, giving Alison a worried look. 'Do you like it? You don't have to use it if you don't want to. I won't be offended.'

Alison reached over and hugged her cousin. 'It's perfect! Just what I need to keep Project Alison on track.'

Though so far, she thought now, as she stacked the last of the cola cans in the cabinet, her journal entries hadn't been anything like what Rosie probably imagined. There was nothing positive or exciting written on the pages yet. She could remember the first entry with depressing clarity:

Sunday 1 February – Project Alison Day 1: Messaged Jenna to tell her I was staying with Rosie for the foreseeable and to send my love to the twins. She didn't reply.

She'd toyed with the idea of messaging again, telling her daughter that she'd be happy to take the girls to Kelsea Sands to see the family if she would like her to, but Rosie had warned her that if she did, she might find herself back at square one before she knew it. Jenna could be very persuasive. Worse than that, though, was the possibility that Jenna would repeat what Joel had said and tell her she wasn't allowed contact with the girls. That would make it all too real and too upsetting.

Monday 9 February – Project Alison Day 9: Visited Mam and Dad. Dad's done an online quiz to see which Doctor Who monster he'd be. Apparently, he's a Slitheen. They're very flat-ulent according to the description. He's bitterly disappointed and says the results are fixed because it should be obvious to everyone that he'd be a Dalek.

Yes, that had literally happened. Mam had thrown up her hands in despair and said, 'He doesn't even watch *Doctor Who*! What's *wrong* with him?'

Wednesday 11 February – Project Alison Day 11: Went to work early for the bakery shift. Lifting those cinnamon buns out of the oven made me want to cry. Treated myself to two cherry tomatoes.

Should have got a medal for that, she thought, heading back to the till where someone was waiting to be served. Ignoring a cinnamon bun! When she wrote that entry tonight she'd add a gold star sticker. She deserved it for her restraint.

Oh no! There were two bags of crisps and a big bar of chocolate on the counter. She swallowed hard, sure that the customer would hear her stomach growl with longing.

'Are you paying for petrol, too?' she asked, without even glancing up at the greedy swine who was about to stuff his face with all those treats.

'Alison?'

She raised her face and stared in horror into the eyes of Ian MacMillan. At least, her mother was convinced he was Ian MacMillan, and this was certainly the man who'd been standing in The North Star, his arms full of foil containers, staring in bewilderment as her entire family had gawped back at him. And he knew her name.

'Ian?'

He smiled. 'Wow! Sam said it was you. So nice to see you again. I heard you were living here in Hull.'

'Mm. Yeah. I heard *you* were back in Kelsea Sands.'

Was it her imagination or did his smile waver? 'Yes, that's right. After all this time.' He cleared his throat. 'And yes, I'm paying for petrol. Pump number three.'

She nodded and rang up his purchase, including the goodies that were lying there so tempting on the counter.

'I thought you were a teacher?' he asked, sounding puzzled. 'I'm sure Mum said—'

'Yes, I was. I left the profession and now I work here.'

She could see he was curious about why someone would leave teaching to work in a petrol station, but she wasn't about to offer him any explanation. It was none of his business anyway.

'That's twenty-six pounds thirty with the petrol. Do you want a carrier bag?' she asked, nodding at the chocolate and crisps.

His face went a little pink as he tapped his debit card on the reader. 'Yes, please. Awful, isn't it? I shouldn't be eating this junk, but I do like to have something in the cupboard if I'm peckish. Truth is, I'm the world's worst cook.'

Despite herself, Alison smiled. 'That's what you think. I could challenge you for the title.' She dropped the crisps and chocolate into a carrier bag and handed it to him, along with his receipt. 'You know,' she murmured, 'you could have got all that a heck of a lot cheaper in a supermarket.'

'I know.' He shrugged. 'I was only going to get petrol, but I felt unaccountably hungry. I've been at Wansbeck's,' he explained. 'I needed a new bed. Have you ever been in there? It's quite expensive.'

She nodded slowly. 'Yeah, I know it. My late husband worked there for years.'

'Oh, heck!' Mac gave her a look of anguish. 'I'm so sorry. I didn't know.'

'What about? Him working there or that he was my late husband?'

'Both. Honestly. I feel terrible now.'

'Why?' she asked. 'People are allowed to talk about him, you know. He's not a taboo subject. If we don't mention him, it's like he never existed, and he did. Talking about him brings him close again, even if it's only briefly.'

'How long has it been?' he asked quietly.

'Nine years.' She hesitated. 'I'm sorry about your mum, Ian. She was a nice lady.'

'She was, yes. Thanks. And it's Mac, by the way.'

'What is?'

'My name. No one calls me Ian any more.'

She suddenly remembered Emmy telling her that fact when she'd called at The Hub. She also remembered that he'd been asking about her.

'Okay. Right.' She wanted to ask him why he'd changed his name but didn't feel able. Anyway, why should she care? It was up to him what he called himself. No doubt it was for some swanky, professional reason.

They stared at each other for a moment, clearly neither of them sure what to say next.

'Well...' Ian, or rather Mac, shrugged. 'It's been ages. Forty years or more.'

'At least,' she agreed. 'More like fifty really. I don't think I saw much of you at all after primary school.'

'No.' He gave her a wry smile. 'I suppose you didn't. And we both went to university, of course.'

'Yes, but I went to Hull University and came home every night,' she reminded him. 'Whereas you – you went off into the big, wide world and never came back.'

'No, except I'm back now,' he pointed out. 'I can hardly believe it myself.'

'I don't suppose Stella can either,' she said without thinking. Remembering his sister's bitterness about the will, she could have kicked herself. 'I mean...'

Mac – oh wow, it was going to take a while for her to get used to calling him that! – looked down at the floor. 'I don't suppose she can. Well, I'd better get off home. Do you live near here then?'

Alison hesitated. 'Not too far away usually,' she said at last, 'but right now I'm staying with our Rosie at Tide's Reach.' There was no point in lying. After all, Kelsea Sands was so small she was bound to bump into him sooner or later, and anyway, it was incredible that news hadn't reached him of her move already. It was only a matter of time.

'Tide's Reach?' he asked, his brow creasing in confusion. 'You mean, in a caravan?'

'Yes, Rosie owns one there and she stays there most of the year.' Alison gave him a forced smile. 'I figured I'd have a change of scene, so I'm living with her for a few months. You know what they say: a change is as good as a rest.'

'So they do.' He smiled warmly at her and Alison's heart gave an unexpected little skip. His eyes really were startlingly blue, she realised. His hair had quite a bit of grey now, and his face was lined, but he was an attractive man. She'd never thought of him in that way until she'd spotted him at the pub; he'd always just been the annoying school swot to her, but now she realised he was actually rather nice-looking and wondered why she hadn't noticed before.

She realised he was watching her and cleared her throat. 'Well, it was nice to meet you again after all this time. No doubt I'll see you around.'

'No doubt.' He nodded at her and turned away, heading towards the door. She took a deep breath and mentally shook her head. It must be the lack of sugar that was making her feel so lightheaded and peculiar all of a sudden.

Mac stopped and turned back to her. 'You know you said you were the world's worst cook?'

She frowned. 'Actually, you said *you* were. I just said you might think twice about that if you'd tasted my cooking.'

She was being pedantic and she knew it. Why was she suddenly so nervous?

'Okay, well, it seems we're both pretty rubbish at cooking, whichever way you look at it,' he said. 'How do you fancy eating out tonight at The North Star? It would be nice to get a decent meal.' He sounded awkward and unsure. 'Might stop me pigging out on chocolate and crisps. And it would be good to catch up, too.' He held up his hands. 'Only if you want to, of course. No pressure.'

'I can't,' she said. 'Rosie's cooking tonight. She's got it all planned.' Besides, after working a double shift she knew that if she went into The North Star at the end of such a long day she might just give in and order something sweet and comforting as a reward, which would undo all the good work of the last couple of weeks. She wasn't about to confess to Ian MacMillan that she was diabetic and had to be careful what she ate. She needed Rosie to keep her on track.

'Ah, right.' He shrugged. 'Of course. Sorry. Hope you didn't mind me asking.'

'Of course not.'

'Well, see you around, Alison.'

He turned to leave, and she found herself saying, 'How about tea tomorrow? I'll be leaving here around four, so if you're free we could grab something at The North Star around five-ish?'

There was something vulnerable and rather sweet about his smile. 'That sounds brilliant,' he told her. 'Five-ish it is. I'll see you there.'

Project Alison – Day 11 cont.: Bumped into Ian MacMillan at work and agreed to have tea with him. He's got the bluest eyes I've ever seen, even bluer than our Rosie's. I want my bloody head read.

'Oh, God, Alison,' she groaned as he headed out on to the forecourt, looking far more handsome than any man in his sixties wearing a wax jacket and jeans had the right to. 'What the hell have you done?'

15

What was I thinking? Mac wondered as he sat in The North Star and waited for Alison to join him at the table. He'd arrived a whole hour early – too nervous to hang around at home – and had found himself keeping Briar company at the bar before bagging the table under the largest of the bay windows half an hour before Alison was due to arrive. He figured that if conversation ran dry, they'd at least be able to look out into the darkness and gaze at the distant lights that gleamed from the Lincolnshire shore, rather than stare dumbly at their plates.

Despite the bitterly cold February weather, Kelsea Sands was looking beautiful today in the gathering dusk. The tide was out, and the Humber mudflats seemed to stretch on forever as he gazed out of the window and watched a ship in the distance, heading inland towards Hull. He could see the North Sea in the distance where the river tumbled between the Lincolnshire coast and Kels Point in its rush to join it.

He'd forgotten this. Somehow, in all the years since he'd left this place to go to university, the memory of how utterly incredible Kelsea Sands was had faded. In the years that followed, as he pursued his career, married, had children, ran his business, this tiny village in Holderness had seemed like a distant dream. In his busy, suburban life it had hardly seemed possible that such a place could really exist.

In his mind it had almost become like Narnia, or one of Enid Blyton's secret islands – some magical place he'd read about once, long ago, when anything had seemed possible.

It was almost funny, he mused, how he'd always put off coming back here when his mum was alive. Rather than go back to that forgotten little corner of East Yorkshire, he'd invited his mother to visit *him* instead, believing that he was bestowing some great favour upon her. She rarely left Kelsea Sands, and he'd reasoned that it would do her good to get away, especially as Stella and Gavin had promised to care for the animals while she was gone.

He'd honestly believed that he was giving her a treat when he'd welcomed her to his home in Oxfordshire for the first time. He remembered, with some shame, the showing off he'd done as he'd taken her round the town he lived in, assuming that she'd be impressed and even awed at how pretty it was, how lovely his house was and how well he'd done.

When it came to the day she'd been due to leave, he'd suggested that she stay an additional week, thinking she'd jump at the chance. He'd been stunned when she'd declined his offer and given him a regretful smile.

'Thanks, love, it's good of you to ask, but I can't wait to get home. I miss the river and the sea air. Can't beat that when all's said and done. Mind you, I'm glad you're settled here. I can see it suits *you*.'

The implication being that it definitely didn't suit her.

He smiled to himself now, remembering how crushed he'd felt at the time. He really hadn't understood her longing to return to this insignificant little patch in a forgotten corner of England. He'd been away too long.

Being back here now, he realised all too well why she'd yearned for Watersmeet, and these views over the Humber to Lincolnshire.

Oxfordshire was stunningly beautiful, but his mum had Holderness in her heart forever. Now he remembered why.

The sound of chair legs scraping on the slate floor brought him back to the present and he realised it had grown dark outside. He turned, his heart thudding as he saw Alison. She gave him a nervous smile as she sat down, dropping her shoulder bag in the seat next to hers.

'You made it then.'

He'd said it as if she lived miles away and had faced some epic journey to get here, not a half-mile stroll.

'I did. Amazing, right?' She rolled her eyes, and he knew she was thinking much the same thing. He was so out of practice at this! He would never have asked her normally, but Evan's words had come back to him as he'd stood in that petrol station.

'*You mustn't be alone, Mac. Someone in your position – you need people to talk to.*'

He was right. The one thing Mac had learned over the last few years was that no man was an island, and he should have people around him. If he was going to stay at Watersmeet he had to keep himself occupied. He needed friends. He had a feeling that Evan could become one if he let it happen, and maybe Alison could be another. It was a start anyway.

'It's been a lovely day, hasn't it?' she said. 'I mean, it was still cold but did you see the blue sky! The blue makes such a difference, doesn't it? Nothing more depressing than grey skies.'

She was rambling and he realised she was just as nervous as

he was, which made him feel better. He wanted to put her at her ease.

'It will soon be spring,' he said comfortingly. 'It's just around the corner.'

'I love spring,' she told him. 'It's my favourite season. I'm glad I'll be here for it.'

'Me too,' he said, then gulped. 'That *I* will be, I mean. It's been a long time since I saw spring in Kelsea Sands.'

She nodded. 'I still can't believe you're back. I heard – I mean, everyone's saying...'

She squirmed and he took pity on her. 'Go on,' he said gently. 'What are they saying?'

'Well, about the will and that. They reckon your mum left everything to you and poor Stella got diddly squat.'

He flipped a beermat repeatedly between his fingers. 'Not true,' he said at last. 'Stella got plenty. I got the house because Mum wants me to look after her animals, and she knew Stella already had somewhere to live and—'

Realising what he'd said, he broke off and swallowed. Bloody hell! How could he have been so unguarded as to let that slip?

Alison laughed. 'What, and you didn't?'

'Well, you know what I mean. She was settled,' he said, hoping his explanation would satisfy her. 'And I... wasn't.'

'You weren't? How come?' She leaned back and held up her hands. 'Sorry! That's none of my business. You don't have to tell me.'

'Shall we order a drink?' he asked. 'Then we'll have a proper catch-up. What are you having?'

She nodded. 'Diet Coke, please. No ice.'

'Good to keep a clear head,' he said, smiling. 'I'll have the same. Well, maybe not the diet version but a Coke sounds good. Won't be a minute.'

He wandered over to the bar where Seb's lad Sam had evidently replaced Briar, and was perched on a stool, reading the local newspaper.

'All right, Sam? Can I order, please?'

Sam glanced up and smiled, shifting off the stool immediately. 'All right, Mac. Ah, Briar said you were on a date. I see she's arrived.' He nodded knowingly to where Alison was sitting, gazing out of the window into the darkness.

'Just two old schoolfriends catching up,' Mac said. He hesitated. 'Your dad could join us, if he likes. He was in our class, too.'

Sam's face clouded over. 'I wish. Even if I asked him he'd say no. He barely shifts out of his room these days except to wander down to Kels Point, and he hasn't done much of that over the winter, what with the rain and that. I'm hoping that, come spring, he'll get a bit of his get-up-and-go back. Mind you, it's been three years now, so maybe it's got up and gone.'

'I'm sorry, lad.' Mac shook his head. 'Do you think he'll ever come back to work? He's young to have given it all up to do nothing.' *Oh, the irony!*

'You're telling me.' Sam sighed. 'I keep hoping but... Ah well. What can I get you, Mac?'

'A Diet Coke and a regular Coke, please. No ice.'

'Steady on. I don't want to have to carry you both home.' Sam laughed and poured two drinks into glasses. 'There you go, mate. Do you want to start a tab? Pay before you leave.'

'Great. Cheers, Sam. Give Seb my best, won't you? Tell him if he ever wants to come round to Watersmeet for a chat I'm usually in. It would be great to see him again.'

'Will do. Thanks.'

Mac carried the drinks carefully back to the table and sat down with a sigh.

'Oh dear. That sigh sounded ominous. What's up?' Alison asked, taking her glass from him with a nod of thanks.

Mac glanced towards the bar, but Sam had gone back to his paper. 'We were just talking about his dad,' he explained. 'It's a crying shame, the way Seb's hiding away from the world like that since his wife died.'

Alison took a sip of her Coke. 'I guess everyone reacts differently to grief,' she said cautiously. 'But you're right. It's been three years, and though I feel for him – God knows, I really do – I think it's time he stopped wallowing and started living his life again. Donna wouldn't want this for him.'

'What was she like?' Mac asked, having never met Seb's wife.

'Donna? She was lovely. Proper landlady material, all jolly and friendly and welcoming. She was the heart of this place.' She glanced around. 'It's not really been the same since she died.'

'I don't know how it stays open,' Mac murmured. 'I've been in here three times now since I got back, and there's never been more than a handful of people in. How do they keep going?'

Alison laughed. 'Oh, don't be fooled! It's quiet now, but you wait until spring. When the crowds return to Kels Point and the nature lovers and birdwatchers come back and invade the wetlands this place'll be heaving. Always is.'

'I remember when I was a kid,' Mac mused. 'Mum and Dad used to come here for the shanty night on Saturdays. Me and Stella used to climb on the benches outside and peer through the windows to see what was going on. The windows were open in the summer, and the music used to blare out, so Stella used to sing along with it. She loved it.' He shook his head, smiling at the memory. 'Hard to imagine her singing along with sea shanties these days.'

'Hard to imagine you climbing on benches and looking through the windows,' Alison said wryly.

'What do you mean?'

She laughed. 'Well, you were such a goody-two-shoes! Can't imagine you doing anything so rebellious. Shouldn't you have been at a Scout meeting or something?'

He took a long drink from his glass of Coke. 'Ah. That's how you saw me, was it?'

'It's how you were!' Alison spluttered. 'You were always so neat and tidy with that bloody satchel of yours, and you went to Cubs and then Scouts. I mean...'

'I couldn't help having a satchel,' he protested. 'Mum bought it for me! What was I supposed to do? Throw it in the river?'

'Yes!' She burst out laughing when she saw the shock on his face. 'Sorry, but you were such an easy target at school.'

'Don't I know it,' he said grimly. 'I've still got the bruises.'

Her laughter died. 'What do you mean? You weren't ever beaten up or anything, were you?'

He stared at her in amazement. 'Are you serious? Are you honestly telling me you didn't know?'

Alison put down her glass looking horrified. 'Aw no, Mac, I didn't. I swear it. I knew there was some gentle teasing but that's all. Who bullied you?'

'Who didn't?' He shrugged. 'Not all the verbal stuff was gentle, but I could shrug it off. Well, I say I shrugged it off. It hurt, I can't deny it. But it wasn't as bad as the physical bullying. I lost track of how many bruises I had.'

'I'm so sorry.'

Her eyes had filled with tears, which made him uncertain whether he should feel glad that she cared or sorry that he'd made her so uncomfortable. For his own part, he was just relieved she hadn't known. He'd always suspected she'd been all too aware and just hadn't been bothered.

'No need to be sorry,' he said. 'It was a long time ago. It really doesn't matter now.'

'But it does,' she said. 'I was so happy at primary school. I loved it there. Do you remember Miss Sayers? She was my absolute favourite teacher. She encouraged me so much and made me feel I could do anything.'

'Is she what made you go into the same profession?' he asked, noting the sparkle in her eyes when she talked about their old teacher.

'I think she was, actually,' Alison admitted. 'I wanted to do for other kids what she'd done for me.' She rolled her eyes. 'Not sure it worked out that way, but I gave it a good go.'

He nodded. 'What made you give it up then? If you don't mind me asking? Was it your husband's death that caused you to leave or—?'

'No, I'd left a year before he died.' She hesitated. 'We'd talked it over, you see. We had plans. He knew that teaching wasn't what it used to be, and I was increasingly unhappy, and he said we could manage without my salary and that I shouldn't waste any more of my life on something that was making me so depressed.'

'That was kind of him. Very understanding.'

'He was a kind and understanding man.' She took a large gulp of her Coke. 'Then he got ill, and it all went pear-shaped. We were going to downsize and buy a campervan. Do some travelling. He was going to decrease his hours gradually until retirement. We were going to have a bigger garden, and I was going to make it beautiful...' She blinked away tears and Mac wished he'd never started this conversation.

'I'm sorry,' he said. 'You don't have to talk about it if you don't want to.'

She cleared her throat and sat up straighter. 'Nothing else to say really. I carried on alone for a year, then took a job at the petrol station. Four shifts a week. Not a great deal of money but enough. Drew had always been careful, you see, and he'd taken out life insurance. The mortgage was automatically paid off upon his death, so I could manage. I mean, I'm not rich by any means, but I'm not struggling either, so the job was never about the money. It was about having company, I suppose. Getting out of the house.' She gave him a challenging look. 'There's nothing wrong with working in a petrol station, is there? I could have gone back to teaching if I'd wanted.'

'Nothing wrong with it at all,' he said, surprised. 'And if you'd wanted to teach, you'd never have left, would you?'

'I didn't want the responsibility any longer,' she said simply. 'I like the fact that I can go to work, do my job and come home without having to stress about what's happened that day and what might happen tomorrow.'

He could relate to that. 'The main thing is you're happy doing what you're doing. There's more to life than money.' He gazed out of the window for a moment, almost forgetting she was there. 'The root of all evil,' he murmured.

'Well, that might be true, but we don't get very far without it, do we?' she said. 'Anyway, enough about me. What about you?'

His guard immediately came down and he nervously drummed his fingers on the table. 'What about me?'

'Well, anything really! You left here to go to university, didn't you? Where did you go and what happened after that? Your mum gave us the odd update, but it was a long time ago and I can't really remember what she told us.'

He smiled to himself, thinking that it was highly doubtful

Alison had even listened to anything his mum had told her. She hadn't been the slightest bit interested in him at school, so why would she start to care afterwards?

'I went to university in the Midlands,' he said. 'Believe it or not, I intended to become a teacher myself, but I changed my mind before I went on to do my PGCE, thank goodness. I'd have been a terrible teacher.'

'I'm not so sure about that,' she said, smiling at last. 'You were always so sensible at school, as I recall. I can just imagine you standing in front of a group of children, inspiring them. Besides, you know how it feels to be treated badly at school. I reckon you'd have been on the lookout for that. It's a shame you changed your mind.'

'Well, maybe.' He shrugged. 'We'll never know now, will we? The Cliff Notes version is that I left university, got a job in finance, made a gifted and fun best friend who got me into the company he was working for, made quite a bit of money, formed a partnership with said best friend, bought, developed and sold commercial property and had quite a comfortable life, thank you very much. That's pretty much it.'

She frowned and he waited for the inevitable question, which wasn't long in coming.

'But what about your personal life? You were married, weren't you? Your mum said—'

'Oh, yes.' He forced himself to sound cheery. 'I got married, too! Lovely woman and we were very happy. The marriage worked perfectly until it didn't, but I don't regret it. Not for a moment.'

It wasn't a lie. He didn't regret the marriage. It was how it ended that he hated.

'And do you have children?'

He steadied himself before replying. 'I do. A boy and a girl.

Well, a man and a woman now. They're in their late twenties.' He could hardly believe it when he thought about it. His children had grown up while he was busy looking the other way. 'How about you?' he asked, anxious to change the subject. 'Do you have children?'

'One,' she said. 'A daughter, Jenna. She's a teacher, too. And I have twin granddaughters. They're seven.'

'Oh wow! You're a grandma!' He puffed out his cheeks. 'I still can't get my head around us being old enough to be parents, let alone grandparents.'

'I know! And look at us. We've hardly changed a bit,' she said, her large, pale blue eyes twinkling. 'So what do you do now? Are you still running the property company with your friend? Where are you based?'

He bit his lip, wondering how to answer her questions. Should he be flattered that she was interested? Or was she just looking for something to talk about?

'I got out of the business a few years ago,' he said finally. 'It's based in Oxfordshire, where I lived, but it's not for me any more.'

'So what do you do then?' she asked. 'Only, with you inheriting Watersmeet... I mean, do you intend to stay here?'

He tried to sound casual. 'Why not? Mum wanted me to have the place and to look after the animals, so I may as well do that. As for work, well, right now I'm not. Working, I mean. There's plenty of time to figure out if I want to do something else with my life. At the moment I'm not sure. I'm at a bit of a crossroads.'

'It's nice though,' she said. 'That you can take your time while you figure it out.'

'Yes,' he said heavily. 'I suppose it is. I'm very lucky.'

'And Watersmeet is so beautiful,' she said. 'It's always been my favourite house in the village. Not that I've ever seen inside it, but it looks lovely from the front gate and from the footpath.'

'Shall we order some food?' he asked, passing her a menu.

She looked confused for a moment, then nodded. 'Oh yes, sure. I totally forgot about eating.'

They perused the menu for a few minutes, each trying to decide which dish they fancied and whether they should choose from the main menu or go for a special.

In the end, Mac ordered a burger and fries, and Alison said she'd just have the chicken salad as she really wasn't that hungry.

Mac placed his order at the bar and carried two fresh glasses of Coke back to the table.

'Shouldn't be long,' he said.

She thanked him for the drink and said he really must tell her how much she owed him because she'd happily go halves.

'It's on me,' he said, thinking of his monthly allowance which had just gone into his account.

'No, I couldn't possibly!'

'I insist.'

'Well...' Alison tilted her head to one side, and he thought for a moment that she looked just the same as that cheeky young girl he'd known and loved back in primary school. She'd always been so pretty. 'In that case, we'll have to do this again some time, so I can pay for you!'

'You're on.' He smiled at her, his mind racing almost as quickly as his pulse, suddenly. 'I don't suppose...'

What was he thinking? Making friends with someone was one thing, but getting too involved was a bad idea. Was this pushing it?

'What?' she asked curiously. 'Go on.'

'Well, you said you'd never seen Watersmeet. I was wondering if you'd like to visit and have a look around? I can introduce you to the animals. You'd have to see them to believe them.'

Her eyes lit up. 'Really? I'd love to!' She hesitated. 'I know this sounds cheeky, but would I be able to bring Rosie?'

'Rosie? Oh, your cousin?' He hardly knew what to say to that strange request. 'I, er, suppose so. Any particular reason?'

'She's always wanted to see inside Watersmeet,' she confessed. 'And if I go and she doesn't, she's going to be proper miffed. Do you mind? Really?'

He couldn't help but laugh. 'No, I don't mind at all. She'd be very welcome. Are you free tomorrow?'

'I'm at work tomorrow,' she said. 'But the day after? It's my Saturday off this week.'

'Perfect,' he told her.

And maybe then he'd have two new friends instead of one. Because that's all he wanted, wasn't it? He didn't need any more complications in his life. Just friends would be absolutely perfect.

Saturday 14 February – Project Alison Day 14: Messaged Jenna last night because I couldn't stand it any longer. Told her that I'm settling in and that she really ought to visit soon. Her gran and grandad would love to see her. No reply. Not going to message her again. Today I'm going to Watersmeet. Taking Rosie with me. That should ensure there are no awkward silences. Oh, I hope it isn't too awful! Tea with Mac was fine but after all, I hardly know him and going to his house seems a bit much. Can't believe I said yes! Then again it will be great to see inside Watersmeet at last. And there are the animals after all.

'Ooh, I can't wait for this,' Rosie said, as they approached the five-barred gate which marked the entrance to Watersmeet. 'Thanks ever so much for making him invite me, too. But, er, do you think I'll be playing gooseberry? I mean, you do realise that today is Valentine's Day?'

Alison had completely forgotten. 'That doesn't mean anything! I think he just wanted a bit of company, that's all.

Maybe he's a bit lonely here. Must be a big change for him after running a business in Oxfordshire and having his family around him. I'll bet he forgot it was Valentine's Day, too.'

'Hmm. Maybe. Fancy him being divorced.' Rosie gave her a knowing look. 'Good to know, right?'

'Don't go getting any ideas. I've told you, we're just old schoolfriends. You'd better not drop any hints either.'

'Hints? Me?' Rosie's eyes widened in innocence. 'Would I?'

'Yes, you would. And your hints are as subtle as a brick.' Alison tutted. 'Don't make me regret bringing you.'

'I'll be good. Brownie's honour.'

'You got chucked out of the Brownies,' Alison reminded her, and Rosie winked.

'Maybe you'd better not mention that, with him being a Cub and a Boy Scout,' she said with a grin. 'He might ban me.'

'Don't be daft, Rosie,' Alison said as she opened the gate. 'And don't mention the whole Cub and Scout thing, please. I told you he got bullied at school. I don't want him to feel he's being bullied all over again.'

'As if I would! And you really didn't know about it? The bullying, I mean.'

'Not a clue.' Alison still felt awful about it. 'If I had, I'd have done something. Said something. You know I would. I never could stand bullying. Poor Mac.'

'You soon got used to calling him that,' Rosie observed as they headed up the drive towards the large, red-brick house. 'You haven't called him Ian once since you got back from the pub.'

'It's funny,' Alison admitted, 'but he suits Mac far more than he ever suited Ian.'

'Blimey,' Rosie said as they passed a rather ancient mud-spattered estate car on the drive, 'that's seen better days.'

'Haven't we all? You'd better be on your best behaviour, Rosie. I mean it.'

Something about Rosie's expression made her throw up her hands and exclaim, 'What?' But whatever her cousin had been about to say had to wait because at that moment the front door opened and there was Mac, and by his side a Jack Russell who took one look at them and began to yap, loudly and persistently.

'Shut up, Carne,' Mac said, more as if it was out of habit than because he actually thought the dog would obey.

Carne ran out of the house and circled Alison and Rosie, stopping to sniff their ankles occasionally and letting out intermittent yaps for no good reason that they could see.

Eventually he wagged his tail and ran back in the house, turning to face them, as if inviting them in.

'I think you passed the test,' Mac said, rolling his eyes. 'Come in. You must be Rosie.'

Rosie held out her hand politely. 'That's right. Pleased to meet you, Mac. Thanks so much for inviting me.'

Clearly surprised at her formality, Mac shook her hand. 'No problem at all. Nice to meet you, too. Hello again, Alison.'

Alison nodded and smiled at him and stepped into the hallway behind Rosie. They glanced around, suitably impressed by the interior, which was clean and spacious and surprisingly light.

'Right,' Mac said, sounding a little awkward. 'First things first. I haven't been away from Yorkshire long enough to forget that the most important thing in any visit is to offer a brew. I'll put the kettle on. Come through.'

He headed down the hallway, Carne dancing around his legs and threatening to trip him up at any moment, and opened a door which led into a large kitchen–diner.

'This is gorgeous,' Rosie breathed. 'I never expected this, did you, Ali?'

Alison wasn't sure. She supposed with Mrs MacMillan living alone for so long it might have been assumed that the house would be old-fashioned and run-down, but somehow, she'd expected it wouldn't be. She'd always had a feeling that the inside of Watersmeet wouldn't disappoint, and she'd been right. Her mam hadn't given much away other than to bang on about the photos of Mac that she'd spotted all over the place from the moment she'd walked inside the house. She noticed that there were none on display now.

'Mind you,' Rosie said thoughtfully, 'My mam did say your mam had workmen in a couple of years ago, come to think of it, although we didn't know why. We thought maybe your roof needed fixing or summat. Hard to see what's going on here, what with all them trees out front.'

It had clearly been a source of frustration to Rosie for many years that the only partial view of the house was over the five-barred gate, although it was possible to sneak a peek into part of the garden from the footpath that skirted the side of the property along the riverbank.

'She had the kitchen and bathroom fittings updated every ten years or so. My mother was very houseproud,' Mac said, filling the kettle. 'Everything had to be immaculate when Stella and I were growing up. We weren't allowed to move the curtains or the cushions, and she banned us from touching the dining room table. She used to inspect it every morning, checking for fingerprints, and woe betide us if she found any.' He laughed as he rummaged in the cupboard for mugs. 'Christmas morning, we had about half an hour to look at our toys and then they had to be bundled upstairs into our bedrooms out of the way, as she didn't want the mess.'

'Sounds like a barrel of laughs,' Rosie murmured.

Alison said nothing. She remembered the little boy in her class whose hair was always neatly brushed, whose clothes were always pristine and perfectly ironed, who carried a little satchel around with him every day, despite his classmates' jibes.

He was the only one who hadn't brought toys to school after the Christmas holidays. The class had been invited to bring in a favourite game or toy that they'd received for Christmas, but his mother hadn't let him, in case it got damaged or stolen. She remembered the teasing he'd got from some of the other boys and felt a sudden wave of sadness and compassion for him.

'How did she cope with dog hair then?' Rosie wanted to know.

'And cat hair,' Alison added, spying a large ginger cat that was curled up on a special bed hooked to the radiator.

Mac found the teabags and dropped them in a pot. 'That was the odd thing about my mother,' he admitted. 'Me and Stella weren't allowed to make any mess at all, but her animals... They could do no wrong.'

'How weird,' Rosie mused.

'I suppose,' Alison said thoughtfully, 'that no one's really black and white, are they? We're all very complex with our own quirks and idiosyncrasies. We don't fit patterns, much as society tries to make us.'

'Hell's bells,' Rosie gasped, spying the cat suddenly, 'that's enormous!'

Mac laughed. 'Alderman Mrs Beddows.'

Alison and Rosie looked at each other and Alison burst out laughing.

'What a bloody name!' Rosie said, shaking her head.

'Of course!' Alison nodded, understanding. 'I knew I'd heard the name Carne before.'

As if hearing his name, the Jack Russell trotted over to her, and she reached down and patted his head.

'What am I missing?' Rosie asked, clearly baffled.

'Winifred Holtby's book, *South Riding*,' Alison explained. 'It's set in Holderness in the 1930s. Robert Carne and Alderman Mrs Beddows are two of her main characters.'

'Bit too deep for me,' Rosie said with a shrug.

'Wait till you meet the rest of the animals then,' Mac said. 'Sugar?'

'Two for me, please,' Rosie said. 'Can you make it strong enough to stand the spoon up in? Can't stand wishy-washy tea.'

'No sugar, please,' Alison said. She was determined to persevere, even though tea still tasted awful without it. Coffee was even worse, but she was certain she'd get used to it. After all, she'd once drunk both with full fat milk and now she couldn't bear it. It was just a question of forming new habits. That's what she kept telling herself anyway.

They sat at the table and sipped tea, making small talk. Rosie was a godsend, chattering away about her life in the caravan and her jobs at the park clubhouse, the chippy and the pub.

'You're glad to be back then?' Mac asked her curiously. 'Twenty years is a long time to be away.'

'Not as long as you were away,' she reminded him. 'I was chuffed to bits to move back here. I'd missed it loads. I expect you were the same.'

'To be honest,' he said, 'I never gave it much thought.'

Rosie and Alison stared at him.

'What? Really?' Alison asked, amazed. It hardly seemed possible to her. She'd spent most of her adult life since leaving Kelsea Sands wishing she could go back somehow.

Mac shrugged. 'Why would I? I'd left. It was behind me. My life was busy enough, what with everything that was going on.'

'Well, so was mine,' Rosie said defensively. 'I had a twenty-year relationship and a job and a house to look after. Didn't stop me missing home.'

'I don't see the point of looking back,' he admitted. 'The past has gone. You've got to focus on today.'

'And the future,' Rosie said thoughtfully.

He shook his head. 'I don't think about the future. It doesn't really exist, does it? We've only got now, so that's all that really counts.'

'Bloody hell, you're a cheerful sod, aren't you?' Rosie said, laughing.

'I prefer the past,' Alison admitted. 'Everything was so much nicer then.'

'Really? You think?' Mac visibly shuddered. 'I don't think so. Not for everyone anyway.'

Alison's expression softened. He must be thinking about being bullied at school again.

'Well,' she said, 'I get that not everything in the past was perfect, but even so...' She sighed. 'It's a safe haven, isn't it? Somewhere where all the good stuff is locked away and no one can ever touch it. Whereas, what's to come is scary. Unknown. And now is...' She sighed. What was now anyway? 'Confusing. Uncertain. Difficult.'

Last night she'd craved a pepperoni pizza, but Rosie had made them tuna salad. Difficult didn't begin to cover it.

'Would you like me to show you round the house now?' Mac asked brightly, as if he'd heard the tone of gloom in her voice and had decided to do something to lift her spirits.

Rosie beamed at him. 'Ooh, yes, please!' She drained her mug of tea and sprang to her feet, ready and eager for a tour. There was nothing Rosie liked more than looking round other people's houses. She was completely addicted to *Location, Location, Location*.

Watersmeet was even bigger than they'd expected. Downstairs was the kitchen–diner, and a room that Mac referred to as a snug, which was actually a good-sized living room big enough to house two sofas, a bookcase, a coffee table and a television unit, complete with a small but attractive fireplace and open fire. There was a second reception room that was much larger, with a massive picture window giving views over the garden, plus a larger fireplace with a wood burner. There was a downstairs cloakroom and a room that Mac said briefly had once been his father's office, then an extension on the back which contained yet another cloakroom and a large utility room.

At the mention of Mr MacMillan, Alison wanted to ask more about him, and she knew Rosie was dying to, but something in Mac's voice told them he didn't want any further conversation about his dad, so they said nothing.

Upstairs there were five large bedrooms – two with en suite bathrooms – and a large family bathroom with another separate toilet.

'Wow, you're never going to get caught short in this house, are you?' Rosie asked, laughing. 'I've counted six toilets in this place now. Do the cat and the dog get one each, too?'

'It was because of Dad's work,' Mac said briefly. 'They used to have people round for dinner to discuss business, and because of its remote location they were always invited to spend the night. Mum hated the thought of sharing the facilities, as she put it, so the house was reconfigured accordingly. It all became a bit pointless in the end.'

After his dad left? Alison vaguely remembered some sort of scandal that had been the talk of Kelsea Sands when she was little, but she wasn't sure what it had been about. She'd have to ask her mam.

'It's massive,' Rosie said as they padded downstairs in their socks, having taken off their shoes because of the beautiful, thick carpet.

'I suppose it is,' he agreed. 'I hadn't thought about it much.'

He hadn't? Alison wondered what his home in Oxfordshire had been like then. It sounded like he was used to luxury.

'Come and look at the animals,' he said, smiling. 'I think you'll enjoy meeting them.'

Rosie and Alison exchanged glances. Everyone in Kelsea Sands knew Mrs MacMillan had kept some strange pets. They'd all seen the Highland cattle grazing in the fields and there'd been the odd glimpse of ponies in the distance from the footpath, but they'd never seen them close up. Sometimes, there'd been trays of eggs on a box outside the gate, and a sign:

Free range hen's eggs £2 per half dozen. Duck eggs 60p each. Please use honesty box.

She wondered if everyone had paid for the eggs. She had no doubt that the villagers would have, but there were a lot of strangers here, especially in spring and summer. Then again, she didn't think money had ever been an issue for Mrs MacMillan, who was rumoured to have come from an extremely wealthy family.

The hens and ducks were the first to be introduced. Mac led them to a large, shady area at the end of the garden where there were two secure runs, with wooden houses in each.

There was a pond near the runs, which was essential for the ducks.

'Meet Jane, Elizabeth, Mary, Kitty and Lydia Bennet,' he said solemnly, as he showed them the hens. 'Ex-battery hens, taken in and lovingly restored to full health.'

'Oh, bless them,' Alison said. 'How long have they been here?'

Mac shrugged. 'Honestly, Mum rescued so many of them that it's hard to keep track of how long these particular ones have lived here. Every time a couple of them died she adopted another two to replace them and even gave them the same name so there's always a full contingent of the Bennet Sisters.'

'I'll bet they've been here a while,' Rosie said, 'since they've got their feathers and they're looking really healthy and happy.'

'They don't live for that long, though,' Mac admitted. 'They tend to have a shorter lifespan than other hens, even after they've been rescued. But they maybe get a couple of years of freedom before they pass on, which is something.'

'Poor little things,' Alison said tearfully. 'After all that suffering!'

'You could say that, or you could say how lucky they are that they get to end their days in such happy circumstances,' Mac pointed out. 'Come and meet the Dickensian Ducks.'

Nancy, Estella and Peggoty were, he explained, three large white Aylesbury ducks named after Dickens' characters.

'They look like Jemima Puddle-Duck,' Rosie observed, who wasn't familiar with the works of Charles Dickens but had been a huge fan of Beatrix Potter back when she was a child.

'I think Jemima was modelled on an Aylesbury duck,' Alison agreed. 'They're so pretty, aren't they?'

'And very friendly and amiable,' Mac added. 'I was a bit wary of them at first but they're no bother. I'm just glad Mum didn't get any geese. I think they're way too scary for me!'

'They make great guard dogs, though,' Rosie told him. 'Well, guard geese. Better than a burglar alarm.'

They carried on to the winter fields, where the two magnificent red Highland cattle grazed.

'Let me guess,' Rosie said. 'Bonnie Prince Charlie and Flora MacDonald.'

'They're not literary characters, though,' Alison said. 'Go on. Surprise us.'

Mac laughed. 'Would you believe, Ellen MacKenzie and Jamie Fraser?'

Rosie whooped and clapped her hands. 'At last, someone I've heard of! *Outlander*. Yay!'

'Ellen's Jamie's mum, isn't she?' Alison asked. 'In the books, I mean.'

'And here, too,' Mac told her. 'When Mum rescued her, she was in calf, and young Jamie Fraser here arrived not long after they arrived at Watersmeet.'

'He's very handsome,' Rosie said, leaning on the fence and watching the cattle admiringly. 'Are they safe?'

'Gentle as anything,' Mac said. 'Believe me, I wouldn't be able to cope if they weren't. They're beautiful, aren't they? I never thought I'd get fond of cows, but they've won me over.'

'Strictly speaking,' Rosie said smugly, 'Ellen's a cow, but Jamie's a bull.'

'Strictly speaking,' Mac corrected her, 'Jamie's a bullock. That was the first thing Mum took care of, as soon as he was old enough. Come and meet the ponies and then we'll get back inside the warmth.'

It was another lovely sunny day, but the winter sunshine struggled to provide much heat and despite the blue skies it was still cold.

'Not as cold here as it is near the sea,' Rosie remarked.

'You're not kidding,' Alison agreed. 'It's quite sheltered here today in comparison. Once you get to the beach, you'll really feel it. The wind blowing off the North Sea is biting.'

Mac frowned. 'Are you warm enough in that caravan?'

'Oh yes! We've got central heating and double glazing. It's lovely and snug in there, don't worry about that.'

He nodded and led them to the paddock where the two ponies immediately wandered over to introduce themselves.

'Aw, they're lovely,' Alison said, rubbing the bay pony's nose. 'I've caught sight of them a few times in the distance. Your mum's had them quite a long time, hasn't she?'

'They were her first rescues,' Mac said. 'We'd always had cats and dogs, but nothing bigger here. Then she wrote to me about, ooh, must be fifteen years ago now, and told me she'd taken in two ponies whose owner didn't want one of them any more because he had leg problems which meant he couldn't be ridden. That was Jacob Armitage. Nothing else wrong with him, but they said they couldn't afford to keep him as a pet, so Mum stepped in and offered to take him. She bought Heatherstone off them, too, because they'd always been together and she didn't want them separated, and they've lived here ever since.'

Alison tilted her head, thinking. 'Jacob Armitage and Heatherstone...' She sighed, exasperated. 'Nope, sorry. I'm not getting it. Who are they named after?'

Mac laughed. 'Bit obscure if you haven't read it, but they're named after characters in *Children of the New Forest* – I guess with them being New Forest ponies. It wasn't Mum who named them, by the way. They were already called that, and I think that's what gave her the idea to name all her animals after book characters from then on.'

'That one looks like he's covered in frost,' Alison said, nodding at Heatherstone. 'How old is he?'

'Twenty-two now,' Mac said. 'Jacob's twenty-four. The frosty look is because Heatherstone's a roan, which means his base coat is bay, but it's interspersed with white hairs. Jacob's a pure bay but you can see how grey he is now on his muzzle and round his eyes especially, and he's lost muscle mass with age. They're both in good health, though. The vet came out to look at them the other week and he's pleased with them.'

'You sound like you know a bit about horses,' Rosie observed.

'A bit. I used to have riding lessons at the stables in Weltringham,' he said briefly. 'Many, many years ago.'

Alison remembered the stables all too well. She'd wanted riding lessons, too, but her dad was scared of horses and had been convinced she'd be trampled to death if she went anywhere near the place.

'They're still there,' she told him. 'The stables, I mean. Different owners of course, but you can still have riding lessons if you ever need a refresher course.'

Mac laughed. 'You must be joking! My old bones couldn't stand it these days. No, I'm happy enough with the company of these two.'

After fussing over the two ponies for a while, the three of them headed back into Watersmeet, glad to step back inside the warm and welcoming kitchen.

'I love it here, Mac,' Alison said. 'It's a gorgeous house.'

'It is,' Rosie agreed. 'Even better than I expected it to be. Bit big for one person, though, isn't it? You'll be rattling around in here all by yourself without any company.' Her eyes slid over to Alison, whose face burned as she gave her cousin a warning look.

'You've got a great-sized garden,' Alison said, determined to change the subject. 'What are you planning to do with it? It looks a bit neglected.'

'Mum was never really interested in gardening,' he admitted, 'and to be honest, I know next to nothing about it myself. I guess it's just a case of keeping the lawn down in warmer weather and getting rid of any weeds.'

'That seems a shame,' Alison said. 'It could be beautiful. I love gardening. I always wanted a big garden but ours is really small. We'd planned to buy somewhere with a bigger garden – sacrifice the house for land, if you like. We didn't need a big, three-bedroomed house any more so it made sense. But as it is...' Her voice trailed off and she shrugged.

Mac nodded. 'That is a shame.'

'Maybe Ali could help you with the garden,' Rosie said brightly. 'I'm sure she'd have loads of ideas for what you could grow in it, and she'd be able to help you plant it all out, wouldn't you, Ali?'

Alison gritted her teeth. Could her cousin be any more transparent?

'I'm sure Mac doesn't need any help from me,' she said firmly.

Mac dug his hands in his jeans pockets and leaned against the worktop. 'If you've got any ideas I'd be happy to hear them,' he said. 'I haven't a clue, and of course I'd pay you if you don't charge the earth.'

'I wouldn't charge you anything,' Alison assured him, surprised that he was agreeable to the suggestion. 'It would be a pleasure to help, although it does depend on time.'

She thought wistfully that if Jenna didn't allow her to see the twins she might have a lot more time on her hands after all, but she did hope that wouldn't be the case. She hadn't wanted to be their main caregiver, but that didn't mean she didn't want to see them at all, and she was missing them. She wondered how Jenna was getting on and if she'd managed to sort out alternative arrangements for picking them up and dropping them off at school. She felt a sudden longing to see her daughter and give her a hug. Put all this mess behind them. If only.

'Well,' Mac said, 'there's no rush. Let's see how it goes, eh? Now' – he pushed away from the worktop and clapped his hands – 'shall I put the kettle on again? I might have some biscuits in the cupboard, too.'

He turned away to wash his hands and Rosie and Alison exchanged glances. Biscuits! How was she going to refuse those? But Rosie was giving her a stern look, and she knew she'd have to find the strength somehow, because it was certain that Rosie would make sure she didn't eat anything she shouldn't.

Her cousin was doing her job far better than Alison had imagined she would. More's the pity.

17

Evan's home was an attractive semi-detached house with a large front garden and a drive, down a pretty street in Millensea.

Mac pushed open the gate and took a steadying breath before heading towards the front door. He couldn't help wondering if he was imposing on the vet. What had he been thinking, inviting himself round for tea?

Well, he hadn't really. That had been Evan's idea. But it had been Mac who'd called him, wanting to chat. He couldn't believe he'd done that now.

It had been because of Seb. He'd gone for a stroll up to the church early on Sunday morning, wanting to wander around the churchyard, look at the inscriptions on the gravestones – and make another attempt to decipher most of them – and sit on the bench and gather his thoughts. He liked to go out early, and as soon as he'd fed the animals and seen to their needs he'd left Watersmeet and headed out.

He hadn't expected to meet anyone. The road was always so quiet anyway, but at this time of the morning it was rare to see people out and about. But to his surprise, as he turned into the gateway of St Helen's, he saw someone coming out of it.

The two men had paused, staring at each other for a moment.

'Seb?' Mac's uncertainty gave way to delight, and he reached out a hand to his former schoolfriend. 'It *is* you! How are you?'

Stupid question. He only had to look at Seb to see that he wasn't good. There were dark shadows under his eyes, and he looked pale and gaunt, like he wasn't eating properly and hadn't seen daylight for a while.

Seb shook his hand limply. 'Ian. I heard you were back.'

'Mac,' he said immediately. It was almost a reflex now. 'I'm called Mac now, not Ian.'

Seb just shrugged. 'Well, nice to see you.' He held the gate open for Mac. 'You going in there?'

'Yes. It's a good place to think in peace, isn't it?'

Seb turned to look back at the church. 'Aye. It is.'

Mac frowned. 'Your wife's not...' Stupid question. There'd been no burials in this churchyard for decades.

Seb shook his head. 'No. She was cremated. What she wanted.'

They stood in awkward silence until Mac said gently, 'I'm sorry to hear about her, Seb. It's a crying shame.'

'Aye,' his old friend agreed.

Mac couldn't believe this was the same young lad who'd been so full of fun and mischief. Seb had never bullied him, had never mocked him for doing all his homework on time, studying hard for exams and refusing to join some of the other boys in the toilets for a crafty smoke each break. Although Seb had messed around in class and hadn't been above a crafty smoke himself, he'd just accepted Mac for who he was, and Mac would be forever grateful to him. It was heartbreaking to see the haunted look on his old friend's face now.

'You know I'm back at Watersmeet permanently,' he said, hearing the words as he said them and marvelling at how he'd got to this position. 'I'm just across the road from you. You'd be very welcome any time you fancy popping round for a drink and a chat. I did tell Sam.'

'Aye, he mentioned.' Seb nodded. 'Thanks.'

'Okay…'

'I don't go out much,' Seb muttered. 'I'm not good around people these days.'

'You don't have to entertain me, Seb,' Mac told him. 'You can sit there and say nothing at all if you like. It's just good to get out of the house sometimes, isn't it? I know I could do with some company.'

'Aye, well.' Seb dug his hands in his coat pocket. 'I'll think about it. See you, Ian—Mac.'

He'd walked away before Mac could say anything else, and as he'd stared after the clearly broken man, Mac had realised Seb had sunk so low that it was going to take a hell of a lot of time and patience to bring him back – and only then if Seb *wanted* to be brought back, which was by no means certain.

It had got Mac thinking about what Evan had said. *'You mustn't be alone, Mac. Someone in your position – you need people to talk to. If you need a listening ear, I'm here. You understand?'*

He was right. Whatever happened, he couldn't allow himself to wallow alone at Watersmeet. He'd made a start, inviting Alison and Rosie round, but they were busy people and had lives of their own. He needed more than just the two of them. And Evan had made it very clear that he would be there for him if he needed him.

So Mac had rung the vet up and had been relieved when Evan sounded delighted to hear from him.

'Come for your tea,' he'd told him. 'We're free on Tuesday, Thursday and Friday this week. Whichever suits best.'

'Tuesday would be best,' Mac said. 'I need to go shopping in Millensea anyway, so I could pop to the supermarket after I've been to yours. I'm running out of everything.'

'Tuesday then, after surgery. Come and meet the wife. She loves having someone to cook for. She's always telling me I don't appreciate her efforts and she's probably right. I'm just as happy with egg and chips.'

Mac laughed. 'Thank you. I'll see you on Tuesday. About six?'

Now, as he rang the doorbell, he could feel his legs shaking with nerves, which was ridiculous. Trouble was, he was so out of practice at living a normal life, doing normal things. It had been a week and a half since Alison and Rosie had visited him, and he was only just recovering from that!

The door was opened by a tall woman with dark hair and a welcoming smile.

'You must be Mac! Come in, love. I hope you're hungry, I've made enough to feed the five thousand.' She ushered him into a wide hallway and called up the stairs, 'Evan! Our guest's arrived.'

'Well, put 'kettle on then,' came the reply.

The woman rolled her eyes. 'All charm, isn't he? Come through to the front room. I'm Tricia, by the way. Evan's better half if you hadn't already guessed.' She laughed and led him into a sizeable front room, separated from a dining room by an arch. There were fireplaces in both rooms, but both had been blocked up and the open fires replaced by modern gas fires. A large table was laid for tea, with three place settings on the spotless white tablecloth.

'Take a seat. Tea or coffee?'

'Whatever you're making,' Mac said, finding it impossible not to warm to this friendly, approachable woman.

'Well, Evan only drinks Yorkshire Tea, and I only drink Maister's own-brand decaffeinated coffee, so there you have it. Incompatible in every detail and always have been. No wonder my mother only gave us a year.' She chuckled. 'Had our ruby wedding anniversary three years ago, so what did she know? So, tea or coffee?'

Mac found he was smiling. 'Tea, please. One sugar. Just a splash of milk.'

'Coming right up. His lordship won't be a minute. He's just soaking off the remnants of another day.' She winked and hurried through to the dining room, which he realised was connected to the kitchen.

He settled back in the sofa and gazed around him, noting the family photographs on the mantelpiece and walls. Children of varying ages and from different eras, wedding photographs, a family portrait. He realised he knew nothing about Evan at all, but it was clear he was a family man through and through. He felt a pang of envy for the vet's perfect life.

'Well, you made it then.' Evan's booming voice interrupted his thoughts, and he half got to his feet in greeting before he was told not to bother.

'We don't stand on ceremony here,' Evan assured him. 'Just make yourself comfy. Home from home. What a day I've had! Cats are the very devil, you know. I'd rather face a charging bull than a cat in a temper. And a very young tortoise! I mean, how are you supposed to know what's wrong with a tortoise? They only have one expression, and how am I meant to examine it? Do I use a tin opener?'

He chortled, just as Tricia arrived with a tray of drinks. 'Take no notice of him,' she told Mac. 'You'd never believe it from the way he talks but he's a marvel with animals. And he's very fond of tortoises. Used to have them when you were a kid, didn't you, Evan?'

Evan sighed. 'I did, but that was back in the days before we knew how cruel it was to keep them the way we did. They need specialist care, you know. Not shoving in a garden and left to fend for themselves and then put away in a cardboard box for the winter and forgotten about. Do you know,' he said, leaning forward, 'not all species of tortoise hibernate? And they should be over three years old before they're put away for the winter anyway? And,' he added, nodding his head furiously, 'they should be checked over by a vet first. And that's not all!'

'Yes, yes,' Tricia said, rolling her eyes. 'But it's quite enough for now, thank you very much. I'm sure Mac doesn't want to know about tortoise hibernation.'

'Hmm.' Evan hitched up his glasses with a sigh. 'I suppose not. Got enough on his plate with his own animals, eh?'

'Ooh,' Tricia said, settling herself beside Mac on the sofa. 'I've heard all about your little menagerie. Evan tells me you have Highland cattle. How marvellous! They're so beautiful, aren't they? I've got quite a thing for them myself, haven't I, Evan?'

Evan groaned. 'Haven't you just!' He shook his head. 'I'm not kidding, Mac. Highland cow tea towels, Highland cow mugs, Highland cow letter rack, even a bloody Highland cow teabag rest, and *she* doesn't even use teabags! I'm surrounded by them. What is it with people, anyway? Why do they feel the need to buy all this stuff? Bet most of them would run a mile if they saw a real one coming towards them.'

'I don't know about that,' Mac said, 'but I reckon if they knew how much looking-after these animals take they'd not be so keen.'

'Are you finding it hard going?' Tricia asked sympathetically. 'It must take some getting used to, especially when you're not used to having animals.'

Mac nodded, wondering if Tricia knew all about him, too. It wouldn't surprise him. Despite their gentle teasing of each other, he suspected that the Joneses told each other everything. He found, to his surprise, that he didn't mind too much.

'Shall we say it's been a learning curve,' he said wryly. He sipped his tea. 'This is lovely. Thank you.'

'I hope there's not too much milk. Evan likes his that strong it would make your eyes water. I don't know why he bothers with milk at all, really I don't. How's your Stella doing, by the way?'

Mac gave her a startled look.

'Tricia used to go to Lightweights meetings with her,' Evan explained. 'Used to be quite chummy with her, didn't you, dearest one?'

'I'll give you "dearest one",' she said, shaking her head. 'He only calls me that when he's being sarky. He never liked me going to that club, did you?'

'I did not,' Evan agreed. 'You were perfectly fine as you were. Just because your Auntie Glenda said—'

'Yes, well, never mind all that,' Tricia said hastily. 'Have you seen anything of her lately, Mac? Stella, I mean. Not my Auntie Glenda.'

'Not for a while,' Mac admitted. 'But funnily enough, she's asked if she can visit me at Watersmeet tomorrow afternoon.'

Evan raised an eyebrow. 'Interesting. Progress, do you think?'

'Who knows?' Mac sighed. 'I'd like to think so, but I have a feeling it might just be more of the same. I guess I'll find out tomorrow.'

'Well, fingers crossed for you,' Tricia said. 'Your mother had every right to leave Watersmeet to whoever she chose, and Stella needs to respect that. I do like her,' she added, 'but I don't agree with her about this. Fair's fair.'

She took a large gulp of her coffee and got to her feet. 'I'd better check the oven. I hope you like shepherd's pie? Evan says you're not a vegetarian.'

'No, I'm not.' Though how Evan knew that was beyond him.

'I had cause to visit the Chambers' home recently,' Evan explained, as if reading his mind. 'They have four goats. One of them was lame so they called me in. Young Briar Chambers works at The North Star and happened to mention that you'd popped in there on several occasions and sampled some meaty treats, including a pasty, and a takeaway Sunday roast.'

Mac laughed. 'I'd forgotten what Kelsea Sands is like,' he said. 'Nothing's sacred, is it?'

'Indeed. Anyway, I'm sure if you'd been vegetarian you'd have mentioned it when I invited you for tea.'

'I'd better strain my veggies.' Tricia hurried out of the living room and Mac and Evan smiled at each other.

'She's nice,' Mac said.

'She's not too shabby, is she?' Evan's eyes twinkled. 'I struck very lucky there, and well I know it.'

'And are these all your children? Grandchildren?' Mac nodded towards the photographs. 'There seems to be a lot of them.'

'Yes.' Evan wandered over to the mantelpiece. 'We had four children. Three boys and a girl. And now we have six grandchildren, so...'

'You're very lucky,' Mac said, unable to keep the envy from his voice.

Evan smiled. 'I agree. We are. Although we've had some difficult times, too.' He picked up a photo of a smiling boy with dark hair and merry eyes. 'Our youngest son, Michael. Died of leukaemia when he was seven.'

'Oh my God!' Mac felt terrible. 'I'm so sorry.'

'It was a long, long time ago,' Evan said softly. 'Not a day goes by when we don't think of him, though. And then there's our eldest grandchild, Ruby. She had an accident when she was ten. Been in a wheelchair ever since.'

'Evan, I don't know what to say.'

'No need to say anything. I'm not looking for sympathy. I'm just pointing out that everyone has their cross to bear. You might think other people have charmed lives, but it's guaranteed that they've suffered at some point. That they're carrying burdens you would never imagine. We all just get on with it, don't we? That's the miracle of the human race, I suppose.'

'I suppose it is.'

'We move on, Mac. We must. We keep going. That's what you're doing now. You're keeping on going. Your mother would be very proud of you.'

'I haven't done anything to be proud of.'

'The very fact that you're here today is something to be proud of. I wasn't sure you'd get in touch, you know. I'm seriously impressed.'

'I actually had visitors at Watersmeet the other day,' Mac told him. 'I invited an old schoolfriend and her cousin round for a tour of the place. You were right. I need people. I bumped into another old friend the day I rang you and it really shook me up. He lost his wife three years ago and he seems to have just given up on life.'

'Are you talking about Seb from the pub?'

Mac rolled his eyes. 'Should have known. Yes, I am.'

'Sad case,' Evan agreed, replacing the photograph gently on

the mantelpiece. 'It's Sam I feel sorry for. That lad gave up his job and his flat to go back there and keep the pub going, because he was convinced his dad would regret it one day if he sold up. Now he's stuck there and there's no sign of Seb making any effort to get back to normal. It's no life for a young man, is it? Who's he going to meet working all hours at that place? The pub is mostly full of middle-aged birdwatchers come spring. The lad should be out clubbing in Hull. Any road, we were talking about you. So, seeing Seb made you think about calling me?'

'Yes. You were right what you said: I need people around me. Doug always told me that, too.'

'Ah yes, Doug. Your mother told me about him. I was sorry to hear he'd passed on. I know your mother was very concerned when it happened. You can imagine.'

Mac could. His mother had known how important Doug was to him. She must have been worried sick that his death would affect him. If it had happened a year earlier, it would have. Ironically, it was only thanks to Doug himself, and everything that he'd done for him, that Mac had found the strength to cope without him.

'You have much more resilience than you believe, you know,' Evan said. 'And if you ask me, you deserve a new start. A second chance. Like Seb's lad Sam. You should find someone.' His mouth curved into a wide smile. 'This old schoolfriend...'

'She's just a friend,' Mac said hastily. 'Actually, we weren't even that at school. I don't think she liked me very much.'

'Well, she must like you now, or why would she bother going to Watersmeet to look around?' He gave Mac a knowing look. 'Or go out for burgers with you at The North Star.'

'How did you...?' Mac sighed. 'Briar Chambers. Though actually, only I had the burger.'

'So, anything in it?'

'No, of course not.'

'But she *does* like you, whatever your relationship was like when you were at school. She's actively chosen to spend time with you. Promising, eh?'

Mac laughed. 'You're incorrigible.'

'Tea's ready!' Tricia called from the kitchen. 'Evan, can you give me a hand with these plates?'

Evan tutted. 'Never get a minute's peace with that one. Up and down, up and down, like a bloody yoyo.' He winked at Mac and ambled into the kitchen.

Mac shook his head, deciding the Joneses were some of the nicest people he'd ever met. And Alison?

Maybe, he mused, Evan had a point. However indifferent she'd been – at best – during their schooldays, it seemed she wasn't averse to his company any longer.

Just as a friend, obviously.

Feeling a sudden optimism, he got to his feet and headed towards the table.

18

Tuesday 24 February – Project Alison Day 24: Had black coffee with no sugar today and for the first time I actually enjoyed it! We're having chicken and vegetables for tea tonight, but I'm pretty sure that Rosie's going to be stuffing her face when she gets to work. Can't say I blame her. I'd sell my mother for a portion of haddock and chips.

Alison and Rosie were walking arm in arm along the beach. Alison had just finished cleaning the caravan, while Rosie had spent the morning cleaning the pub, and was due to head off to the chippy in Millensea after tea for the evening shift. They were making the most of their free time and, rather than slobbing out in front of the television, Rosie had insisted that they go for a walk instead.

'Walking on the sand burns off twice as many calories as walking on the pavement. That's got to be a good thing for you, hasn't it?' She squeezed Alison's arm. 'You're doing ever so well,' she said proudly. 'I still can't believe you resisted those thick, chocolatey biscuits Mac offered us at Watersmeet. They were absolutely yummy. Do you think he believed you when you said you didn't want to spoil your tea?'

'He must think I'm a paragon of virtue,' Alison said with a laugh. 'When he took me out for tea at the pub that day, I only had chicken salad. I didn't even have the dressing that should have gone with it. He must think I eat like a bird.'

'I'm really proud of you,' Rosie told her. 'You've got more willpower than I'd ever have. Have you heard anything from him, by the way?'

Alison nudged her. 'Why would I? No, as a matter of fact, I haven't.' She sighed. 'And I haven't heard anything from Jenna either, which is more worrying. I hope she's okay. What if she's struggling? What if she hasn't found anyone to mind the twins?'

'If she hadn't,' Rosie said firmly, 'she'd have been in touch with you by now, believe me. Stop worrying about her. It's not your problem. Especially not after what that prat Joel said.'

'I do miss her and the girls, though,' Alison admitted. 'I'm not used to going so long without seeing them. I feel as if a part of me is missing.'

Rosie squeezed her arm sympathetically. 'It won't be like this forever,' she told her. 'You wait and see. Jenna will be in touch before long, I'll guarantee it.' Her eyes twinkled. 'I'll bet Mac is, too. I mean, he wants his garden sorting if nothing else.'

'Yeah, thanks for suggesting that.' Alison shook her head. 'Like I said, subtle as a brick.'

'What's wrong with that? He's got a garden he doesn't know what to do with, and you're a person with a passion for gardening but no garden to work on. You're a match made in heaven, if you ask me.'

'Hardly.'

They'd been walking quite a way, and as if of one mind they stopped and turned around, heading back the way they'd come.

'What did you think of him? Really?' Rosie asked. 'He seemed nice to me. Calming. Gentle. I really liked him, did you?'

'He's very nice,' Alison said hesitantly. She didn't want to give Rosie any more daft ideas, after all. 'I think he's been very lucky though, don't you? Had a charmed life really.'

Rosie frowned. 'I don't see how. His mam's just died! Also, he's fallen out with his sister, and he's divorced. Hardly sounds like a charmed life to me.'

'Yes, his mum died but look at the house she left him! And it's not like he saw her regularly, is it? They were hardly close. And Stella's got good reason to be angry with him, although it does seem as if she wasn't left out of the will, even though she gave that impression. I'm sure they'll make it up eventually – though again, he can't have seen much of her, can he? How much does it really bother him if she's not speaking to him?'

Rosie peered at her, surprised. 'Doesn't sound like you, Ali! Thought you'd have more sympathy for him.'

'I do! But... I don't know. He told me himself he got a great job after university, set up a business with his mate which did really well, made loads of money, had a good marriage—'

'Which ended in divorce.'

'Yes, but he doesn't seem bitter about that. He said he doesn't regret it. He's got two kids who, no doubt, are as charmed as he is. They've grown up in Oxfordshire with a wealthy father, so I'll bet they've done all right for themselves. Same as Mac. His parents were loaded, he was teacher's pet at school, probably got a first at university, never known what it's like to be broke or go without... I don't know. I like him. I think he's a nice man. I just think he's been very lucky, that's all, and I wonder if he realises that.'

He's never known loss and grief. Not real *loss and grief. Not like I have.*

'Didn't his dad leave when he was a kid?' Rosie asked. 'And didn't you say he was bullied at school?'

Alison's heart sank. Her cousin was right, of course. She wondered why she was looking for reasons not to like Mac. He'd done nothing to upset her, after all.

'I suppose,' she said, ashamed.

Rosie reared away from her, studying her face closely.

'What on earth are you doing?' Alison demanded.

'Checking you're really you and you haven't been replaced with an alien. The Alison I know and love would never be so bitter and uncharitable, especially about someone who's done nothing but be kind to her.'

'All right, all right. Don't go on.'

'I reckon you like him a lot more than you want to,' Rosie said. 'And I reckon it scares you to death. I reckon you don't want to like him so you're telling yourself a whole lot of reasons why you shouldn't.'

'You reckon a lot, don't you?' Alison said. 'And you're talking rubbish. I haven't given him much thought at all. I've got more important things to worry about, don't you think? Like trying to stick to this bloody diet and worrying about Jenna and the twins. Oh, and I'm taking Mam and Dad to the supermarket in Millensea later to do a late-night shop, which is always fun. Not. They want to go late so they can grab the reduced bargains, so we might pop in and see you at the chippy.'

'Just don't give in and order anything,' Rosie said, 'because I'll refuse to serve you.'

'Thanks very much.' Alison wasn't sure if she was glad or sorry about that. 'Oh, I got the invitation from Niall, by the way. Mam gave it to me when I popped in to see them on my way home from work. Bit random inviting adults to a kid's birthday party, isn't it?'

'It is a bit,' Rosie agreed. 'Maybe it's because it's Poppy's thir-teenth so it's special.'

'Even more reason to just invite her friends, surely?'

'Maybe she doesn't have any,' Rosie said. 'Can't be easy when your dad's the local vicar.'

'Oh well, I expect it will be nice for her, although when I was thirteen, I'd have been mortified if my mam and dad had invited the rellies to my birthday party.'

'Yeah, me too,' Rosie admitted. 'But that's Niall and Kendra for you. It's a different world. And our Poppy's a sweet kid. She's probably happy to have us all round there.'

'There's an invitation for Jenna and Joel and the twins, too,' Alison said.

Rosie pulled her to a halt and stared at her. 'Are you going to tell them?'

'I don't know,' Alison admitted. 'I'm scared.'

'Scared? Of Joel and his big mouth?'

'Of being rejected, I suppose.' Alison gazed out at the sea, shivering as a blast of cold air hit her, and digging her hands into her pockets, wishing she'd thought to wear gloves. 'I could post it on to them, but it would be better to call Jenna, wouldn't it? What if the invitation gets lost in the post? But if I call her and she hangs up on me, or doesn't even pick up the phone, or tells me she'll only take the twins to the party if I'm not going to be there, or—'

'Blimey! Talk about worst-case scenarios!'

'I know. But she's ignored every text I've sent her so what am I supposed to think? It was half-term last week, and usually I'd have had the twins at my house most of the week, but this time there wasn't a peep from Jenna.'

'Even so...'

'I'll think about it.' Alison shivered. 'It's bloody freezing out here, Rosie. Let's go back to the caravan and warm up before my toes turn black and drop off.'

'I had no idea you were such a drama queen,' Rosie said, tucking her arm through Alison's once again. 'I'm learning a whole other side to you, Alison Parker. Who knew?'

19

Alison and her parents had been browsing the shelves of the local discount supermarket in Millensea for over forty minutes, and Alison was beginning to wonder if they'd ever get out of there. She wasn't keen on this shop. It felt cold and impersonal to her, and she missed the warmth and familiarity of Maister's.

There was a branch of her favourite store further up the coast, but Mam and Dad had turned white when she'd suggested going there instead, declaring that they wouldn't pay those sorts of prices if their lives depended on it, and did Alison think they were made of money?

Instead, they trawled the shelves of ShopSmart, her parents arguing between themselves about whether they really needed more tins of baked beans when they already had eight of them in the cupboards at home, before loading their trolley with another four because you never really knew when you might need them.

Mam spent ages rummaging through the reduced-to-clear sections, swooping on anything with a yellow sticker despite the wilting salads and sorry-looking vegetables that looked far from tempting, because she said that every penny counted, and had Alison forgotten they were pensioners?

Yeah, with Dad's private pension from the civil service, she thought wryly.

As they pushed the trolley towards the chiller section Mam told Alison that she must have more money than sense.

'You'd better watch and learn because you'll be a pensioner yourself soon,' she said darkly. 'Then you'll realise how careful you have to be.'

She nodded knowingly at her before adding a packet of deluxe sausage rolls and a luxury-brand cheesecake, the price of which made even Alison's eyes water, because 'Ooh, they do look tasty!'

Dad had a strop because Mam put granary bread in the trolley and he hated 'All them bits that stick between me teeth', so she took it out and put it back on the shelf, only to sneak it back in again when he wandered off to inspect the ice cream.

Somehow, instead of ice cream, he came back with a jar of crunchy peanut butter which, for some reason Alison couldn't fathom, he was adamant didn't get stuck in his teeth at all.

As they stood by the freezer arguing because Mam wanted to buy some chicken pies and Dad said he'd rather get a take-away pie from the pub, because Seb's lad Sam had told him he could, Alison leaned on the trolley and wondered how many times she'd listened to conversations like this. Their shopping trips had been the stuff of nightmares, and she'd done everything she could to get out of going with them when she was a kid.

Saturdays. That had been 'big shop' day for them and just about everyone they knew. Dad had got paid weekly in those days, and in cash, too. He'd handed over the housekeeping to Mam and kept hardly anything for himself because, as he pointed out, what did he need money for? Mam took care of everything.

She smiled to herself, remembering those fabulous Thursday evenings when Dad came home with his wages, and fish and chips from Millensea for tea, and a bag of sweets each as a payday treat.

No late-night shopping in those days. No big supermarket close by either, come to that. And as for Sundays…

'You look happy.'

She blinked and looked up, shocked to see Mac standing in front of the trolley, a basket hooked over one arm. He was the last person she'd expected to find in a supermarket – especially ShopSmart.

'I zoned out,' she admitted without thinking, then nodded towards her parents, realising too late that they'd stopped arguing and were now watching her and Mac with undisguised interest. 'I was just remembering going shopping with these two when I was a kid. They were a bloody nuisance then, too.'

'Of all the cheek,' Mam said indignantly. She gave Mac one of her best smiles. 'It's lovely to see you again after all this time, Ian. How are you?'

'Mac,' he said immediately. 'My name's Mac now, Mrs Wainwright.'

'Oh, of course. Alison did mention. I was sorry to hear about your mum, love. Such a shame.'

Mac smiled. 'Thank you.'

'Alison was telling us all about the animals at Watersmeet,' she continued, blithely ignoring her daughter's glare. 'They sound wonderful. I've always wanted to see them myself but when I visited your mother she was too ill to worry about all that really, and before then I never went round. Sheila didn't really invite people in, did she? She kept herself to herself.'

'She was a right funny onion,' Dad said with a grunt.

Alison felt her face burning with embarrassment, but Mac just laughed.

'She wasn't one for people,' he agreed. 'She much preferred animals.'

'Oh yes, and she had a heart of gold where they were concerned,' Mam agreed hastily, after shooting her husband a look that should have floored him but seemed to have no effect on him whatsoever.

'She *used* to mix with people,' he said, 'until your dad left.'

There was a silence and for a moment Alison held her breath, not sure what to do or say to rescue the situation her tactless father had plunged them into.

'So can we order one of them pies from the pub?' he asked plaintively, apparently forgetting all about Mac and refocusing on his belly.

Mam glared at him. 'No! You can get a pack of four for a quarter of the price of one from the pub! Stop moaning or I won't get you any pies at all this week.'

Alison sighed and turned back to Mac. 'See what I mean? That's why I zoned out.'

He nodded solemnly. 'I understand.'

She couldn't resist a peek into his basket. Three ready meals and a multipack of crisps. *Healthy.*

As if reading her mind, he shuffled awkwardly. 'I know, it's terrible, isn't it? I need to get my act together, but like I said, I'm the world's worst cook.'

Alison gritted her teeth as her dad laughed and said, 'You haven't tasted our Alison's cooking.'

'Thanks for that, Dad.'

Mac winked at her, which made her heart flutter in a very weird way. 'I did try to make sure the ready meals were healthy ones but it's not easy, is it? Maybe I should add some salad or veggies to make it a bit better,' he mused, not sounding too keen.

'There are some proper bargains in the reduced-to-clear section,' Mam said helpfully.

'I thought you were busy arguing about pies,' Alison reminded her.

'Oh, we're done with that. I've got these, look.' She held up a box of ShopSmart bargain minced beef pies and Alison mentally shuddered when she noticed the price of them. What sort of meat would be in those?

'You ought to join forces with our Alison,' Mam continued, giving her daughter a sympathetic look. 'She's trying to eat more healthily, aren't you, love? She's just been told she's a diabetic, Mac,' she added, mouthing the word *diabetic* as if it was some shameful secret.

Alison could have throttled her, because, truthfully, she felt as if it was. 'I'm sure Mac couldn't care less about all that,' she said. 'I'm only *just* diabetic,' she added defensively. 'It hardly counts at all.'

'Best to nip it in the bud now, though. It's all the junk you eat,' Dad said, dropping a four-cheese pizza and a box of chocolate profiteroles into the trolley. 'Alison, where would we find the curry powder?'

'How should I know?' Alison demanded. 'I don't shop here usually,' she told Mac hastily. 'I tend to shop at Maister's.'

'And spend twice as much as you need to for the privilege,' Mam pointed out. She nudged Dad. 'The curry powder will be in the world foods section. What do you need curry powder for anyway?'

'I fancy a curry,' he said forlornly.

She rolled her eyes. 'Then you get a jar of curry sauce! If you think I'm faffing about making a curry from scratch, and me with a broken arm... Honestly! Alison, mind the trolley, will you? I'm just going to take your father to the sauce aisle. Won't be long.'

Alison leaned heavily on the trolley handle and let out a long sigh of relief.

'Are they always like that?' Mac asked, his eyes twinkling.

'Always. They're a pain in the sodding arse.'

'What happened to your mum's arm?' he asked, switching the basket to his other hand.

'She had a fall,' Alison said soberly. 'Broke her arm but not her spirit, as you can tell. She took it all in her stride, like she always does.' She smiled fondly at the thought of her mother's determination to look upon it as a learning curve. 'She's been practising writing with her left hand and now she says she's better at that than she is with her right hand, so she's going to use it all the time now, even when the plaster's off.'

'Great attitude!' Mac said admiringly.

'Yeah...' Alison couldn't deny it. Her mam was something else. Would Jenna ever say the same about *her*, she wondered. Somehow, she couldn't imagine it.

A kind of grief overwhelmed her as she thought about the days when she and her daughter had been so close: when Jenna had cuddled up on her lap while Alison read her stories; when she'd held on to the trolley handle as they'd wandered round the supermarket together; when she'd sat Jenna on the draining board and soothed her as she gently bathed her knees because her little girl had fallen off the swing and now they were all scraped and bleeding.

She blinked away tears as Mac gently asked, 'Are you okay?'

'I was just thinking back to when I was a mum,' she admitted.

'You still are a mum,' he said, surprised, but she shook her head.

'It doesn't feel like that. Jenna and I – we're not really speaking at the moment. Things are... difficult.'

He sighed. 'I'm sorry.'

'Thanks.' She wiped her cheek and straightened, embarrassed that she'd revealed the truth about her relationship with her daughter. He'd only just found out she was a diabetic with a junk food habit, thanks to her parents! 'Truth is, we've all been invited to my cousin's for his daughter's birthday party on the fourteenth of March – Jenna and the twins included – but I don't know whether to tell them.'

He raised an eyebrow. 'Why wouldn't you?'

'It could be awkward,' she mumbled, not wanting to go into all the details about Joel and the horrible things that had been said about her.

'Would you like to see Jenna?' he asked. 'And the twins?'

She hesitated. 'It's not as simple as that.'

'Well, obviously I don't know all the details, but it seems to me that if you're standing in the middle of a supermarket in tears because you miss your family, and you have the perfect excuse to get in touch with them, then maybe it's simpler than you realise. What's the worst that could happen?'

He was right, she realised. Even if Jenna hung up on her, or said no, at least there'd be contact. At least she could say she'd tried. At least there was a chance...

She gave him a watery smile. 'Thanks. I'll call her when I get home.'

'Make sure you do.' He hitched up the basket. 'Well, I'd better get on and finish my shopping. See you around, Alison. Good luck.'

'Ian! I mean, Mac!'

Alison inwardly groaned as her parents hurried towards them, her dad carrying a jar of curry sauce and a packet of chicken breasts in his arms, her mam waving her plaster-encased arm in the air like a white flag.

'I'm glad you haven't gone yet, Mac,' her mam said, rather breathlessly. 'It occurred to me as we were looking at the chicken breasts and we realised it was much cheaper to buy the bigger pack—'

'How is that possible?' Alison asked doubtfully.

'Well, better value then! Anyway, it occurred to us that there's going to be far too much for two of us, so we wondered if you would like to come for tea at ours tomorrow? And you, Alison, naturally. I'd ask our Rosie but she's working at the chippy tomorrow again, isn't she?'

'Yes, but I don't think—' Alison began, but her mam tutted impatiently.

'Oh, I know. You're *diabetic*. Don't worry, we won't give you any rice. I've got some lovely salad reduced to clear in the trolley, so you can have that with it.'

'How delightful,' Alison murmured. 'Can't wait.'

She tried to communicate with Mac by giving him a look of sympathy and mentally telling him that he really didn't have to say yes, and no one would blame him in the slightest.

'He probably takes after his mother,' Dad said. 'It's all right, lad. Not everyone's sociable, are they?'

Alison was pretty sure the horror she was feeling showed on her face, because Mac was clearly struggling not to laugh when he looked at her.

'It's really kind of you,' he said at last. 'I'd be delighted.'

'Smashing!' Mam beamed at him. 'Shall we say five o'clock? We don't like to eat too late, on account of Stan's heartburn, especially if he's insisting on having a curry for some reason.'

Mac nodded. 'Five it is.'

'Cherry, will we need some mushrooms?' Dad asked suddenly.

His wife clapped her hand to her head and groaned. 'We will! Come on, Stan. Back to the reduced-to-clear section.'

They hurried off and Alison shook her head. 'They're absolutely nuts, the pair of them.'

'They're lovely,' Mac said softly. 'You're very lucky to have them.' He reached out and touched her lightly on the arm. 'Call your daughter, Alison. You have such a nice family. Don't let it fall apart, whatever you do.'

She watched him walk away and bit her lip, thinking it over. Then she reached into her bag and pulled out her mobile phone.

It was time to talk to Jenna.

20

Mac was even more nervous about his sister coming round than he had been about visiting Evan and his wife. It was ridiculous. He and Stella had grown up together. She was three years younger than him and had been his best pal when they were little.

Even in the early days of their marriages the two of them had been close. Stella was his son Wyatt's godmother, for goodness' sake, and he and Gavin had got on well, as had Stella and Lynne.

That, he supposed, was part of the problem. He had a feeling that Stella was living in the past far too much and was nursing grudges that she simply couldn't let go. And there was the other problem of course. Gavin. She couldn't let go of him either by the sounds of things.

He'd added a cake and Stella's favourite brand of coffee to the supermarket basket after he'd said goodbye to the Wainwrights, even though he wasn't sure his sister would stay long enough to partake of anything. It depended what sort of mood she was in, and how quickly his words would inflame her. Because they were bound to, he thought wearily. She wanted him to sell the land to her ex-husband. He wasn't going to agree to that. Where did that leave them?

When the rap on the door came, he found himself smoothing down his shirt and swallowing nervously, as if he was going on a first date or something. He glanced over at Mrs Beddows, who stopped washing her paws and eyed him innocently.

'Wish me luck.'

She gave him a look of contempt and went back to washing her paws. It was too late to ask the same of Carne. He'd shot into the hallway and was yapping excitedly at the front door, no doubt recognising their visitor already.

'Good afternoon, Stella.'

She was dressed for the late February weather in a smart navy-blue coat, black knee-high boots, a hat, gloves and a scarf, which was pulled up over her nose as if she was planning on committing a robbery. She might as well have worn a balaclava.

'Come in,' he began, but she'd already pushed past him, ignoring Carne, and headed straight to the kitchen where she plonked herself at the table, dropped her bag in front of her and folded her arms.

'Well,' he said, giving her a resigned look, 'you might as well take your hat and coat off. Unless you're not stopping?'

'That depends on you,' she said, her voice muffled under the scarf. 'Are you willing to have a reasonable discussion or are you going to close me down the minute I open my mouth?'

It was on the tip of his tongue to tell her there was nothing to discuss, but he knew she'd simply storm out without a backward glance, and where would that get them? He missed her. He'd lost enough people in his life. He didn't want to lose his sister for good, too.

'I'm willing to have a reasonable discussion,' he said. 'Tea? Coffee?'

She shook her head, pushing down her scarf. 'Haven't you got anything stronger?' she asked irritably. 'Surely there's some of Mum's wine left? Or have you drunk it all?'

'You're not driving?'

She shrugged. 'I came by taxi so I could have a drink.'

Stella lived in the next village, which was Weltringham, just a five-minute drive away, so it wouldn't have been too expensive – although the nearest taxi company was based in Millensea. Looking at her face, he had a feeling she'd still have demanded wine, even if she'd lived miles away and the taxi had cost her a fortune. Stella never used to drink before dinner, and it was on the tip of his tongue to remark on that, but he decided not to risk antagonising her further.

'Fair enough. I'll open a bottle.'

He wasn't a wine drinker himself, but there was still an unopened bottle in the fridge from when his mum had lived there. He handed it to Stella, along with a glass, and popped another one from the wine rack into the fridge.

'Aren't you having one?'

'No. I like to keep a clear head.'

She unscrewed the cap on the bottle. 'Hoping I'll get drunk and you can wangle an agreement out of me?'

'No agenda, Stell. I just don't like to lose control,' he said evenly.

She hesitated, then nodded. 'Fair enough.'

He made himself a cup of tea and found plates for the cake.

'None for me,' Stella said. 'I've given it up for Lent.'

He raised an eyebrow. 'I didn't know you were religious?'

'There's a lot you don't know about me. Since I moved to

Weltringham I've been going to the church quite regularly. It's only across the road from me, after all. I find it quite a comfort.'

'Right. That's a shame. About Lent, I mean, not you going to church. I got you your favourite. Chocolate fudge cake.'

Stella drained her glass and poured herself another. 'Well, it can't be helped.'

He put the cake back in the cupboard. It wouldn't be fair to eat it in front of her. He carried his tea over to the table and sat down opposite her.

'Are you sure you want to sit in here?' he asked. 'We can go through to the living room, or the snug if you prefer.'

'I'm fine here. It's more businesslike.'

He sighed. 'Do we have to be businesslike? Can't we just be brother and sister for a change?'

'Are you trying to swindle me already?' she demanded. 'I thought you said you were willing to have a discussion.'

'I am! It's just – can't we have a discussion in comfort? Be a bit more relaxed about things?'

'Oh no.' She shook her head determinedly. 'You'll get round me if we do that. I know you. I know how sneaky and deceitful you can be, remember?'

Shame washed over him. 'I'm not that person any more,' he said quietly. 'That wasn't me.'

'You think that by changing your name everything's forgiven?' she asked incredulously. 'You really think that *Mac* isn't responsible for what *Ian* did?'

'Far from it,' he said. 'I know perfectly well what I'm responsible for. I hold my hands up to it all. Everything. But bloody hell, Stell, don't you think I've paid the price for it?'

'You weren't the only one who paid the price,' she said bitterly. 'Lynne and I were best friends. I haven't seen her in years, thanks to you.'

Hardly best friends. Yes, they'd got on well, but they'd seen each other maybe two, three times a year. He thought Stella was exaggerating a bit.

'Sorry,' he said simply.

'Sorry? You have no idea, do you? If it hadn't been for you, Gavin and I—' she broke off, shaking her head, and drained her glass again.

He watched, rather worried, as she poured herself another one. 'Steady on,' he told her. 'It's not a race. What did you mean, if it hadn't been for me?'

'You haven't got a clue, have you?' she said, shaking her head. She stared into her glass, looking thoroughly miserable. 'Bloody hell it's hot in here.'

'You've still got your coat, hat and scarf on,' he reminded her. Not to mention her gloves.

'Oh. Right.' She unwound her scarf and threw it on the table along with her gloves and hat, then stood to unbutton her coat.

Mac took it from her and hung it in the hallway.

'So, what *did* you mean?' he repeated, as he returned to find her staring into her glass again, her cheeks flushed.

'Me and Gavin,' she said sadly. 'We had plans. And you ruined them.'

'What sort of plans?'

She ran a finger around the rim of her glass, saying nothing. Mac watched her for a moment then urged, 'Stella? What sort of plans?'

Stella blinked, as if she'd forgotten he was there. 'Oxford-shire,' she said simply.

'Oxfordshire?'

She sipped her wine, nodding furiously. 'Yep. We'd decided. We were going to sell up Tide's Reach and the house and buy a small hotel in Oxfordshire. I wanted to be nearer to you, and

Oxfordshire was so beautiful. Gavin liked it, too. Thought it was classy. He said the hotel had real potential. Ned and Crystal loved Wyatt and Sarah, and it was all going to be perfect.

'And then it all came crashing down, and after you left Lynne got really funny with us, like she didn't want to be around us, and Gavin said it wasn't worth bothering with the hotel and we should focus on businesses round here because it was cheaper, and he ended up buying the site at Puffin Point instead, and spending more and more time up there, and we drifted apart and...' She gave a noisy sob. 'And then he asked me for a divorce.'

'Stella,' Mac said gently, 'Lynne and I broke up fifteen years ago. You and Gavin only divorced three years ago. It can't have been down to my marriage ending.'

'It was the catalyst!' she said, glaring at him. 'From then on, everything started to go wrong.' She glanced around the kitchen. 'Where is it?'

'Where's what?' he asked, baffled.

'That bloody cake! I'm starving.'

'But you've given it up for Lent,' he reminded her.

'Sod that. Extenuating circumstances.'

He could see himself getting the blame for this as well, tomorrow, but he collected the cake, two forks, two plates and a knife and carried them over.

'You're sure about this?' he asked, knife hovering over the cake.

'Big piece,' she said firmly. 'Enormous.'

As he cut her a slice she poured her fourth glass of wine.

'Gavin,' she said, 'was never the same with me after you left. I don't know why. I tried, I really tried to make it work, Ian.'

'Mac,' he said quietly.

'Whatever. I really tried. He just drifted away from me, and no matter what I did I couldn't get him back.' She dug her fork into the cake, tears rolling down her cheeks. 'He left me. Everyone leaves me in the end. Gavin. Mum. You. Even my own children.'

'Your children?'

'Well, Ned's gone, hasn't he? Went off to university and never came back, just like his bloody Uncle Ian. Business and Tourism Management. Pah! And now he's running a hotel in Wales! I ask you, bloody Wales!'

'But Crystal's around?'

'Hardly ever here,' she said with a sniff. 'More interested in Puffin bloody Point. What's so special about that place anyway?'

'Well...' Mac hadn't been up to that area for years, but he remembered that Puffin Point was a pretty little village with two lighthouses and stunning beaches. Not to mention the tall chalk cliffs that were home to thousands of seabirds – including the famous puffins. He could see the attraction.

'There's nobody left,' Stella said, wiping another tear away. 'Nobody.'

'I'm sorry,' he said, genuinely feeling her pain. He knew how it felt to believe that not a single person in the world would care if you lived or died. It was the loneliest place on earth. 'But it's not true, Stell. Your kids love you. They're just busy doing what you equipped them to do by being such a good mum. Living their lives. Making their way in the world. And Gavin – he still cares about you, I'm sure. You had two children together. Built up two businesses. And as for Mum... Aw, she couldn't help leaving you. You know you meant the world to her. You were here for her, and that will have meant everything to her.'

'Not that much,' Stella said, before downing the rest of her wine. 'She took all the photos of me down after me and Gavin split up, but she had loads of you scattered around the place. I couldn't move without coming face to face with your smug grin.'

'I'm sure she didn't mean—'

'She said it was because they were my wedding photos, and she didn't want to hurt me. She could have dug out other pictures, surely? But no. Not worth the bother, was I?'

She ran a hand across her forehead. 'And this place! She knew how much I needed it, and she left it all to you just to spite me. I wanted it for Gavin, you see. It's not for me, honestly it's not. But Gavin needs the land and if you'd just let him have that he might come back to me. It would give him something to do here, you see. Bring him back from Puffin Point. You do understand that, don't you?'

Mac pushed his cake away, untouched. 'I can't give Gavin the land. You know that.'

'He'd give you a fair price!' Stella grabbed his arm, a pleading look in her eyes. 'Think about it, Mac. Think what you could do with all that money!'

He stared at her, feeling icy cold in the pit of his stomach. 'Are you serious?' So *now* she called him Mac, when it suited her. 'Wow. You really are desperate.'

'Yes, I am!' she cried. 'I love my husband. Can't you understand that? No, I don't suppose you can. The way you treated your family you clearly don't understand anything about love.'

'You know nothing about it,' he said, trying to remain calm. 'You only think you do.'

'I know you drove my best friend into the arms of another man,' she said angrily. 'I know your own kids have nothing to do with you. I know—'

'I think you should go.' He picked up his mobile phone. 'I'll call you a taxi.'

Stella picked up her plate and hurled it across the kitchen. Mac stared at the smashed china and the mess of chocolate sponge on the floor, then at her. There was a silence, only broken when he realised Carne was rushing over to investigate the situation and that he might try to eat the remains of the cake.

He grabbed the little dog and tucked Mrs Beddows under his other arm, shutting them in the living room. Then he took out a dustpan and brush and began to sweep up the mess.

'I'm sorry,' she said, sounding a bit shell-shocked.

'Maybe you should go home,' he told her. 'Things have got a bit fraught, and we're not going to get anywhere today. Maybe another time, when you're more clear-headed?'

She scowled. 'I'm perfectly clear-headed. Are you going to sell this place or not? To me or to Gavin, I don't care which.'

He stood up, the dustpan in his hand, and met her challenging look with one of defiance.

'No,' he said. 'I'm sorry, Stella, but I'm not. Not ever.'

'Right.' She got to her feet and dragged on her hat, scarf and gloves. 'Then I'll see you in court.'

Mac laughed. 'Court? You've got no chance of winning a court case.'

'Watch me. I'll hire the best solicitor I can afford, and I can afford a *very* good one.'

'You'd just be throwing your money away,' he told her.

'Well,' she snapped, her eyes flashing, 'you'd know all about that, wouldn't you?'

He let her go. She collected her coat from the hallway and went outside, slamming the door after her. No doubt she'd go to the pub and call a taxi from there. He just hoped she wouldn't have anything else to drink. He'd call Sam in half an hour and check that she'd got into a cab safely.

What a day! So much for putting things right between himself and Stella. He couldn't help thinking that, this time, maybe he'd lost his sister for good.

21

Saturday 14 March – Project Alison Day 42: It's Poppy's birthday party today. There's going to be posh sandwiches and birthday cake and probably sausage rolls. I love a sausage roll. How am I going to get through this then? Oh, and I'm seeing Jenna and the twins. Just another day. Nothing to worry about at all, right? Feel like I'm being punished for something but can't quite figure out what. Must have been a troll in a previous life.

No amount of pretty stickers and washi tape had made today's entry look any less terrifying to Alison. She was about to see her daughter and granddaughters for the first time in well over a month, and on top of that she was facing all sorts of temptations at a birthday party, and no doubt her parents would make absolutely sure that everyone knew she was diabetic and mustn't, on any account, eat anything 'bad'.

They'd gone on and on about it that night she and Mac had gone round to Sanderlings for tea. It had been mortifying, not to mention annoying. Seeing the three of them tucking into chicken tikka masala with mountains of rice, while she had half the amount of curry dolloped on to a bed of wilting baby spinach – and no chance of a naan bread either – had been almost too much to bear, but when Mam brought out the cheesecake and Dad handed her a pot of natural yoghurt to eat instead she'd almost cried.

She might have done if Mac hadn't been there. In fact, if he *hadn't* been there, she'd probably have ended up sneaking into the kitchen and stuffing her face with cheesecake anyway. But he *had* been there, so she didn't dare risk it. Which, looking back, she was very glad about.

He'd clearly been embarrassed that she couldn't eat what the rest of them were eating, and had looked so awkward about the whole thing that she'd ended up assuring him quite heartily that she didn't mind a bit, and had been really looking forward to her reduced-to-clear vegetables and reduced-to-clear yoghurt, which tasted so sour she wasn't sure it was even safe to eat.

Mac had walked her home after tea at her parents'. He'd insisted upon continuing with her as they reached the gates of Watersmeet, even though she'd pointed out it was only a short walk up the road from there and she'd be fine. She never felt unsafe in Kelsea Sands. He'd been so quiet at first that she'd worried the whole evening had been a disaster, but when she'd tried to apologise, he'd looked horrified that she thought his low mood was down to her or her family.

'It's Stella,' he'd explained. 'She came to see me earlier and things didn't go very well. Honestly, it has nothing to do with you. I really enjoyed tonight.' He'd smiled at her, making her heart skip. '*Really* enjoyed it.'

'Are you ready?' Rosie popped her head round the bedroom door, cutting into her thoughts. 'We're supposed to be setting off in a minute. We don't want to be late. Mam would rather die than let Kendra down.'

Alison rolled her eyes and stood, wriggling around uncomfortably.

'Get you, wearing tights!' Rosie said admiringly. 'You look lovely, Ali. I can't remember the last time I saw you in a dress.'

'I can't remember the last time I wore one,' she admitted. 'It's been stuffed in my wardrobe for about two years, cos it got a bit tight, and where do I ever go to wear a dress these days?'

Realising she had nothing suitable to wear for Poppy's party, she'd called home after work one evening to rummage through her clothes and find something that didn't look too scruffy or too much like it was cutting off her circulation. The dress had caught her eye because it was covered in poppies, and seemed appropriate for Poppy's party, but she hadn't really believed she'd get into it.

When she found that it fitted her comfortably, she'd almost whooped with excitement. On impulse, she'd rushed to the bathroom and pulled out the scales, wondering how much weight she'd lost, because surely she must have lost *something*?

She'd *literally* whooped out loud this time as she discovered she'd lost twelve pounds in just over four weeks. Obviously that rate of weight loss wouldn't continue, but it was a brilliant boost to start her off, and it must be doing something to help her blood sugar levels.

'You're absolutely glowing,' Rosie said, tilting her head and surveying Alison thoughtfully. She smirked. 'All that healthy food must be doing you the world of good.'

She was probably right. Alison had never eaten so healthily in her life. Rosie had set her on the right path, and now she had another ally whose help was making all the difference...

'Your parents are lovely,' Mac had said as they walked

through Tide's Reach towards Rosie's caravan. 'You know they're just worried about you, don't you? I know they did go on about the diabetes a lot, and I saw the look on your face when your mum served up that cheesecake and you got the yoghurt, but it's only because they want you to be well. I could see it in their eyes. They love you to bits.'

Alison had nodded. She knew it, deep down.

'It's just a bit embarrassing,' she said at last.

'What is?'

'Getting diagnosed with type 2 diabetes,' she admitted. 'Feels like an admission of failure somehow. Like if I'd only had more self-control and willpower this would never have happened to me.'

'It's not your fault,' he assured her. 'Society's geared towards getting people to eat unhealthily. Diabetes is an epidemic these days. How many diabetics did you know when we were kids?'

'I'd never heard of it,' she agreed. 'But food wasn't so widely available as it is now. The shops closed at teatime. They closed on Sundays. There were no takeaway deliveries or apps that allowed you to have food delivered to your door in minutes. It feels like we're encouraged to eat non-stop these days. And all the wrong things.'

'I've been thinking about that,' Mac said. 'You know I'm the world's worst cook?'

Alison laughed. 'You might have mentioned it once or twice.'

'Yes, well, I've decided that I'm going to learn how to make some meals from scratch, so I've ordered a cookbook. I wondered if you'd like to learn alongside me? We could help each other out. You could come round to Watersmeet, and we could practise together. Only if you want to!' he added hastily. 'I mean, there's no pressure. I just really want to do this for myself, and I thought if you wanted to do the same, we might as well work as a team.'

Alison liked the sound of them working as a team. She liked it a lot, which wasn't something she wanted to examine too closely.

'That would be great,' she'd told him. 'Thank you. Let's do it!'

What he hadn't mentioned – and what she only discovered a few days later when the cookbook arrived – was that it was full of diabetes-friendly recipes and was aimed at getting your blood sugar levels back to normal. She couldn't believe he'd done that for her, and thought he was quite possibly the kindest man she'd ever met.

Well, apart from her dad, obviously.

And Uncle Christopher.

And Niall.

And Drew of course...

'Ali, have you drifted off again?' Rosie asked impatiently. 'Come on, or we'll have Mam moaning at us all afternoon.'

'Sorry!' Alison shook her head and grabbed her bag. 'Ready.'

'At last! Let's go.'

22

Alison had never noticed before, but Rosie was quite right. Elaine was like a different person when in the presence of Kendra and Niall.

'How can she be so awestruck by her own family?' she wondered aloud, watching her aunt transform into a timid, blushing mouse, who was all 'please' and 'thank you' and 'you're so kind' as Kendra offered her tea and enquired if she'd prefer milk or lemon in it.

'To be fair to Mam,' Rosie said, 'nobody else in our family would even think about offering tea with lemon, would they?'

They watched as Kendra asked the same question of Alison's dad, who threw up his hands in horror and said, 'I want a brew, not a cold remedy!'

Rosie giggled and Alison said, 'Trust Dad.'

Uncle Christopher told an amused Kendra that he'd love tea with lemon, and she gave him a knowing smile before heading into the kitchen.

'Nothing rattles Kendra,' Rosie said. 'Even our peasant

family. Where's Niall anyway? Not like him to be anything but the perfect host.'

'Dad's in the study, finishing up some work,' Poppy said. They hadn't even heard her approach. She was a pretty girl with bright red hair and had a Teenage Queen badge pinned to her T-shirt. 'He said he'll be out in a minute. How are you, Auntie Rosie?'

She grinned as Rosie tapped her on the arm. 'Hey, you! What have I told you about calling me Auntie Rosie? It's just Rosie, thanks very much. I'm fine, thanks, love. Happy birthday! Can't believe you're a teenager already. How are things with you?'

Poppy shuffled awkwardly. 'Oh, you know. All right.'

'As good as that, eh? Oh, to be thirteen again, eh, Alison?'

Alison sighed. If only. How simple life had been back then.

'We haven't seen much of you lately,' Poppy said, twisting a strand of her hair around her finger.

'I know. It's all my shifts. And I'm busy being glamorous, obviously. Bad auntie. I'll make more of an effort in future, honest.'

Poppy nodded and shrugged. 'It's fine. I was just wondering, that's all.'

'Your birthday presents and cards,' Rosie said, as she and Alison handed her two gift bags.

'Cool. I'll open them later when you're gone. I hate opening stuff in front of people.'

'How strange,' Alison said, as Poppy took the gift bags into the kitchen.

'I know! I'd have been ripping the wrapping paper off before you'd let go of the gift bag. The youth of today is a mystery to me. I mean, look at our Ryan!'

She nodded over to where a tall, gangly boy was sprawled on an armchair, his fingers practically flying over his mobile phone as he tapped out a message or replied to a post or played a game or whatever it was he was doing. Fair-haired and dressed in jeans and an old T-shirt, he was all arms and legs. At nearly sixteen, he probably considered this party a waste of his time.

The vicarage, a rather ugly 1970s brick building with a spacious through lounge and a neat, boxy little garden, stood in the shadow of St Saviour's Church, no doubt so that Niall would always be reminded of his duties. The old vicarage was further down the road and was a gorgeous Georgian house with large grounds. Sadly, the church had sold it off years ago and it had been turned into a care home.

Kendra had done her best to make her home more character-ful, but it wasn't easy. There was something quite soulless about it, which was ironic given its purpose.

Rosie yelped as Alison clutched her arm.

'Sorry, sorry.' Alison rubbed her cousin's arm apologetically. 'Jenna's just walked in with the twins. I feel sick.'

'Don't be daft. You've done nothing wrong,' Rosie reminded her. 'Just stay calm. Let her come to you.'

But there was no chance of anything so restrained, because seconds later the twins let out shrieks of excitement and rushed over to Alison, threw their arms around her and hugged her tightly.

'Where have you been?'

'Mum says you're on holiday!'

'We haven't seen you for ages.'

'We've missed you, Grandma!'

Alison blinked away tears and hugged them back, kissing the tops of their heads. 'I've missed you too. And yes, I am sort of on holiday, but only in Kelsea Sands. I'm staying with Rosie in her caravan.'

'In a caravan!' Hallie's eyes widened. 'I love caravans! Can we come and stay, too?'

'We just don't have the room,' Alison began, but broke off as Jenna approached.

'All right, girls, leave Grandma alone. Come and say hello to Poppy and wish her a happy birthday.'

'But we haven't seen Grandma for ages,' Ada protested.

Jenna shrugged. 'You've got all afternoon. Come on, you've got to give Poppy her card and present, remember?'

Reluctantly, the girls allowed themselves to be led away.

'She didn't even look at me,' Alison murmured disbelievingly.

'She looked nervous to me,' Rosie said. 'Honestly, I think she's feeling as awkward about all this as you are. Give it time.'

Niall finally emerged from the study, all smiles and apologies. The room brightened immediately, and Poppy's face broke into the widest smile as he put his arm around her and wished her a happy birthday for probably the tenth time that day.

Alison had always liked Niall, even if she didn't always agree with his beliefs and had puzzled over his decision to become a vicar from a very young age. He was a good, decent man, as kind as Uncle Christopher, and with the same blue eyes and strawberry-blond hair as his sister, although Rosie's wasn't perhaps quite as red-tinted as his.

Tall and broad-shouldered, he made an imposing figure when in church. People listened to him. His congregation was small but committed. He was well-respected and well-loved in his parish, and Alison thought there was no wonder Elaine was so proud of him.

Kendra, who'd made umpteen cups of tea and had been the perfect hostess in his absence, gave him a wry smile and said, 'Well, now her dad's here perhaps we can begin celebrating the birthday girl's big day at last. Thanks so much for coming, everyone. Please don't stand on ceremony. The table's laid and you're very welcome to help yourselves. Tuck in.'

Niall put his arms around her and kissed her. 'You're wonderful,' he said. 'You've worked a miracle with all this. Sorry I was delayed.'

She tapped him playfully on the nose. 'Don't be daft. It's only a bit of party food. I didn't part the Red Sea. No need to apologise.'

'Couple goals,' Rosie said with a sigh.

They headed into the back part of the through lounge, which served as a dining area. Alison swallowed as she saw all the delicious food spread out on the table, and Rosie looked dismayed.

'Aw, Ali, what are *you* going to eat? Look at all this! Can you have *any* of it?'

Alison sighed and patted her handbag. 'Don't worry, I came prepared. I've got a bottle of SlimKwik here and a tiny piece of cheese to nibble on. I'll be fine.'

'You can't just have that!'

'It's okay, honestly.' Alison gave her a bashful smile. 'I'll be eating tonight. Mac's picking me up from here and we're going to go for a walk around Millensea then head back to Watersmeet for tea.'

Rosie's eyes widened. 'Oh, wow! *Again*? This is getting serious.'

Alison's smile dropped. 'No, no it's nothing like that. We're just friends. He's helping me with the diet, I told you, and we're learning to cook together using that cookbook I mentioned. Don't read anything else into it, Rosie, for goodness' sake.'

Rosie sighed. 'I don't see why not. There wouldn't be anything wrong with it if you and he—'

'Well, we're not.' Alison glanced around, anxious in case

anyone was listening who would get the wrong idea. 'I don't need all that in my life. I had a very happy marriage with Drew, and I'm not looking to replace him.'

'No one said anything about replacing him,' Rosie pointed out. 'But a bit of a kiss and a cuddle now and then wouldn't be too much to ask. Blimey, I wouldn't say no if Mac was twenty years younger.'

'Er, do you mind?'

'Mind what? That he's twenty years older than me – near enough – or that he's yours and I should keep my mitts off?'

Alison rolled her eyes. 'You don't have to rub it in how young you are.'

They watched, amused, as Elaine stood with a plate in one hand, delicately nibbling on a sandwich that Christopher had got for her.

'It's going to take her an hour to eat that, the rate she's going,' Rosie pointed out. 'I don't know why Mam's so weird around Niall and Kendra, I really don't. Maybe it's because she's the only churchgoer among us. It's like she can't believe her own son is a vicar, and it somehow makes her inferior to him.'

'Auntie Rosie!' came a voice behind them. 'If I didn't know better, I'd say you were jealous.'

Rosie's face turned pink as they realised Poppy was standing behind them. 'Stop eavesdropping! You weren't supposed to hear that.' She smiled as she saw Ryan hovering behind his sister. 'There you are! Thought you were going to ignore us all afternoon.'

Ryan shrugged. 'Sorry. I was checking my TikTok stats.'

'Fair enough,' Rosie said. 'Where's your other grandma, by the way? Thought she'd be here for your birthday, Poppy.'

'She's flown off on holiday to find herself,' Poppy said.

'Though you'd think she'd have found herself by now, wouldn't you? She's seventy! Flipping ancient.'

'Thanks a bunch,' Alison said.

'Sorry. Didn't know you were seventy,' Poppy said, blushing.

'I'm not! Bloody hell, I'm really glad I came,' Alison said, as Rosie laughed.

'Maybe your gran's having a midlife crisis.'

'Seventy's not midlife!' Poppy said, wide-eyed.

'Not unless you're Moses,' Ryan said. 'Has Mum made any of those mini quiches?'

The party, it turned out, was only for family members. None of Poppy's friends had been invited, but Kendra explained that the birthday girl and her five besties were going bowling the following day and then to a burger bar in town for tea – no adults allowed.

'We were going to have a proper party for her,' she said, 'but she wanted it this way. I suppose it's so she gets to celebrate twice, which is quite crafty of her. Blimey! How have all those sandwiches gone so fast?'

She hurried off to the kitchen to whip up more of them, since Alison's dad had stormed through the first lot like a plague of locusts.

Alison sipped her SlimKwik and tried not to look at the mini quiches and the savoury filo pastry triangles and the little samosas that were calling her name.

'Mum?'

She almost choked on her rather disgustingly synthetic-tasting chocolate drink as Jenna moved beside her.

'Hello, love!' Alison swallowed hard, trying her best to look and sound casual and welcoming all at the same time. 'How are you?'

Jenna, she thought, looked pale and thinner. She'd lost

weight and it was more noticeable than her own weight loss, which was a bit galling. Not a single person had remarked that she'd looked thinner, but there was no mistaking it on her daughter.

Jenna shrugged. 'Fine. You know.' She handed Alison an envelope. 'Mother's Day card for tomorrow.'

'Oh!' Alison nodded. 'Thanks.'

'I didn't know what to get you so there's a voucher inside.' Jenna hesitated then sighed. 'Look, I know a lot's been said and I know we can't turn the clock back, but I want to know if you'd be willing to see the twins. Not overnight or anything,' she added hastily. 'Just for a few hours one day. They really miss you and it's not fair. Whatever's gone on between us we shouldn't make them pay the price.'

'I'm glad you see it that way,' Alison said hesitantly. 'But really, I said from the beginning that I'd be happy to have them, didn't I? It was Joel who said I was banned from—'

Jenna gave her a startled look. 'What?'

Alison frowned. 'Joel. He told me that if I wasn't willing to babysit the twins as usual then I wasn't allowed to see them any longer. Actually,' she added, 'he told me that was your decision, and he was just passing on the message.'

Jenna hung her head and turned away. 'Right.'

Alison touched her arm. 'You didn't know, did you?'

'He was just angry,' Jenna said defensively. 'He could see how upset I was and how much hassle it was causing me, fixing up alternative arrangements. That's all.'

'Really?' Alison eyed her steadily and Jenna's cheeks flushed.

'Look, whatever was said and done the question remains. Will you have the girls for an afternoon? For their sakes, not mine. You got out of the half-term holiday, so you can't say I'm just using you, because I'd have contacted you earlier if I needed you for that.'

'*Got out of the half-term holiday*?' Alison gasped. 'It was *your* half-term holiday, too. It's not like you had to work the entire week and needed childcare, is it?'

'You know as well as I do that school holidays involve work for teachers,' Jenna said frostily. 'I had lessons to plan, marking to do...'

'And every evening free to do it,' Alison pointed out. 'Unless, of course, you'd made other plans?'

Jenna glared at her. 'I can see I'm wasting my time.'

'No, no, you're not. I'm sorry. That was uncalled for.' Alison sighed. 'Look, of course I'll have the twins one afternoon. I'll pick them up and take them out for the day. Your grandma and grandad would love to spend more time with them,' she added, nodding over to where her parents were happily chatting to the twins and her mother was showing off her plaster cast to the girls, who were begging to be allowed to draw on it.

'Okay, but only if you're sure. I wouldn't want to be a burden.'

Alison gave her daughter a sharp look. 'Are you ever going to let this go? I've messaged you a few times now and you've ignored every one. Is this how it's going to be from now on?'

Jenna stared at her for a moment, then she rubbed her temples and said, 'I'm sorry, Mum, it's just—'

Ada came running over and grabbed Alison's hand. 'Can we see the caravan then, Grandma? When are you coming home? We don't like you being away so long.'

Alison and Jenna gazed at each other and Jenna said, 'Whenever you like, Mum. It's up to you.'

'Shall we say next Saturday night then?' Alison said brightly to Ada. 'I'll come and pick you up after work and take you round our posh caravan, then we'll see Great-Granny and Grandad, and maybe I'll take you for dinner at the pub on Sunday before I drop you home. What do you say?'

Ada whooped and ran off to tell her twin sister the good news.

'Thanks, Mum.'

'Are you sure you're okay, Jenna?' Alison asked anxiously. 'If there's anything—'

'I'm fine. Just tired. You know what teaching's like.' Jenna managed a wan smile. 'Takes it out of you, doesn't it?'

It had certainly taken it out of Alison, but she'd had only one child to care for at home, and a supportive, loving husband. Joel was never there, and even though he clearly wanted to protect and defend his wife, was that enough? Jenna needed him by her side.

Should she put her own selfish needs aside and go home? If her daughter needed her...

'Jenna—'

Her voice was drowned out as a chorus of 'Happy Birthday' erupted and everyone sang to the birthday girl, who stood looking suitably embarrassed until they'd finished. As the cheering and clapping began Jenna moved towards the table where the twins were urging Poppy to blow out her candles and make a wish.

Alison took a step forward.

'Don't even think about it.' Rosie's hand was tight on her arm. 'I heard every word, and I know what you're going to do. Leave it, Ali. Please.'

'But she needs me,' Alison said sadly.

'She needs to sort out her life if she's not happy with it,' Rosie said firmly. 'Just as you're doing right now. If you go back things will slot into place exactly as they were before. You'll be busy and stressed and resentful, the diet will go out the window and you'll be right back at square one. You need to fix yourself, and if Jenna's not happy she needs to fix *her*self, too.'

As Alison hesitated, Rosie's voice softened. 'Look, I know how you're feeling, and I get that you think she's your responsibility, but she's a grown woman. You need to focus on your health right now – physical and mental. Please, Ali.'

Alison nodded. Rosie was right. If she went home things would never change, and she needed to remember how unhappy she'd been. She had to think about getting her blood sugar down and figuring out what she was going to do with the rest of her life – because the truth was, she was happy in Kelsea Sands, and though she'd never imagined it possible, she was quite happy living in the caravan with Rosie. She'd never felt more relaxed, and her stress levels had only risen when she thought about Jenna, which said a lot.

She would take the twins on Saturday, as agreed, and if she was allowed, she would see them every weekend, or every other weekend. But that had to be the limit of her involvement for now. She couldn't get dragged back into a situation that was wearing her down. Not until she was stronger in her own mind about what she wanted for herself and her future.

23

'Do you remember,' Alison said, 'when we were kids and this place used to be heaving?' She and Mac were leaning on Millensea's sea wall, gazing down at the beach, which was completely empty of people. 'Look at it now.'

Mac laughed. 'Yes, but it's the middle of March and half past five. Most people are tucked up warm at home, eating their tea. I'm sure it still gets busy in the summer.'

'Ah,' Alison said, 'but there's busy and there's busy. I've not seen it like it used to be for years. Decades.' As a gust of wind blew her hair in front of her eyes for the umpteenth time, she tucked it behind her ears yet again. 'I remember when this beach was packed. There used to be donkey rides along the sands, and the ice cream van was parked near the slipway. The amusement arcades were blaring out pop music, and you could hear the bells and whistles from the machines and the sound of coins dropping everywhere.' She gave a wistful sigh. 'It was magical.'

There used to be a bus service from Kelsea Sands to Millensea back then, and like most of the villagers she'd paid regular visits to the town. Then the local bus company had sold out to a larger company, which had promptly scrapped the service, despite promising to keep it running. The village had become even more isolated.

'The real death knell for Millensea came when they closed the market,' she continued. 'Everyone used to come here on a weekend for that, didn't they? I'll never understand why they shut it down.'

'The council sold the land to build a supermarket,' he pointed out. 'The very one we both shop in.'

'ShopSmart?' Alison wrinkled her nose. 'I was only there because Mam and Dad insisted on it. I'd have gone to Maister's.'

'Not everyone can afford to go to Maister's,' he said quietly. 'This isn't exactly a booming area, is it? ShopSmart's been a godsend for a lot of locals.'

'But if the market had stayed open it would have meant more money coming in for Millensea!'

He shrugged. 'Some would say that a lot of the market stall-holders came from Hull and further afield, not from here. And the day trippers who came for the market often used to bring a picnic with them, rather than spend money on burgers and fish and chips. I know we did. You could argue that the market didn't benefit Millensea as much as we think, and the supermarket's benefitted the residents more.'

Alison didn't see it that way. 'The market was such a big attraction that it enticed people to buy caravans here. People used to stay on the holiday parks and spend in the shops and amusements.'

'Plenty still do.'

'Hmm.' She nodded down at the beach below where a vast number of huge grey boulders were stacked up all along the edge of the sea wall. 'They don't help, do they? So ugly. We had lovely clear sands when we were kids. Who wants to sit on a beach full of hideous boulders?'

'Firstly, the beach isn't full of boulders,' Mac pointed out reasonably. 'Look how far the sands stretch! And more importantly, they're helping to keep the erosion at bay. If they hadn't been put in place, we might not be standing here now.'

Alison gave an exasperated sigh. 'Do you always see the good in everything?'

He grinned. 'It's not that. I just think maybe you live in the past too much. You see it as some sort of wonderful haven where nothing bad ever happened and everything was so much better.'

'Well, it was,' she said heavily. 'And so much simpler, too.'

'I think you're being very selective with your memories,' he said. 'And yes, Millensea was probably busier back then, and yes, I'll admit it does look a bit run-down these days, compared to what it was when we were kids. But so do most seaside towns, let's face it. They don't have the pull they used to. And councils are broke, so it must be hard for them to maintain them as well as they'd like.'

'I suppose...'

'I think the Promenade Gardens look lovely,' he added, turning round to look at the sunken area of land that had once been a mere but which had been filled in back in the early twentieth century to form a leisure area, where people of the town could stroll, sit on benches, listen to the music coming from the old bandstand and admire the beautiful flowerbeds. In recent times the old bandstand had been replaced with a modern canopied stage, and a cafe had been added. 'The council runs a few events from there, too. *And* they're free.'

'How do you know all this anyway? You've been away for years!'

'There's an amazing thing I've discovered recently,' he dead-panned. 'It's called the internet. It will blow your mind.'

'Very funny.'

'Seriously, though, don't you think there's something charming about this place? I know it's not got the seaside glamour and all the bells and whistles of somewhere like Scarborough or Burlington-on-Sea, but there's something about it, don't you think?'

Alison was quiet for a moment. She let her gaze wander beyond the Promenade Gardens to the row of amusements, now dominated by Games Master, an amusement centre and cafe which had taken the place of three of the old independent companies. Other than that, the row looked pretty much as it had when she was a kid.

You could still get a good fried breakfast from some of the cafes inside them, and on the end of the row was the Seaside Shop, which sold buckets and spades and all the usual paraphernalia for a seaside holiday, along with sticks of rock and ice cream.

Across the road, next to the small children's fairground, was her favourite childhood cafe. The cheeseburgers there had been to die for. Ordering a cheeseburger and a milkshake, she and her teenage pals had felt as if they were living in the film *Grease*. It had all seemed so exotic and wonderful back then!

The town still had its old pubs, its fish and chip shops and its little gift shops. Sadly, the old Woolworths where she'd spent many a happy Saturday afternoon with her schoolmates had been replaced with a large frozen food shop, and there were more charity shops and takeaways, and even the odd empty unit, but even so, it was still recognisably Millensea, and it had still given her a thrill when she and Rosie had spotted the sign welcoming them to the town earlier that day, and they'd caught a glimpse of the white lighthouse which stood in the centre of the town. It hadn't been a functioning lighthouse for decades, and was now a tearoom and museum, but it looked beautiful. Familiar. Comforting. Not many seaside places had a lighthouse down a street, had they?

'I've been sent an appointment,' she said, unable to hide the gloom at the thought of it. She hadn't even mentioned it to Rosie because she really didn't want to talk about it, but somehow Mac had a way of coaxing her to talk without even trying.

He turned to face her. 'What sort of appointment?'

'Retinal eye screening,' she said. 'Apparently, even though I'm not on any medication or anything, I'm still classed as diabetic, and I need to get my eyes checked.'

'Well, that's good, isn't it?'

'No,' she said stubbornly. 'It isn't. I've heard it's really uncomfortable, and to be honest...'

'What?' he asked curiously.

She heaved a sigh. 'Okay, the truth is I hate hospitals and doctors and anything medical. I'll avoid them as much as I possibly can. I know you won't understand, and you'll think I'm stupid but—'

'Since Drew's illness?' he asked gently.

She nodded tearfully, grateful that he seemed to understand after all. 'It was all so awful, and I've been scared ever since. I just want them to leave me alone, but they keep calling me in for this, that and the other, especially since I turned sixty.'

'I know what you mean,' he said. 'I had to send in a sample a couple of months ago. You don't want to know what of.'

'I can guess. I got the same kit through the post.'

'Did you send it back?'

She shook her head. 'Why invite trouble?'

'You know that's a ridiculous way to look at it, though?'

She bit her lip. 'Yes,' she said eventually. 'But the thing is, it's like I said, they've bombarded me with stuff! It's too much.'

'You just need to take one thing at a time then,' he said. 'Go to this retinal screening. Then, when that's over with, send off the bowel testing sample.'

'And then I suppose I have to book a cervical smear.'

'Have they asked you to?'

'Yes.'

'Well...' He shrugged. 'Aren't we bloody lucky? We live in a country where we get all these screenings for free. It's amazing.'

Alison stared at him, feeling suddenly stupid and a bit ashamed.

'Maybe,' she said cautiously, 'you're right. Maybe I do bury my head in the sand. And maybe you're right about me living in the past, too. I suppose it's safer there. You just never know what's going to hit you in the future, do you? I guess the two things are connected.'

'I don't think about the future too much either,' Mac confessed. 'I worry about today, and that's it. It's all we've got when you think about it, and it's more than enough to deal with.'

She frowned, noting the faintest hint of sadness in his voice.

'Have you heard anything from Stella since her last visit?' she asked, realising with some guilt that she'd not even asked him since that night he'd first walked her home after tea at her parents'.

Mac considered for a moment. 'No,' he said at last. 'Not a word. I saw Crystal the other day, though.'

'Your niece? How is she? I haven't seen her around, even though I'm on the caravan park.'

Crystal, she knew, often helped her father, Gavin, at either Tide's Reach or his other caravan park further up the coast at Puffin Point. Alison hadn't seen her for a few years, though.

'She's mostly working at Puffin Point,' Mac said. 'She likes it there. Apparently, Gavin's bought a hotel there, and that's their latest project. She only comes back here now and then if she's desperately needed. They mostly leave it to the staff these days.'

'Well, it's a small caravan park,' Alison agreed. 'Not like the one at Puffin Point, I guess.'

'She seems happy enough anyway,' he said. 'The main thing is, she doesn't seem to bear me any grudges. It could have been awkward, but she didn't seem to mind. I asked her if she'd seen anything of her mum, because I know Stella's missing her, and she told me she'd seen her a few days ago and she's been to a solicitor about the will, but that he'd told her there was nothing she could do as there was no reason to contest it. It wasn't like she'd been cut out of it anyway. She got thousands.' He rubbed his eyes, as if weary of it all.

'I can sort of see her point, though,' Alison said cautiously. 'Not that she should contest the will or anything, but it is odd that your mum left Watersmeet to you when you lived in Oxfordshire and Stella only lives in Weltringham.'

'Stella would have sold it to Gavin,' Mac explained. 'That's what Mum was afraid of. Gavin needs more land to expand Tide's Reach. It's crumbling away fast, as I'm sure you've noticed, and he can only move the caravans so far back before he encroaches on farmland. He tried buying some of the land off the Fosters, but they weren't having it, so Stella thinks Watersmeet land could be a sort of extension for him, with it only being half a mile up the road.'

'Stella and Gavin have been divorced a couple of years now, though, haven't they?'

'Three,' Mac said. 'But she'd still do anything for him. Mum told me Stella never wanted the divorce. She only went along with it because it was what Gavin wanted, and having talked to her that day it's very clear that she's never got over him.'

'Poor Stella,' Alison murmured. 'That must be so hard for her.'

'Which is why Mum didn't trust her not to offer the land to him if she got her hands on Watersmeet. Hence her leaving it to me to keep it safe.'

'And you didn't mind leaving Oxfordshire to come all the way back up here?'

He paused. 'No,' he said finally. 'It was no trouble.'

'What about your kids, though? You must miss them. Are they coming up to visit you soon?'

'Shall we head back to the car?' he suggested. 'I'm getting hungry now and we need to cook our tea before we can eat.'

He pushed away from the sea wall and led her along the road to where his car was parked. She couldn't help noticing that it was fifteen years old, which seemed odd considering he'd been a wealthy businessman. Maybe he just wasn't into material things and didn't care about money or possessions or how he looked to other people. It would explain him shopping in ShopSmart anyway.

They got into the car, glad to be out of the brisk wind, and Alison glanced in the mirror, groaning as she saw the state of her hair.

As she rummaged in her bag for a comb, Mac said, 'Sorry. Didn't mean to ignore your questions.'

She looked up, surprised. 'It's okay. None of my business, is it?'

He drummed his fingers on the steering wheel. 'Thing is, I haven't seen my children for a while.'

'O-kay.' Alison quickly combed her hair, her eyes never

leaving his face. Even though he was in profile she could see how tense he was. 'Well, you don't have to tell me if you don't want to.'

'It's only fair, since you told me about Jenna,' he said.

She smiled. 'You don't owe me anything for that. Honestly.'

He turned to face her, and she saw anguish in his eyes. 'I think I'd quite like to tell you.'

She didn't know what to say to that, so she just nodded and slipped her comb back in her bag.

'Truth is,' he said quietly, 'I haven't seen them at all for about twelve years.'

'Oh wow,' she breathed. 'That *is* a long time.' She simply couldn't imagine going that long without seeing Jenna. It would kill her.

'After... after our divorce, the kids sort of drifted away,' he admitted. 'I saw them on the occasional Saturday for a while, but it was... difficult. I couldn't always have them when their mum wanted me to have them, or when they weren't at school.'

'Because of your job?' she asked, curious.

'For a lot of reasons,' he said evasively. 'Anyway, over time they stopped bothering about it, I guess. Terry became more of a father to them. He saw so much more of them, and he was there for them in ways I couldn't be.'

'Terry?'

'He was my best friend. The one I told you about. The one who I ended up going into business with?'

'Oh, of course.' Alison frowned. 'Sorry, but why did he become a father figure to your children?'

Mac gave a heavy sigh. 'Because he married their mum. My ex-wife, Lynne.'

Alison gasped. 'Bloody hell! That must have been a complicated situation.'

'It was.' He gave her a grim smile. 'Not the easiest of times, let's put it that way. I was devastated when I found out they were together, and things went from bad to worse. In the end I cut off all contact with Terry and Lynne completely. I had to. But it meant that seeing the kids got harder and harder and it just...' He rubbed his forehead then looked at her, and she saw the shame in his eyes. 'It just trickled away,' he admitted at last. 'I haven't heard a word from them in all that time.'

'I see.'

'So now you know why it was no wrench at all to move up here. I had nothing to keep me in Oxfordshire. Nothing at all.'

'Your business?'

'I sold my share to him,' Mac said. 'It seemed the easiest thing to do. The only thing to do, to be honest.' He blew out his cheeks and tried to smile. 'Pretty messy, eh? Now do you understand why I find Kelsea Sands so peaceful? It's been like the answer to a prayer. I'm only sorry it took Mum's death to bring me home. I should have come back a lot sooner.'

Alison noticed that he still called Kelsea Sands home, just as she did. After all this time.

'Well,' she said gently, 'hindsight is a wonderful thing, isn't it?' She tentatively reached out and put her hand on his arm, and he smiled before placing his own hand on top of hers.

'Right,' he said. 'Watersmeet. Time to get cooking because, I don't know about you, but I'm starving.'

24

Monday 23 March – Project Alison Day 51: Haven't written in this journal for a few days. It's been all go here!

Picked the twins up on Saturday after work and took them to see Mam and Dad. Mam let them sign her plaster cast. Dad regaled them with thrilling tales about Kelsea Sands and Kels Point during the World Wars. I had to wake them up to take them back to the caravan, but apart from that little interlude they really enjoyed themselves. We all had Sunday dinner at The North Star yesterday before I took them home. I think they've fallen in love with Kelsea Sands.

Going to the hairdresser's today. Rosie thinks I need a change of image, but she can think again. I'm a bit wary about going somewhere new. It's hard to trust hairdressers when you don't know them, but I'll probably just have a trim so it should be okay.

Finally told Rosie this morning about Mac's ex-wife marrying his ex-best mate. She's as appalled as I am. Poor Mac! He's had such a hard time of it and he's always so calm

and kind. We cooked salmon burgers last night with ginger
and soy sauce and a bit of coriander. They were yummy. Had
another lovely evening at Watersmeet and then Mac walked
me home again...

'I'm just saying,' Rosie said, as she adjusted the towel around her shoulders, 'that Mrs MacMillan kept very quiet about Mac losing his kids and his business. We all thought he was doing really well in Oxfordshire and had a brilliant life. You said it yourself! You thought he was charmed. If Mam had known anything about it you can be very sure I'd have heard, so it's all been hushed up.'

Alison looked at her disbelievingly. 'Why would Sheila MacMillan go around telling your mam, of all people? Or anyone else's for that matter! It's nobody's business, and I only told you because – well, it's you. But don't go saying anything to anyone, Rosie. I mean it.'

She glared at her cousin's reflection in the mirror, and the hairdresser, who was fastening a cape around her, laughed.

'Well, don't worry about me, love. I won't say anything. I haven't the foggiest idea who you're talking about.'

It was a good job there wasn't a hairdressing salon in Kelsea Sands, Alison thought, because news would spread like wildfire – even more than it usually did. Here in A Cut Above in Hilderstead she felt reasonably safe discussing the issue with Rosie, if not entirely comfortable.

'Right,' said the hairdresser, 'what are we having done today?'

'Be radical,' Rosie advised. 'Honestly, Jade, she's been having her hair cut at the same salon in Hull for donkey's years, and it's always the same. She needs something doing with it, if you ask me.'

'Well, I think that's up to her,' Jade said, her eyes twinkling with amusement. She lifted some of Alison's locks and let them drop, eyeing them critically. 'It is quite fine, though. Have you ever thought about getting it cut shorter?'

'Shorter?' No, Alison hadn't. She'd had it past her shoulders for as long as she could remember and couldn't imagine it short. It was easy to put up in a ponytail or a bun at this length.

'Just to give it a bit of bounce and body,' Jade suggested. 'The length of it is weighing it down. How do you fancy a chin-length bob? You've got great bone structure. You should show it off.'

Alison wasn't sure but Rosie was full of enthusiasm. 'Oh, go on, Ali! Be daring. New you, remember? It could be part of Project Alison. Hey, Jade, do you think she could do with a bit of colour?'

'I'm not dyeing my hair,' Alison said.

'Maybe a few highlights?' Jade suggested. 'You're very lucky. You've hardly got any grey, but a few blonde highlights would blend with what you do have. Nothing too extreme. Just to brighten your face a bit.'

Rosie was leaning so far towards her it was a wonder her chair didn't tip over. 'Oh, go on, Ali! You'd look brilliant with highlights, and I think a bob would really suit you. Do something different for a change. Go on!'

'And when did you last change your hairstyle?' Alison demanded.

Rosie looked wounded. 'I don't need to! My hair suits me perfectly.'

'Thanks very much.' Alison sighed as the hairdresser watched her reflection hopefully. 'Oh, go on. Might as well give it a go.'

'The bob or the highlights?'

Alison shrugged. 'Both.'

'Woohoo!' Rosie punched the air. 'You're going to look fab, Ali. Trust me.'

It was almost two-and-a-half hours later when they left the salon, and Alison felt like a new woman.

'Honest to God, it's taken years off you,' Rosie told her.

'It's taken nearly eighty quid off me, too,' Alison said wryly.

'Totally worth it.' Rosie linked arms with her. 'Come on, I'll treat you to a cup of tea at the cafe over there. Help you get over the shock.'

The Trusty Teapot was just across the market square from the salon, so it was only moments later when they settled themselves at a table and ordered a pot of tea for two, politely refusing cake or scones to go with it.

'You know, you didn't even flinch when you said no then,' Rosie observed. 'A month ago you'd have been dithering about turning down cake but look at you now.'

'It's becoming second nature to me,' Alison said, surprised. 'I'm feeling a lot better, especially since I've started eating proper meals again. The SlimKwik wasn't great, but with the recipes from Mac's cookbook and all your support and help it's getting easier to keep going. I can't thank you enough for inviting me here and looking out for me, Rosie.'

'Don't be daft. It's a pleasure.' She smiled a thank you as the waitress placed a pot of tea and two cups and saucers on their table, along with milk and sugar. She stirred one spoonful of sugar into her tea and said, 'Did you notice? I've cut down from two sugars. I'm going to cut it out completely eventually. Taking a leaf from your book.'

'That's great. I thought black tea and coffee with no sugar would be vile, and to be honest, at first they were. But now I prefer them that way. It's just a habit really, isn't it?'

They sipped tea and admired the decor in the cafe, which was fairly plain but pretty, and spotlessly clean.

'Heard you outside the caravan last night,' Rosie said suddenly. 'I wasn't eavesdropping deliberately, honest! But you know how thin those caravan walls are...'

Alison blushed and Rosie gave an exasperated squeal and punched her lightly on the arm. 'Oh, come on, Ali! I've been so patient, and I've been dying to ask you, but it *sounded* like Mac kissed you last night. Am I wrong?'

Alison's face burned even more, and she was sure she must look scarlet by now. 'Shh!' She glanced around but no one was taking any notice. Why would they? It was only to her that it was a huge deal. And to Rosie, obviously. 'If you say one word about this to anyone, I'll leave Kelsea Sands and never come back.'

'Bit dramatic,' Rosie said. 'Anyway, as if! Leave the handsome Ian MacMillan behind? I don't think so. So you *did* kiss then?'

'It was nothing,' Alison insisted. 'Really. Just a peck on the cheek.'

'Oh.' Rosie looked bitterly disappointed. 'Well,' she said thoughtfully, 'it's a start.'

'Give it up, Rosie,' Alison advised. 'We're just friends.'

'Are you kidding me? He bought a cookbook for you. He's had you round at his house God knows how many evenings and afternoons now, cooking and eating at his place—'

'Only when you've been at work,' Alison said quickly. 'And the times you weren't he invited you, too.'

'I'm not complaining about that,' Rosie said impatiently. 'I'm just pointing out that he's gone to an awful lot of trouble for you.'

'He's a kind person,' Alison said. 'He wants to help me. Besides, it's helping him, too. He was sick of beans on toast. This way we both improve our cooking skills, and we get to eat healthily.'

'And is that all you're doing at Watersmeet?' Rosie asked curiously. 'Really?'

'No. I've helped him with the animals a few times. I've got quite fond of them actually. And we've discussed the garden – what he might like to do with it. That kind of thing.'

'Riveting,' Rosie said, clearly disappointed. 'Have you thought about trying to move things on?'

'Rosie, I told you already, I've had a happy marriage. I'm not looking for anything else but friendship.'

'Well, I think you deserve better. Drew would understand. You know he would. It's been nine years, Ali! It's not like you've rushed into anything, is it?'

'I think we're both cautious,' Alison mused. 'And remember, he's been badly hurt by his ex-wife and his best friend. How awful is that? I can't imagine anything worse than being let down so badly by the two people you should be able to trust more than anyone in the world.'

'Yes, that is horrible,' Rosie agreed, pouring the last of the tea from the pot after checking Alison didn't want it. 'How long were they having an affair before Mac found out?'

'I have no idea. He hasn't volunteered any more information than I already told you, and I can't exactly ask him. It would be insensitive to push it. But you can see why he'd be hesitant about starting a relationship with anyone, can't you?'

'But are you happy with that?' Rosie persisted. 'Really? You're okay just being friends? He might be sixty-two, which obviously is *ancient* to me, but even I think he's a good-looking man, and quite the catch. Are you sure you don't want to—'

'We're fine as friends,' Alison said firmly. 'And less of the "ancient", if you don't mind.'

Rosie sighed. 'All right then. Fair dos. Mind you, when he

sees your new hairdo, he might have a change of heart. Fingers crossed, eh?'

Project Alison – Day 51 cont.: Had another lovely evening at Watersmeet and then Mac walked me home again...

He kissed me! It was so lovely and so sweet. I had a funny feeling he was going to do it because we've been getting closer and closer and we kept giving each other these looks all evening. My stomach was spinning round like the washing machine!

And then when we got to the caravan and he said good-night I thought, well, maybe I'd got it all wrong. But then he suddenly reached out and stroked my cheek, and kind of waited for me to see if it was okay, and when I smiled and did the same to him, he just pulled me closer – ever so gently – and kissed me, really lightly on the lips. And I put my arms around him and then he, well, he kissed me a bit less lightly, and before I knew it, we were properly kissing!

I haven't had a kiss like that in years. And then he said, 'Is this all right?' And I said, 'More than all right.' And he smiled at me, and we kissed again, and then he said goodnight and I went into the caravan and it was a really good job Rosie had gone to bed because she'd have been able to tell straight away. I couldn't wipe the smile off my face!

But it's early days and I'm saying nothing – not even to her. It might be a one-off for all I know. And Mac's been through a lot, and maybe he's just lonely. And then there's Drew... We'll see. It's all a bit new and scary. But nice. Really, really nice.

Went to the hairdresser's as planned. Only intended to get a trim but ended up getting a cut and colour. I was a bit nervous, but it looks great. It was time for a change, I think.

I keep imagining Jenna's face when she sees it.

Just imagine what she'd say if she ever found out about Mac kissing me! Oh God, what am I doing? Feels like everything's moving very quickly and maybe I should slow it down.

But I'm probably getting way ahead of myself. It was just a kiss after all.

Bet he's forgotten all about it.

25

Mac was quite glad to discover that Tricia wasn't at home that evening. He liked her very much, but he needed to talk to Evan, and it was going to be awkward enough without having Evan's wife bobbing in and out with cups of tea – as lovely as she was.

'Tricia's relieved you're here tonight,' Evan told him as he led him into the living room. 'She's going to one of them make-up parties at her friend's down the road. I don't know why she does it, you know. She'll go there and spend a small fortune on eye stuff and lipsticks and whatever it is they wear, then she'll come home and put it all in a drawer and it'll never see the light of day. You should see how much of it she throws away.'

'I expect it's more of a social thing,' Mac suggested.

'It would be cheaper to go to the pub with her friends,' he said with a grunt. 'Anyway,' he added, brightening, 'she hasn't cooked for us because I told her we'd get a takeaway. We never have takeaways and I've been fancying a Chinese for bloody months. What do you say?'

Mac smiled. 'Sounds good to me.'

It was almost an hour before the takeaway was finally delivered, and Mac and Evan sat on the sofa, trays on their laps, tucking into various dishes and agreeing that this was probably the tastiest meal they'd ever eaten in their lives.

'Don't ever tell Tricia I said that,' Evan warned.

'I won't. I won't say anything to Alison either. She's cooked me a few meals recently and I wouldn't want to hurt her feelings.'

'Terrible cook?'

'No. Actually, she's come on in leaps and bounds. We both have. But it's all healthy stuff, and there's something irresistible about a mixed curry with rice, isn't there? And these little spring rolls. And those prawn crackers.'

'Forbidden fruit always tastes the sweetest,' Evan agreed. 'Best to limit it to the occasional treat, though.' He took a bite of a spring roll and chewed thoughtfully. 'You've mentioned her a few times now – this Alison. Getting serious, is it?'

'She's just a friend,' Mac said, his cheeks burning.

'Hmm. Tell your face that.' Evan grinned. 'There's no shame in it, you know. I'd be delighted for you. Just what you need, if you ask me.'

Mac swallowed a piece of curried chicken and took a gulp of water – not because the curry was hot but because his face was. This was what he'd come here for, wasn't it? To talk things over with Evan. Get his perspective on a situation that Mac felt was running away with him.

'Thing is,' he said uncertainly, 'it's kind of moved on from friendship.'

Evan beamed at him. 'Excellent! I'm so pleased for you.'

'It's complicated though, isn't it?' Mac asked desperately. 'I'm not sure I'm doing the right thing.'

'Whyever not? You clearly like the woman. You've certainly spent enough time with her recently. The two of you must be cordon bleu chefs by now!' He narrowed his eyes. 'When you say "things have moved on from friendship", what exactly do you mean?' He threw up his hands, almost knocking the tray off his lap. 'No gory details, please! I'm an old man. My heart couldn't stand it.'

Mac laughed. 'Nothing like that. But... Well, I tend to walk her home after she's been at mine, and – well – we kiss outside the caravan.'

'Kiss outside the caravan?' Evan roared with laughter. 'Sounds like a teenage romance movie.'

'I know. Pathetic, isn't it?'

'No, no! That's not what I meant.' Evan looked deeply apologetic. 'I'm sorry. I really wasn't making fun of you. It's quite sweet. It just sounded so funny, that's all. The way you put it. So, it's just a kiss?'

'Every evening I see her,' Mac admitted.

'Do you really like her then?'

Mac prodded a prawn with his fork. 'I really do,' he said at last. 'To be honest, I always did. She was my childhood sweetheart.' He gave Evan a wry look. 'She just didn't know it. I was mad about her when we were at primary school, but she never showed any interest in me whatsoever.'

'Well, she's showing interest in you now.'

'Yes, but, she's a widow. I have to be careful.'

'How long has she been a widow, did you say?'

'Nine years.'

Evan waved a hand dismissively. 'Nine years! Well, she's hardly rushing into anything then, is she?'

'I know, but it's still delicate, isn't it? She loved him. A lot. And I know she still misses him.'

'Well, of course she does. He was her husband. You'll have to learn to accept that, Mac, if you're to have a future with her.'

'I do accept it, of course I do. It's not just that, though. Alison's not the problem, is she? It's me. I'm the bloody problem.'

Evan sighed. 'I don't see why.'

'Really? After everything that's happened?'

Evan leaned back in the sofa and helped himself to a large piece of curried beef, which he chewed thoughtfully as he contemplated the issue.

'Well,' he said finally, 'I'm not an expert on these matters, of course, but haven't you been taught to live in the present? Forget about the past. Don't worry about the future. Concentrate only on today. Isn't that what Doug always said to you?'

'He did.'

'And what would Doug be telling you to do now?'

Mac thought about it. 'I think... I think he'd be telling me to go for it,' he admitted at last. 'I think he'd be saying that I've worked hard to put my life straight, and that I've paid the price for what I did in the past. I think he'd tell me to grab a chance of happiness while I can, because you're a long time dead.'

Evan nodded. 'Well, there you go then.'

'What if I let her down though? If things go wrong between us... Look, Evan, right now I'm doing okay. I'm settling in at Watersmeet. I'm happy looking after the animals. All right, I still haven't figured out what I want to do with the rest of my life, but I feel calm and stable and happy. If it wasn't for the people I've lost along the way, and all the hurt I've caused, I'd say life's pretty good. But if Alison and I go any further – if we get really involved – I'm making myself vulnerable again.'

'Go on,' Evan said, listening intently. 'In what way?'

'If I let myself fall in love with her and then we row or break up... would I be able to stay this balanced and steady? Or would I end up back where I started? How do I take the risk?'

'I suppose,' Evan said thoughtfully, 'you have to decide if the risk is worth taking. There's nothing else for it. You either choose to remain as you are and potentially miss out on something wonderful, or you go for it, knowing that it makes you vulnerable, but it could also be the best thing that ever happened to you.'

'Which do I choose?' Mac asked, feeling anguished. 'What do I do?'

'Only you can decide that,' Evan said. 'I think, the way you and Alison are going, feelings are only going to grow and deepen anyway. Maybe you're at the point where it's either let her go now to save the potential pain, or go all in: decide this is what you want and that you're going to do everything in your power to make it work.'

As Mac rubbed his forehead worriedly, Evan asked gently, '*Is* it what you want? Is she worth the gamble?'

They stared at each other and Evan sighed. 'The risk. Is she worth the risk? I'm going to make us a cup of tea while you think it over.'

Mac pushed his food around on the plate, mulling over the conversation. Alison was wonderful, and he was waking up happy for the first time in years. He'd been terrified, kissing her for the first time, but she'd been so warm and welcoming, and clearly glad that he'd done it. In the days that had followed it had become something they did – a kiss outside the caravan before they said goodnight. Half the time it was Alison who initiated it, and he'd got the distinct impression recently that she'd be happy to go further.

And he wanted to. Oh, a part of him longed to. But the fear...

'Is she worth the gamble?' Evan had asked.

The truth was, Mac wasn't sure anything was. He had way too much to lose.

26

Friday 27 March – Project Alison Day 55: Horrible day ahead! Going to the hospital for retinal screening. Really scared. What if it hurts? Rosie's working and I'm not allowed to drive because the drops will affect my vision, but Mac's offered to take me. Hope he waits outside while I have it done. If he hears me scream, I'll die of shame!

'Are you sure you want to come in with me?' Alison cast a sideways glance at Mac as he walked beside her, car keys rattling in his hand. It had taken them ages to find a parking space and they'd driven round and round the various areas of the hospital, until they'd finally found a free space in the very spot they'd first checked. Typical!

Mac had got out of the car and seemed to take it for granted that he was going inside with her, which made Alison very nervous.

'Of course. You don't want to go in there by yourself,' he said, nodding to the smart new building where the diabetic unit was housed. 'Anyway, you might be in there ages. You'll need someone to talk to. And so will I.'

She nodded, determined to look as if none of this bothered her at all. She took a steadying breath and pushed open the door, trying to stay calm as she headed to the reception desk, despite the weird hospital smell and the sight of NHS uniforms.

The receptionist directed her to take a seat in the waiting room, and she and Mac found two chairs next to each other and sat down.

She wanted to make conversation with him, she really did, but she was too nervous. Her mouth was dry, and she felt sick. Every time a nurse came out and called another name her stomach lurched with dread.

'How are you feeling?' Mac asked gently.

'Fine.' She meant to sound bright and cheery, but her voice cracked, and it sounded as if she was about to choke instead.

He held her hand in his, holding her steady, reassuring her without a word.

'Alison Parker?'

'Oh, God!'

'It's okay,' Mac said. 'I'll be right here. Don't worry.'

'You can come through if you like,' the nurse told him. 'Not into the room, but there's another waiting area nearby and you can sit with her while the eye drops take effect.'

'You don't have to,' Alison said weakly.

'Don't be daft. I want to.'

Still holding hands, they followed the nurse through the double doors.

'Just in there, Alison.' The nurse nodded towards another set of doors. 'Follow me,' she told Mac, 'and I'll show you where you can wait.'

Reluctantly, he let go of Alison's hand. 'You've got this,' he murmured, and she nodded, because she didn't want to look like a total wimp even though she knew she was.

Another nurse was waiting inside for her, all youth and vitality and cheeriness. She beamed at Alison.

'Don't look so worried! Is this your first retinal screening?'

Alison nodded. 'I–I've heard it's really painful.'

'Stings a bit,' the nurse said. 'Probably like getting shampoo in your eyes or something. But it wears off very quickly, honestly. The trick is to blink really rapidly as soon as the drops go in.'

'I don't like anything near my eyes,' Alison admitted.

'Oh heck, me neither,' the nurse said, laughing. 'Don't fret, Alison. You'll be fine, and it'll be over before you know it.'

After checking a few details with her and getting her to read some letters from an eye chart, the nurse stood over her and administered the drops. Immediately Alison could feel the effect.

'Blink, blink, blink,' the nurse instructed, and Alison blinked for all she was worth. Before she knew it the stinging faded, and it was done.

'There you go,' the nurse said brightly. 'Now, you just need to go through to the other waiting area and give it a while for the drops to work. You might find your vision goes a bit blurry. Did you bring sunglasses, by the way?'

Alison nodded. 'Although it's not too bright today, is it?'

'You'll need them, believe me,' the nurse said. 'Turn right when you go out of here, then right again and you'll see all the chairs. Someone will fetch you when you're ready for the screening.'

Alison nodded and thanked her. She found the seating area almost immediately and was relieved to see Mac patiently waiting for her. Two other people were sitting together, talking quietly to each other.

Mac smiled and got to his feet when he saw her, guiding her

into the chair even though her vision seemed perfectly fine at that point. 'How was it?'

'Not as bad as I feared,' she admitted.

'I didn't hear the screams,' he said, winking at her. 'You were obviously very brave.'

'Hmm.' She felt quite wrung out from all the stress and relief, and slumped in her chair, not able to chat.

Luckily, he seemed to understand that, and sat quietly with her, not attempting to engage her in conversation.

By the time she was called again, her vision was a little blurry, and she followed the nurse into the examination room a little unsteadily.

The screening process itself was simple enough, and not that dissimilar to screenings she'd had at an optician's. There were a few flashes as photographs were taken of the back of her eyes and then it was done.

'See you in a year,' the technician said.

Alison wrinkled her nose. 'If I reverse the diabetes and I'm not on any medication, will I still have to come?'

The technician laughed. 'Afraid so. We've got you in our sights now, so to speak. You'll get an appointment next year, and then if everything goes well it will be every two years.'

Alison sighed. 'Fair enough.'

Mac was hovering outside, and he slipped his arm through hers. 'All okay?' he whispered.

She nodded. 'That part was fine. I just can't see that well. It's a bit blurry still.'

'Don't worry. I won't let you bump into any doors.'

As they headed through reception to the main doors, someone pushed it open, and she winced.

'I forgot to put my sunglasses on!' She rummaged in her bag and found them, thankfully slipping them on. 'Everything looks *way* too bright!'

Mac led her to the car and made sure she was settled, even though she assured him she was perfectly fine.

'So,' he said, as they drove away, 'another thing ticked off the list. Well done!'

'Yeah, I've got to admit I feel miles better knowing that's out of the way,' she said.

He glanced at her but said nothing. He didn't have to. She knew perfectly well what he was thinking.

'On Monday I'll book that smear,' she said, feeling a sudden warmth and pride as he gave her an approving look. 'Another thing ticked off then, isn't it?'

'You're brilliant,' he told her. 'I'm so proud of you.'

'Thanks, Mac,' she said softly. 'For everything. I don't know if I'd have had the nerve if you hadn't encouraged me. And thanks for bringing me, too.'

'No worries at all.'

She hesitated. 'Would it be cheeky if I asked you to stop at my house? I need to check if I've had any post and make sure everything's okay.'

'Of course. You'll have to direct me.'

Her vision was blurry, but not so blurry she couldn't see where she was going. Around a quarter of an hour after leaving the hospital they pulled up outside Alison's house.

'Would you like to come in?' she asked.

Mac gazed over at the house then back to her. 'Are you sure?'

'I might bump into things,' she said with a grin. 'I need you to guide me.'

He gave her a knowing look. 'Hmm. You might be milking this a bit now. Come on then, let's go.'

It felt weird unlocking the door and walking into her house with Mac at her side. She waited for the feeling of guilt to kick in. After all, this had been Drew's house, too. But strangely there was none of that. What there was, however, was the realisation that this place no longer felt homely or comfortable. She had the oddest feeling that she didn't belong here any more.

Mac bent down and scooped up a handful of letters and handed them to her as he glanced around the hallway.

'Nice house,' he said. 'Nice area, too.'

'Come through,' she said. 'I'll make us a cup of tea.'

'I think *I'll* make us a cup of tea,' he said firmly. 'I don't want any accidents with boiling kettles while you're still wandering around with those sunglasses on.'

She laughed and removed the sunglasses, then led him through to the kitchen, where French doors looked out over the small garden.

'Oh,' Mac said, as he filled the kettle at the sink, 'I see what you mean. Not much scope out there for your gardening plans, is there?'

The garden looked even tinier now she was used to the huge garden at Watersmeet. Surrounded by a six-foot wooden fence, it was quite depressing really, despite the border full of daffodils that had flowered in her absence.

'Not really,' she said, somewhat distracted as she noticed one particular letter that she'd been waiting for. She tore it open as Mac flicked the kettle on and said, 'Where do you keep your cups?'

Alison's eyes scanned the letter, her heart thumping with anxiety and dread. Then she let out a sigh of relief, clutching the piece of paper to her chest.

Mac raised an eyebrow. 'Good news?'

'The best. My bowel test results.' She waved the letter at him. 'No problems.'

His face widened in a smile. 'You did the test?'

'I did.' She'd been too scared to mention it to anyone, even Rosie. Scared she might jinx it. But now she felt free and light as a feather.

'Come upstairs,' she said impulsively, dropping the mail on the table and holding out her hand.

He stared at her, and she laughed. 'I mean to look at the view. It's why we bought the house really.'

Carefully, she led him up the stairs, hoping she'd left her bedroom in a tidy state. Thankfully, she had, and she led him straight to the glass door at the far end of the room, where a Juliet balcony gave them a view of the footpath below and the dock behind the house. Beyond that lay the glorious Humber Estuary.

'Oh, wow,' Mac said. 'I wasn't expecting that!'

'I know. Isn't it brilliant? I always wanted to move back to Kelsea Sands but Drew's work and my work were in West Hull, and you know what the traffic can be like. And then there was the little problem of properties hardly ever coming up for sale in the village. But this view – it meant I could look out and see the Humber and know that I wasn't so far from home after all. The water was flowing towards Kelsea Sands, and it made me feel connected to my family. And further down in the other direction is Hessle Foreshore, and Jenna lives there with the twins. Not on the foreshore but close by. Somehow, we're all together.' She gave an embarrassed laugh. 'I expect that sounds stupid.'

'No,' he said. 'No, it doesn't. Not at all.'

They gazed out at the river. 'Just up there,' he said wonderingly, 'is Watersmeet. That's so strange.'

She nodded. 'I love the Humber,' she told him. 'It's so amazing. The Ouse and the Trent and the Don all feed into it—'

'And the River Hull,' he reminded her.

'Naturally. I love the River Hull, too. It's one of the things I do enjoy about this city. There's water everywhere! All these channels criss-crossing the place, and you can't get from one side of the city to the other without crossing a bridge over the river. Isn't that fabulous?'

'Not so much in traffic jams, or when one of the bridges is up to let a ship through, or being repaired,' he said, his eyes twinkling. 'But I know what you mean. You're like me. You love being near the water. Even when I was in Oxfordshire I had to be beside the river. It's so soothing and calming, isn't it? Even the sea, which is quite tempestuous at times. We're lucky at Kelsea Sands to have both.'

'It puts everything into perspective. No matter what happens, the North Sea tide comes in and out, and the Humber keeps flowing. When you look at it, it makes you feel like – I don't know – that somehow, everything will be all right. And at the same time, like none of it really matters anyway, because we're just temporary little blips on the landscape, and the water will be there long after we're gone.'

She shook her head. 'Sorry. Did that sound depressing?'

'No, not at all. It's something I've thought myself. In fact, I find it quite a comforting thought.'

He smiled at her, and she smiled back, realising that he understood what she was talking about and she had no need to justify herself or apologise.

'So, three things ticked off,' he said.

'I'm getting there, aren't I?'

'You're amazing.'

There was a long silence, then, 'Tea,' he said, half-regretfully.

'Oh yes. That kettle will have boiled by now,' she agreed.

She closed the balcony door and took his hand. Something had shifted between them. She could sense it, and it made her happier than she'd felt in a long, long time.

27

Saturday 28 March – Project Alison Day 56: Going for tea at Mac's. Rosie said I might as well just move in with him. I asked her if she minded that I was spending so much time with him, but she looked at me as if I was daft and said she was over the moon for me. She's going round to her mam and dad's to watch another Harlan Coben thriller. We can't get Netflix in the caravan, and besides, she knows I don't like anything too tense, so she's making the most of it while I'm out.

I offered to help cook tonight but Mac says he's got it all under control and it's my reward for being so brave at the retinal screening yesterday! He's so lovely. I can't believe my luck really, and I'm sure Drew would approve. He'd be happy for me. I know it. I just don't know how Jenna would take it.

But then, there's no need for her to know, is there? I don't know where this is going. Mac might not feel the same way I do after all, and I can't exactly ask him, can I? But sometimes I think I can see it in his eyes, so...

'Can you believe it's nearly April?' Alison mused, as they leaned against the fence, arms folded, watching Jamie Fraser and Ellen MacKenzie grazing contentedly in the dusk.

She and Mac had eaten a delicious meal of slow-cooked beef casserole and had decided that, rather than sitting around watching television or talking, they'd burn off some of the calories by walking around Watersmeet and saying goodnight to the animals. Mac had to shut the ducks and hens up anyway, and Alison said she'd like to go with him.

They'd put the Bennet Sisters and the Dickensian Ducks away for the night, made sure the ponies had water and hay and were healthy and happy, and had now arrived at the cattle pasture. They'd left Carne in the garden, where he was having his usual mad half hour, galloping up and down and tiring himself out before bed. Mrs Beddows had done one of her vanishing acts. Mac suspected she was in someone else's house, conning them out of food.

'The clocks go forward tonight. Well, tomorrow morning. An hour less in bed,' he said.

Alison kept her gaze firmly on the cattle, not wanting her expression to reveal that she'd had a sudden image of herself and Mac waking up together in his bed. What, she wondered, was his bedroom like? She'd seen it, of course, when he'd given her and Rosie a tour of Watersmeet, but she hadn't really taken much notice. She couldn't even remember which bedroom was his. Would she ever get the chance to find out?

She hid a smile as, in her mind, she heard Rosie's voice saying, *Blimey, Ali! What's come over you? Good for you, I say. Now, how are you going to move things forward a bit?*

But then there was also the thought of Jenna, and what *she'd* say. She pushed that image away. She didn't want anything to spoil this perfect moment, as she and Mac stood in the gathering dusk on the shores of the Humber, watching these beautiful red beasts grazing.

They'd been moved from the winter fields back to their favourite pasture. Mac's friend Evan had told him that they liked to watch people passing by, and now that spring was upon them there'd soon be plenty of people wandering along the footpath by the river, gazing in admiration at the two noble Highlanders.

'Egg production's picked up, too,' Mac said. 'The ducks and the hens had a little gift for me this morning. I'll be eating eggs for breakfast, dinner and tea at this rate.'

'Your mum used to sell the eggs,' she told him. 'She used to put them outside and leave an honesty box there.'

'An honesty box.' She loved the way his eyes lit up when he smiled. 'I think it's fantastic that we live in a place where you can put eggs outside for sale and just leave an honesty box there, don't you?'

Her own smile faded. 'Except, I *don't* live here. Not really. And I'll be going home soon.'

It was hard to believe that in little over a month Project Alison would be over, and she'd be back in Hull. She couldn't believe how fast time was flying by.

'Will you miss it?' he asked, turning away from her to focus on the Highlands.

'I won't miss the commute!' She had to make a joke of it, because if she didn't, she might just cry.

'Fair enough.'

'I don't know what I'm going to do with myself really,' she admitted. 'I feel like I'm at a crossroads in my life. I have no idea what's next.'

'What do they call a deer with no eyes? No eye-deer,' he joked.

'That,' she told him sternly, 'wasn't even funny the first time I heard it back in primary school.'

'Aw, come on. It was a *bit* funny!'

Seeing his pleading expression made her laugh. 'Okay. Maybe a teensy bit.'

'I'll take that. And if it's any consolation, you're not the only one at a crossroads. I really haven't got a clue what I'm going to do with myself. You know, it seemed easy enough before – winter, hibernation, that sort of thing. But now it's spring and I feel as if I can't hide away any longer. It's time to do something with my life, but what?'

'Would you be interested in buying and selling commercial property again?' she asked, tentatively, not sure if his old profession held too many unhappy memories.

'No,' he said briefly. 'I've moved on. That's something Ian did, not Mac.'

'You really do separate the two, don't you?' she said curiously. 'Ian and Mac. Like they're two different people.'

'They are,' he said firmly. 'I left Ian behind in his old life. Now I need to figure out what kind of life Mac's going to have.'

She wondered if it was because of the bullying that he wanted to leave Ian behind, though it seemed to her that life had been very cruel to him in many respects. What with the kids at school assaulting him, and then his business partner and so-called best friend betraying him in the worst possible way with his then wife. Even his children seemed to have abandoned him. It didn't seem fair that someone as lovely and kind-hearted and gentle as he was should have been so badly treated. To think, she'd once believed he had a charmed life!

'Well,' she said, 'what sort of thing would you *like* to do? Have you any ideas?'

'Not really. I just know I'd like to make a difference, before it's too late. Do something good, you know? Help someone, somehow.'

That was so typical of him. She'd never met anyone with such a pure soul.

'I do know how you feel. I've been thinking for ages that I should be doing something more with my life than working in a petrol station.'

'Do you regret leaving teaching then?' he asked. 'Because you said yourself you weren't happy doing that any longer, and at least with the petrol station you have no responsibility.'

'No, I'm not thinking about teaching.' She sighed. 'I wish I knew what I *was* thinking about. It's just... well, I know this may sound odd, but I keep thinking about Drew. He was so young. Far too young to die. We had all these plans, and then it was all taken away from us. And I think, I'm still here, and what am I doing with this extra life I've been given? The trouble is, what *can* I do at my age?'

'I think we're both very, very fortunate that we can afford to take our time to think about it,' he said.

'I know. Look at our Rosie. She's got three jobs: cleaning at the pub and the caravan park and working in the chippy in Millensea. Bless her, she works so hard and for very little financial reward. But the thing is, she's happy. Really happy. And I think that's the difference, isn't it? Take Jenna, for instance. She and her husband have both got good jobs with prospects, but are they happy?'

She frowned as she realised that, actually, she didn't think they were. When was the last time she'd seen her daughter laughing or really enjoying herself? When was the last time the two of them had gone out socialising together, or even on holiday? What sort of life was that? What was the point of it all really?

'And the twins,' she continued sadly, 'never get to see them. You know, they spend most of their time watching YouTube or glued to their tablets. I try to take them off them and they act as if I'm that horrible Miss Trunchbull from *Matilda*! They don't seem to have a proper relationship with Jenna and Joel at all.'

'I can hardly talk,' Mac said sadly. 'I have *no* relationship with Wyatt and Sarah. It's funny, when Stella came round to see me, she was upset about her own kids. Ned's working in Wales and Crystal's mostly up at Puffin Point, working with her dad. Stella really misses them. It seems to be a common theme.'

'I guess there are a lot of parents in our position,' she agreed. 'When you think of all the divorced couples out there, and the weekend dads, and the frantic pace of modern life, and the lack of communication...'

The sun was setting. It was harder to see the cattle now. He took her hand, and they began to walk back towards the house.

'We were lucky,' he said. 'Growing up in a place like this at a time when it was a much slower pace of life. No tablets, no internet, no social media. Don't get me wrong, I don't think everything about those days was better than it is now. It's like I said before, it's easy to look back at the past with rose-tinted glasses and stuff yourself on a big bucket of nostalgia, but there were bloody hard times for many people. In some ways, life's so much easier now. But...'

'But there's a lot of pressure on parents,' she said. 'And a real lack of communication between some parents and children. Not all, by any means. But some. I know with Hallie and Ada, when they're not glued to the internet, they're rushing off to parties at fun palaces, or going to dance class or gymnastics, even at the age of seven. And Jenna and Joel are working so much, and now they're probably paying for childcare...' Her voice trailed off as the guilt attacked her again. 'I don't know what's going to happen when I get home,' she admitted miserably.

'With you and Jenna?'

'With all of it. I feel bad for her if I don't have the twins, because I know how stressed she must be, but I'll feel tired and fed up if I have them too much, and – oh, I hate to say this, but *resentful*. I don't want to look after them all the time. I suppose what I want is an impossible dream. I want Jenna and Joel to wake up and realise that their daughters' childhoods are slipping away, and they're missing them. I want them to ease back on the work and spend time with their children before it's too late. But how can they? Life just doesn't work like that, does it?'

But did Joel really have to go to so many conferences and training courses? And did Jenna really have to prove herself so she could one day be a head teacher? And anyway, she'd found time to flirt with a colleague, hadn't she? Time to arrange a night of passion with him while her husband was away. Time to dupe her own mother into babysitting her children so she could get up to all sorts in secret.

She was going round in circles, and she knew it.

'Modern life,' she said with a sigh. 'If only everyone could have the sort of childhood we had.'

Mac squeezed her hand. 'Hmm. Well, the good bits of it, anyway.'

They wandered up the path towards the house, and Alison thought how lovely it looked in the gathering darkness with the kitchen light shining through the window and the outside lamp casting a warm and welcoming glow to guide them home.

Home. What am I thinking? Watersmeet isn't my home!

'Do you want to watch the next episode of *Poirot*?' she asked, still thrilled that she'd found someone who shared her love of cosy detective stories. They'd been treating themselves to an episode most evenings after tea and she looked forward to curling up on the sofa in his snug, with him beside her, all warm and cosy in the lamplight with the fire crackling in the grate and the thick curtains shutting them off from the world.

He didn't reply, seeming deep in thought.

'Mac?'

'Sorry! What did you say?'

'Penny for them.'

He grinned. 'Not worth a penny. Just daydreaming. What were we talking about?'

'*Poirot*,' she said. 'I was asking if you wanted to watch another episode before I go home?'

He hesitated and she felt a momentary disappointment. Had he decided their evenings were getting too boring and cosy? She'd wondered the same thing, recently, but couldn't deny that she enjoyed just being here at Watersmeet with him. It was enough. She didn't need nights out and excitement. She'd done all that years ago. But maybe it was all getting a bit samey for him, and she couldn't blame him if it was.

'We don't have to,' she said quickly. 'If there's something else you'd rather be doing? I mean, we could go over to the pub if you'd prefer?'

'It's not that. I love *Poirot*. I love watching it with *you*. I love our cosy evenings in the snug, don't you?'

She smiled, relieved. 'I really do. So, if it's not that, what is it? Because there's something on your mind, isn't there?'

He drew her to a standstill just outside the kitchen door, and turned to face her, wrapping his arms around her waist. 'I was just thinking,' he said slowly, 'and you can tell me to get lost and there'll be no hard feelings, honestly there won't, but I was just wondering...'

She eyed him curiously. 'Just wondering what?'

He closed his eyes for a moment then said quickly, 'If you'd maybe like not having to rush home after we've watched it? If you'd like, maybe, to stay the night?'

Alison's stomach whooshed with nerves, and her pulse raced. She swallowed, feeling terrified and exhilarated and doubtful and excited all at once.

But looking at Mac, she could see he was experiencing the same sort of emotions, and that his pulse was probably racing, too, and that at this moment they truly were at a crossroads. Which road should they take? Was it too soon? Did they know each other well enough? Did it really matter?

She thought of Drew and felt a momentary sadness that he wasn't here with her right now. But Drew had gone, and life had gone on without him. And she'd had to go on with it, just like the river, flowing endlessly to the sea. Life was all about moving forward. She'd done way too much looking back, longing for the past. Maybe it was time to look to the future.

'I think,' she said, squeezing his trembling hands, 'I'd like that very much.'

28

So this was what Mac's bedroom looked like. He'd very thoughtfully gone to freshen up in the main bathroom, leaving the en suite for her own use. He had a spare toothbrush she could use, and he'd even put out a pair of his pyjamas for her if she wanted to wear them.

She'd washed and brushed her teeth, combed her hair, and stared at her reflection in the mirrored bathroom cabinet, wondering what the heck she was doing. Then she'd slipped on the pyjama top, which was too big for her and fell to just above her knees. Ignoring the bottoms she'd scurried out of the bathroom and clambered into bed, then sat there with the duvet pulled up under her chin, looking round her and trying very hard not to feel sick with terror.

His room, she thought, was a bit odd. This bed, she remembered, was brand new, as was the headboard, and it was a king size one with a good quality mattress by the feel of it and looked rather sophisticated. But the rest of the bedroom – well, it looked a bit like a teenage boy's room. The curtains were very retro, and the wallpaper... Ugh! Even the carpet looked old and a bit faded.

It occurred to her that, apart from the new bed, it probably hadn't been touched since Mac had left for university in 1982, which explained a lot. She supposed she should be thankful there weren't any posters on the walls. Staring at images of a young Debbie Harry and *Charlie's Angels* would have done nothing for her self-esteem.

Speaking of which... She anxiously rubbed her chin, relieved to discover that Hagrid, as she and Rosie now referred to the lone whisker, hadn't started to grow back yet, after being plucked out a few days ago. Imagine the embarrassment of that!

And that gave rise to lots of other thoughts about hair that might be surplus to requirements. It was a different age now. Woman did certain things to themselves that she never would have thought of back in her courting days, and men might expect a particular look. And she hadn't even shaved her legs for a couple of days!

She pulled out the pyjama top and peered down, inwardly groaning. She couldn't deny that her stomach wasn't flat like Farrah Fawcett's had been. Had *anyone's* stomach been as flat as Farrah Fawcett's? She wondered about Mac's ex-wife, Lynne. Did *she* have stretch marks and drooping boobs? Did she visit a beauty salon for regular bikini waxes? Was she a whizz with a Bic razor? Or maybe she was old school and let nature take its course?

Bloody hell, this whole thing was a minefield! She'd never had to worry about all this with Drew. They'd been together for so long that it had never crossed her mind that he might be judging her appearance when they were in bed together. But Mac was a whole new entity, and for all she knew he might keep score, marking her out of ten for various aspects of her body.

She could see it now:

Legs – Bit short and slightly on the hairy side. Very Ernie Wise. 6/10

Stomach – Podgy and saggy. Stretch marks. 5/10

Hips – Good grief! They're enormous! 3/10

Breasts – What breasts? 1/10

Personal Grooming – Hell's bells! Beam me up, Scotty! 0/10

'I don't even know if I can still do this,' she murmured to herself, her panic increasing. 'I'm an old lady. What if there's a no entry sign down there? You hear about such things, don't you? It might be Mission Impossible. Hell, when did I last trim my nose hair?'

Hair! It was proving to be the bane of her life. She'd always had fine hair on her head and worried that she didn't have enough of it. Now she was obsessed with the possibility that she had way too much of it – just not in the right places.

What was she playing at? She was far too old for this sort of shenanigans. Past her best. She should be put out to grass, like old Jacob Armitage and Heatherstone. And there was Mac, all sexy and vibrant and utterly gorgeous. He'd wonder what the heck he'd got himself into. Could she bear to see the look of horror in his eyes when he realised what he'd saddled himself with?

There was a faint tap on the door.

'Yes?' she squeaked, then shook her head. *Yes?* What did that mean? This was his room, not the head teacher's office. 'You can come in.'

But only if you really, really must.

Evidently, he really, really must. He popped his head round the door and said, 'All right?'

Seeing her tucked up in bed, he entered the room and closed the door behind him. He was wearing a clean T-shirt and boxer shorts. He looked lovely, and she envied the fact that he didn't have to worry about whether he'd shaved *his* legs – or anything else for that matter. Men had it so easy, didn't they? She'd bet he hadn't given a thought to how he looked or what she'd think of him.

He climbed into bed beside her. They both sat there, frozen.

'I wasn't sure if this was your side of the bed or not,' she said at last. 'I always sleep on this side you see and...'

He swallowed. 'I usually sleep on this side, so it's perfect.'

'Oh good. That's good, isn't it?'

'Really good.'

Silence.

'I like your...' She cast around for something she admired in the room. 'Headboard.'

'It's new. I ordered it that day when I got the bed from Wansbeck's. Remember?'

Ah yes. The shop where Drew had worked.

She saw the look of horror in his eyes when he realised what he'd said. Well, this was going well.

'The bed's very comfortable,' she told him, bouncing gently up and down on the mattress.

'Isn't it? I tried it out in the shop. I've never bought a bed before. I was a bed-buying virgin.'

He gave her a feeble smile that didn't mask the terror in his eyes.

Oh wow, he's as scared as I am.

The realisation made her suddenly calmer. Braver.

'I feel like an actual virgin right now,' she told him. 'I've never been so scared in my life.'

He gave her a worried look. 'There's no pressure, you know. If you don't want to do this, you don't have to. Please don't feel like I'm expecting anything to happen. We can just have a cuddle and go to sleep if you like.'

'Maybe,' she said thoughtfully, 'we should just see how we feel when we've got used to being in bed together. We could just talk for a while. See what happens.'

'And if nothing happens that's absolutely fine.'

'Absolutely.'

'That's good then,' he said.

They both heaved sighs of relief and lay down, staring up at the ceiling.

'It's a shame I haven't got a television in here,' he said.

'Yes. We could have watched another episode of *Poirot*.' She gave him an innocent look, and he burst out laughing and slid his arm under her shoulders. She turned on to her side and snuggled into him, her head resting on his chest.

'This is nice,' she said happily.

'I'm sorry,' he told her. 'I'm so out of practice with all this.'

'Oh, me too! It's been ten years since...'

Since Drew had got ill and any thoughts of romance had gone out of the window. Life had become all about hospital appointments and doctors and medication and tests. Hard to think about making love when you were in permanent panic mode. And then he'd been too ill, and it was the last thing either of them had cared about. It was just about survival. And when she'd reached out to touch him at night, it wasn't to initiate sex, but to check he was still with her. That he hadn't left her while she'd been sleeping. And one morning, when she hadn't been looking, he had.

A tear rolled down her cheek and a sob escaped before she could stop it.

Mac pulled away and stared at her, horrified. 'Alison? What is it?'

'I'm so sorry,' she said. 'It's not you, honestly. It's just...'

She couldn't speak.

He stroked her hair. 'Drew?'

Miserably she nodded. She'd blown it and she knew it. How could any man be turned on when the woman he was in bed with was sobbing over her dead husband?

'It's just, the last time I was in bed with a man, it was him. And he'd passed away in the night. And I didn't even know.'

'Oh my God.' Mac pulled her closer and held her tightly. 'I'm so sorry. This must be bringing back all sorts of memories for you. Look, if you want to go home, I'll take you. It's no problem. Or if you'd rather I slept in another room—'

'No! No, honestly. I like you being here. I want you to be here. *I* want to be here.' She put her arm around his waist as if to make certain he couldn't leave. 'It just brought it all back, like you said. I really am sorry. I know I've ruined it.'

'You haven't ruined anything. If you can't talk to me about it, who can you talk to? I thought he must have died in a hospital or a hospice. I can't even imagine what it must have been like for you.'

'Horrible,' she admitted. 'But it was nearly nine and a half years ago, and Drew's gone. He's not suffering any more. I can't stay there with him any longer, can I? It's like you said. We move on. We have to.'

'The last time I was in bed with a woman,' Mac said slowly, 'was with Lynne. That was over fifteen years ago now. You can imagine how out of practice I am. Well, you can see it for yourself. Here I am lying beside a beautiful, funny, intelligent woman, and all I've done is tell her I wish I had a television set in my room.'

Despite herself, Alison started to giggle, and a few moments later he was laughing, too.

He kissed the top of her head. 'We're a right pair, aren't we?'

'We are. I was scared stiff, you know. I thought maybe you'd give me marks out of ten for physical appearance.'

'Are you kidding? What do you think I am? But if I was going to do that, you'd get ten out of ten every time.'

She pulled a face. 'You haven't seen what's under this pyjama top.'

'Well, no,' he said quietly. 'I haven't.'

Uh-oh! Now she'd done it.

'I'm scared again now,' she admitted.

'No need. I'm not going to do anything. I think this is such a big deal for us, and it's been such a long time. Let's just cuddle up and talk until we drift off to sleep. There'll be other nights. Lots of other nights.'

'You're so lovely,' she told him.

'I know,' he said, squeezing her to him and kissing the top of her head again. 'You're a lucky woman.'

She kissed his chest and snuggled further into him, feeling relaxed and warm and safe.

This isn't at all how it was meant to go, but it feels right, and I'm happy.

She realised, with surprise, that she genuinely was. This kind, sweet, gentle man *made* her happy. He made her feel secure and like nothing would ever hurt her again.

I think I love him! How has that happened?

Her eyelids drooped and she allowed them to close. Her last thought before she fell asleep was, *I hope to God I don't drool on him.*

29

The sunshine streaming through the unlined curtains woke Mac up, and he mentally groaned, swearing to himself for the umpteenth time that he'd buy some new ones, because those rubbishy ones hanging at the window were so old and thin they were practically useless.

As he wondered what time it was and considered whether he should get up, because the animals would need seeing to and it was clearly daylight, he remembered that the clocks had gone forward earlier that morning and it was now an hour later than it should have been.

And as he remembered that he remembered something else, and his eyes flew open in shock, and he found himself staring at Alison, who was sound asleep beside him.

Something within him lurched with joy, excitement and disbelief. It had been many, many years since he'd woken up to find himself beside someone – let alone someone he cared about so much. A few months ago, he'd have said this would have been an impossible dream. Yet here she was, flesh and blood and completely real.

He hardly dared breathe as he studied her face as she slept. She was even prettier now than she'd been as an eighteen-year-old, the last time he'd seen her before leaving Kelsea Sands behind. He couldn't believe she'd been worried that he'd criticise her looks in any way. There was nothing to criticise. She was perfect. Not just physically but as a person, too. She listened to him, she understood him, she cared about him, she made him laugh. She'd given him hope.

Mac had seriously thought this part of his life was over. After everything had fallen apart with Lynne, he'd believed he'd be alone forever, and a large part of him knew that was only what he deserved. He'd never imagined for one moment, when he returned to Kelsea Sands, that he'd find someone who seemed to like him as much as he liked her. Especially not Alison, of all people!

Yet here she was. Fast asleep in his own bed, looking like an angel in his pyjama top. He thought about the previous evening and cringed with embarrassment. It hadn't gone at all as he'd hoped. Bloody hell, had he really said he wished he had a telly in here?

But she'd been as nervous as him, he remembered. And then there'd been the shadow of Drew hanging over them. He didn't blame her for crying, and he understood totally why she'd been so upset, but it had added another layer to his insecurities.

He wasn't lying when he said he was out of practice. He wasn't sure he even remembered what he was supposed to do. And if the last person Alison had slept with was her husband, that would have been, as she said, ten years ago, before he'd got ill, when Drew was only in his early fifties and probably looked a heck of a lot better than Mac did right now.

No matter which way he looked at it, there was no escaping

the fact that he was sixty-two years old, and hardly the stuff of women's fantasies. What if she found him unattractive? What if he disappointed her? Hell, what if he couldn't even manage to do it at all?

He'd been literally shaking when he got ready in the bathroom last night, and seeing her sitting there in bed waiting for him had nearly made him turn around and head straight back in there. It was like she was watching him, judging him as he walked towards the bed, mentally assessing whether he was worthy of her and if he'd be up to the job.

Well, he hadn't been, had he? In fact, he hadn't even attempted it. And now he wasn't sure that he ever would. Despite what he'd said last night about them having lots more nights ahead of them, the fact remained that she was going home in a few weeks, he hadn't told her everything about himself, and she might not want anything to do with him when she found out the truth. Even putting those two *huge* factors aside, he wasn't convinced he'd have the nerve to suggest she stay the night again.

As lovely as it had been to fall asleep with her in his arms and to wake up beside her the next morning, it wasn't what he'd promised her, was it? Not literally promised her, but the implication had been there, and he couldn't help but feel he'd let her down. God, what a bloody mess he was! She'd be far better off without him.

He rolled over on to his back and contemplated what to do now. He didn't want to risk waking her up and face all that awkwardness again, but at the same time he *wanted* her to wake up. He wanted to talk to her, to reach out and touch her, just to stroke her face and experience the joy of starting the day with her. And he had the animals to see to. But if he moved and she woke up and she was embarrassed or upset to find herself there...

He realised that his sixty-two-year-old bladder had made the decision for him, and he slipped out of bed as quietly as he could and headed into the main bathroom. Washing his hands a few minutes later, he stared at his reflection in the mirror on the wall and shook his head.

'You absolute moron. What a bloody mess you've made of everything.'

He sighed and picked up his toothbrush. Might as well clean his teeth and get dressed. But would that be rude? Would Alison consider it a snub, a rejection if he wasn't in bed beside her when she woke up? Oh, hell! Why was everything so complicated? He was so useless at all this!

But the Bennet Sisters and the Dickensian Ducks needed to be let out and he couldn't put that off. Maybe if he was quick, he could see to the animals then sneak back upstairs without Alison even knowing.

He quickly pulled on the jeans he'd left in the bathroom the previous night and padded downstairs, slipping on his trainers, which were in the hallway. He opened the kitchen door and Carne jumped off his bed and rushed over to him, wagging his tail furiously.

Mrs Beddows was nowhere in sight. He unlocked the back door and he and Carne stepped outside into a landscape where British Summer Time had officially arrived, the sun was actually warm and the skies were clear and blue.

He breathed in the fresh air and gazed, as he always did, across the river, feeling a peculiar sense of wellbeing and contentment. Then he remembered he was in a hurry, and leaving Carne sniffing around the lawn, he rushed to release and feed the ducks and hens and check on the ponies and the Highlands.

Returning to the house, he met Mrs Beddows stalking home after a night on the tiles.

'I won't ask,' he told her. 'A lady's entitled to her secrets.' Though how much of a lady she was was anyone's guess.

He filled the water bowls and gave both the cat and the dog their breakfast, then hesitated. Should he make breakfast in bed for Alison? Or should he let her sleep? Should he try to sneak in beside her and pretend he was still asleep himself, or should he admit he'd already been downstairs to see to the animals?

After changing his mind several times, he finally made two mugs of tea and carried them carefully upstairs, placing them quietly on the bedside table. She was still sound asleep, and he slowly removed his jeans, hardly daring to breathe, then climbed into bed beside her.

Slowly, slowly, he slid down the bed, pulling the duvet over himself and let out a small sigh of relief.

'You took your time.'

He turned to face her, and she opened one eye and smiled at him.

He grinned back. 'Sorry. Did I wake you?'

'Yes, but I'm glad you did. You gave me the chance to clean my teeth. Morning breath.'

He laughed. 'I went downstairs to see to the animals.'

'What a responsible person you are,' she told him. She opened her other eye and smiled even wider. 'Ooh, have you made tea?'

'I have. Do you want it now?'

'In a minute. Thank you.' She sighed and rolled over on to her back. 'That was the best night's sleep I've had in ages.'

'I expect this bed is a lot more comfortable than a caravan bed,' he said.

'It wasn't that.' She turned to look at him, stroking his face. 'It was because you were there beside me, and you made me feel safe.'

He was so touched he could barely speak.

'Well,' he managed at last, 'I'm very glad about that.'

'So am I.'

'Alison, I'm sorry. About last night, I mean. I know it didn't go as expected.'

'No, it didn't, but that doesn't matter, does it?'

He eyed her worriedly. 'It doesn't?'

'Not at all.'

She shuffled closer to him – so close their noses were almost touching. Her eyes were so wide and blue and innocent, and she had such soft, velvety skin. His fingers stroked her cheek, and she closed her eyes briefly, a smile playing on her lips.

He moved very slightly closer and kissed those lips, unable to resist a moment longer. Her eyes opened, and he saw a look in them that he recognised, because it reflected an emotion that he was experiencing himself. His hand cradled her face, and he kissed her again, his other arm slipping around her shoulders, pulling her half on to him. She moaned, her leg rising over his, while his tongue probed her mouth and he heard her breathing quicken as his own heart thudded with excitement.

She pulled back and shrugged off the pyjama top. Her expressions and little gasps encouraged him as he explored her with his hands, tentatively at first, but with increasing confidence as desire overrode everything else.

His fear ebbed away. His doubts might never have existed, as they put the past behind them and moved forward together into something that felt so right, so perfect, he could only wonder what the rest of his life had been for.

Because this – this was all that mattered, and all he cared about. This woman, lying beneath him, gazing at him as if he was the most wonderful man who'd ever lived, showing him with every sound, every slight movement, every touch, that she wanted him, needed him – she was *everything*.

It was a long time before they remembered the tea. And by then it was stone cold.

30

They had a leisurely breakfast of omelette made with cheese, spinach, and a few mushrooms that hadn't gone into the beef casserole. They sat at the kitchen table, sipping coffee and smiling at each other, as if they'd discovered something amazing and it was their secret – something no one else would ever know or understand.

Afterwards they took Carne for his morning walk, strolling up Weltringham Road towards the sea, arm in arm. Alison realised there was no longer any question over whether they were just friends, or even whether they were casually 'seeing each other'. Things had moved way beyond that, and she knew Mac shared her feelings without either of them having to say a word. It was as if, she thought, it was meant to be. Like there was something inevitable about it all. She would never understand how she'd barely noticed him when they were at school together.

But then, if she had, she might never have married Drew, and she could never regret that. She would never stop loving her husband or being grateful for the years they'd spent together.

She felt so fortunate that she'd been given the opportunity to share her life with not one, but two amazing, kind, gentle men. All women should be so lucky.

She thought about Jenna and wondered what her relationship with Joel was really like, and why her daughter would risk losing everything she had for the sake of a meaningless fling.

But she didn't want to dwell on sad things or worrying things right now. It was Sunday morning, and spring was in the air, and she wanted to savour every moment of this beautiful day.

They reached the church and stopped a moment to lean on the metal gate and gaze at the sad, empty building.

'Our Rosie was in the Brownies there,' she told Mac. 'For a short while anyway, until she got kicked out.'

His eyebrows shot up in surprise. 'She got kicked out of the Brownies? Never! No one ever gets kicked out of the Brownies!'

'Rosie did. I'll tell you about it one day. And I remember seeing you in your Cub's uniform. Aw, you did look cute in your little green cap.'

He nudged her indignantly. 'I was a very good Cub. There was certainly no question of me getting kicked out of there!'

'I used to like going to that church,' she admitted wistfully. 'It wasn't like Niall's church in Millensea, or the one at Weltringham. They're much bigger and grander, obviously, and far older. But there was something warm and cosy and friendly about this little place. Don't you think?'

'I do. Though Mum stopped going after Dad left. We never went to Sunday services after that.'

He'd never spoken about his dad to her before, and she wanted to ask him so much but didn't want to spoil things between them. If he wanted to tell her, he would. When he was ready.

'Did she lose her faith?' she asked instead. 'I don't think my mam and dad ever had any faith, but Mam liked to hedge her bets, so we'd go to church maybe three or four times a year. She never missed the Easter and Christmas services though. Aw, it's such a shame it had to close. Look at it now. So sad.'

'I don't think it was so much that she lost her faith,' Mac said. 'I think she was ashamed. Ashamed that Dad had left her. Us. She didn't want to face people. That's when she really turned to animals. She said they didn't judge her.'

'I don't think anyone would have judged her,' Alison said, shocked.

'Maybe not.' He shrugged. 'That's how it felt to her, though. The disgrace. Divorce wasn't common in those days, and to be an abandoned wife was something shameful. She thought people would blame her. Say she'd done something wrong.'

Alison nodded. 'I understand that.'

'She *didn't* do anything wrong,' he told her quickly. 'It was him. He wasn't cut out for family life.'

'Did he—I mean, was there someone else?'

'I don't think so.' He turned, checking on Carne who was busy sniffing the hedgerows, his little tail wagging furiously. 'I only saw him once after he left. When I was at university. He came to see me. I don't even know how he knew I was there. I never mentioned I'd seen him to Mum, and she never said anything, so...'

'What did he want?'

'To tell me he was sorry for abandoning me.' Mac gave a short laugh. 'I told him not to worry. I was perfectly happy without him.'

'And were you?' she asked gently.

'Not really.' He gave her a knowing smile. 'Well, not when I was younger anyway. I always wondered, you know. Why? What had I done wrong? But by the time he got in touch I'd realised it wasn't my fault, and I was way past caring. He never sent Mum anything towards my keep, you know, and when I brought that up, he said, "Well, why should I? She had way more money than I ever did."

'I told him I didn't think that was the point, and that surely he'd wanted to contribute to his own child's upbringing? And he laughed and said, "You've got a lot to learn, lad." I always swore I'd never be like him, you know,' he added. 'I promised myself I'd be the best father in the world, and that my kids would always know how much I loved them, and that I'd always be there for them. Boy, was I ever fooling myself.' He shook his head. 'Come on. Carne's getting a bit antsy now.'

She took his arm, and they continued walking. Just past the church was a five-barred gate – the entrance to a footpath that led to the fields behind the church and, beyond that, the wetlands. It was overgrown with bushes and trees, and long grass made the footpath barely visible.

Mac pulled her to a halt and nodded. 'Look at that.' He scooped Carne up in his arms as Alison turned to look and saw a life-size statue of a deer facing them.

'Oh, wow,' she breathed. 'How have I never noticed that before? How long has it been there?'

He grinned. 'No eye-deer.' Then, as she nudged him, his smile turned to a frown. 'Er, you do realise it's not a statue, don't you?'

She laughed. 'Don't be daft. Of course it's a statue. No way would a real deer stand so still and stare at us like that. It would be long gone.'

Carne yapped furiously and the 'statue' turned its head and cantered away, disappearing into the undergrowth.

Alison's mouth fell open in shock and Mac lifted her chin, laughing. 'Told you.'

'Oh my God,' she said. 'This place is absolutely perfect.'

'It is,' he said, as they continued their walk. 'I'd forgotten, and I don't know how I'd forgotten. I can't imagine living anywhere else but here now. I just wish...'

He didn't finish the sentence.

'You just wish what?' Alison urged.

'I just wish Wyatt and Sarah could see it. I wish I'd brought them here when they were little. I wish they'd got to see more of their grandma. I wish they could see Watersmeet and meet Jacob Armitage and Heatherstone, and Ellen MacKenzie and Jamie Fraser, and Mrs Beddows and the Dickensian Ducks and the Bennet Sisters. Yes, and even this annoying little swine,' he added, rolling his eyes as Carne tugged on the lead.

'More than anything,' he said, 'I wish they'd come to see me, and believe me when I tell them that I love them so much, and I'm so sorry we lost touch, and I'd do anything to change what happened.'

'Well,' Alison said slowly, 'have you tried to tell them that?'

'No,' he admitted. 'I gave up years ago.'

'But why? Why don't you try again?'

'After all this time? What if they put the phone down? What if they don't want to know me? What if they hate me and they tell me so? One thing believing they do. Quite another hearing it from their own mouths.'

'You know,' she said, 'you told me that I lived too much in the past, and you were right. But if you ask me, your problem is that you won't look to the future.'

He swapped the lead to his other hand. 'I don't know what you mean.'

'Yes, you do. You say you only think about today because that's all we've got. And you're right. Today *is* all we've got. But our today is shaped by what we did yesterday, and our tomorrow is shaped by what we do today. If you want your future to be a good one, you have to lay the foundations in the present. You have to start fixing things now, Mac, because one day, your today is going to be your last, and if you haven't done everything you can to put this right it's going to be full of regret.'

He said nothing, and his stride lengthened as if he was trying to walk away from her. But Alison wasn't giving up and she kept pace with him. They headed rapidly down the road, the sea growing ever closer, and Carne's ears pricked up with excitement, his nose sniffing the salty air in anticipation.

As they finally reached the beach, Mac unclipped the lead, and Carne raced off along the sand, yapping joyfully at the rolling waves.

Mac dug his hands in his jacket pockets and turned to Alison.

'When I – when I was going through a hard time, and my marriage had ended, and things were... Well, they were really bad. Back then, my mother used to write to me. Proper letters, written with her fountain pen on thick, unlined paper. She always found me. I moved around a lot, but she tracked me down. I didn't reply, but she never stopped writing. And one day, three years ago, I picked up the phone and I called her, and we talked and talked.'

She waited, her heart aching as she heard the grief in his voice.

'She never said a single word about all the letters I hadn't answered. She was just glad to hear from me. After that, I called her every week.'

His eyes gleamed with unshed tears. 'She never gave up on me, Alison. Why did *I* give up on *my* kids? Why am I such a coward?'

She moved to him and put her arms around his waist, resting

her head on his chest. 'You're not a coward,' she told him. 'You've just had a lot to deal with, and maybe you made mistakes. But now you know that, and you want to put it right.'

'They might not be as forgiving as Mum was,' he murmured into her hair.

'No, they might not,' she agreed. 'But you'll never know unless you try, will you?'

He rested his chin on her head, holding her close, sheltering her from the sudden gusts that blew in from the North Sea. He made her feel safe, protected, cared for. She knew he could do the same for his children if they'd give him another chance, but he had to give *them* a chance first. He had to try, or he'd never know.

'I'll write to them,' he said at last. 'You're absolutely right. It's time I started to put plans in place for the future. I need to talk to Gavin about something, sort things out with Stella. Most of all, though, I want my children back in my life so badly, and I have to make the first move. I can't guarantee they'll want anything to do with me. They might even hate me. But I'll try. I won't give up on them. Not again.'

'I'm so proud of you,' Alison whispered.

She wasn't sure he heard her, what with the wind rushing round their ears, and the pounding of the waves, and Carne's happy barking. But she thought maybe he could feel it as she stood there with him, holding him tight, silently sending him all the love and support she knew he deserved.

31

'Well,' Evan said, raising his glass and clinking it against Mac's, 'here's to new beginnings and happy endings. I couldn't be more pleased for you.'

They were sitting in the light, spacious restaurant at Captain Taylor's Hotel on the promenade at Millensea. Large bay windows ran the full length of the room, providing enviable views out to sea. On a day like today – the last day of March – where the sky was cloudless and the sun shone, even a slightly run-down little seaside town like this looked beautiful.

It was Tuesday lunchtime, and Evan had an hour before returning to work, so they'd taken the opportunity to meet up for a tasty meal of fish and chips, washed down with alcohol-free beer.

It had been Mac's suggestion to meet. He wanted to tell Evan about his plans for the future and ask him what he thought of them. He'd had no intention of telling him how things had moved on with Alison, but somehow he couldn't contain his happiness, and he'd given his new, but already dear friend a very discreet version of events.

'It seems to me,' Evan said, 'that things are finally coming right for you. Your mother would be delighted. She always said that Kelsea Sands would be the place you'd find your happiness. She kept telling me so. "If I can just get him to come home, Evan," she'd say, "I just know everything would be all right then." Leaving Watersmeet to you was never just about the animals, you know. She wanted you to have a home where you could live the sort of life you deserved.' He looked up at the ceiling and raised his glass again. 'Well played, Sheila, my dear. Well played.'

Mac thought Evan was getting slightly carried away. 'It's not as cut and dried as all that, is it?' he said.

'I don't see why not,' Evan said comfortably. 'Sounds to me like you've got great plans for Watersmeet, of which I heartily approve, and I'm sure your mother would, too. And you've clearly got the girl. What more do you need?'

'My children, for a start,' Mac reminded him. 'I've written to them, care of Lynne and Terry's address, but there's no guarantee they'll reply. Lynne and Terry might not even pass the letters on.'

'What's for you won't go by you,' Evan said. 'You've told me you'll be persistent, and persistence pays off. Water cuts through rock, not because it's stronger but because it keeps on going, wearing the rock away through time. All those vast valleys and gorges cut out by water!' He gave him a resigned look. 'You only have to look at our vanishing shoreline to know that. Persistence, Mac. That's what it takes.'

'Maybe,' Mac said doubtfully. 'But then there's Alison.'

Evan sighed. 'You really know how to kill a mood, don't you? What more do you want from her? Is it the L word?' He nodded. 'If you want my advice, you need to say it to her first. Women like that sort of thing. Once she's sure you love her, she'll be happy to say it back, you wait and see.'

'How can I tell her I love her?' Mac demanded. 'Don't you think there's something more pressing I should tell her first?'

Evan looked confused. 'There is? Like what?'

As Mac stared at him, his expression changed. 'Oh! Yes, I see what you mean. Well, I suppose you have a point,' he said, almost reluctantly. 'I mean, she probably does have to know, doesn't she? Well...'

'Yes,' Mac said firmly. 'She does. I can't build a future with Alison on anything less than complete honesty. There's been way too much deceit and lying in my past, and I can't start a new life without coming clean about my old one.'

'Fair play,' Evan said. He gulped some of his beer and pulled a face. 'It's not the same, is it? What I wouldn't give for a pint of Guinness right now, but I have house calls later and I can't exactly go on the bus. What can you do?' He sighed regretfully. 'So, when are you going to tell her?'

'I don't know,' Mac admitted. 'I'm terrified. I have no idea how she's going to take it, and I can't help thinking I should have come clean before we – you know.'

'But if you *had*, you might never have – *you know*.'

'Thanks for that,' Mac said, aghast. 'So you *do* think she'll break up with me after she knows the truth?'

Evan threw up his hands. 'It was a joke! Just a joke. If you're honest with her and explain what was going on at the time, and how you felt, and why you did what you did, I'm sure she'll understand. Your mother did.'

'My mother adored me.'

'Sounds to me like Alison adores you, too.'

'I wouldn't go that far,' Mac said, his eyes widening. 'It's very early days. Fragile. It could so easily be broken.'

'Then, maybe don't tell her until it's not so fragile?' Evan suggested cautiously.

Mac shook his head. 'It wouldn't be fair. She deserves the truth. And like I said, I can't start a new life with this hanging over me.' He paused, thinking. 'I'll invite her round for tea tomorrow night. Tell her everything.'

'Hmm. You do know tomorrow's April Fool's Day?'

'That ends by lunchtime, doesn't it? Anyway, it has nothing to do with anything. I need to get this off my chest and then, if she'll still have me, Alison and I can begin our new life together.'

'At Watersmeet?'

Mac smiled. He couldn't help it. Just the thought of Alison sharing his home with him gave him a warm, happy feeling inside. He just had to hope that she understood what had happened. If he lost her now, he didn't know how he'd ever get over it.

'It's such a gamble though,' he murmured, his heart thudding as he realised what he had to lose.

'*Life* is a gamble,' Evan said kindly. 'From the minute we're born we're battling the odds, aren't we? Every decision we make could take us lower or higher than we've ever dreamed. And we keep gambling, flipping over the cards, throwing the dice, making bets on our future. If you think about it, it's hardly worth worrying. The odds are stacked against us from the start, because we all know how the game ends, for each and every one of us. Maybe it's the game itself that's the thrill. Why else would we keep playing it?'

'And if I lose this throw of the dice?'

'Then you go off on another path, and you find something else you care enough about to gamble on. You think you won't, but you will. We're all gamblers. We can't help it. There's always another game to play, another challenge to face, another risk to take. We move on, Mac. We move on and we survive.' He shrugged. 'Until we run out of chips and the game's over. Who knows after that?'

'This is a cheery conversation,' Mac said.

'What I'm trying to say is, if you love her, and it's quite obvious by the pathetic expression on your face that you do, then you're going to have to take a chance and tell her the truth.'

'But you know me,' Mac said quietly. 'You know what might happen. What I might do if I'm thrown off balance.'

'And I'll be right here to kick you up the backside and get you on an even keel again. But trust me, it won't. You've been down that road before and you know where it leads. You have support systems in place.'

'Doug's gone,' Mac reminded him.

'Doug was just a tiny part of it. You know where to go, what to do. But I honestly don't think you'll need it. You're older, stronger, wiser, and you've got so much to look forward to. These plans of yours – wonderful! A house that you love. Relationships with your sister and your children to focus on and mend. You can do this, Mac, with or without Alison. You must believe that. Sooner or later we all have to stand alone. It's the way of the world.'

'Bloody hell. I feel like I'm sitting here with Confucius,' Mac joked. 'When did you get to be so philosophical?'

'I've watched a lot of Jim Carrey interviews.' Evan glanced at his watch. 'I'll have to go. Duty calls.' He got to his feet, passing Mac enough money to cover the cost of the meal plus a generous tip, despite Mac's protests. 'You're going to be okay, you know, whatever happens. But I'll be rooting for you, and I really, genuinely hope that it goes well. Let me know, won't you? I shan't get a wink of sleep until I know you two have booked the church.'

Mac shook his head, laughing, as Evan headed out. He was

lucky to have such a funny, kind and understanding friend. It was more than he deserved.

And Alison? If he lived to be 120, he'd never be able to make up for what he'd done and earn the right to have a woman like her by his side. But maybe Evan was right. Life was a gamble, and sometimes you just got lucky.

And sometimes you had to stop asking if you really deserved that luck and just appreciate it for what it was and enjoy every moment while it lasted.

The rest of his life would begin tomorrow night.

He could only hope the cards would fall in his favour.

32

'I'll bet you feel so much better now that plaster cast's off, Auntie Cherry,' Rosie said as they slipped into their seats at a table in the Driftwood cafe. 'It must have been a right pain for you.'

Alison watched, smiling, as her mam stretched out her arm, examining it. 'Oh, it wasn't that bad, and I'm amphibious now, so that's a good thing.'

'I think you mean ambidextrous, Mam,' she said, shaking her head affectionately. 'Unless you're turning into a frog or something.'

'Well, whatever, I can do all sorts with my left hand now, which I think will be very useful for the future. You never know when you're going to need skills like that. If I were you two, I'd start practising now.'

'I'll take that on board,' Rosie said, giving Alison an amused glance. Her expression changed as Alison quickly turned over her mobile phone, and she sat back in her chair, arms folded. 'Oh yes? Something you don't want us to see?'

Alison blushed. 'Don't be daft.' She gave Rosie a subtle kick under the table, but Rosie didn't do subtle.

'Ow!' She reached down and made a huge song and dance about rubbing her leg. 'What did you do that for?'

'I think,' Mam said, 'that she's trying to tell you not to open your big mouth in front of me.'

'Mam...' Alison hardly knew where to look. 'It's not that, honestly. It's just—'

'Hello, ladies. Nice to see you all in here.' Mrs Miller arrived at the table, beaming at the three of them. 'Aw, Cherry. You've got your cast off! Smashing. Bet that's a relief.'

'Don't get her started,' Alison advised. 'How are you, Mrs Miller? No Emmy today?'

'I'm right as rain, love, and our Emmy's just through there in the shop dealing with some customers.' She nodded at the archway. 'What can I get you all?'

'Just three teas, please,' Mam said.

'By, I'll never make my fortune with you three, will I?'

'I thought you'd be busier now,' Rosie said, 'what with Tide's Reach being open again and the birdwatchers and hikers out and about.'

'Oh, don't worry about that. You should have been here earlier. Couldn't move in here for people wanting cooked breakfasts, and they'd no sooner gone than the lunchtime crowd arrived. Trouble is, I don't have enough tables. I could do to expand through there, but that would mean losing the shop, and we need a shop, don't we? God knows, we've lost everything else here.' She sighed. 'Anyway, that's a worry for another day. Three teas coming right up.'

The moment she'd moved away, Alison's mother leaned forward, her face bright with delight. 'So, this text message. Is it Ian? I mean, Mac? Go on, you can tell me. I promise I won't say a word to your father. We all know how he loves to gossip.'

Dad? He's the last one to gossip. It's you I'm worried about.

Alison glanced around the cafe then leaned forward, her arms folded on the table. 'It's nothing much. He's invited me round for tea tomorrow night, that's all.'

Rosie wrinkled her nose. 'Oh, is that it? Well, nothing new about that. He's always inviting you round for tea.'

'Yes, but usually I'm helping him make it. He says he's cooking, and he wants me to arrive just in time for him to dish out so I don't get caught up in the prep, and... and he said he wants to talk to me about something.'

'OMG!' Rosie squealed and clapped her hands.

'You know,' Mam said thoughtfully, 'you'd never believe you're forty-three, our Rosie.'

'Thanks, Auntie Cherry.' Rosie rolled her eyes. 'Did you not hear what Ali just said? Mac's invited her round for dinner and he's got something he wants to talk to her about.'

'Yes, I broke my arm, not my eardrums,' Mam said with a tut. 'Now, Alison,' she said, turning to her daughter with an earnest expression on her face, 'you need to be ready. When a man says he wants to talk to you about something it quite often means one thing – and it's not a proposal of marriage. It's manspeak. They have their own language, you know. A sort of code that we're expected to understand. It could be that what Ian really wants—'

'Mac,' Alison interrupted automatically.

'All right, all right,' said her mother, with an impatient wave of her mended arm. 'It could be that what *Mac* really wants is a bit of how's-your-father.'

'How's-your-father?' Rosie bit her lip and gave Alison a sly look.

'Rumpy-pumpy,' Alison's mother explained.

Rosie shrugged, her eyes wide with innocence. 'Sorry, Auntie Cherry. I'm not following.'

Alison averted her gaze as her mother sighed with exasperation and said, 'You know! A bit of the other. Getting his leg over.'

Rosie threw up her hands. 'I'm sorry, I just don't know what you mean.'

'For goodness' sake! Sexual intercourse!'

'Auntie Cherry!'

'Mother! Wash your mouth out with soap,' Alison commanded, as she and Rosie burst out laughing and her mam gave them an indignant look.

'Oh, I see. You were having me on. Well, you can joke all you like but it's a serious business. Now, Mac is a lovely young lad—'

'Of sixty-two,' Rosie mumbled.

'And I have every respect for him, but the fact remains he's a man, and men have needs. It's as well to be prepared.'

'Don't worry, Mam,' Alison said sweetly, 'I won't let him touch me.'

'What? Are you insane?'

Alison stared at her. 'You said I should be prepared!'

'Yes, and so you should! Put your best bra and pants on, and for goodness' sake, shave your legs. And take a toothbrush in case he wants you to stay over, because you don't want to put him off you before you've even got started, especially since you don't know what he'll be cooking. And if there's garlic bread on offer, avoid, avoid, avoid, and make bloody sure it goes in the bin before he can eat any.'

Alison was speechless, which was a shame because it gave Rosie the perfect opportunity to say airily, 'Oh, that ship's already sailed.'

'I can't believe you just said that!' she gasped, as her mother whooped and clapped her hands.

'You know, you'd never believe you're eighty-four, Auntie Cherry,' Rosie said sarcastically.

'Is this true?'

Alison groaned inwardly as her mother leaned over and grasped her arm, her eyes bright with excitement. 'Have you and Mac done the dirty deed?'

'How many euphemisms can you come up with in one afternoon?' Alison shook her head in wonder. 'All right, just keep your voice down, will you? Rosie, remind me never to tell you anything in confidence ever again.'

'It's only sex, Ali,' Rosie said, her eyes twinkling. 'We've all done it. And anyway, it's your own fault. You should have given me all the details, but you won't, which I think is dead mean. Do you know, Auntie Cherry, she won't tell me anything about it! I mean, what's the point of doing it if you're not going to spend hours relaying every detail to your favourite cousin afterwards?'

Alison's mouth fell open as her mother nodded. 'It does seem a bit mean. So come on, love, spill the beans. I mean,' she added hastily, 'I don't want any of the ins and outs, so to speak, but just tell me if it was worth it. Was Mac good in bed?'

There was a clattering sound and they all turned, stunned to see Stella standing in the archway between the shop and the cafe, a carrier bag lying on the floor and cans of baked beans and chopped tomatoes rolling along the slates.

'Bloody hell,' Alison murmured, horrified.

'Oh heck,' Rosie said. 'Awks or what?'

'Stella, love,' Mam cried, waving to the white-faced woman as if she'd just spotted her best friend. 'How smashing to see you. How are you? Would you like to join us? We're about to have tea.'

Stella bent down and gathered her spilled shopping. Stuffing it in the carrier bag, she walked hesitantly over to the table.

'You and Mac?' she asked Alison. 'My brother?'

Alison's heart skipped. She hated confrontations. 'Er, yes.'

'Since when?' Stella demanded.

Alison looked round at her mother and cousin for support. 'Well, not long,' she said faintly.

'Long enough, though,' Rosie said defiantly.

'Clearly,' Stella said. 'Well, I'm glad to see he's got over our mother's death so quickly. I'd hate to think he was grieving or anything silly like that.'

Alison's eyes narrowed. She might not like confrontation, but she wasn't about to let Stella get away with that. 'He loved your mother very much. Of course he's grieving for her. He misses her.' She hesitated, hardly wanting to be nice to this woman at all, but knowing Mac wanted to build bridges with her. 'He misses you too.'

'Sure he does.' Stella gave a bitter laugh. 'If Ian – or Mac as he insists on calling himself these days – really missed me, he'd do as I asked and give me my due. By rights Watersmeet should be mine anyway and everyone knows it, but I've said I'll accept half of it and I've offered to buy his half from him. What more can I do? He's just so bloody unreasonable. And now I know why. He's got some stupid notion of playing happy families with you!'

'He's building a new life for himself,' Alison said, forcing herself to stay calm, even though she was seething. 'Can't you just accept that and move on? Let him be happy.'

'Let him be happy?' Stella gave her a pitying look. 'You really don't have the first idea, do you? You think you know him? You don't. He doesn't deserve to be happy.'

'Well,' Rosie said angrily, 'your ex-husband clearly doesn't share your opinion of him.'

Stella and Alison both turned to look at her, each clearly as surprised as the other.

'Gavin?' Stella asked. 'What's he got to do with it?'

Alison heard the catch in her voice and felt a sudden stirring of sympathy for her. She had to remember that Stella was still missing her ex-husband and was acting out of character. She never used to be like this. Everyone said how kind and lovely Stella was, though you'd never believe it lately. What had happened to her?

She wanted to warn Rosie to leave it. She knew Mac wouldn't want his sister hurt and she had a feeling any mention of Gavin would only inflict more harm upon her. But Rosie had the bit between her teeth, and she wasn't about to mince her words.

'I was chatting to him this morning. He called the caravan park while I was cleaning Time and Tide, and he mentioned Mac had rung him to chat, and they were going out for a drink on Saturday for a catch-up. So it seems Gavin doesn't bear any grudges towards him, doesn't it? Maybe you should take a leaf out of your ex's book.'

Stella stared at her for a long moment, until even Rosie shifted uncomfortably in her chair. Then, without another word, Stella marched out of The Hub, slamming the door behind her.

'Well,' Alison said faintly, 'that's done it. Poor Stella.'

'Poor *Stella*?' Rosie demanded. 'Did you hear the way she was speaking about Ian?'

'Mac,' Alison's mam reminded her.

They all sat there, rather subdued.

Mrs Miller came through, all smiles, carrying a tray with three mugs of tea on it.

'Are you sure you wouldn't like something to go with that?' she asked. 'I've baked some of my blueberry muffins.' She nudged Alison. 'Our Emmy said you were very partial to my blueberry muffins.'

Alison could only shake her head. Even if she wasn't on a

diet, just thinking of Stella's stricken look as she left the cafe, and the pain in her eyes that revealed all too clearly how hurt she was that Gavin – who everyone knew avoided Stella as much as he possibly could – was going out socialising with her brother, she felt every mouthful would stick in her throat.

33

After a meal of baked sea bass with roasted peppers and potatoes, Alison and Mac were sitting in the snug, a glass of wine in her hand and a glass of orange juice in his, while a strange and unsettling silence hung over them.

Alison was wondering how to break it to Mac that Rosie had dropped the news about his forthcoming meeting with Gavin on Stella and had quite possibly set back any hopes he might have about a reconciliation with his sister any time soon. She could tell, though, that she wasn't the only one with something on her mind. Mac was quite clearly anxious about something.

She cleared her throat. 'I, er, called the surgery this morning. I've booked that cervical smear. Told you I would, and better late than never.'

He smiled. 'Well done! You're doing brilliantly, you know.'

'Thanks.'

There was another silence and Alison wondered if Mac had discovered what had happened at the cafe. Maybe Stella had already called him and read him the riot act. Maybe he was angry, or worse still, disappointed that she and her family had blurted out that she and Mac were a couple, and that he was meeting Gavin.

'Mac,' she said hesitantly, 'I should tell you—'

'Alison, there's something I have to say—'

They broke off, then smiled awkwardly at each other.

'You first,' he urged.

'No honestly, you go,' she said.

There was the sound of a banging door and they both frowned. Mac got to his feet. 'What the—?'

There was another bang, then another. Someone was checking the rooms. Mac and Alison headed towards the door of the snug, but before they could open it, it was thrown open and crashed against the wall.

Stella stood in the doorway, like Cruella de Vil in *101 Dalmatians*. All it needed was a flash of lightning behind her and the scene would be complete. She looked furious and was clearly drunk.

'Well, well, well,' she sneered. 'Look who's here. Little brother and his bit on the side.'

'Stella!' Mac grabbed her arm and pulled her, protesting, down the hall and into the kitchen. Alison followed, her heart thudding. Was Stella's strange behaviour down to her and her family? 'You've been drinking again. Look, sit down and let me make you a black coffee. Please tell me you haven't driven here.'

'What would you care if I had?' she demanded, as he pressed her into a chair.

'I'd care a lot. Believe it or not, I don't want anything to happen to you. And I don't want anything to happen to anyone else either, which it could well do if you're careering along the roads in this state.'

Alison stood uncertainly in the kitchen doorway. Carne

jumped up on to Stella's knee and she threw him off with a contemptuous cry.

Uninjured apart from his pride, the dog ran to his bed and put his head on his paws, watching her with a wounded look in his eyes.

Mrs Beddows, who clearly had more common sense, stalked out of the kitchen and into the boot room, no doubt to make her escape through the cat flap.

Mac busied himself making coffee, casting apologetic looks at Alison now and then as he tried to soothe his sister.

'What's brought you out here at this time of night?' he asked, laying a hand on her shoulder. 'What's upset you?'

She shrugged it off. 'As if you didn't know.' She glared at Alison, who shrank back, knowing she'd have to come clean.

'The thing is,' she said huskily, then cleared her throat. 'The thing is, we sort of let slip that you were meeting up with Gavin on Saturday night, and Stella got a bit...'

'Ah.' Mac crouched down beside his sister and took hold of her hands. 'Stell, it's not what you think. I'm just meeting up with him to discuss a few things, that's all.'

'About this place? About Watersmeet? Or...' There was the faintest trace of hope in her eyes as she willed him to tell her they were going to talk about her.

Alison could feel it. She sensed Stella's desperation for her brother to put her case to Gavin, and for her ex-husband to admit to him that he still loved her.

Mac sighed. 'It's just a business idea, that's all. Nothing to do with caravans or... or anything else you might be thinking.'

'A business idea,' she said flatly.

'Let me make you that coffee,' he said, getting to his feet and dropping a kiss on the top of her head.

For a moment she said nothing, staring straight ahead of her in a daze. Then her gaze lifted, and she seemed to suddenly remember Alison's presence in the kitchen.

'Did I interrupt?' she asked nastily. 'Were you about to have sex? You never did answer your mother's question, did you? *Is* Mac good in bed? No, on second thoughts, don't tell me, I really don't want to know, although I expect everyone else in The Hub was agog. Voices do carry, and there were quite a few people in the shop.'

Alison's face burned as Mac turned to look at her, shock registering in his eyes.

'It wasn't like that,' she said feebly. 'Really it wasn't.'

Stella laughed. 'Sorry, did I say something I shouldn't? How careless of me.'

Alison glared at her, furious that she was so bitter and twisted that she would do anything to spoil things for her brother.

'Stop being a bitch,' she said coldly. 'You know as well as I do that it wasn't like that, and Rosie would never have said anything to you about Gavin if you hadn't been so nasty about us in the first place.'

Stella leaned forward, her finger jabbing in Alison's direction. 'Don't call me a bitch! You have no idea. You think you're better than me, don't you? You think you've got it all figured out. Keep his bed warm, get your feet well and truly under the table here. You think he can make you happy? My friend, Lynne, thought he could make her happy, too, but he didn't, did you, *Mac*?' She laughed. 'Oh, sorry! That wasn't *your* fault, was it? It was that nasty Ian. Nasty Ian's gone now, so good and kind Mac is blameless. No one can accuse him of anything because he's a different person now. Isn't that right, *Mac*?'

Mac looked stricken. 'Stella, please. This isn't the way—'

'So, you *haven't* told her then? I suspected as much. Well, maybe *I* should.' She turned to Alison, a smirk on her lips. 'Do you know why my dear mother left Watersmeet to him instead of leaving it to me? You know, the dutiful daughter who stayed close by and looked out for her every day while big brother was miles away, ruining his life and everyone else's.' She glanced round at Mac, who'd gone very pale suddenly. 'Because,' she said coldly, 'she felt sorry for him, didn't she? You see, my brother didn't have a home of his own. In fact, for a couple of years he was actually sleeping in his car. Isn't that right, brother dear?'

Mac stared at the floor as Alison stood frozen, not knowing what to say.

Eventually, she ventured, 'Well, when marriages break up things happen, don't they? I'm sure there was a good reason...'

Mac groaned and turned his back on her, and suddenly Alison felt scared. She had a feeling she was about to hear something she really didn't want to.

'There was a *very* good reason why he ended up homeless,' Stella said. 'You see, *Alison*, my brother destroyed his life and ruined the life of his wife and children.'

'Lynne had an affair with his best friend!' Alison said hotly. She looked over to Mac, silently pleading with him to state his case and put Stella back in her place, but he didn't turn round. He remained standing in front of the sink, his hands gripping the edge of the draining board.

'He drove her to Terry, and thank God Terry was there for her, because where would she have been without him?' Stella shook her head. 'Lynne was a lovely woman. My friend. And the children – Wyatt and Sarah – they were my own flesh and blood, but I hardly see them now, because of him!'

'I don't understand,' Alison said desperately. 'Mac, what's she talking about? Please.'

Mac turned to face her. 'I was going to tell you,' he said, a plea in his eyes. 'I swear it.'

'Oh, you swear it!' Stella continued. 'And how many times did you swear to Lynne that you'd never do it again, eh, Mac? How many times did you tell your wife and kids that things would be different? How many chances did they give you, until you brought them to the edge of ruin?'

Alison's legs felt shaky, and she sat at the table opposite Stella. Mac sank to the floor, his arms folded protectively around himself, avoiding Stella's eyes as she glared at him.

'He's a gambler, Alison!' Stella spat out. 'Don't you get it? He went through all the money, all their savings, everything. Luckily, everything in their business account had to be co-signed, so he couldn't rip Terry off, but he emptied his own personal account. How big was that overdraft, Mac? How many payments on the mortgage did you miss? How many final demands were there when Lynne finally found them stuffed in your desk drawer?'

Mac sat very still, hugging his knees, saying nothing.

'The house was about to be repossessed,' Stella told Alison. She seemed calmer suddenly, almost weary. 'Terry stepped in. He bought Mac's half of the business and gave the money to Lynne to bring the mortgage payments up to date and pay off the debts, but she couldn't keep it up on her own after Mac left, so she sold the house and Terry put a roof over her head and took care of her and the children. *His* children.' She jerked a thumb in Mac's direction. 'More than he ever did. No wonder she fell in love with him.'

Mac gave a short laugh and rubbed his face but didn't argue.

'He drifted off, sleeping on the sofa at various friends' houses, until their patience ran out, because even then he was gambling, weren't you? They had people coming to their door –

bailiffs. He'd racked up credit card bills he couldn't pay. In the end he ran out of friends and was living in his car. How pathetic is that?'

She burst into tears. 'But hey, no worries. Mother to the rescue. With a wave of her magic wand, she leaves him Watersmeet, and here he is, back on his feet, a beautiful house and now a woman to share it with – as if his wife and children never existed. As if *I* never existed.'

Mac shook his head. 'You weren't left out of the will, Stella. You got plenty.'

'I got control of you,' she said scornfully. 'That's the thing, Alison. This so-called man is so pathetic, so untrustworthy, that our mother couldn't be sure he'd even pay the bills here, or feed the animals, so although she left him enough money it was all tied up with conditions. I have to make sure that when he asks for cash, he really needs it. I have to check that it genuinely is for animal feed, or vet's bills, or maintenance on the outbuildings and house. How pathetic is that? And yes, he even gets a monthly allowance, so he doesn't have to worry about getting a job, but it's only just enough to feed and clothe himself, so don't get any grand illusions about living the life of Riley with him. If Mum had left him it all in one go it would have been gambled away by now, wouldn't it, Mac dear?'

Mac said nothing.

Alison put her head in her hands, trying to process everything she'd just heard. The picture Stella had just painted sounded so unlike the Mac she knew and – yes – loved that she couldn't believe it was true. And yet, Mac had made no attempt to deny it. Even now he was just sitting there, not even trying to defend himself.

Stella put her hand over her mouth. 'I think I'm gonna be sick!' she wailed.

Mac leapt to his feet and ushered her into the toilet off the hallway.

Alison hesitated, then she stood and let herself out of the back door, as quietly as possible. She made her way round to the front of the house, hurrying down the drive and along Weltringham Road. Stella's car was nowhere in sight, so it was probable that she hadn't driven after all. She shivered, remembering she'd left her coat hung up in the hall, but realised she wasn't even cold. She just felt sick – sick to her stomach.

She'd really thought she could trust Mac, but it was clear he wasn't the man she'd thought he was.

'Alison!'

As she heard his voice she picked up speed. She didn't want to talk to him. She just wanted to go home.

She heard footsteps as he ran up behind her and shuddered as he laid a hand on her shoulder. He removed it instantly, hurt in his eyes as he handed her the coat.

'You forgot this. I didn't want you to be cold,' he said miserably.

'And that's it, is it?' she asked. 'That's all you have to say? Why didn't you tell me?'

'I was going to,' he said. 'I swear it. That's what tonight was all about. I was going to cook dinner then sit down with you and explain everything to you properly.'

'Twist the truth, you mean?'

'No.' He shook his head, denying the possibility. 'I wouldn't lie to you, Alison. I'm not that person any more. What Stella said—'

'Was it true?'

He flinched. 'It's not as straightforward as that. Stella only knows some of the story anyway.'

'But?'

He sighed. 'I *was* a gambler. I *am* a gambler. She's right. I ran up debts and nearly lost the house. I sofa surfed for years. I was in a hostel. I lived in my car. I was in another hostel. It was a mess. *I* was a mess. I went to Gamblers Anonymous. I followed the programme – went to meetings every week. I turned my life around, Alison. I had a sponsor. Doug. He was brilliant. He helped me see things differently.'

He threw up his hands helplessly. 'What else can I say? I was addicted. I still go to meetings sometimes. I'm always going to have to be careful. Mindful. But I'm not the same person as I was back then. I promise you. Please, just give me the chance to explain properly.'

'I thought you just did,' she said.

'It wasn't how Stella thought. Lynne and Terry – they were having an affair for years before I found out. When I did, I was devastated. It felt like everything I'd believed was a lie. I fell to pieces, and I was so, so low. Then I found a scratch card on the floor.'

He gave a bitter laugh. 'One bloody scratch card. I won two hundred quid on it, and that's all it took. There was this rush of excitement, and just for a moment I felt happy. And I wanted to feel that way again, so I bought another one, and then another. Before I knew it...' He groaned. 'You have no idea what it's like. I'd bet on anything. I was in the casinos, I played cards with the blokes who worked for me, I'd be in the bookies. Then came the phone apps. I didn't even have to leave the house to lose my money any more. I couldn't stop. I just wanted the pain to end, and when I was gambling it did.'

'So this is Lynne's fault?' Alison asked. 'Hers and Terry's?'

'No! No, I can't say that. Plenty of wives have affairs – even with the husband's best friend. It's not an excuse. It's just a reason. Why it started. The addiction was all me. The weakness, it was mine. My responsibility. The lies. The deception. The hiding of bills and statements. The recklessness of almost destroying my family's future. That was me. That was Ian. That's why I left him behind, because I'm not that person any more. I'm just not. You have to believe me.'

Alison nodded. 'I understand addiction, Mac,' she said gently. 'And I can't even begin to imagine how painful this must have been for you, or what you and your family went through. But can you, hand on heart, tell me that you'll never, ever gamble again?'

Mac stared at her. 'Wh-what?'

'You heard the question,' she said. 'Can you swear it?'

Mac swallowed. 'I can't. I want to, but it would be a lie. I'll always be a gambling addict. That's why I focus on one day at a time. We're taught to do that, you see, at Gamblers Anonymous. It saved me. Following the steps. Going to meetings. But honestly, I can't promise that I won't slip up ever again because I just don't know. Right now, I feel as if it will never happen, because I'm in such a good place and I'm happy. Well, until tonight. But who knows what's around the corner? It wouldn't be fair of me to say otherwise. You deserve better than that.'

'Thank you,' she said tearfully. 'I appreciate that. But you see, Mac, I can't live like that. The fear of you going back to that kind of behaviour. I told you once that I'm pretty risk averse, and I really am. I just want a steady, quiet life. I can't cope with any more drama. I've had more than enough of it already. I just need to back away right now, because if I don't... I'm so sorry, Mac.'

Tears glistened in his eyes, but he didn't try to convince her to change her mind. He stepped back and nodded silently, letting her walk away.

She knew he was watching her as she walked, and that he'd keep watching until he couldn't see her any longer. Part of her longed to turn around and run back to him, tell him that it didn't matter and she didn't care what had happened in the past. But she couldn't, because she was too afraid of the future, and what it might bring if she trusted him.

She simply wasn't brave enough.

34

Gavin hadn't changed that much. He was older, of course, but weren't they all? He had a bit more grey in his hair, a few more lines around his mouth and eyes, a bigger paunch than he used to have, but basically he was still Gavin. Still the man who'd been his brother-in-law for years. Who used to be one of his best friends.

Mac held out his hand to shake and Gavin laughed and pulled him close for a hug, clapping him on the back.

'Bloody handshake, you daft bugger! How long have we known each other?' He sat down in the armchair opposite Mac and gazed around him. 'Where have you brought me to? Bit boring, isn't it?'

They were in a hotel in Hull. Gavin had sounded delighted when Mac called him a few days ago, and told Mac he'd be happy to meet him on Saturday, and could they meet in the city because he was catching a train up to Puffin Point later – a little problem with too many speeding points on his driving licence which was bloody inconvenient – and it would be easier to meet near the station, away from... everything.

He hadn't been specific, but the implication had been that he didn't want to bump into Stella.

Mac had suggested this hotel because it wasn't far from the interchange and there was free parking, and because Alison had once mentioned that it did a good selection of non-alcoholic beers and offered a fine choice of coffees, which he thought would come in useful should he decide he'd prefer a hot drink.

'That's because I'm boring, too,' he told Gavin.

'Give over! Ian MacMillan, boring? No way.'

'Mac,' he said wearily, wondering when he'd ever get to stop correcting people about that.

'Oh yes. Crystal did mention. She said you were looking well and she's right. A damn sight better than the last time I saw you anyway.'

The last time they'd met, Mac had been a sobbing, broken mess. He'd just learned that Lynne had moved in with Terry, and his children were now under his ex-best friend's care as well as his roof.

'It's all my fault. All my fault,' he'd wept as Gavin had put him to bed on the sofa in his hotel room and told him not to worry and everything would be fine.

By the time Gavin woke up the following morning, Mac had gone – too ashamed to face his brother-in-law and too heart-broken to sit and talk about Lynne's new relationship, which he knew Stella would want to do the minute she arrived that morning to join Gavin, who was having business meetings in London at the time.

Not that Stella would have been intentionally cruel, but she had a habit of wanting to fix things, and she would believe that she could fix Mac, and in turn, fix his marriage. Mac knew it was beyond fixing, and he couldn't deal with going over and over how he needed to sort himself out. He *knew* he needed to sort himself out. He just didn't believe it was possible any more.

'Yes, well,' he said now, giving Gavin a wry look, 'I don't suppose I could have looked much worse, could I?'

They ordered two coffees, because Gavin simply couldn't bring himself to even try non-alcoholic beer, and settled down in the armchairs with their hot drinks like, as Gavin put it, a respectable old married couple.

'How are you doing though?' Gavin's tone was gentle. The jokes and smiles had been replaced with genuine concern. 'Can't have been easy for you, moving into Watersmeet, especially with your kid sister pulling the purse strings. Bit harsh of your mother to do that to you.'

'She needed to be certain I didn't blow the money,' Mac said with a shrug. 'I can't blame her for that.'

Gavin gave him a puzzled look. 'But if you wanted money, you could sell Watersmeet any time you wanted. There's nothing to stop you from doing that, as I understand it. It doesn't make any sense.'

He was right. It didn't. As Evan had explained, his mother had given Stella control over his inheritance so the two of them had to be in contact. She hadn't wanted them to lose each other again, because she loved them both so much, and wanted them to stay close.

She'd left Watersmeet itself to him with no strings attached. Nothing to say he couldn't turf the animals off the land and sell the whole place, lock, stock and barrel.

What made her think he wouldn't?

But he hadn't, had he? Because the thought of letting her down after all she'd done for him had been too much to bear. And because the animals depended on him, and Watersmeet was the first place they'd ever been truly loved and cared for.

And because, deep down, he'd fallen in love with the place, and the thought of staying there and making a home for himself – somewhere he could, one day maybe, invite his children to stay – was what kept him going most days. It was all he'd had to cling on to, until Alison walked back into his life.

And now she was gone, and he couldn't believe it, and a part of him was terrified. Because what if the pain of her loss tipped him over the edge once more? It was what she'd expect, no doubt. Stella. And maybe even Alison. But she couldn't stay with him to make sure he didn't gamble. He wouldn't want her to.

He just didn't know how he was going to start over yet again, putting aside the dream he'd begun to build. The dream he'd begun to believe in. A home, a wife, a family – because Alison came with the whole mad Wainwright clan in tow, he had no doubt about that, and he loved it. It had all collapsed around his ears, and here he was again. Just him. Trying to believe he could be better this time.

'Well,' he said with a shrug, 'that's Mum for you. She must have had her reasons.'

She believed in me. She trusted me. There *was* no other explanation. Her faith in him was humbling and made him quite emotional. He was relieved when Gavin changed the subject.

'So, this business venture,' Gavin said. 'I like the sound of it very much. It seems to me that you've got a good idea there.'

'It does?' Mac asked hopefully. 'You don't think it's a bit vague?'

'Well, a bit, but most business ideas start that way. I think it's got great potential.' He sighed. 'I can understand the need for it, too. The way the world is today, we all need somewhere we can escape to. Somewhere we can chill out, with no internet, no mobile phone or laptop, no fancy gadgets, and no bloody twenty-four-hour news channels. Just the stars and the river, and peace, and time. I could do with a bit of that myself.'

'But it's more than that,' Mac said. 'It's like I told you – so many parents are estranged from their children for whatever reason. Weekend dads. Parents who work too hard and never get to spend any time with their kids. Families who've lost touch and don't know how to reconnect. Watersmeet could be somewhere they come to stay for a few days, and with no other interruptions, they get to talk to each other.'

'They can do that in McDonald's though,' Gavin said.

Mac laughed. 'No, they can't! Not like this anyway. I was thinking about them sleeping under the stars, sitting round a campfire talking, maybe doing some beach activities, learning to cook together – whatever they feel like. I was in the Cubs and Scouts long enough. I could certainly put together some activities that they'd enjoy – all optional of course. And then there's the animals. Nothing bonds people more than stroking Highland cattle, or grooming old ponies, or collecting eggs from hens and ducks.'

He remembered the evenings he'd spent with Alison, leaning on the fence, admiring Ellen MacKenzie and Jamie Fraser. How they'd ushered the ducks and the hens into their little houses, making sure they were safely shut away for the night. Checking the old ponies were all right and had enough food and water.

'It teaches responsibility, too,' he said. 'We all need to learn that, don't we?'

'So, this "sleeping under the stars" bit. You're thinking of providing tents?'

'Possibly,' Mac said.

'Sounds a bit grim. Not many people would pay good money to stay under canvas with no mod cons. You'll need something a bit more glamorous than that if you're going to make this pay.'

'Not static caravans,' Mac said, shaking his head. 'I'm not having water pipes laid all over the place, and electricity cables, and gas bottles, and cars parked up. Before I knew it, I'd be opening a clubhouse and a launderette.'

'I wasn't thinking static caravans,' Gavin said, waving his hand as if dismissing the idea. 'You've made your feelings perfectly clear on that score.'

'Glamping pods then? Yurts?'

Gavin rubbed his chin. 'I was thinking something with a bit of rustic charm. What about shepherd's huts? You'd need planning permission, of course, because you're planning to make money from them, but they look really classy.'

'Shepherd's huts?' Mac leaned back and tilted his head, thinking about it. 'I hadn't thought...'

'Well, maybe you should. They're increasingly popular, you know, and you don't need to connect them to any mains if you choose off-grid models. You can make them look smashing inside. I've got a pal in the trade who sells them, either ones you put together yourself or ready to move into. He'd put a few your way, if you're interested.'

'I'm not sure,' Mac said doubtfully. 'I mean, they sound great, but they also sound expensive, and I'm not exactly rolling in money.'

'You have your inheritance,' Gavin pointed out. 'And it's yours whenever you want it. All you have to do is get Stella on board. If you can convince her that this is a good investment, she'll hand over the money and away you go.'

'As easy as that?' Mac gasped. 'You have *met* my sister?'

'Oh, yes,' Gavin said dryly. 'I know her quite well. But she's always had a soft spot for you, and if you just—'

'Not any more,' Mac said glumly. 'Truth is, right now she hates my guts.'

'No, she doesn't, Mac. Right now she hates herself, and she's taking it out on you because you're the one person guaranteed not to turn your back on her.'

'Is there really no way back for you and her?' Mac asked. He groaned and gave Gavin an apologetic look. 'Sorry, mate. The times Stella asked me that about me and Lynne and I wanted to throttle her in the end. If there was a way back, we wouldn't be divorced, would we? She wouldn't be living with bloody Terry. She wouldn't have taken my children to live in his sodding detached house with the massive lawn and the ride-on mower.'

'You should have told Stella what really happened,' Gavin said. 'If she'd known that Lynne was carrying on with Terry behind your back all those years, she'd have gone a lot easier on you.'

'Yeah, but she wouldn't have gone easier on Lynne,' Mac said. 'She'd have gone round there and played merry hell with her. You know what she's like. And my kids would have found out what their mother had been up to, and I didn't want that. God knows, I'd let them down enough. I didn't want them to think their mum had, too. They needed *someone* to believe in.'

'Well, you're a lot nobler than I'd have been. Letting her have all the profits from the house sale, too. You could have got half of that, you know. You always were too decent for your own good.'

'I wanted my kids to have financial security. It was the least I could do for them. Besides, I'd only have lost it on a roulette table or a card game or a horse race. Hell, I was such a mess.'

'That was an addiction,' Gavin said firmly. 'One you've put behind you and more than paid the price for.'

'What you said on the phone, about never wanting Watersmeet. Did you mean that?'

Gavin puffed out his cheeks. 'I have never, ever told Stella I wanted Watersmeet,' he said. 'Truth is, Mac, I'm thinking of getting out of Kelsea Sands all together. Tide's Reach is falling into the sea and there's only so far back I can move the caravans. The Fosters won't sell me any land, and to be honest I've lost interest. We've expanded the park at Puffin Point and it's doing really well now, competing with the big holiday park companies. And then there's the hotel. That's my pet project. I'm selling the house to invest in that. Going to live in. I'm looking forward to it. I'll be Puffin Point's version of Basil Fawlty.'

'All you need now is a Sybil,' Mac said.

Gavin shuddered. 'No chance. I'm single and happy. Women are too much like hard work. No, I'm sixty now. I just want a bit of peace and to focus on my work. I'm sorry things didn't work out with me and Stella, but that's the way it goes, isn't it?'

'She still loves you. You know that, don't you?'

'Yes. I know. I'm sorry about that, but what can I do? I don't hate her. I'm quite fond of her. But love... No, that's long gone. You'd think three years after our divorce she'd understand that, wouldn't you?'

Mac felt a wave of sadness for his sister. Poor Stella. She'd lost so much when she and Gavin had divorced. Not just the man she loved, but her home and her job, too, because it was impossible for her to continue working with her ex-husband every day. She simply couldn't face it. Her confidence low, she'd withdrawn into herself, living on the divorce settlement and moving to a smaller house in Weltringham, because with Gavin and the children gone, a larger house would just remind her of all she'd lost.

He wished he could make her happy, but it was beyond his power. He couldn't even make himself happy. Every time his thoughts strayed to Alison he felt his heart fracture just a little more and a lurch of panic, because what if it became too much and he gave up? It was how it had all started before. Losing Lynne. What if losing Alison sent him back to that hell? What if he lost control? What if he didn't have the strength to hang on to Watersmeet and he let his mother and all the animals who depended on him down?

Was he capable of being the man his mum had clearly thought he could be?

A meeting, he thought. I'll go to a meeting this week. I'll go to every meeting they hold if it will keep me on the straight and narrow.

'So these shepherd's huts,' he said, 'how much are we talking? Just so I know how much I'm going to have to grovel to Stella for.'

'I'm not sure, but I'll text Rupe and ask him.' Gavin took his phone out of his jacket pocket and began to tap out a message.

Mac took his own phone out, wondering wistfully if there'd been any message from Alison. Not that he expected one, of course, but even so...

He frowned and stared at the screen in bewilderment. A notification from his bank. It was impossible!

He quickly opened his mobile banking app and checked his account. There was no mistake. Thirty thousand pounds had just been paid into his account by Stella. Had she heard about the shepherd's huts? Had Gavin mentioned them to her? Was this some sort of deposit or...

And then, with sickening clarity, he understood.

He put the mobile phone back in his pocket, his mind whirling. He had thirty thousand pounds in the bank. His to do what he liked with.

Forty minutes later, he hugged Gavin goodbye outside the train station.

'The shame of it,' Gavin said. 'Having to catch a train at my age.'

'Nothing wrong with taking a train. Better for the environment.'

'There you go again. Too bloody noble. Great to see you again, Mac. Let me know if you make any decisions about those shepherd's huts.'

'I will. Thanks, Gavin. For everything.'

Gavin nodded. 'Take care of her, won't you? Stella, I mean. She's a pain in the backside a lot of the time but she's a good woman at heart. I don't like to think of her hurting, you know?'

'I know.' Mac forced himself to smile. 'I'll do my best.'

'And tell her the truth. What really happened. Get her on your side. It's the only thing to do if you're going to get this business off the ground.'

Ten minutes later Mac was in his car, heading home to Holderness. Gavin had asked him to take care of Stella, but he was no longer sure he could. Everything had changed, and he didn't know how he felt any more.

Driving back towards North Bridge, which crossed the River Hull, his gaze strayed to the huge casino with restaurant and bar that stood on the front. He'd never been in there before. It hadn't existed when he'd left home all those years ago, and he'd had no desire to visit it since his return.

He thought about the thirty thousand pounds he had in his bank account, and how it had got there.

He hesitated, just for a fraction of a moment, then indicated left, turning towards the car park that belonged to the casino.

35

Thursday 9 April – Project Alison Day 68: Another shift at the petrol station. Rosie was just coming home from cleaning Time and Tide when I set off. I gave her a hug and told her she was brilliant. She didn't know what to make of it but I couldn't tell her. She'd be too upset, and she'd argue about it all, and I haven't got the energy. I don't seem to have the energy for anything these days. Mam says it's all this dieting, but I'd never felt healthier until a week ago.

God, it's only been a week. How is that even possible? I miss him so much, but I know I did the right thing. I just hope Rosie understands. I'm so glad I got my bags into the boot before she came home. I'll text her when I finish work, let her know not to expect me. She's at the chippy tonight so she won't come looking for me. I just need to go home and start my life over. Figure out what's next. Make it up with Jenna if I can. What a bloody mess.

Alison had just arrived at her house from a shift at work. Not the caravan. Not home. Flicking on the light switch in the hall, she went from room to room, drawing curtains and switching on lamps, trying to make the place look cosy and lived-in again.

She put the carrier bag on the kitchen table. Teabags. Coffee. A ready meal that was the healthiest she could find in the fridge at the petrol station. No milk because she no longer took milk in tea or coffee. Definitely no sugar. No bread or butter.

Tomorrow she'd do a proper shop in Maister's and fill the fridge with healthy food. She'd order a copy of that cookbook for herself, because she had no intention of letting things slide. Not after she'd come this far.

Maybe she'd buy Jenna a bunch of flowers and take them round to hers. It was the Easter holidays after all. She'd posted the twins' Easter eggs and Easter cards to them last week. It had cost her a fortune. She could have saved her money and delivered them in person.

She was supposed to be having the girls this weekend at the caravan. She'd promised they could have the twin room again, and she'd sleep on the sofa. They were so excited and now she was about to let them down.

Maybe she could make it up to them somehow. Take them to the cinema to watch a film. Treat them to popcorn.

She remembered suddenly that she still hadn't used the handmade voucher that Rosie had written for her as a birthday present. She should have held her to it. Oh well, maybe next year.

Tears pricked her eyes, and she sank into the chair and put her head in her hands. She missed Rosie already, and she missed her mam and dad.

'Don't be so stupid!' she told herself. 'They're only twenty-four miles away, not on the dark side of the moon. You can visit them any time you like.'

But how could she, without the risk of bumping into Mac?

She didn't think she could face him. It was too painful. Did that mean she'd lost Kelsea Sands, as well as everything else?

When her phone rang, she barely had the energy to take it out of her bag. Only the thought that it might be about the twins or her parents made her look at it.

Rosie.

Alison closed her eyes. The last thing she needed was her cousin firing questions at her. Then again, she owed Rosie so much. The least of which was an apology and an explanation.

'Hello.'

'You don't have to say anything,' Rosie said immediately. 'I checked your wardrobe and your drawers. You've gone back to Hull, haven't you?'

'I'm so sorry, Rosie. I just...'

'Yeah. I get it. You miss Mac and I don't blame you. Are you okay?'

'Not really,' Alison said with a sniff.

'Do you want me to come round? I'm supposed to be at the chippy in half an hour, but I can call in sick. Some things are more important.'

'No! You can't do that. Besides, you can't afford to. I'll be okay, honestly. I just need a break.'

'Funny that, isn't it?' Rosie said wistfully. 'You only needed a break from Hull so you came to Kelsea Sands. Now it's Kelsea Sands you're running away from.'

Put like that, Alison sounded like a total wimp. 'I'm not running away,' she said. 'Not really.'

'Oh. My mistake. Sorry.'

There was a short silence, then Rosie said, 'Oh, come on, Ali, don't be so daft. Get yourself back here and sort this out. Not tonight maybe, but tomorrow when you've slept and you're feeling refreshed.'

'What would be the point?' Alison asked.

'You love Mac. You know him!'

'But I don't, do I? That's the trouble. He's not what I thought at all.'

'Yes, he is. You just have to believe in him.'

'And what if I do believe in him and then he lets me down? What if it all goes wrong? How would I deal with the fallout then? I can't go through what Lynne went through. It would break me.'

'But that might never happen!'

'Things go wrong,' Alison cried. 'Look at you and Craig. Twenty years you were with him. You gave up everything for him to move to Sheffield, away from your home and your family, and in the end it finished, and you had to come home and start again.'

'So what?' Rosie asked.

'So *what*? Twenty years! You never married, never had children. All those years wasted.'

'Not wasted. I loved him. He loved me. Why is it a waste when I have twenty years of happy memories to look back on?'

'But... it ended. Don't you regret it?'

Rosie was quiet for a moment, then she said, 'Your marriage ended. Do you regret that? All *those* years wasted?'

Alison gasped. 'How can you say that? Drew didn't leave me! He, he...'

'Died, Ali. Drew died. Because life's a risk, and you two gambled and eventually you lost. But, oh my God, while you were winning, wasn't it perfect? Wasn't it bloody lovely and happy and wonderful? If you'd known he was going to die in his fifties, would you have said no to marrying him?'

Alison's eyes were blurry with tears. 'It's not the same.'

'It is, though. None of us have any idea what's ahead. You

didn't know the Mac of yesterday. What he did then is none of your business. But who he is now, that's the Mac you know and love, and you're throwing him away – why? Because at some point in some mythical future he might let you down? He might get run over by a bus, too. So might you. Not in bloody Kelsea Sands because the buggers cancelled our service, but you know what I mean. You were so happy, Ali. Don't let go of that happiness for *what if*. Grab hold of it. Hold on to it. Live it. Enjoy every bloody moment cos you never know when it will be over.'

'I've got to go,' Alison said weakly. 'I need to get something to eat and then get an early night. I'm on the bakery shift tomorrow. At least I won't have that awful commute.'

'No, well, I'm sure that makes everything worthwhile then.'

'I'm sorry, Rosie.'

There was a loud sigh. 'No, love. I'm sorry. Sorry for you. I'll leave you to it. I need to get ready for work anyway. Take care of yourself, won't you?'

'I will.'

'And Ali?'

'Yes?'

There was a pause, then Rosie said, 'Me and Craig? I wouldn't have missed it for the world.'

36

'That's two duck eggs and three hen's eggs today. Not bad at all.'

Mac gazed down at the basket over his arm and nodded approvingly at the little haul, then rolled his eyes. Look at him, walking around like Little Red Riding Hood. Whoever would have believed it?

He'd got used to the routine now, having figured out that it was best to collect the duck eggs in the morning, as they tended to lay at night, whereas the Bennet Sisters laid throughout the day until mid-afternoon, so he usually waited until around three o'clock to collect theirs.

He glanced at the pond where Peggoty and Nancy were swimming in the water, while Estella was lying close by, drying off after a previous dip. He couldn't believe that he knew which duck was which. When he'd first arrived here, they'd all looked the same to him, no matter how many times Gilly Foster had pointed out their differences. He was, he had to admit, extraordinarily fond of them. Of all the animals and birds. Maybe he really was cut out for this Doctor Dolittle lark, after all.

Smiling to himself he strolled up the garden path and into the kitchen, placing the basket on the worktop.

Carne trotted in behind him, never wanting to be away from him for too long.

'You should be outside,' Mac told him. 'It's a beautiful day. Don't be cooped up in here. Take a leaf out of Mrs Beddows' book.'

Where she'd vanished to again he had no idea, but she could take care of herself, and she'd be home when she felt like it. No doubt about that.

'Mac?'

He spun round, his heart thudding with sudden hope at the tentative voice behind him, but his spirits fell when he saw Stella standing there, her hands wringing together and her posture revealing that she was nervous as hell. As well she might be.

'Oh,' he said dully, turning back to the sink and reaching for the handwash. 'It's you.'

'I was watching you out of the window in the snug,' she said. 'You looked really happy. *Really* happy.'

He mentally shook his head as he washed his hands. He knew exactly what she was implying.

'*Are* you happy?' she asked cautiously.

'Well, my sister seems to think she can let herself into my house any time she feels like it, and the woman I love has moved back to Hull and wants nothing more to do with me, so no, I wouldn't say I'm exactly thrilled, but I'm getting by. Is that what you wanted to hear?'

He dried his hands and threw the towel on to the draining board, then turned to face her. She swallowed, looking terrified and, despite his anger, he felt himself soften towards her.

'Why did you do it, Stella? To teach me a lesson? To prove a point? To ruin my life?'

Stella gripped the back of the chair.

'Because you could have done, you know. You *could* have ruined my life! Do you know that?' He gave a bitter laugh. 'Well, of course you know that. That was the intention, wasn't it? See me back in the hell I'd finally managed to drag myself out of. God, you must really hate me.'

'I don't hate you, Mac. I don't!' Tears rolled down Stella's cheeks and she sat down at the table, staring at him in anguish. 'Please tell me you haven't done anything stupid. I'd never forgive myself if you have.'

'You mean, please tell you I didn't go straight to the casino and blow that thirty thousand pounds which you kindly transferred to my bank account last week?'

She nodded dumbly.

Mac fumbled in his jeans pocket and took out his mobile phone. He tapped it a few times and waited until her phone pinged.

Stella retrieved it from her handbag and tapped the notification. Her mouth fell open as she stared at the photo he'd just sent her.

'You *did* go to the casino! Oh, Mac! I'm so sorry. I'm so, so sorry!'

She took out a tissue and began to sob noisily with genuine regret. Mac couldn't stand it any longer.

He sat down next to her and put his arm around her shoulders.

'If I was going to go into the casino, would I really have taken a selfie outside it to show you? Don't be daft, Stell. I took the photo to show you that I was strong enough *not* to go into the casino. Look, I'll prove it.'

He opened the banking app on his phone and passed it

across to her. She gazed at it for a moment then looked at him in
wonder.

'It's all there. You didn't touch it!'

'No. I didn't touch it. I didn't gamble, Stell. I promise.'

He was stunned when she threw her arms around him and
sobbed on to his shoulder.

'I'm so glad! And I'm so sorry. Oh, Mac, I've been such a
bitch. Alison was right about that. I don't know why I did it, I
really don't. Well, that's not true, I do know, sort of. I was all
mixed up and angry and hurt and I just wanted...'

'To force me into selling Watersmeet? Is that what it was? Did
you think that if you could get me gambling again, I'd get into so
much debt that I'd have to part with it?'

She pulled away, wiping her nose on the tissue. 'No. I don't
think so. I didn't really think beyond you losing that money. I
didn't really think at all. I was just so angry, and I thought I
wanted to teach you a lesson, but as soon as I'd done it I
panicked and regretted it, but I couldn't stop it. It was too
late. So...'

'So,' Mac said, 'you rang Gavin and told him what you'd
done.'

'He called you?'

'He did. Checked up on me. I told him what I'm telling you.
I'm fine. I wasn't even tempted. I've got way too much to lose, and
believe it or not, I really like my life now. I love it here. I'm not
about to throw that away again.'

'Oh, Mac,' she breathed. 'I'm so glad! And I'm so proud of
you.'

He'd never expected to hear those words from his sister, and
he swallowed. 'Thank you. But Stella, it could have had a very
different outcome, you understand that? Especially since Alison
– what happened with her. I was vulnerable, just like I was when

I found out about Lynne and Terry, and I could have gone down the same path. What you did was awful. Cruel.'

'I know. I know it was, and I can't tell you how sorry I am.' She rubbed her eyes then looked at him with genuine pain. 'Gavin told me, Mac. He told me what really happened. About Lynne and Terry's affair. All those years! And about you giving her your half of the house proceeds and walking away with nothing. Why didn't you tell me?'

Mac sighed. 'He shouldn't have done that. I asked him not to, and I explained my reasons. I don't want the kids to ever find out what really happened. They'd lost all faith in me, and I didn't want them to lose faith in their mum. Please tell me you haven't contacted Lynne. I couldn't stand it. I don't want any of that raking up again.'

'I haven't, I swear it. I mean, I would have done if I'd known back then. I'd doubtless have gone round there and bawled her out, and you're right, the kids would probably have found out all about it because I'd have been so furious about it all.'

She squeezed his hand. 'I still *am* furious about it all. She let me think it was all your fault. She made me despise you.'

'Stella,' he said firmly, 'it *was* all my fault. The gambling bit anyway. Yes, Lynne and Terry behaved badly, deceiving me for all those years and betraying my trust, but they didn't force me to throw away every penny I had on the horses, the cards, the roulette wheel. That was all me. My responsibility.'

'It's an addiction,' she said sadly. 'An illness. I didn't understand, but I think I do now. A little bit anyway.' She raised embarrassed eyes to him. 'Drinking,' she said quietly. 'I think... I think I've got a bit of a problem with it.'

He nodded. 'You think? Or you know?'

She took a deep breath. 'I know. I've started to rely on it way too much. I've been so unhappy, Mac, and the alcohol seemed to take the edge off it, however temporarily. But it's no solution, is it? I mean, alcohol's a depressant in itself so it's the last thing I should be doing. I've...' She shook her head and gave a small laugh. 'I've been to an AA meeting in town. I stood up and said I was an alcoholic. Me! I'm so ashamed.'

He squeezed her shoulder, remembering his own battle, and thinking of Alison and her junk food habit, and of Doug, who'd stopped gambling and helped him so much but had been unable to kick the heavy smoking habit which had eventually led to his own untimely death.

People suffered and struggled so much, and they used all sorts of different props to help them through. It was easy to judge from the outside, but how many people could claim they didn't have *something* they relied upon to cope? It was just that some addictions seemed to be more socially acceptable than others. But all of them had the potential to be dangerous, one way or the other.

'Well done, Stella,' he said. 'I'm proud of you, too.'

'It was after I transferred the money to you,' she explained. 'I couldn't believe I'd done it. I was drunk, of course, and when I sobered up – oh, God. I was so disgusted with myself, and so terrified. I just didn't know what to do. That's why I called Gavin. He always knew what to say. I thought he'd fix it for me. I thought...'

'That he'd come riding to your rescue and everything would resolve itself?'

She nodded. 'When he made it very clear that he'd check on you, but he wasn't going to come round and see me, I realised it really was over. I've been such a fool, haven't I? Gavin doesn't want me back, does he?'

Mac hesitated, not wanting to hurt her, but he realised there was no point sugar-coating this particular pill. She was going to have to swallow it, as bitter as it was.

'No,' he said, his eyes brimming with tears as she gazed up at him. 'He's moved on, and you have to as well. And you can,' he added quickly. 'You've got me. You'll always have me. And Crystal and Ned.'

'I don't deserve you,' she said.

'Of course you do. We'll help each other.'

'I don't know what I'm going to do, though. I'm sixty this year and look at me! I'm lost. Completely lost.' She burst into tears and Mac hugged her tightly.

'Help me then,' he said impulsively. 'Come into business with me. Help me turn this place into a refuge for people to reconnect with nature, with their loved ones, with themselves.'

She blinked away the tears and frowned. 'What do you mean?'

Briefly he told her about his plans for Watersmeet.

'Shepherd's huts? But you were so against a caravan park.'

'There'll only be three or four shepherd's huts at the most. That's if we can get planning permission, of course, but I don't think it will be a problem. There are a couple of houses along this road that have a static caravan in their gardens which they rent out to birdwatchers and the like. It sort of sets a precedent, doesn't it? And shepherd's huts are so unobtrusive. They won't even be connected to the mains.'

He tapped his phone, showing her the website of Gavin's friend, who made and sold them. 'See? Off-grid ones. They'll have wood-burning stoves so people can stay warm in them, but no electricity or water or waste pipes.'

'Then, how...?'

'The extension at the back of the house,' he said. 'The utility room and downstairs cloakroom. There's plumbing already there. We could turn it into a shower block with a couple of toilets.'

'And what about food and drink?'

'Bed and breakfast,' he said with a grin. 'I'd make them breakfast every morning and take it to their hut, or they could eat in here if they wanted. And I'd provide dinner if they paid extra, or they could go over to The North Star. I could even make them packed lunches. The point is, they'd be warm, comfortable, fed, and there'd be no distractions. Nowhere to plug in their mobile phones or laptops or games consoles. No TV. Just nature and each other, or themselves if they wanted to be alone. You see?'

'And you really want to do this?' she asked.

'I really do, but I know nothing about running a business like this. You're the one with the hospitality background. What do you say to helping me out?'

Stella shook her head in wonder. 'You'd really let me be part of this, after what I've just done to you?'

'You're my sister, Stella,' he told her kindly. 'I love you. I'd be so happy if we could do this together.'

She fell against him, and he hugged her to him, stroking her hair as she cried softly against his chest.

'So,' he said at last, as her sobs turned to sniffles, 'what do you say? Partners?'

She nodded and smiled up at him, her eyes red from crying but also bright with a new optimism.

'Partners,' she said.

37

Monday 27 April – Project Alison Day 86: This might be my last entry in this journal. I haven't written in it for ages and there doesn't seem much to say, except that today I'm going to the surgery to get my blood pressure taken, get weighed, and have my bloods taken again to see if my blood sugar levels have dropped. If they haven't, I might as well give up now, because I've done all I can. I deserve a medal.

No word from Mac. Of course, I don't want there to be. There wouldn't be much point, would there? Jenna is talking to me again, so that's something. It's a bit awkward, but we're trying. I haven't seen Joel, and I don't want to. I've gone right off him. Not a word of apology from him about what he said to me.

Had the twins on Saturday but only for the day. Took them to the park. It was lovely. They wanted to go to Kelsea Sands again, but I told them Mam and Dad were busy, and Rosie was at work. They were really disappointed. I'm having them again the Saturday after next, so maybe I'll take them to see

Niall and Kendra in Millensea. One beach is as good as another when you're that age, right?

Oh, and my cervical screening results came through. All fine. Another thing ticked off the list, as Mac would say.

Rosie rang to wish me good luck for today. She offered to come with me, but I told her I didn't want her driving all that way just to hold my hand. I'm a big girl. I can do this. Funny, it really doesn't feel like such a big deal any more – going to the doctor's, I mean. Life is certainly strange, isn't it?

'Alison,' the nurse said, beaming at her with delight, 'you've worked a miracle!'

As Alison stepped off the scales she couldn't help smiling at her obvious approval. She might well approve, too. Alison had lost thirty pounds in three months. Her blood pressure was normal, and the nurse was already sure that her blood glucose levels would have dropped – it was just a question of by how much.

'What have you been doing? I'd like to tell my other patients the secret,' she said, as Alison sat back down.

'I followed the recipes in a diabetic-friendly cookbook,' Alison said with a shrug. 'I taught myself to cook from scratch. I think that made a difference.'

With Mac's help. She hadn't taught *herself* to cook from scratch. They'd taught each other. She wondered if she should add that it had got a lot easier over the last three weeks. It was amazing how being heartbroken dulled your appetite.

'Well, I'm proud of you,' the nurse said. 'Call the surgery in a few days and we'll have the results for you. I have a good feeling that you'll be out of the diabetic range, but I'll keep everything crossed for you. The main thing now, of course, is to keep going with it. You've still got some weight to lose to be in the ideal range for your height, and of course, we need to keep that blood sugar steady, don't we?'

Oh, do we? I'm so glad we're doing this together.

But the nurse was so happy for her, and so full of compliments that Alison couldn't help but feel good about herself, so she smiled and thanked her, then left, promising to keep up the good work.

She headed through reception, waving a cheery goodbye to the receptionist, and went through the automatic doors into the car park.

'Hiya, Mum.'

Shocked, she stared at Jenna, who was standing nearby.

'What the heck are you doing here?' She glanced at her watch. 'It's eleven o'clock. What's wrong? Why aren't you at work?'

'I'm playing hooky.' Jenna gave her a sheepish smile. 'I rang in sick. Sod it.'

'You did what? *You?*' Alison couldn't believe it. Jenna, the woman who wanted nothing more than to be every pupil's favourite teacher and be promoted to head teacher by the time she was forty-five had played hooky? It had never been known. 'Has something happened?'

'Sort of.' Jenna glanced upwards and wrinkled her nose as spots of rain started to fall. 'Come and sit in my car. Let's talk.'

Feeling she was in a dream, Alison followed her daughter to where her smart new car was parked. Well, nearly new. She'd only taken delivery of it last week. The family was certainly aspirational.

'Nice,' she said, admiring the interior as they sat inside, while the rain began to pour down, bouncing off the windscreen. 'Very smart.'

'I doubt it will stay that way for long,' Jenna said. 'You know how much mess the twins can make.'

'Don't I just!' Alison said with feeling.

'Bloody April showers,' Jenna said wistfully. 'It was such a lovely day yesterday, too. I hope it's not an omen.'

'An omen of what?'

Jenna turned to face her, her cool facade dropping. 'Mum, why didn't you tell me?'

Alison frowned. 'Tell you what?'

'About the diabetes!'

Alison heaved a heavy sigh. 'Bloody Rosie.'

'Don't blame her! She shouldn't have had to tell me. *You* should have! She called me last night. She told me you were going to get your bloods checked today and that you might be really nervous, because we all know what you're like about going to the doctor's. She wanted to be with you, but she was needed at work, so she asked me if I'd go with you, and I told her I had work, too, and she said she'd clean forgotten. But I don't think she had, do you? I think she just wanted me to know. And then I got stuck in traffic and missed your appointment anyway and... How did it go?'

'Okay, I think,' Alison said, feeling slightly stunned at Jenna's little speech. It was the most her daughter had said to her in months. 'Are you telling me you called in sick to be with me for my blood test?'

Jenna's face crumpled. 'Yes! And I missed it! I'm so sorry.'

'There's no need to be sorry,' Alison assured her, handing her a tissue as Jenna began to cry. 'I was absolutely fine. Honestly.'

'But you're scared stiff of doctors. Everyone knows that. Ever since Dad.'

'Yes, well, I'm not so scared any more. I've had that many tests lately it doesn't bother me at all.'

'Tests?' Jenna's eyes widened. 'What sort of tests?'

'Nothing sinister. Just routine stuff. When you get to my age they want to check everything. And besides, you know what it's like when you're a woman. It never ends, does it?'

'Oh. Oh, you mean like a mammogram?'

Alison groaned. 'Bloody hell. I'd forgotten about that. That'll be next, no doubt. Something to look forward to, eh?'

'But everything's okay?' Jenna asked anxiously.

'I'm fine, love. All results are good so far. Just got the blood sugar test to come back now and then that's it. And I've lost so much weight and eaten so healthily that I'm feeling positive about that too. My blood pressure's normal again. The nurse is really pleased with me.'

Jenna surveyed her thoughtfully. 'You look fabulous,' she said. 'Really well. I guess going away to Kelsea Sands did you the world of good.'

'Mm. It did.' Until it didn't.

'I thought... I thought it was all because of me, you see,' Jenna said. 'You going away. I thought you'd left home because you didn't want to be at my beck and call, and I felt awful. I didn't know you were going away to get healthy.'

'Well,' Alison said slowly, 'it *was* partly because of you. Not that I wanted to get away from you,' she added hastily. 'It was just... it was all getting too much for me. Looking after the twins all the time and working at the petrol station and worrying about Mam and Dad. My blood pressure was creeping up and up and I was comfort eating way too much. I had to do something. I had to reset my life. I'm sorry if I made things difficult for you. I know it can't have been easy, finding someone to take care of the twins.'

'No,' she admitted. 'It wasn't.'

'So, who did you find in the end?' Alison asked tentatively.

'Me,' Jenna said. 'I started juggling things around to make sure I could pick them up and take them to school as much as possible. And I started doing my marking and lesson planning when they were in bed, or at gymnastics, or dance class. I've never seen so much of them since my maternity leave ended.'

Alison stared at her. 'I don't know what to say. How are you finding it?'

Jenna smiled. 'You know what? At first it was awful. I was in tears nearly all the time, and I was so bloody angry at you for dropping me in it. But the truth is, you did me a favour. I *like* spending time with my girls. I've realised I hardly knew them at all, but now... now we talk. We go out. We have fun. They're so good to be around. They really make me laugh.'

She stared out of the window. 'I think I've realised that there are more important things than being promoted to head. Truth is, I don't care about that any more. I don't think I've really cared about it for years. I was just stuck in this hamster wheel, going round and round because I didn't know what else to do. You helped me step off it. You *forced* me to step off it. I was furious! But now, I'm so grateful.' She turned back to Alison, smiling. 'Thank you, Mum.'

'Well,' Alison said, 'I never thought I'd ever hear you say *that*!'

'No, me neither.' Jenna laughed. 'And now,' she said, folding her arms and eyeing Alison knowingly, 'I want to hear all about this Mac person that Rosie told me about.'

Alison scowled. 'She never did!'

'Oh, we had quite the chat,' Jenna confirmed. 'I'd forgotten how much fun Rosie can be, you know. It was so lovely to talk to her properly after all this time. And she couldn't wait to fill me in on my mother's holiday romance. So go on, tell me all about him.'

'There's nothing to tell,' Alison said, her voice suddenly croaky. 'It was nice for a while, but it's over now.'

'Yes, I know. And I know why, too.'

'You've got to be kidding me,' Alison said weakly. 'She never told you *everything*?'

'Well,' Jenna said, 'if she didn't, I dread to think what she left out. The mind boggles.'

'That bloody woman!'

Jenna took her hand. 'She's really worried about you, you know. She says you're making a terrible mistake. She thinks Mac's perfect for you and you're walking away from something that could be so good for you.'

'Did she tell you why I walked away?' Alison asked, her eyes pricking with tears.

'Yes, she did. The gambling. I get it, Mum, I really do. But it seems to me, from what Rosie's told me, that he's not that person any more. He sounds lovely. A real gentleman. And he clearly thinks the world of you. Whatever he was before, does it matter? He's shown you who he is now. You clearly like him as he is or you wouldn't be looking and sounding so upset right now.'

Alison nibbled her thumb nail, staring out across the car park. She could see her own little car waiting for her.

'He's not your dad, Jenna,' she said quietly. 'He's nothing like him really.'

'How could he be? Dad was a one-off,' Jenna said. 'But you wouldn't want to replace him, would you?'

'No. No, I wouldn't. Not ever.' Alison turned to face her daughter. 'You do know how much I loved your dad, don't you?'

Jenna's eyes widened. 'Of course I do!'

'Do you really think I drove him to his grave? I need to know what you really believe. Please tell me the truth.'

The shock in Jenna's eyes told her everything she needed to know.

'You didn't say that, did you?' she said gently.

'Who the hell told you I did?' Jenna gasped. She stared at her mother for a moment, then her face fell. 'Joel?' she asked weakly. 'He didn't. Please tell me he didn't.'

'Yes, he did. The same night he told me I was banned from seeing the twins.'

'Bloody hell.' Jenna shook her head, dazed. 'You must have hated me so much.'

'No! I've never hated you. I thought... I thought maybe you hated *me*. He said you'd blamed me all these years, and I didn't want to believe it, but when you're feeling low already it's easy to fall for someone's lies.'

'I know,' Jenna said grimly. 'Believe me, I know. Mum, I've never blamed you for Dad's death. Never. I know how close you two were, and I think you're amazing, the way you've got on with your life without him. But look, now you have the chance not to be alone any more. And Dad would be so happy for you. You know he would. Can't you give this Mac bloke a chance? You deserve a fresh start. Kelsea Sands has always been your dream. Your happy place. This could be the new life you deserve.'

'I can't go back to Mac just because he lives in Kelsea Sands.'

'That's not what I mean! But don't you think it's all meant to be? It's how it feels to me anyway. He may have made some terrible mistakes in the past but he's a different person now. He's even changed his name, for goodness' sake.'

'Rosie really didn't leave anything out, did she?' Alison shook her head. 'He's a gambler, though. An addict.'

'Everyone's addicted to something. Look at you with all the junk food you used to eat.'

Alison raised an eyebrow. 'You think that's the same?'

When Jenna said nothing she asked curiously, 'And what about you? What are you addicted to?'

Jenna didn't reply.

'It could all go wrong,' Alison said after a moment's silence. 'Not every love story has a happy ending, and what would I do then?'

Jenna laughed.

'What's so funny?' Alison demanded.

'Seriously? Don't you get it yet? *No* love story has a happy ending. Not a single one. Sooner or later one or the other of us has to say goodbye, whether that's because of a break-up or because – well, like you and Dad. One of us is always going to be left alone to pick up the pieces. That's the way it goes.'

'My God,' Alison said weakly. 'What an awful thought!'

'But it's true. And that's why you've got to grab every chance of happiness you can and enjoy it while it lasts. Don't worry about what might happen at some point in the future. Live, laugh, love. That's what they say, isn't it? And it's true. Just go for it! Let tomorrow take care of itself.'

'Is that what you were doing?' Alison asked. 'Grabbing a chance of happiness while you could? Is that what your little fling was about?'

When her daughter didn't reply she said, 'Jenna, are you all right? Is there anything you want to tell me?'

Jenna seemed to hesitate, then shook her head. 'I'm fine, Mum, and this isn't about me. Are you listening to me? You've got a good man waiting in Kelsea Sands for you. Someone who really cares about you, and who's fought a hard battle to get to this point and turn his life around. Are you really going to walk away from someone who's made you so happy, just because of his past mistakes and the chance that things might go wrong in the future?

Because if you are, you're not the woman I thought you were.'

'And who did you think I was?'

Jenna smiled. 'Someone who's strong, resilient and unbelievably kind. Someone who wouldn't punish someone for messing up in the past. Someone who's had to deal with the worst possible thing that could ever happen to her, but picked herself up and kept on going. My mum.'

They sat quietly, staring out of the window as the clouds parted and the sun peeped through at last.

'The rain's stopped,' Alison said quietly.

'It always does in the end,' Jenna told her.

Alison leaned over and dropped a kiss on her daughter's cheek. 'I love you, you know. Never doubt it.'

'I love you, too. Now, are you going to get out of this car and get your sorry arse back to Kelsea Sands, or do I have to drive you there myself?'

Alison laughed. 'You'll need to pick the twins up soon. You won't be driving me anywhere.'

'So?'

'So...' Alison took a deep breath. 'I guess I'm going home.'

38

Mac stared at the letter on the doormat. It wasn't possible. Was it?

He bent down and picked it up, his eyes scanning the neat, loopy handwriting, his fingers gently caressing the expensive-looking envelope. Had it got lost in the post? His mother had been gone for months now. Surely, even the post in Kelsea Sands wasn't that unreliable?

He checked the postmark and frowned. This had been posted on Friday 24 April. It couldn't be from his mother. Well, of course it couldn't.

What's wrong with you, you moron? She'd hardly have written a letter to you addressed to Watersmeet, would she?

But who then?

He carried it through to the kitchen and sat down, staring at it for a moment before finally starting to open it, carefully, gently, bit by bit. It was too beautiful to be torn open like a bill or an appointment letter.

Carefully he pulled out the piece of paper inside. It wasn't the same as the ones his mother had written all those letters on, but it was similar enough. Good quality writing paper, and the actual writing itself... Not a fountain pen, but some sort of gel pen, he guessed. Still, it was lovely handwriting.

His eyes scanned the contents of the letter, his pulse racing and his heartbeat quickening as he did so.

Dear Dad,

Thanks for your letter. It was quite a shock to receive it and I'm sorry it's taken me so long to reply, but as you can imagine I've had to think about what I wanted to say to you.

Like you said, it's been a long, long time. You say you never stopped loving us or thinking about us, but from where we're standing it's not that easy to believe it, you know? It's always felt to us like we no longer existed as far as you were concerned. It hurt. It still does if I'm being really honest with you.

A couple of years ago, Mum told us all about your gambling. We didn't know. They'd never said anything about it at the time. All we knew was that you'd walked out and left us, and Terry took us in. He's been really good to us. Like a proper dad. I can't tell you he hasn't.

Anyway, when Mum finally told us the truth, we were shocked. Wyatt says it doesn't make any difference and it's no excuse for what you did. But I read up on gambling addiction after Mum told us, and I sort of think it wasn't all your fault. Addiction's like an illness, isn't it? A disease.

I'm really glad to hear that you're not doing that any more, and that you've made a new life for yourself at Watersmeet. I'm sorry about Grandma MacMillan. She was nice. I wish I'd seen more of her, but I guess it's too late now.

You might like to know that Mum and I are in partnership. We run a property development company. We buy up houses and flats, do them up and sell them on. Terry's retired, and he sold the business and helped us set up ours. He says he's quite happy to sit back and let us keep him in the style to which he's become accustomed, haha!

Wyatt's not part of all that, but he doesn't want me to discuss him or what he does. He's not ready for any communication with you yet, so I have to respect that. He takes his time, but he usually gets there in the end. Sorry, but it's up to him, you see?

Anyway, I think that's all I wanted to say for now. This feels really strange to be honest, but I'm glad you reached out.

Maybe one day I'll come up to Kelsea Sands and see this amazing Watersmeet for myself? Auntie Stella always said it was beautiful, and I've looked it up on Google Maps, which isn't exactly the same but it's a start. It looks really cool.

Let's just stay in touch and see how it goes, okay? I'm glad you're well and I hope to hear from you again soon.

Take care.

Sarah xx

Mac closed his eyes, holding the piece of paper to his face and inhaling the scent of it. This was from his daughter. His flesh and blood. He'd never thought to hear from her again, but she'd written to him. He'd given her his mobile number, thinking she'd text him at best, but she'd written an actual letter, just like his mum used to.

His throat burned and tears pricked his eyes. She hadn't slammed the door on him. She'd said she wanted to stay in touch. That maybe one day she'd even come and see him. He could hardly believe it.

He put the letter down on the table, buried his head in his hands and let the tears fall.

Carne let out an excited yap and Mac wiped his eyes as he looked down at the little dog, who was dancing around his legs, his tail wagging frantically.

'Don't get upset,' he told him. 'You know I'll be okay. It's not the first time you've seen me cry, is it?'

Carne yapped again and Mac shook his head and looked up. He froze, wondering if he was hallucinating. Standing in the kitchen doorway was Alison.

'I did knock on the front door,' she said, 'but no one answered, so I thought you might be with the animals.'

Carne danced around her like a mad circus dog.

So that's what you were trying to tell me.

He wanted to say something, but he didn't know what. His mind was blank. All he seemed able to do was stare at her.

'Can I come in?' she asked after a moment.

He blinked and tried to pull himself together. 'Yes, of course. Sorry.'

She stepped inside and he hurriedly indicated that she should sit down at the table opposite him.

She ignored his instruction and sat next to him, giving a curious glance at the letter in front of him.

'It's from Sarah,' he told her.

Her smile lit up her face, the way it always did, and his heart did that funny little dance in response, the way *it* always did. He couldn't believe she was here, and he stared at her, not wanting to take his eyes off her for a moment in case she vanished.

'Really? That's fantastic! I'm so pleased for you.' Then her smile faltered, and she said, 'It *is* good news, right?'

He pushed the letter towards her. 'Here, read it for yourself.'

'Are you sure?'

He nodded. 'I would never have written to her if you hadn't given me the courage to.'

'You would. Eventually.' She quickly read the letter, and her smile returned. She laid her hand on his arm and his stomach flipped over. 'This is brilliant news. So promising. You must be over the moon.'

'I am. I mean, I know Wyatt's not interested yet, but she says he likes to take his time. She didn't say it was a definite no, did she?'

'She didn't.'

'And even if it is… I mean, I never thought Sarah would get in touch, but she has. It's good, right?'

He was jabbering and he knew it. Nerves had got the better of him.

'It is,' she said soothingly. 'I'm really happy for you, Mac.'

He put the letter back in its envelope with shaking hands. 'So, what are you doing here? I never expected to see you. This is quite the day.'

'For me, too. I went to the doctor's yesterday. I thought you might like to know that Project Alison has gone very well. I'm thirty pounds lighter, my blood pressure's normal and the nurse is pretty confident about my blood results. I'll find out for sure in a few days, but it's looking good.'

'That's great. I'm so pleased for you.' He smiled. 'I knew you could do it.'

'I might not have done without your help,' she said. 'I wanted to say thank you.'

'It was all you,' he told her. 'I didn't do anything.'

'We both know that's not true,' she said, squeezing his arm.

He glanced down at her hand and hesitated, then covered it with his own hand, hardly daring to breathe in case he'd made a terrible mistake.

'I've missed you,' she said. 'And I'm sorry.'

'Sorry?' He narrowed his eyes. 'What have you got to be sorry for?'

'For being an idiot. A coward. For running away. For turning my back on the best thing that's happened to me in a long time.'

'Alison—'

'No, let me say this, Mac. I know you can't promise me you'll never gamble again. Truth is, I can't promise I won't put weight back on again. All we can do is try, right? We both have so much to lose. But at the same time, we both have so much going for us. Life is good. It could be even better if we're together. I know there are no guarantees, but I'm willing to take the chance if you are.'

Was she really saying this? On top of the letter from his daughter, Mac felt as if he was in some sort of lovely dream. If he was, he hoped he'd never wake up.

'I never told you,' he said. 'I love you.'

'Oh, but you did tell me,' she said, smiling. 'Maybe not in words, but you told me every day, with everything you *did* say, and everything you did for me. But I never told *you*, did I? So let me tell you now. I love you, Mac. I love you very much. And I don't want to waste another moment of my life being without you. Will you give me another chance?'

She put her arms around him and he held her tightly, burying his face in her hair, breathing in the scent of her, as she stroked the back of his head and told him everything he'd longed to hear, of how she wanted to make a new life with him, be here with him in Watersmeet, of a future she couldn't wait to start building.

He had so much to tell her. So many plans. So much to look forward to. But right now, there was only thing he could say.

He pulled away and cradled her face in his hands, kissing away her tears.

'I love you so much. Welcome home, Alison.'

EPILOGUE

Saturday 9 May – Project Alison Day 98: On Tuesday I rang the surgery and my HbA1c results had come through. 40! I'm no longer even in the pre-diabetic range. Mac and I celebrated by taking the family out today to The North Star for lunch. I had chicken salad. Dad had a starter, a main and a pudding, because Mac was paying.

Jenna came too, and she brought the twins. Joel was busy. Funny that. They all seem to really like Mac, which is a relief. Jenna and Kendra never stopped talking to each other. You'd think they'd never met before! I think Jenna's finally relaxing and letting people in. She looked so pretty this afternoon. It made me happy to see her laughing and joking, and the twins were thrilled to be back in Kelsea Sands with all their family.

They nagged and nagged to go to Watersmeet and meet the animals, so we've said they can stay in a couple of weeks, once I've got settled in. Everyone's volunteered to help me with the move from Hull, and Uncle Christopher said he can recommend a good estate agent to handle the sale of my house, though maybe I'll think about letting it out instead for now.

Everyone was very interested in the brochure for the shepherd's huts. Stella's already planning a website and social media accounts. We haven't even got planning permission yet, but she's so excited that no one had the heart to remind of her that.

Dad wanted to know what duck eggs taste like and Mac said he can have all the duck eggs he wants for free, which pleased Dad no end. Mam said Dad thought of nothing but his stomach and she sometimes wondered what she'd ever seen in him, and Auntie Elaine said they were both an embarrassment and she couldn't think of a couple better suited to each other.

Rosie didn't say anything because she was too busy crying. Her mascara ran and everything. I asked her what was wrong, and she said she was so bloody happy for me she didn't have the words, so I gave her a big hug and reminded her that she still owed me a night at the pictures and those nachos and dips, and she said surely I'd be too busy settling into Watersmeet to even think about going into town.

That's Rosie for you.

I looked around the table and my heart was just about fit to burst. I have the most wonderful family in the world.

I guess this is the end of Project Alison. Final entry and all that. What an incredible three months it's been. I feel kind of sad to close the journal for the last time. But Mac's looking at me now, and he's got that expression in his eyes, and it's late anyway and I really do have to go to bed.

And anyway, I have another project to focus on now. Project Watersmeet. And I have a feeling it's going to be absolutely amazing.

This is Alison Parker signing off.
Over and out.

* * *

MORE FROM SHARON BOOTH

Another book from Sharon Booth is available to order now here:
https://mybook.to/KelseaSandsBook2

ACKNOWLEDGEMENTS

Thank you so much for reading *Take Me Home to Kelsea Sands*. I really hope you've enjoyed your first visit to my fictional village on the very real Holderness coast in the East Riding of Yorkshire.

Kelsea Sands may not be an actual place, but it's very much inspired by the real-life village of Kilnsea, which sits next to Spurn Point (Kels Point), a spit of land that curves out between the Humber Estuary and the North Sea.

Wild and beautiful, Spurn Point is nicknamed 'Yorkshire's Land's End' for very good reason. It feels like you're at the end of the world when you're standing on that shoreline, never mind Yorkshire!

Kilnsea is a quiet village with an interesting past. The area was a hive of activity during the two World Wars, and there really are the remains of an old battery on the beach.

There's also a lovely pub with views over the Humber, an old church that's no longer in use and a caravan park. But I must stress, none of the characters in this book are based on any actual people. They are all the products of my imagination.

But the deer... The deer was real, and what a fabulous treat that was to see it standing behind the gate watching us. Alison's reaction was exactly my reaction, and my husband had to lift my chin just as Mac lifted hers!

And with that, my first thank you must go to The Husband, who has driven me to the Holderness coast countless times, and has kept me company as I explored Kilnsea and the surrounding area, taken photos for me (his camera is much better than mine) and indulged me by taking no notice of the satnav and following little tracks and lanes so we could discover places we'd never have otherwise visited.

We both have happy memories of days spent by the sea in Holderness. We each holidayed there with our respective families as children, we "courted" there as teenagers and we brought our own children back frequently.

Still, it never fails to shock us how much of the land we used to walk on has now disappeared. Huge chunks of the chalet park where our families once stayed have fallen into the sea. Roads end abruptly. The coastline creeps ever closer to family homes and businesses.

The Holderness coast is possibly the fastest eroding coastline in Europe, and it's heartbreaking to see how much has changed even since our childhoods.

I wondered how it felt to live in a place teetering on the edge of the sea, never knowing how much longer you'd have your home. You'd have to have a lot of resilience, plenty of humour, and a determination to live your life to the full each day. And as I was thinking about people who displayed those traits, my characters started to form in my imagination, and before I knew it I had a whole series in mind! Such is the life of a writer...

My thanks, as always, go to the team at Boldwood Books – especially to my wonderful editor, Francesca Best, who has been so supportive and is very good at seeing what works and what doesn't. Also to my copyeditor, Helen Woodhouse, who has done a brilliant job on this book – particularly in untangling my rather chaotic timeline!

Thank you to my proofreader, Anna Paterson, for all your hard work.

Many thanks to Debbie Clement for the fabulous cover,

which I absolutely love, to Niamh, Claire, Nia, Wendy, Issy and Megan in sales and marketing, to Ben, Kate, Kathryn, Hayley, Grace, and of course, Amanda. If I've left anyone out, I apologise. There are so many names to learn! And thank you, also, to the other Boldwood authors who are so supportive and always there with advice and tips and general reassurance.

Finally, a big thank you to you, the reader, without whom none of this would be possible. I look forward to telling many more stories in the future, and there's no one I'd rather share them with than you.

Love Sharon xx

ABOUT THE AUTHOR

Sharon Booth is the author of feel-good stories set in charming, quirky locations, and now writes cosy romances with a magical twist for Boldwood. She lives with her husband in East Yorkshire, England.

Download your exclusive bonus content from Sharon Booth here:

Visit Sharon's website: <u>www.sharonboothwriter.com</u>

Follow Sharon on social media:

f facebook.com/sharonboothwriter

⊙ instagram.com/sharonboothwriter

▶ youtube.com/@sharonboothwriter

BB bookbub.com/authors/sharon-booth

℗ pinterest.com/sharonboothwriter

ALSO BY SHARON BOOTH

Ghosts of Rowan Vale

Kindred Spirits at Harling Hall

Loving Spirits at the Vintage Teashop

Christmas Spirits at Honeywell House

Kelsea Sands

Take Me Home to Kelsea Sands

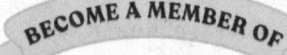

BECOME A MEMBER OF

THE
SHELF
CARE
CLUB

The home of Boldwood's
book club reads.

Find uplifting reads,
sunny escapes, cosy romances,
family dramas and more!

Sign up to the newsletter
https://bit.ly/theshelfcareclub

Boldwood

Boldwood Books is an award-winning fiction publishing company seeking out the best stories from around the world.

Find out more at www.boldwoodbooks.com

Join our reader community for brilliant books, competitions and offers!

Follow us
@BoldwoodBooks
@TheBoldBookClub

Sign up to our weekly deals newsletter

https://bit.ly/BoldwoodBNewsletter